ANASTASIA NOVYKH

SENSEI
OF
SHAMBALA

SENSEI
Publishing house
Kiev 2009

"Sensei of Shambala" by Anastasia Novykh, Book I

At first glance, the story of a youth meeting **Wisdom** seems naïve. But this ordinary perception is just an illusionary barrier, a skillful trap set up by our ego on the path to the perfect **Spirit**. The one who will overcome it will **discover** more for himself than **he** would dare to hope for. Hail to the winner – because **Knowledge** will be his prize, because **truth** will be unveiled.

This book was written based on the personal diary of a former high school senior girl reflecting events of the years 1990-1991.

The books of Anastasia Novykh are phenomenous for the fact that every person sees as if in the mirror something of his or her own, purely personal. This book discloses the inner world of a sixteen-year-old girl, who suddenly encounters death face to face. This pushes her to reconsideration of her own life and search of answers to the everlasting questions: "What are we living for? What is the sense of life? Who am I really? Why are most of people on earth – believers? For if they believe, they must be hoping for something. What is the path by which the great achieve their inner immortality? What is hidden beyond cognition of the Human nature?"

Ungovernable energy of inner exploration leads her to meeting with a most erudite man, a martial-arts master and a very enigmatic Person, Sensei. Unordinary soul-staggering world-view of Sensei, his fascinating philosophy and knowledge of the world and of humans, dynamic martial-arts, worldly wisdom, alternative medicine, ancient spiritual practices (including effective techniques for tackling negative thoughts), human abilities phenomena. This and much more the girl learns, having touched upon the world of Sensei. But most importantly, she finds answers to her principal inner questions and learns from the personal experience that people are granted the most powerful creative force from above – the power of belief and love.

ISBN 978-966-2296-10-5

© Anastasia Novykh, 2009
© Translation by Anna Lanovaya, 2009
© Sensei Publishing house, 2009

Prologue

The silent, warm summer night has long entered its sovereign rights, relieving the bustling day with all its important and troublesome running about. Its deep, dark veil was calming and sweetly lulling all living beings, slowly submerging them into a deep sleep. This charm didn't affect only hearts in love, for whom eternity seemed to pass in an instant. On the sea shore, in an uninhabited place, a lonely fire crackled, casting mysterious shadows. A formless creature sat alone in front of it. Its only witness was an infinite universe, brightly illuminated by starlit worlds, and the moon, inviting eternity with its silvery sparkling path on the water surface. All around was such a stillness that even the sea couldn't dare to disturb it with the soft noise of its waves. Time seemed to have stopped, losing all its meaning. It was the moment of eternity.

The creature started to move, making

strange sounds, and slowly divided itself into two stirring parts. Human speech could be heard in the air, "God, how good can it be sometimes in this sinful world."

"Honestly, I don't even want to leave."

"That's what I'm telling you."

The fire was blazing brightly, jealously trying to win back a piece of space from the night. Its luminous glares with variable success were first swollen by the darkness and then fearlessly running far ahead, illuminating nature with its natural tones.

"So, what will your decision be, Rigden?"

"My conclusions are, of course, sad. But I think it is still worthwhile to wait a little for a final decision... I suppose it's worthwhile to remain here for some time."

"It's not all that bad. If you decide to stay, give them another chance and let me..."

Suddenly, from nowhere, a light breeze flew over the sea, breathing life into the moonlit path, which charmingly sparkled with its silver hues, alluring leading into a hazy distance. It was as if nature was teasing the creature, embracing it on the one hand with its eternity and on the other with its natural earthly beauty. Apparently, some innermost mystery, known only to it, was hidden in this delicate gust.

1

It's not a secret that destiny guides a man by a complex journey of the finest interrelations, natural phenomena, and intricately bound paths of occurrences and coincidences. At the very end it leads to a concrete event, a final crossroads of the life's path. And here a human dares to hope that he will get a chance to choose. But the same implacable power of destiny, through a net of logically bound circumstances, unnoticeably helps him to make his choice. Because a chain of events, by its plan, inevitably should draw together people who don't know each other yet and who, living in their own small world, don't even realize it at the moment. But this acquaintance will make them work together, mutually seeking the same goal, generating a great number of key events in the lives of other people.

I shared the same fare. I was born in a remote Russian village. My parents were in the military, fulfilling their duty in an honest and fair way. And their command, in the same honest and fair way, was sending us into different parts of our boundless motherland – the Soviet Union. That's how our family got to Ukraine, to "the country of blooming chestnuts," where we settled down in a rose-scented miner's land.

I should say that I'm quite an outgoing person with various interests. It was never a problem for me to find a common language with new people. That's why I quickly joined a group of like-minded people in my new home. Together we had different hobbies, including ballroom dancing and going to the cinema, cafes, and the theater. In general, as they say, my life took its normal course.

Everything was nice... up to a certain moment. Destiny has its own plans. Unexpectedly for my relatives and moreover for me, at the very peak of my youth, it threw me into such an arduous trial that I almost died in it because of complete hopelessness and animalistic fear of death.

2

At the beginning of the last school year, I started to have headaches that were strong and chronic. My parents took me for a checkup. Doctors discussed the results mostly alone with them, which disturbed me a lot. It gave rise to shady concerns that one after another started to torment my soul. This complete uncertainty was the worst thing of all.

And all those circumstances were terribly scary up to a certain point, when I overheard by chance my mother's conversation with a doctor:

"...But there should be some way out, shouldn't there be?"

"Of course, a way out can always be found. You see, this small tumor can grow progressively larger over time, and that's very dangerous. It is best to perform an operation now before it's too late... Besides, in Moscow, there is a very good clinic that specializes in these kinds of problems with skilled specialists. The only problem is that it's hard to get there. The waiting list is scheduled for years ahead. But the girl needs it, as you understand, as fast as possible. Otherwise... it's hard to predict the development of this disease, especially if it's a brain tumor. Sometimes one can live a year, and sometimes even longer... In any case, you shouldn't lose hope. Maybe you have connections that will let you get there..."

I wasn't listening to the rest of the conversation. Only one phrase was pulsating in my head: "One year... and the end!" Emptiness and hopelessness gripped my soul. Noisy hospital fuss was gradually fading out, giving way to a rising whirl of thoughts: "I will die in the prime of my life! But I haven't even started to live... Why me? What have I done to deserve this?!" It was a scream of despair. Tears streamed down my cheeks. It became unbearably stuffy in the hospital crypt, and I ran to the exit. The doctor's voice was ringing in my ears like a threatening echo: "One year! One year...One!"

Fresh air hit me in the face with its dizzy aroma. Little by little I came to my senses and looked around. After the rain, trees stood as if in a fairy tale, with brilliantly sparkling pendants. Purity and renewal was shining all around. Warmth, coming from the ground, was covering the asphalt with a light haze, creating an unreal impression of what was happening. God, how wonderful everything was! This beauty of nature that I had never noticed before now gained some new meaning, a new charm of its own. All small problems that had brought me so many worries every day now seemed to be so trivial and stupid. With bitterness and anguish, I looked at the bright sun, fresh green grass, cheerful bird flitting, and thought: "How foolishly I have spent my life. It's a pity that I didn't have time to do something really worthwhile!" All previous resentments, gossip, vanity — all lost its meaning. Now all those around me were lucky people, and I was a prisoner in a death castle.

For some time I was terribly depressed. I lost interest in school, everyday life, all of my previous hobbies. I was avoiding my parents, locking my bedroom door, and indifferently turning pages of books and magazines. I really wanted to cry to somebody, to tell someone how much I was afraid of dying before I had started to live. My closest friend was, of course, my mother. But how can a mother's heart endure such a soul-screaming confession from her child? One day, sitting at the table, alone with my heavy thoughts, I took up a pen and described all my feelings on a piece of notebook paper. I felt a lot better. Then I started a diary. Later on it became my best "friend" that patiently endured all my thoughts about my non-ordinary destiny.

The only thing that somehow distracted me from my gloomy thoughts was communication with my friends. Of course, I didn't tell them anything about my disease. I just didn't want to see them, like my parents, with mournful eyes and faces full of condolence. That would have killed me once and for all. Their funny chatter amused me, they discussed problems that seemed complete nonsense. Now I looked at everything in the light of some different vision, jealous of any human who should leave this mysterious, still unknown world in his heyday. Something in me had definitely changed and broken down.

3

When friends finally managed to drag me out to the cinema from my voluntary home imprisonment, I was surprised to find that I started to perceive even movies completely differently. It was a time when martial arts just started to come into fashion. In newly opened cafes, they showed the most popular martial arts hits for a ruble or three. The athleticism of the athletes, unusual cases of their self-recovery, their will, and their spirit power intrigued me. I knew that it was all the play of actors. However, I couldn't stop thinking that many scenes were based on real phenomenal facts from the history of mankind. That stimulated me to search for articles, books, and magazines on that issue. My evident interest in these phenomena spread to my friends. With hunting passion, they began to find rare books wherever they could.

Amazed by the extraordinary capabilities of these people and by the depth of their understanding of this world, I felt that it had awaken in me some kind of internal power... hope, vague anticipation that the death of my body is not my end! That insight so touched me and inspired something inside of me that I quickly started not only to get out of my depression, but even felt somehow a new impulse for life even though my mind, like before, was aware of inevitable death because few people had ever recovered from cancer. But the new understanding didn't dispirit me and didn't cause fear. Something inside of me simply refused to believe in it. And what's most interesting, it unconsciously started to resist my heavy, dark thoughts.

This new feeling again made me revisit my life and how foolishly I've lived it. I didn't do anything bad in it. But it was absolutely obvious that every day, every hour, I was justifying my own egotism, selfishness, laziness. I wasn't striving to know myself but rather how to gain more points in society through that knowledge. Or, to make a long story short, in all my life, studies, and family life, only one thought was hiding behind it all: "Me, myself and I." And the realization that this small bodily empire of "me" was coming to the big end, that is, to the real death, gave birth in me to all that animal fear, horror, despair, and hopelessness that I had been so intensively experiencing in the last couple of weeks. I realized that death is not as fearsome as its foolish anticipation. Because in reality, it's not the bodily death you are waiting for, but the crash of your egotistic world, which you've been building so hard all your life.

After that realization, I clearly understood that the life I lived and what I've done in it is a sandcastle on the sea shore, where any wave will wash away all my efforts in a second. And nothing will be left, only emptiness, the same one that was before me. It seemed to me that most people around me also waste their lives with sandcastles, thoroughly building them, some closer and some further from the coastline. But the result will inevitably be the same for all of them - one day all will be destroyed by the wave of time. But there are people who sit on dry land and impartially observe this human illusion. Or maybe not even observe, but look afar, over it, at something eternal and unchanging. I wonder, what do they think about, what is their internal world like? After all, if they have comprehended this mortality, it means that they have realized something really important, something really worth spending their life on.

These questions began to worry me more than anything else. But I didn't find answers to them. Then I turned to the literature of major world religions. The great figures, such as Buddha, Jesus, Mohammed, were those who had already been observing from the shore. But how did they get there? It's written everywhere: by concentration, faith, prayer. But how? Explanations of their followers were so confusing, so odd and veiled, that my brain was falling asleep when my eyes were making efforts to read the same words ten times over. The teachings of those geniuses were interesting, but they only reflected the common truth of all mankind. Perhaps the essential grain of knowledge was hidden in between the lines. But, alas, I was just an ordinary human being, not the "chosen" one, so I wasn't able to grasp it with my mind although reading of certain lines did evoke something inside of me.

Then a new question arose. Why are there so many people in this world who believe? If they believe, it means they hope for something in the future. In all world religions, there is life after death. Even after throwing away the legends and myths, then possibly there really is something - but what? How does it express itself? How does it manifest itself?

I've tried to get deeper into the paths of religion but just got more confused. The only thing that I understood was that there is one thing that unites all the world religions – and it was the power of faith of the people, their attempts to understand God and themselves. And I discovered that people were searching for the very same thing in their search, and they achieved some results on their way, and in fact many of them didn't belong to any religion. They just were wise and talented individuals.

Then, what's the matter? Why is this phenomenon inherent to human nature? What's behind it? There were plenty of questions, but too few answers. That gave me cause to search further.

Gradually, everyday life was getting back to normal. Moreover, some unusual courage started to arise in me because in my case I had nothing to lose. Therefore I had to quickly realize all my desires. "If I could spend every remaining day effectively, that could substitute for my whole life." Arming myself with such a motto, I started to look intensively for books on that issue, go in for sports, catch up with school, and attend different hobby groups. All my days were fully filled up, and I didn't have time to think about the bad. Even though the headaches reminded me about the worst, despite it all, I kept eagerly searching and attempting to understand everything new that I didn't know or wasn't able to do.

While my parents were trying to find different loopholes in order to get into the Moscow clinic, my ungovernable strivings brought me to study Kung-fu. Our group didn't miss any film about our eastern martial arts heroes, and with a sinking heart we watched triple somersaults, overturns, undercuts, and jumps of sportsmen. And when they started to open Wushu schools in our town, where they were actually practicing Kung-fu, our group got extremely excited. We visited one school after another. But in the first school, the teacher was too angry and ignorant; in the second, the teacher considered himself to be almost Bruce Lee, even though he was only teaching ordinary wrestling mixed with boxing; in the third, the guy was simply a cheater and a drunkard. We were looking for a teacher who would be like the heroes we had seen in the eastern martial arts films. And, as they say, the one who's looking will always find. But what we found was more than unexpected because it surpassed our ideals even in our dreams.

4

After a few unsuccessful visits to several schools, we were told to try a school located in the outskirts of our town, near an old mine. We didn't believe that we would see anything better than what we had seen in the town center, but something was definitely drawing us there. After spending half a day questioning a great number of locals, we finally found it.

"Indeed," in a low voice confessed my friend Tatyana, "this place is, of course, quite scary. If we will be practicing here, I will die from fear. I already have goose bumps."

I too felt a light shiver, even though the weather was quite warm. Approaching a dilapidated old building, blooming with moss, even always-silent Slava couldn't keep quiet:

"Well, well! I think we've just wasted our time. Don't tell me that someone is practicing in this out-of-the-way hole. I bet, only mice are practicing here at night."

Andrew, whose face and figure were slightly reminiscent of the Russian Schwarzenegger, concluded significantly, "Generally speaking, the outside form always corresponds to its contents. It's very likely that we'll reinforce that saying."

And having pulled the handle of a worn-out door, he heard crafty words cited by Kostya with regret: "I'll bet the doctor's in your body yet."

With loud laughter, we rushed into the sports hall. But our cheerful mood quickly changed to mute amazement because inside there were around sixty people.

"Oho," Slava whistled, "there you are!"

But I wasn't listening to my friends' puzzled remarks. My eyes were immediately fixed on a fair-haired man. Even though that man didn't differ from the others standing in the crowd, something in him was definitely intriguing me. "God, his face looks so familiar," I thought. His appearance reminded me of someone I knew well. But who? I started to dig intensively in my memory, recalling all my friends from different cities, my numerous relatives and their friends. But all my attempts were in vain. I was awaken from that wild stream of memories by the melodic voice of Sensei (the Teacher) who turned out to be that mysterious young man.

"So, newcomers," he said with a smile, "why do you stand like a girl after her first kiss? Here you either practice or leave. It's your choice."

That voice!... I was so amazed. For sure I'd heard his voice once somewhere. But where and when?

Our small company went together to the locker rooms. And all that time, buzzing thoughts continued to demand satisfaction of their useless curiosity. Getting ready for the training, I tried to ask other people around me about Sensei, to find out where he was from. But it turned out that nobody knew anything clearly. This intrigued me even more.

Unlike slow Tatyana, I quickly put on a white kimono and went to the sports hall hoping to find more answers there. But there I got only more questions.

What struck me at first was the fact that there were people of all ages, from fourteen to fifty years old, and that was strange by itself. I'd not seen something like that in any previous school. I thought: "What can unite so many people of different beliefs, ages, and life experiences? If it's only the martial arts, then what kind of master and psychologist do you have to be in order to attract and interest all of them?"

When the training began, the second thing that struck me was the ideal discipline and friendly atmosphere that surrounded us. Nobody here forced anybody to do anything, but no one ever thought of breaking the discipline. Everyone sincerely tried to do his best, and that was astonishing in comparison with our previous unfortunate experiments. Our company tried to show ourselves only from our best side, intensively puffing, groaning, and sweating. But even during that activity (painful, as it seemed, for my badly trained extremities), one thought didn't leave me: "How was it possible to create such a discipline without, as they say, carrot and stick? What have all these people found here for themselves that they train their bodies with such enthusiasm? And why do they all train in silence?!" My feminine mind finally rebelled. "Why won't anybody say at least one word!" For my curious, talkative nature, this was a complete disaster. But I hoped to gain at least something during the training.

After the warm-up, we heard three strong claps of the sempai (senior disciple). It was a kind of a signal. People started to form a circle by sitting on their knees on the floor. When everybody sat down, the Teacher went out simply and easily to its center. He began to tell the history of the Tiger style as if he were telling it not to the crowd of silly disciples, but to his old friends. For the first time, I learned that the Tiger style is the only style that preserved its original martial spirit without any changes.

It appeared in China. One of the Shaolin masters observed the behavior of tigers and created his own style distinguished from the others by greater aggressiveness and danger. The style has no sportive roots. Its martial spirit was transmitted from Teacher to disciple, changing his consciousness to the level when he begins to feel and to think like a tiger. By its wisdom it's only inferior to a more ancient style called Dragon.

"All right, theory is just a theory; it's time to warm up a little," Sensei said.

He called three fighters - strong, tall, athletic guys – to the tatami and demonstrated a couple of defense and attack techniques from this style. First he showed the moves at high speed, where the real blows were happening. Honestly, I, and probably many others too, didn't even notice when the Teacher struck the blows. All that my eyes could record was the fact that Sensei passed by three fighters and waved his hands for a second. I didn't even realize what had happened before they had time to fall. The same happened during the demonstration of defense techniques. The speed of the blows seemed to be unreal to me. And my brain, unwilling to comprehend that, suggested artfully: "Maybe they fell down on purpose, probably pretending." But it was impossible that the men's faces, distorted by pain, were faked. Sensei came up to them calmly and helped restore their breathing by poking his fingers into some points on their bodies. After that, the boys were able to recover from the pain and shock and continue the training. That entire scene was accompanied by silent contemplation of the amazed crowd.

After that the Teacher started to explain the technique of the Tiger style in detail, slowly showing each movement and the targets for the blows. I thought that these movements were too complicated to be able to be thrown in a split second.

Having split up into pairs, people did their best and repeated diligently what they'd just seen. A plump man of about fifty years old was puffing not far from me, comically ejecting his short hands and legs. His face, with chubby, bulged-out lips, looked like a big dumpling and was neatly shaved. His wise eyes looked through thick glasses. A small bald spot, with errant hairs turning gray, was shining on his head. "And how did he get in here?" I thought. "It's hard to tell by his appearance that he has been practicing martial arts all his life... What is he looking for here? Has he decided to master Kung-fu in his old age?!"

My thoughts were interrupted by Sensei's voice correcting the attack technique of a pair of young, strong boys near me.

"Who strikes like that? What are you doing, Valentin Leonidovich? You are a future doctor, aren't you? You should understand why you strike, where you strike, and what is going on during this process. Your goal is to cause a painful shock, not just to flap your hands. A blow should hit the exact location of the nerve or nerve plexus. It should be instantaneous. The faster, the better. Why? To cause a spasm in the muscle tissue. In its turn, the transmitted nerve impulse, through reflex channels of the nervous system, will cause intense irritation of the nerve-knot, which will inevitably lead to inhibition of a certain part in the brain cortex. In other words, the man will fall into a stupor caused by the nerve shock..."

A crowd of curious guys began to gather around him during this conversation. Sensei continued to explain, "But the blow should be delivered taking into consideration that every human being has its own anatomical peculiarities. That's why not everybody will be affected by an ordinary blow to this anatomical point. So in order to be one hundred percent sure, you should strike not with a straight "tsuki" (blow) but a blow with a twisted fist at the moment of the contact, so that the blow goes deep inside. As a result, a big "damage zone" will appear...

"This strike goes into the point between diaphragm and solar plexus. Why exactly there? Because there passes one of the twelve pairs of cranial nerves, the so-called "nervus vagus" or the vagus nerve. It not only passes that point but also forms the nerve plexus which forms two vagus trunks close to esophageal opening. And what is the vagus nerve? It is, first of all, innervations of respiratory organs, the digestive system, the thyroid and parathyroid glands, adrenal glands, kidneys. It also takes part in innervations of the heart and vessels. Therefore the correctly delivered blow to this point causes an intense irritation of the nervous system, which temporarily distorts functioning of the cerebellum. And the cerebellum, as you know, is responsible for coordination of all movement functions. Man is momentarily disoriented. In other words, it means that you have time to make a certain decision. For example, to deliver another blow or to run away.

The last word caused a lot of selfish smiles on the faces of the surrounding people, including myself. "What? To run away?!" I thought to myself dreamily. "If I've just dealt such a powerful blow, I would, I would... wouldn't chicken out, that's for sure!"

At this moment, the Teacher looked at the smiling crowd and said seriously, "And why not run away, if that's the best way out in this situation? In some cases it's a lot better to get hit ten times in your own nose rather than to kill... to take somebody's life."

His words made me shake and turn red, ashamed by my own egotistic thoughts and megalomania. With bitterness, he brought me back to the tough reality of my existence.

"Because human life is invaluable," Sensei went on, "your objective is to cause only a muscle spasm, a painful shock, in order to prevent the undesirable development of the situation. And in no way should you injure internal organs, break ribs or something else; that is, you should not cause serious after-effects to your opponent. That's why we spend so much time here, in order to master the right technique of blows. Otherwise, if you deliver a powerful, uncontrollable strike, it is possible to cause great harm to the body or even to bring to death. What for?!... You should respect human life because one day you may happen to be in his place... Or maybe one day he will save your life. Because it is very likely that when you are in trouble it will be this human who will appear to give you a helping hand and save you. Because life is unpredictable and anything might happen in it, even the most unbelievable, what you yourself can't imagine."

Throughout the rest of the training, I was very impressed by this peculiar, easily understood lecture of profound anatomy and unusual philosophy. It completely captured my thoughts, and from time to time I found myself thinking over what I had heard.

Three claps of the senior sempai meant the end of the training. When everyone traditionally lined up, he commanded:

"Dojo ni rei" (which means a bow to the martial spirit of the sports hall).

"Sensei ni rei."

The Teacher also politely bowed in response and said, "We'll meet as usual at the same time. And now whoever needs to, change, and whoever needs to, stay."

"There you are! And who needs what? Who stays? I want, too..." I thought to myself. But the majority ran in single file to the changing rooms, carrying me along. Running past Sensei, I saw the chubby man in glasses approaching him.

"Igor Mikhailovich," he said to the Teacher, with respect in his voice. "Concerning our previous conversation. Here, I brought something for you..."

The rest I couldn't hear in the noise of laughter and jokes of guys running close with me. In the women's changing room, a storm of emotions already began to roar, caused by the discussion of the most vivid moments and Sensei's explanations. All this was happening amidst women putting on many layers of clothes on their wet bodies.

A girl with bright curls was changing next to me. Getting acquainted with her, I asked, "Have you been training here for long?"

"No, only for three months."

"And does he often tell and show such things?"

"Well, probably when it's necessary. But, when he is in a good mood, he shows much more...Today it was nothing out of the ordinary."

"Not so bad, nothing out of the ordinary", I thought to myself. "I can't imagine what something special would be then?!"

"What style did he master, the Tiger?"

"Not only. I've heard from the senior guys that have been training here for a long time that he perfectly mastered the Dragon, Snake, Wing-chun, Cat, Mantis, and Monkey styles, and a whole range of other styles that I just can't remember."

I gave her a distrustful gaze, "When did he have time to master all that? He looks like a young man. People sometimes spend their whole life mastering just one style."

"I was also surprised at first," she went on. "But the guys say that, according to the Teacher, a young body doesn't mean the age of the soul." My new acquaintance answered, shrugging her shoulders.

"Who is he, then?!" I started to become nervous, and my old thoughts, together with this new information, once again began tormenting my unsatisfied curiosity.

"An ordinary man," I heard in reply.

Having changed, our company crowded before the exit and contemplated with admiration the unusual technique of a couple of athletically built guys who were training with the others who had stayed. I'd never seen such genuine, naturally beautiful undercuts, overturns, elusively smooth withdrawals, even in movies. But what struck me the most was the speed of their movements. "Is it really possible to move at such speed and still be able to orientate yourself so well in space?" I thought to myself. "Great! And where is Sensei among them?"

Sensei turned out to be sitting quietly aside, looking through a pile of papers and books with bookmarks, presented by Dumpling. Two more men were sitting nearby carefully listening to the explanations of the Teacher. Then Dumpling unfolded a yellowed map, and all four inclined over it as if it were a priceless treasure. Sensei started to mark something there with a pencil, constantly commenting and explaining it. I really wanted to get my curious nose in there, but at that time we were gently pushed by guys trying to get out.

"Hey, guys! Why are you standing here? Don't you know the law of this dojo? You either train here or you stay on the other side of the door. If you want, go back in, and if you are going out, go out, don't disturb the others."

Together we streamed out outside. "It's not fair!" I thought jealously. "They've stayed, why can't we?" But, of course, I didn't say anything aloud.

5

We spent almost one whole hour waiting for the only bus in that district, strenuously tamping the earth that was called the bus stop. But the bus didn't come. So we walked to the tramway, which the locals said was fairly close: only some thirty or forty minutes of walking. But because we weren't familiar with the area, we spent an hour and a half getting there. But nobody paid attention to those unpleasant circumstances. Everybody passionately shared impressions of the training.

"So," said Kostya smiling, "are we going to the next training?"

Almost simultaneously we all said, "Yes!"

"I don't know about you," said Andrew, the biggest fan of martial arts among us, "but I think I found what I wanted, at least for now. Cool training!"

"Yes," Kostya interrupted him, "today I learned a lot more than during all our visits to different schools."

The guys nodded in agreement. Suddenly Slava stopped, tapped himself on the forehead, and said with horror, "Shoot! We forgot to ask how much it costs!"

Andrew placed his hand on Slava's shoulder and reassured him, "Don't worry, old man, I've asked Sensei. He said: 'The more the better. But not more than five rubles. Preference will be given to the pure gold of royal coinage'."

Everybody laughed. Slava even took a deep breath of relief, which was understandable because he was a good guy but from a poor family. He could not afford to pay for the training in the other schools. To get fifteen or twenty rubles a month meant a real fortune for him. Loudly recalling some episodes that happened during the training and the Teacher's funny jokes, we didn't even notice how we got to the tram stop.

6

The working week had begun. We got very interested in the vagus nerve story and body innervations in general. For the remaining days of the week, we tried to uncover details from our biology and anatomy teachers. But they didn't give us any concrete answer, saying only that most likely it had to do with advanced anatomy, which was studied in medical universities. This fanned the fire of our interest even more and gave us an impulse to search for these kinds of books through our friends and relatives.

All that time, I was trying hard to search through my memory in order to figure out where I knew Sensei from. I even took time and went through all my family photo albums. But my attempts were in vain. As before, life went on in a continuous search for answers to unknown questions.

We could hardly wait for the next training. So as not to be late, we departed two hours earlier. When our company arrived at the sports hall, we were surprised to discover that we weren't first, even though there was still half an hour before the training. There were thirty people already waiting, like us unwilling to miss something interesting right from the beginning. Our guys, getting acquainted with some of them, jokingly came to the conclusion that we, in comparison to those poor guys, live quite close by. Because they lived in such distant districts, some people had to spend almost half a day on their journey, changing a couple of different types of transport and wearing out their soles walking a great many miles. And only a few lucky ones drove here in their own cars.

"So, guys," Andrew concluded, "you may show off and yell that we are locals!"

Sensei arrived soon, surrounded by a group of guys. People started to smile and act friendly. Separate groups merged into a single crowd greeting the Teacher and entering the open sports hall. We also got caught up in this wave of good feelings. But our joy didn't last long.

At the very beginning of the warm-up, two respectable looking men walked in and, approaching Sensei, began whispering something to him in a familiar way. Having agreed upon something, the Teacher entrusted the senior sempai to continue the training, and having slipped on a jacket right over his kimono, walked out with them. From that point forward, there was endless suffering of our extremities.

The senior sempai, obviously planning to train us the same way he trained his muscular body, carried out a warm-up in a tough tempo, as if we were being prepared for a gold medal. There was such a difference between Sensei, with his graduated exercises, and the senior sempai, who tried to make us Olympic champions with a full set of medals before the Teacher returned. At the end of the warm-up, we heard the command to relax, which for some reason was named by the sempai the "dead body position." People in the sports hall, including me, fell down to the floor with such a loud sound that it really seemed that exhausted dead bodies were lying all around. Later, I found out that the sempai interpreted some commands in an unusual way because he was a policeman.

After that exhausting warm-up, we started to repeat after our chief instructor basic exercises mastering blows, blocks, and stances. I had the impression that I was in the Japanese army, where soldiers executed commands in an exact and simultaneous manner, loudly counting in reply in their native language.

When Sensei walked in, I breathed in with ease. He took his jacket off and continued the training as if nothing had happened. Having noticed a mistake made by a young man standing in the first row, he corrected him courteously: "The correct blow should be delivered with this part," he circled the area on the bones of the forefinger and middle finger. "This way... You shouldn't use these two neighboring fingers (ring finger and pinkie finger) because the incorrect blow can seriously damage your wrist."

And, already addressing the crowd, he added: "It's necessary to work hard and long on yourselves not just to correctly deliver blows, but also not to harm yourselves. A straight fist blow, as I have already said, is one of the basic martial arts techniques. And without thorough preparation, the fist can be easily hurt. If you train every day, the flexor tendons of the fingers, which are located over here, will part over the sides of the metacarpophalangeal articulations II and III of the fingers in such a way that the bones will become protected and dense. Only then will you be able to easily deliver blows without harming yourselves."

Someone asked him, "To achieve that, should we start hitting something very hard?"

"No need for such a sacrifice," objected Igor Mikhailovich. "Start hitting a punching bag. Or, if somebody doesn't have one, use a sand bag. I think everyone can make one at home. But what's important is to slowly exercise the blow, gradually increasing speed. And don't be lazy, really work at full power. Then the result will come."

The training ended with another demonstration of new techniques from the Tiger style and practice of the previous moves. And again, after the training, puffy Dumpling posed questions to Sensei. There were many people around who wished to talk to Sensei or to listen to him. But Dumpling impudently crawled through the surrounding crowd, including us, and took the Teacher aside, obviously considering his question more important. Not being able to wait for the end of their conversation, we went home.

7

A couple of days later, we got a good news: somehow Kostya managed to get the university manual of anatomy through friends of his parents. Our joy was infinite. First, of course, we satisfied our curiosity about the vagus nerve by touching and detecting its routes in our bodies. Kostya wasn't too shy during this experiment and conducted his diagnostics right on Tatyana, making her squeak and us laugh. Then we examined more thoroughly the structure of our hands. And later we started to examine in detail, with evident interest, our bones, muscles, tendons, nerves, organs, and brain. I can't say that I didn't know it before. In general, we studied all of this during anatomy classes. But it was the first time that I looked at it from a different point of view. And it was the first time I was interested in it not because of school, but rather to know it for myself.

I really wanted to examine my muscles and joints in order to understand why and how we move. How do muscles take part in our exercises, and how are they reflected on our internal organs? What happens during the blow? What is pain from the physiological point of view? Why do people suffer at all? And finally, what is going on in my own brain? Perhaps, the last thought was the most important because subconsciously it had been tormenting me.

The guys commented on what we had seen during the training just as passionately, but they were motivated by their own reasons. We agreed unanimously that we didn't know anything in this sphere and that we should fill this gap together. In order to do that, we spontaneously created a special card game. We drew separate cards for bones, muscles, blood and nerve vessels, the lymphatic system, organs, and the brain. Then we made attempts to put that puzzle together, one by one, trying to identify them not just by name, but also by the corresponding functions. At first, of course, it was hard. But all this was accompanied by such jokes, such a passion that, whether you wanted to or not, you'd remember.

Before the next training session, we formulated a couple of questions on biomechanics of the blow and decided to ask Sensei after the training in order to find a reason to stay longer. But that day, life itself gave us an opportunity to do this without our secret conspiracy plan.

At the end of the training, Sensei organized free fights. People sat down on the floor, creating a big circle, and fighters were selected and invited by Sensei two by two into its center. Andrew was chosen, and his opponent was a novice, also brawny and athletically built, chosen by Sensei. Having made a traditional bow to each other, the guys started the fight. For some time, they fought as equals. But Andrew turned out to be faster and nimbler, and that let him win. The approving clap of Sensei meant the end of the fight. Our guy helped his competitor stand up. Bowing to each other and to the Teacher, they took their places.

And when more serious fighters began to walk out to the improvised ring, Andrew couldn't stand watching. Inspired by his recent victory, he volunteered to fight again. He lost almost immediately. This circumstance greatly fanned his dissatisfaction with himself. Infected by his emotional mood, our company screwed up all its courage and asked Sensei to stay for additional training. The Teacher anwered smiling, without objections, "You know the law of this dojo: If you want to train, you stay and train."

That day, fortune was on our side because Dumpling was not present at the training to irritate us with his importunity. Access to Sensei was free, and we could ask him about all aspects of the training that interested us.

While the majority of the crowd was leaving, all the rest were perfecting their blows' weak sides. The ones we named "speedy guys" worked on their own level, and the rest of us on our own. But Sensei was closely watching all and correcting the mistakes he noticed. In the already deserted building, he showed us new kata (shadowboxing), which united the speed of undercuts, blows, overturns, and sharp withdrawals. When I started to practice them, Sensei suddenly came up to me from behind and, putting his hand on my shoulder, said "You better not do this."

I turned to him in surprise: "Why?"

At this moment our eyes met at a close distance. I had such a drilling feeling as if someone were looking through me from head to toes with an X-ray. I've never seen such a gaze. It was very unusual, piercing, and strange.

"Because."

That answer puzzled me a little. I was standing quite confused, not knowing what to say.

Keeping silent for a while, he finally added: "It would be better for you to do these kata."

Sensei showed me movements that smoothly changed one into another, with deep breathing following them. All that time I was repeating after him almost automatically. And when he went to help others, endless questions started to flash in my head: "What did he mean? Can it be that he knows about my diagnosis? But how?! I didn't tell any of my friends, and so far I didn't show it in any way during training." And during this process of thinking, I made an unbelievable discovery. At school, home, at ballroom dances, I had sometimes a sudden, throbbing, continuous headache, but here, no matter how much I tortured my body, this headache had never appeared. "Why? What is the reason for that?"

Being deep in my thoughts while working on new techniques, I didn't notice how people crowded around Sensei, having interrupted their exercises. And when I finally realized that, I joined the listeners in order not to miss something important.

"Can you tell us how we can learn a technique of the real blow, just by training our muscles?" Andrew asked.

"No. First of all, by training your mind," Sensei replied.

"And what does it look like?"

"Well, to be clearer, let's say it this way... A muscle is like a mechanism that executes its function. It has certain programs coming from the brain in the form of neuron impulses. As a result of the work of such programs, signals arise in the brain that cause contractions of a group of muscles. Thus it results not only in movements of extremities but also in complex moving acts. It means that our training leads to a purposeful perfection of our brain and therefore of our muscles. The better and faster the trained brain works, the faster and better the muscles work."

"And what about the highest mastery of martial arts fighters?" Kostya asked, joining the discussion. "I've read somewhere that masters can deliver a blow before they even think of it. How does it happen and why?"

"Well, guys. You touch upon such a serious subject. But I'll try to explain in a few words... The whole trick is not just to simply train your muscles but to imagine a concrete situation, or your opponent. And the most important is to know exactly where you hit, into which tissue, and what is happening inside of that body, what's the power level of the blow, and so forth. If a man strikes thoughtlessly, just to practice, then all his efforts are in vain! A true fighter, while practicing on a makivara, first of all works with image. He imagines how the opponent opens up, and at that moment he delivers a blow, being conscious of all possible consequences. In other words, he trains his brain."

"And what is happening in the brain during that?" one of the senior guys asked.

"The brain evaluates the situation through visual perception, analyzes it and makes a decision. Then it sends that command to the cerebellum or, in other words, to the motion center. And from there, through the nerves, the corresponding signal arrives into the muscles. All that activity is being fixed in the memory. Then, during the fight, this memory unconsciously returns but without a complex chain of analysis and commands in the brain. In other words, when an opponent just opens up, a master has already counteracted automatically. Let's say it's a different frame of mind, a different innervation, and different workings of the brain."

"Does it happen on a subconscious level, from the physiological point of view?" asked Kostya, showing off his erudition.

"You are absolutely right. Complex reflex motion reactions proceed now on the level of unconditional reflex," said Sensei smiling. He added, "in the school anatomy program such things are described as conditional and unconditional reflexes. The unconditional are genetic by nature. They determine the regulation of the internal medium of the body and preservation of the species. And to the conditional belong the acquired reflexes arising as a result of accumulated experience and new skills. But even they are based on unconditional reflexes. Human beings have a lot of unconditional reflexes, connections, reactions regulating the spinal brain, the after brain, and the middle brain, the subcortical sections of cortexes of the cerebral and cerebellar hemispheres..."

"And is 'the highest art' what you told us at the beginning?" Andrew asked with excitement.

"No, it's only a first step to real mastery. In 'the highest art,' the major work is based on pre-vision. It is the work of epiphysis which is located above the cerebellum in the epithalamus area of the thalamencephalon."

"And is epiphysis just a section of white matter?" asked Kostya.

"No, it's the so-called pineal gland that weighs only one carat. However, it plays a huge role in the vital activity of the body. It is one of the most mysterious parts of the human brain and of the human as a whole. Unfortunately, science doesn't know anything about its true functions."

"And who does know?" asked curious Kostya.

"Those who need to know," Sensei answered with a cunning smile and went on. "So, working on pre-vision, a master subconsciously obtains the ability to catch his opponent's thoughts. It means that, as soon as the opponent thinks about striking somewhere, the master has already simultaneously taken the exact counteraction that is necessary. All that happens unconsciously, in a few split seconds."

"I wonder if only masters of martial arts face this phenomenon of momentary speed?" Andrew asked thoughtfully.

"Why? Not only. Many people often face these phenomena of mind. Some acquire it after long special training. For example, circus acrobats that catch knives or arrows at great speed. Other people have experienced the influence of unconditional reflexes in their lives. Let's say you are seriously scared by someone or something, for example, by a dog; you can momentarily execute a series of movements. And only later when the danger has passed you realize how fast you have done it. This ability is implied from the very beginning in human genes. Otherwise, people wouldn't have survived in ancient times when they had to save themselves by running from mammoths, saber-toothed tigers, or other predators."

We stood silent, enchanted by Sensei's words. At that time somebody knocked on the door. It caught me off guard, and everything inside of me contracted. It wasn't a time when people were out just for an evening walk. Sensei calmly opened the door under the watchful eyes of our company.

"Oh, it's good that I've caught you here," an unknown man greeted him shaking his hand. "I was just about to look for you at home. You see, there is such a case..."

"All right, wait a second," remarked Sensei. Turning to us, he said, "Guys, you have fifteen more minutes and then we have to go home."

Half an hour later, we were standing outside, waiting for the others. Igor Mikhailovich closed the sports hall and quickly said goodbye to us, then drove off in a car.

"Well," I was getting angry with myself, "I wanted to ask Sensei after the training about his mysterious 'because,' but it didn't work out. I should have asked him in the sports hall. But there are too many curious ears over there. That's the trouble!"

On the way home, everyone thought about his own experiences. And this was not strange, after such trainings there was always something to think about. Some of us thought silently and some aloud. For almost half of the way, Andrew was trying to convince us or most likely himself that he had lost just by accident.

"It's a pity that I didn't have nunchaku with me. Never mind, I will bring them to the next training. And then I'll show them!"

That spectacle promised to be really thrilling, as we knew how good Andrew was with nunchaku. It was his favourite skill.

8

Our company looked forward to this training like no other before. We came early. The sports hall was open. Some guys, having changed, began to warm up. Sensei stood aside and talked with enthusiasm to a gangly old man who was so skinny that his kimono was hanging on him like on a coat-hanger. Not far from them, together with a group of men, stood Dumpling. By the expression on his face, one could see that he didn't hear the funny jokes of his fellow company. It seemed like his ears had turned into a radar that was picking up the slightest sound coming from Sensei and the old man.

"Gosh!" I thought with indignation, "He is here again!"

Following us, a couple of guys from our dojo loudly walked in, in an elated mood. They were accompanied by a proudly walking, untidy looking man, about forty years old, with a week's worth of old bristle on his face. The guys greeted Sensei and announced with evident pleasure:

"We have just met a very interesting man, very sensitive... His name is Vitaliy Yakovlevich."

At these words, the disheveled man made a ceremonious bow with his head and again put on his self-satisfied air.

"He possesses extraordinary abilities, and he politely agreed to demonstrate them to our group..."

Sensei made a polite bow in reply and said, "It would be very interesting to see."

"And very edifying," added Vitaliy Yakovlevich meaningfully, raising up his forefinger.

Our huge curious crowd began to gather around him. Meanwhile "the sensitive one," with an air of great expertise, took out of his jacket's torn pocket a dozen of common kitchen spoons wrapped in a piece of dirty rag.

"What do you think," Kostya quietly whispered to Andrew. "Where has this Neanderthal man got these goods of human civilization?"

"I think he has stolen them from somewhere, probably," replied Andrew.

"I wonder, does he even know how to use them?" Kostya asked, smiling.

Meanwhile, Vitaliy Yakovlevich, in an emphatic manner, undressed down to his waist and, having uncovered his wrinkled fat stomach, began to diligently stick the back sides of spoons to his chest. Our guys burst out laughing, and Kostya added:

"Wow! That's why they say that equipment in the hands of a savage is just a pile of metal!"

A slight wave of amazement ran through the crowd. Spoons got really stuck, and "the sensitive one" was now grandly walking with a puffed out chest as if it were covered with medals of honour.

One of the guys asked, "How are you doing this? How can you explain it?"

It seemed like this was the question Vitaliy Yakovlevich was waiting for. With obvious pleasure, he started to talk instructively about bioenergy and informational fields, biological human magnetism, its phenomenal manifestation only through chosen people, and its all-powerful influence. His speech finally reached its culmination. Walking in front of the astonished crowd with his naked torso covered with the hanging spoons and convincingly gesticulating, "the sensitive one" was passionately declaiming, "...this powerful, pulsating emanation born from the Power of the World's Universal Reason embodies the last step to the perfect spirit. It is able to surround the human mind with the power of its aura. And not only to separate itself from the human body but also to exist out of the body together with the soul. I would say, existence beyond the border is quite conscious. Having accumulated the energy of this cosmic emanation, I have discovered a fantastic super power in myself. I got an invaluable gift of magnetism, clairvoyance, and healing. I have the power to heal miraculously all diseases. I cure through an all-penetrating, omnipresent double flow of emanation, which appears to be an initial cause of all energy and informational fields of the great Universe. With my positive pole I restore power, body, and human aura and also take away the evil eye..."

I noticed that, even though this peculiar lecture was not quite clear to me, my thoughts started to search for the ways of a possible cure in it. "Maybe he will be able to heal me?! Although, of course, it's very hard to believe, but maybe..." Encouraged by the elusive hope, I started to listen much more diligently to the convincing speech of "the sensitive one," already not paying any attention to his appearance.

"... My might, as I was perfecting it, became immense...Here, as you can see, this is one of its manifestations," and he pointed out the stuck spoons.

It looked quite strange. Making circles around the listening crowd, he stuck his stomach out further and further and slightly leaned back, like a penguin. I looked at Sensei. He stood, with hands crossed on his chest and a slightly lowered head, probably already tired of listening. He was smiling ironically.

"...I achieved this perfection due to some mysterious knowledge that is not known to anyone on Earth except the chosen ones. On the basis of that secret information, I developed my own system of spiritual development. But it's not available to every mortal. Even that one, who due to the hardest work and through the atonement of sins and privations will reach the tenth level of my system of perfection, won't be able to realize by himself the great mystery of this teaching. Because it reveals itself only to best of the chosen ones. Only people like me who are able to unite the perishable body with the great spirit, the spirit of Universal Reason, possess the all-mighty of God!"

It seemed like those words were the last drop on Sensei's nerves. Judging by his light wave of movements, it seemed to me that he would lose his temper and punch this man with so much force that even the so-called power of this "alien" wouldn't be able to save him. But despite my forecast, Sensei, clearly enunciating every word, said:

"Mister, isn't it too much responsibility to take on yourself? So far, you haven't demonstrated to us anything that would have proved your words."

"What do you mean, haven't demonstrated?!" Vitaliy Yakovlevich demanded angrily. "Don't you see this?!"

"All this is rubbish," continued Sensei. "Anybody can do it. And there is nothing extraordinary or special in it. You simply need to wash yourself more often."

The whole crowd rolled with laughter. Kostya, hitting himself on the forehead, said in excitement, "Of course! I remember I've read about this trick. He just has a sticky and wet body; that's why the spoons got stuck."

The self-proclaimed Ruler of the Universe and the whole Earth became even more furious and shouted across the sports hall towards Sensei, "What? You are too young to make judgements about such great knowledge! What else can you do except flap your legs?"

Sensei gazed at him seriously. Then he came up and easily took one of the spoons that were slipping away. Everybody around them froze. The Teacher stretched out his hand, holding the thin end of the spoon, and started to make a series of breathing exercises, working on deep breathing. In a minute, his face relaxed and his emotions disappeared. His eyes changed, and it seemed to me they became fathomless. He froze for a split second, fixing his eyes on the spoon. His figure seemed to look like a great sculpture. And at that moment the spoon started to bend fast like a soft fading flower, as if it weren't made from tough metal but from some plastic material. I couldn't believe my eyes. Impossible, but it's a fact!

Sensei regained his usual appearance in a few seconds and calmly said to the shocked Vitaliy Yakovlevich as he returned the bent spoon, "When you can demonstrate for us at least this simple trick, then we will listen to you with great pleasure."

And quickly turning to the crowd Sensei added, "I would like to inform those that haven't changed yet that the training will start in two minutes. The ones who don't make it in time will have to do the push-up penalty."

Having heard these words, we rushed to the changing rooms, outrunning each other, missing the most interesting part: how this newly born God-like bum recovered from his stupor.

"Senior sempai! Why are there strangers inside?!" We heard the voice of Sensei behind us.

During the warm-up I revised my thoughts: "How could I even allow the thought that this bum is able to help me somehow?! Well... But on the other side, in my desperate situation, all I can do is believe in miracles and hope for the best. Here you grasp at any straw just to survive. That's why these silly thoughts arise, because of an internal, almost panic level of fear. No. I should control myself. Anyway, I will find a saving loophole. I'll try to survive. I shouldn't lose hope, and I will fight to the very end!" The most amazing thing was that my firm belief was based on some deep, subconscious feeling, on that something I was looking for so hard. But all this became apparent in vague guesses.

Meanwhile, the warm-up ended up and we started to exercise the bases under the supervision of the senior sempai. Sensei was sitting on a bench discussing something with the gangly old man. "I wish I could hear what they are talking about," I thought to myself. But evidently those curious thoughts were present not only in my head. During the training, despite the fact he was a man with grey hair, Dumpling was always trying, as if by accident, to take a place closer to the Teacher. And with each try he caused in me an indescribable feeling of envy and jealousy. And judging by the accusing gazes of our guys, I was not the only one who felt it.

During the noisy and monotone basic exercises and loudly announced commands, I again got deep into my thoughts. "How did Sensei manage to bend the spoon? And why did he call that phenomenon simply a trick? If that was a trick, then, in my understanding, it should have been thoroughly prepared. But he just took the spoon and bent it with his gaze alone."

I could say that I believed and disbelieved it at the same time. I believed because somewhere I've read about people who possessed such abilities. I recalled that there were described people-magnets. But any objects, regardless what material they were made of - wood, metal, plastic - would stick to them. I remember that I was amazed most of all by the weight those people could hold up: more than ten kilos!

It was a paradox, but I didn't believe that I had seen all that with my own eyes, as they say, "live." Or rather, this disbelief was caused by my reluctance to realize that this fact itself was real. Everything seemed so mysterious. I would have understood if our crowd had been hypnotized, had had it explained to use beforehand what we would see. But Sensei just took it in silence and did it. How?!

Nevertheless, the fact that it was possible was very important for me. It was some kind of, not yet known to me, firm platform formed by Sensei's knowledge. And my subconscious was intensively grasping it in every way possible, resisting those antagonistic thoughts. I don't know why, but I started to trust that interesting man. At least, he obviously knew where there is truth and where there is fiction.

After the basics, finally came the moment long expected by our company. This part of the training we used to call "the free style program" because people, having split up into pairs, were exercising old techniques or some peculiar techniques from the previous trainings. Andrew picked up his nunchaku and being followed by our curious glances came up to the Teacher.

"Is it possible to do something against nunchaku?"

"And do you know how to use them?" Sensei replied with a smile.

"Of course!" bragged Andrew self-satisfied. "I haven't put them down for four years. One could say, I eat and sleep with them."

Andrew demonstrated a couple of, in our opinion, complex movements.

"Not bad," Sensei said.

"And still, is it possible to do something against nunchaku?" Andrew repeated his question, obviously provoking the Teacher.

"Of course... For every Vijai there is a Rajah."

"What?" Andrew asked again, not understanding the last phrase.

"I mean, for every power there is a counter-power. Nunchaku is not an exception."

"Can you show me?"

"I can, but then it will not be fair, you with nunchaku against me... Take somebody else with you."

We looked at each other with astonishment. Nevertheless Andrew went along to look for a partner, and our company to look for the second weapon. To our regret there were no more nunchaku. Instead of that, we found a lot of two-meter-long poles in the sports equipment room.

But although we found weapons fairly easily, finding a partner for Andrew was more difficult. Senior guys flatly refused the proposal to take part in this fight and laughed: "No, thanks, guy. You'd better do it alone."

Finally, Andrew managed to convince a man among the newcomers. Meanwhile, Sensei was peacefully chattering with that skinny old man in the white kimono.

"Here, I found one!" Andrew happily announced to the Teacher.

"You have found one, great. Let senior sempai second us. At his clap, start to attack with full contact. Is that clear?"

That was all Andrew was waiting for. He nodded with obvious pleasure. Sensei walked out into the middle. Andrew stood facing Sensei, and the man with the pole chose a position from the rear right of Sensei. It came to a thrilling moment. All participants were battle-ready, except Sensei. He was standing relaxed, thinking about something and slightly playing with the tips of his black belt, embroidered with gold hieroglyphs.

At the senior sempai's clap, Andrew zealously rushed into a frontal attack, spinning his nunchaku with the speed of the blades of a working propeller. Meanwhile, the other man jumped up quickly and started striking with the pole. What happened next happened in an instant. Sensei hadn't changed his position from the moment the attack was begun but rather kept standing in a deeply thoughtful pose. As soon as his opponents achieved a critical distance with regards to his body, he, without changing his stance, quickly threw his hand forward... if "threw" is the right word because in reality his hand shot out like an attacking snake. The nunchaku folded, spun on it, and flew towards the second fighter. The Teacher accompanied them with a twist of his wrist, slightly changing the trajectory of the flight. The nunchaku made half a turn in the air, aligned, and like the butt-end of a stick, hit the exact middle of the forehead of the man attacking from behind. The second nunchaku's stick, continuing its flight, hit the pole. And the pole, correspondingly changing its trajectory of movement, hit Andrew right in the head. As a result, two unsuccessful fighters clumsily fell down to the floor, not even realizing what happened. And Sensei continued to stand thoughtfully, as if all the turmoil around had clearly nothing to do with him. And then, having come to himself, he asked his "opponents" carefully:

"How are you, guys? Did you get hurt badly?"

"No," Andrew answered confused, intensively massaging a puffed out bump on his forehead. "It's all right."

The other man also nodded.

"I am sorry, I miscalculated a bit," apologized Sensei. Coming up to his previous interlocutor, he said, as if nothing had happened, "You know, I have a great idea! What if..."

Meanwhile, observing the fight, the crowd buzzed in discussion with noises of laughter and amazement about such a quick fight. And one of the senior guys whom Andrew had asked to help said with laughter, "Yeah right, Sensei miscalculated, aha! Don't worry, guys, that's all right. We went through such 'miscalculations' already many times, and all due to our own stupidity."

When Andrew realized what had happened, he simply tormented Kostya and Slava with the same question: "How can that be? One movement... not even a strike?!" Kostya perplexedly answered, "How can we know? Sensei is over there, ask him."

But the Teacher was always busy until the end of the training, first demonstrating new techniques, then showing complicated strikes to the senior guys, then answering endless questions, and at the end of the training talking to the old man. However, Andrew made up his mind to clear that up right then, no matter how.

We got that chance only when the supplementary training was over. We quickly changed and waited at the exit, like guards, as we decided to get what we wanted. But it turned out that Igor Mikhailovich and his guys were going towards the same tram stop. On the way, we started our interrogations.

"How did you manage to best two armed opponents with only one movement?" Andrew asked his sore question.

"Well, weapons have nothing to do with it. This is the technique of using the opponent's force. By the way, it is used in many other styles, for example, Aikido, Jiu-Jutsu, Wing Chun, and others. You need only to catch a moment and use it right away."

"In general it's clear, but in this case, what style did you use?"

"Nothing special," cunningly answered Sensei, shrugging his shoulders, "a little bit of everything."

"But still?" queried Andrew.

"Well, here all you have to know is the physical law of acceleration, distribution of the gravity center in biomechanics, and a little bit of the Snake style."

"Oho!" whistled Andrew.

"And what did you think? All great things are ridiculously simple, but it takes a lot of hard work to master them."

While Andrew was thinking over that phrase, Slava quickly asked, "Is it possible to explain that case with the spoon?"

"Of course, it is possible," Sensei said with a smile. "There is nothing concealed that will not be disclosed, or hidden that will not be made known."

"So, what was that?"

"Ah, just trifles. There is nothing special in ordinary Qigong, or rather one of its modifications."

"And what is 'Qigong'?" Now it was my turn to ask a question.

"I've read somewhere that it is just a breathing technique," Kostya added.

"Yes, many people think so," replied Igor Mikhailovich. "But in reality, Qigong is a meditative and breathing system that allows a person to master his hidden psycho-physical potential. Though in fact it is one of the simplest types of spiritual practices."

That phrase roused the interest of our company and something trembled inside of me after these words. But as soon as I opened my mouth to ask about how we could learn it, Kostya squeezed in with his favorite manner of verbiage: "Well, 'If but a friendly hint be thrown / 'Tis easier than to feel one's way.'"

"Oh, you like Johann Wolfgang von Goethe, do you?" demanded Igor Mikhailovich. "Then, if you've read carefully, he also said the following: 'Now of the wise man's words I learn the sense: / Unlock'd the spirit-world is lying, / Thy sense is shut, thy heart is dead! / Up scholar, lave, with zeal undying, / Thine earthly breast in the morning-red!'"

At that moment, you should have seen the surprise on Kostya's face. He was so much impressed by these words that he wasn't able to immediately find the right answer. That was the first person in his life (except his parents, of course) who talked to him at his 'high intellectual' level. "It serves him right," I gloated in my thoughts. "He used to pose as the only man of great erudition in this world."

"I've read quite a lot of books," our 'Philosopher' started to defend himself, more trying to uphold his pride rather carrying on the topic of the discussion. "And it was written there that the spiritual world is only a fairy tale for kids."

"Who knows," Sensei said indifferently, continuing to quote Goethe, "'Parchment, is that the sacred fount whence roll / Waters, he thirsteth not who once hath quaffed? / Oh, if it gush not from thine inmost soul, / Thou has not won the life-restoring draught.'"

"Hmm! It's easy to say 'the life-restoring draught,'" puffed Kostya. Keeping silent for a while, he added, "As Moliere said, 'Not all things that are talked of turn to facts; / The road is long, sometimes, from plans to acts.'"

"What do I hear?" Sensei joked, "'If we are too wise, we may be equally to blame. / Good sense avoids all extremes, and requires us to be soberly rational.'"

"It sounds familiar..."

"That is from Poquelin, his expression from 'The Misanthrope'."

"Who is that?"

"Well, Jean-Baptiste Moliere. Poquelin is his real surname."

Even in the dim light of street lamps, we could see how Kostya turned red in the face.

"But... but... Eastern wisdom says that a really wise man foresees the end before starting any doing."

"Absolutely right. In other words, it means that a human being possesses mind, and his real power is in his thoughts. Even in the modern world, to put it in scientific terms, you may find, for example, the confirmation of it in the saying of Tsiolkovsky, 'A thought precedes an action, a fantasy precedes a precise calculation.' As you see, in human society nothing has changed throughout the ages. And why? Because, as Valentin Sidorov correctly emphasized, 'The nature of your thought is your own nature. / Master your thought and you will know yourself. / And you will be the ruler of your own.' The real power is the power of mind."

"Yes," uttered Kostya, concluding, "'A head without mind is like a flashlight without a light bulb.'"

"Wonderful words of Leo Tolstoy," agreed Igor Mikhailovich to the complete surprise of the 'Philosopher'. "If you remember, he also has this beautiful saying, 'Thought is the beginning of all. And you can rule your thoughts. That is why the most important thing in self-perfection is to work with your thoughts.'"

Kostya nodded uncertainly. It seemed to hurt his pride even more. So, for the next twenty minutes we witnessed a grand battle with aphorisms, quotes, sayings of native and foreign writers, poets, philosophers, scientists, and I didn't even know most of their names. Meanwhile, I was trying hard to join this dialogue with my essential question, and I was impatient to ask it. But Sensei's polemics with our 'Philosopher' flew uninterrupted, gradually reaching its culmination. I have already got completely angry with Kostya that he took such priceless time just to satisfy his mania of brilliant erudition. But he was so possessed by the discussion that it seemed nothing else in the world existed for him.

At the very end, already coming to the tram stop, after probably going through all his memory, he recited his favorite expression. "Well, as Villon said, 'I know all, save myself.'"

"So, 'You gaze today, while You are You — how then tomorrow, when You shall be You no more?'"

"And who is that?" Kostya almost screamed, completely losing his temper.

"Oh," drawled Sensei with pleasure, "that was Omar Khayyam, a famous Persian poet and philosopher, and a great scientist who was considerably ahead of his time. His full name is Ghiyath al-Din Abu'l-Fath Omar ibn Ibrahim Al-Nisaburi Khayyami. He lived in the eleventh century. His wisdom was highly esteemed even by the Seldjuk rulers of Iran, though he was from Khorasan, a small village near Nishapur. He had very interesting philosophical thoughts. According to his views, the Soul is eternal. It came from the Nowhere into the human body and will return to the Nowhere after death. This world is a strange land for it."

"I wonder," said Tatyana, joining the conversation, "where is the soul located inside of the human body? Just like this philosopher thinks, in the heart, or not?"

"No, he thought that the heart was born on the earth and it is only a part of mortal human flesh, although it's the best and the most 'spiritual' part. Through the heart in particular speaks the soul. But the heart, in his opinion, knows only this world and existence... He has the following interesting lines, when the heart asks the soul about the mysteries of the Nowhere."

Sensei reflected on it for a bit and said, "'I sent my Soul through the Invisible, / Some letter of that Afterlife to spell: / And by and by my Soul return'd to me, / And answer'd "I Myself am Heav'n and Hell.'"

"And what is that 'letter'?"

"It is believed to be 'Aleph' "a first letter in his native language; it's also the number one. As he thought, it is a symbol of the One Existing, a symbol of the Universal Unity." Having looked at Kostya, Sensei ironically added, "What else can be argued about?!"

Kostya was completely confused, not knowing what more to say. I hastened to use that opportunity and exclaimed in a single breath, "How can we learn that system of techniques to master the hidden psychophysical potential?"

"It's very easy. There is no secret at all. The most important thing is, as they say, to have a great desire, and the chance will come soon."

"So, can we learn it from you?"

"Of course."

"And when can we start?" asked Andrew, apparently thinking the same way as me.

"Well, if you are so interested in it, you are welcome to join. I devote an hour and a half for these exercises, twice a week."

"How much does it cost?" asked Slava.

"Do you think it's possible to evaluate spiritual knowledge with money?" said Sensei, surprised. "You guys pay too much attention to this 'paper'. We train just for ourselves, for our own spiritual development. If you want to train, come and train."

Our company fixed in detail a date and a time of the next meeting.

"Eugene will show you the way," added the Teacher.

Eugene turned out to be a tall, lightly-haired, athletically built guy, one of those 'speedy' guys always with Sensei.

"We certainly will come," Andrew answered for all of us.

At that stage we said goodbye to each other. I was beside myself with joy. Finally I got close to what I had been looking for for so long. It seemed I needed to make just one step and maybe I would be able to cross over this abyss and climb out to the solid surface of Existence. I felt that intuitively, with a sort of sixth sense. Although my mind didn't see any real chance to survive. Despite that, as they say, the Soul was singing.

All the way, the guys passionately discussed today's training and what awaited us the day after tomorrow at the spiritual training. Enthusiasm overfilled everyone but Kostya. He was puffed, like a turkey, with gloomily knitted eyebrows.

"Kostya, will you come?" asked Andrew, clapping him on the back.

"I'm not sure, maybe we shouldn't go," mumbled the dissatisfied 'Philosopher'. "We're not the circus clowns to learn those tricks. We'll just waste our time for nothing there."

"Are you stupid, man?" Andrew retorted 'politely'. "Where have you seen a circus clown who can bend spoons just by looking at them?"

"And who teaches others to do it for free," Slava added his strong argument.

"That's what I'm saying. You must be insane! That distresses me!"

"And yet I understand "most kindly would you be," our discontented 'Philosopher' sarcastically replied.

"All right, guys, don't quarrel," said Tatyana. "You should better advise me how to convince my parents to let me go to this training."

"How?" answered Andrew. "Like in this joke, 'A daughter came back home late and her father asks her, What would you call that? The girl replies, I don't know what it's called, but from now on, it will be my favorite hobby."

Everybody laughed. Having agreed upon a new meeting, we went home.

9

We waited impatiently for that day. Finally, on Thursday our company arrived in full in a good mood at the destination point. Arriving at the stop, we discerned two men silhouetted in the dark.

"Oh, there is Eugene over there," said Andrew merrily.

As it turned out, Eugene was with his friend Stas. Having greeted each other, we moved into the unknown, or to be more exact, pitch-dark direction.

"They should've at least hung lamps here," remarked Tatyana, once again stumbling over something.

"Aha," agreed Kostya, "it's not a residential area but a real steeplechase zone."

"Why should they waste the government's money for electricity?" grinned Eugene. "Besides, we already know everything around here perfectly by touch. Moreover, it's unlikely that strangers would like to come to this area, especially by their own will."

"And why is it so?" asked Slava anxiously.

"This place is unusual, remote. Not every beast will run over here, not to mention people. And dogs, do you hear how they howl?"

And really, somewhere close by in the village, a couple of dogs were drawlingly howling.

Tatyana slightly shivered, grabbing my hand.

"And dogs feel danger well," he continued.

"Come on, stop scaring people with fairy tales!" said Andrew, trying to make a joke.

"They aren't fairy tales at all. Try to live here for some time, and you'll find out what sort of devilry is going on here... if you survive, of course."

After that statement, our good mood quickly disappeared. For some time we walked silently looking around. But no matter how much we tried to peer into the pitch darkness, nothing could be seen. Only dim silhouettes of old houses. And what was strange, there was no light there. Dogs alone with their mournful howls showed at least some signs of life in this Godforsaken place.

"Where are we going?" panicked Kostya.

"Where?" mimicked Eugene. "Right where you've ordered... to the black glade."

"Where?!" we exclaimed, horrified, almost at once.

"Gosh, don't yell like that" said Eugene, rubbing his ear deafened by our wild outcry. "I told you, we are going to the black glade."

And stumbling over another pothole, he slightly cursed, "What the hell?! Evil forces try to set a trap everywhere. It's very likely that they will drag away those who remain behind."

Tatyana, who was holding my hand just to be safe, grabbed Kostya's hand with her other hand. I felt how she started to tremble all over. Slava, slightly lagging behind after those words, quickly moved ahead of us. Andrew was walking silently and looked around.

"Where have you seen evil forces and a black glade?" Kostya uttered with fear. "Why should they be here? Absolute nonsense..."

"Where? Over there!" Eugene confidently waved his hand somewhere to the side.

"Why have we come here?" mumbled Tatyana with fear and trembling. "We could have been at home, without caring about anything."

"But you wanted to learn black magic. And now you say 'Why have we come?'" Eugene answered, shrugging his shoulders.

"To learn what?" we asked again all together in amazement.

"I can't believe it!" Eugene made a surprised face. "Didn't you know that Sensei is the most powerful wizard, so to say, the right hand of Lucifer?"

Now it was our turn to stare wide-eyed.

"Who? What? And who is Lucifer?" An avalanche of questions rushed on Eugene.

"All right," our guide grandly stopped the torrent of our questions. "I will explain everything to you now. 'Lucifer' means an angel of light, the right side of God. For the majority of people, he is known under different names. For example, Satan or Devil, whatever you prefer. He is a ruler of the Earth. Second, I emphasize once again that Sensei is his right hand. And his power doesn't have boundaries. For him to bend spoons, it's nothing. He is able to do such things that you can't imagine even in your most dreadful dream! And third, you are very lucky that you can master what you want. You can get extraordinary abilities almost for nothing. Just for a soul about which you don't know anything and you don't even feel. But why am I telling you all this? You will see it now yourselves."

"There you are! I think we got into trouble," Tatyana really got scared.

"That's it!" cried Kostya in a low voice. "And what did I tell you? We shouldn't have come, but you didn't listen. I told you something's fishy here. But I was also stupid, a dummy, I dragged myself with you. What should we do now?"

The panicy fear of Kostya spread to Slava, and he whispered to us, "I think it's high time to run away from here."

"Where?" hissed Kostya. "Do you remember how many times we turned, going in different directions?"

"I don't care!" declared Andrew. "Let's assume that Sensei is a wizard; that's his personal problem. What's important is that he knows much more than me. I won't miss an opportunity to learn that."

"Me either," I responded. I thought to myself, "I shouldn't care at all because this is my chance to survive. And if not, then I have nothing to lose anyway. But maybe it will help..."

We came out on a curved path along a long, lonely fence. At that moment moonlight shone through the clouds. Suddenly, right before us a big black cat jumped on the fence, his eyes burning like yellow-green lights. Caught by surprise, Tatyana and I screamed and hid behind the guys' backs. However, our defenders also froze, rooted to the ground. Only our guides alone continued calmly on their way. Eugene, having seen our stupor, mysteriously whispered, "It's just the beginning." The cat, without paying any attention to us, grandly kept walking along the lone fence, and as if on purpose, in the same way they were guiding us.

"Fie, fie, fie," spit Slava over his left shoulder.

"You should have made the sign of the cross," Andrew said sarcastically.

"Sounds good," Tatyana licked over her dry lips. "They say, if a black cat crosses the road, you should hold on to one of your buttons. Then the evil forces won't even notice you."

Just to be on the safe side, I touched a button with shaky hands. Our company hurried to catch up with our fellows, continuously looking at the dark shadow of the cat.

The path took us to a small glade. The big full moon was ominously creeping out from the clouds. What we saw completely shocked us. In the middle of the glade, with his back to us, stood a man in a black garment with a hood thrown over his head. His figure phosphoresced with the faintly-cold moonlight. Over it ascended light smoke. All around was a weighty, eerie silence. Looking at this scene, we all lost our ability to speak. In that moment, the big black cat jumped right to our feet, stopping all possible movements of our extremities. The last thing our frightened small group managed to do was to instinctively grab our saving buttons. Jumping off in a cheeky way, that beast rushed to the dark figure and started to rub against his feet, to our unspeakable horror.

Looking at such a sinister picture, everything in my mouth dried up, and a shiver ran along my entire body. In spite of my desire to run away, my body stood still, unable to move. I looked at the guys. Tatyana almost crawled over Kostya and grabbed him with a death grip. Kostya himself looked like a plaster monument. Slava stood with an open mouth and wide-open eyes. Even Andrew, despite his earlier optimism, was stamping out with his teeth a fine, nervous quiver. His face was covered with sweat.

Eugene, looking back at us, obediently went up to the dark figure. Raising his hands, he solemnly pronounced, "Oh Great magician, wizard and sorcerer, ruler over all the nations, whose power and might over all land, water, air, and fire stretches over the entire Universe. Your loyal disciples have fulfilled their holy duty. Take in your bosom these lost souls, in order to restore your true and fair authority and power on Earth!"

Eugene made a low bow. During his speech, Sensei turned to him in surprise.

"What? What?" he asked. "Which might, which power? What are you talking about?"

Eugene and Stas both rolled with laughter.

"What's the matter? What are you laughing about?" asked Sensei, while smoking a cigarette. "And where are the other guys? Have you met them?"

Drowning in laughter, Eugene waved towards us, "They are still in a stupor over there and can't come out."

"What kind of stupor?" asked Sensei, not understanding and looking into the dark. "What nonsense have you told them?"

But Eugene couldn't stop laughing, hopelessly waving his hand.

"What a clown!"

"Sensei, don't you know Eugene?" replied Stas, dying laughing.

Looking at all that turmoil, Andrew was first to understand what was going on. Shamefully pulling his hand away from the button, he sighed with relief.

"Well, guys," said Andrew, coming out from the darkness to them. "That was great. The joke was good, but who's going to wash my pants now?!"

This comment provoked an even bigger storm of laughter. Sensei said with a smile, "What did this clown make up this time?"

Andrew started to tell in detail how this "guide" led us through the village, changed according to his stories into the Brocken mountain. We also joined him, enriching the story with our impressions. At the very end, our entire big company, together with Sensei, roared with uninterrupted laughter, recalling our recent feelings.

"I just came earlier today," explained Sensei, laughing through tears. "The light in our village was cut off. Probably the cable was damaged somewhere."

"What a story," Tatyana uttered with her clear voice. "I don't want to mention what we suffered from Eugene, but there was also this cat!"

Meanwhile, the small ball of our big fear sat peacefully, frightened by human laughter.

"It's Samurai," Stas waved his hand and explained. "Sensei's cat. He always follows him."

"Stas, you should have clued us in to what was going on," Andrew said with a smile.

"How?" he shrugged his shoulders. "You dashed aside from every shadow, and if I were to start making faces, we would have had to search for you all over the village."

The guys laughed, having imagined this picture.

"I say," Eugene justified, "it was an ordinary joke. Like Ostap Bender said, 'The most important is to bring confusion into the enemy's camp... Because people most of all are afraid of the unknown.'"

"That's right," said Sensei. "Fear begotten by imagination sees danger even where there is no danger at all. There is one ancient eastern legend about fear. A wise man met the Plague on his way and asked, 'Where are you going?' It answered, 'To a big city. I have to kill five thousand people there.' In a few days the same wise man again met the Plague. 'You said that you'd kill five thousand people but you've killed fifty thousand,' he accused. 'No,' objected the Plague. 'I've killed five thousand; the others died from fear.'"

Having discussed all the funny details of this journey and having dispersed the myth of our unjustified fears by humor and laughter, we switched to more serious topics. Our group was joined by three other guys: Ruslan, Yura, and Victor (senior sempai). A little later came Nikolai Andreevich ("Dumpling"), who turned out to be a psychotherapist. Meanwhile we were talking about Qigong.

"What does the word 'Qigong' mean?" Slava asked Sensei.

"Well, translating this word literally from Chinese, Qigong refers to work with the energy of the air, because 'Qi' means 'wind, gas, breath,' and the syllable 'gong' means 'work, action, or deed.'"

"And this system was invented by the Chinese?" asked Andrew.

"Not really," answered the Teacher. "It is the Hindu system of self-regulation, which migrated to China at the beginning of a new era."

"I've read that there exist different types of Qigong." As always, Kostya put in his remark. "I think there are two different schools."

"There are a lot more of them," said Igor Mikhailovich. "In the modern world there are plenty of different schools of Qigong. For example, Confucian, Buddhist, medical, military..."

"Medical?" I shuddered. "What does it heal?"

"Many diseases."

"So, we need only to breathe the right way?" Andrew interrupted my next question.

"Not only. You also need to think the right way. There is a saying that 'a thought guides Qi, and Qi guides the blood.' Blood is like the ambulance of the body; it includes all necessary medical supplies. In the very ancient medical treatise Huangdi Neijin, it is said that 'when a thought rests in stillness it is free.' It means that you can master Qi. The human who thinks the right way has good health."

"To put it short, a sound mind can only exist in a healthy body," Kostya made a conclusion for himself.

"Not really. I would say, with healthy thoughts there will be a sound mind, and with a sound mind will be a healthy body."

"Could you please explain to me, you always emphasize the importance to think the right way, both during physical trainings and now," remarked Andrew. "But for some reason, before I thought that all we need is just to act the right way. Because thoughts can be different during the choice of action: both good and bad."

"That's where you waste priceless time on the struggle with your own self. You shouldn't have to choose between a good and a bad thought because you shouldn't have any negative thoughts in your mind at all. The goal of the highest Art, the Art of Lotus, is to learn the proper way of thinking; in other words, 'to kill a Dragon inside,' or 'to conquer a Dragon.' Have you heard of such an expression?"

"Yes."

"That is the purpose. The greatest victory is the victory over yourself. What does that mean? It means to win your own negative thoughts, to control them, and to control your emotions. I repeat once again, there shouldn't be anything negative in your mind. Only positive thoughts! Then you won't need to spend time fighting with yourself, and your doings will always be positive. Peace should be first of all inside of you. Peace and harmony."

"So, it means that human thought is reflected in any action?" asked Andrew, thinking about something known only to him.

"It is not only reflected, it guides all action. Because the thought is material."

"Material?" It was Nikolai Andreevich's turn to be surprised.

"Of course. It's a much finer substance, not studied enough yet. But it does exist, it is real, its movements are traced. There have been many effective experiments on psychics and psychic phenomena. There were experiments with our own psychics; for example, Nina Kulagina, Julia Vorobieva, and many others. I don't even mention the rich world practice. This research is conducted all over the world, although it is known by different names. For example, in England it is known as mental investigation. In France it is 'metapsychics', in countries of Eastern Europe 'psychotronics', in the U.S. 'parapsychology', in China 'investigations into extraordinary functions of the human body', and so on.

"And if you look deeply into the history of mankind, you will find there is much evidence that it was known from the earliest of times. In all mythical, magical, and religious views and teachings of people, a firm belief exists that it is possible to influence anyone and anything through thoughts, regardless of the distance, time, and space. In other words, generally speaking, this knowledge has always existed."

Nikolai Andreevich joined again in the polemics, "Well, now you have given us examples of local psychics who became known to us just recently. Why weren't there such people earlier in the Soviet Union? I've been practicing psychotherapy for many years. But studying the mind of different people, my colleagues and I have never come across such phenomena. It's true that recently there were people talking nonsense and considering themselves to be sensitives. And they even tried to prove it. But in reality, it was just their sick imagination, while real psychics didn't exist in the Soviet Union."

"Why didn't they exist?" Igor Mikhailovich was surprised. "They existed, and there were a lot of them! From time immemorial in Russia there existed many of such people. But how were they treated? In ancient, unenlightened times, very seldom were they considered saints, but in the majority of cases, those who refused to obey the church were burned in a fire, put on stakes, depending on the whim of the king.

"Only starting from the second half of the eighteenth century, after the opening of the Academy of Science, the phenomena of the psychic life of human beings started to be researched in Russia more seriously, from the medical point of view. And about one hundred years later, research in that sphere was conducted by many prominent scientists; for example, by one of the founders of your own science, Vladimir Mikhailovich Bekhterev. When he was the head of St. Petersburg's imperial military and medical academy, he himself financed the creation of an entire research institute for the study of brain and psychic activities.

"And during Soviet times? Almost from the start of its existence, supreme attention was paid to the study of psychic phenomena of the brain and of one of its main mysteries - thoughts. It can be proved by historical fact that those investigations were held by the order of Vladimir Ilyich Lenin under the personal control of Felix Edmundovich Dzerzhinsky in the special department of the Secret Service that was dealing with secrecy and protection of state secrets. This department even had a special neuro-energetical laboratory. This elite special department used in its work various healers, mediums, shamans, hypnotherapists."

"God, and why did they need all those 'healers'?" Nikolai Andreevich was really surprised.

"Well, all that was for the same reason: the extraordinary abilities of those individuals. They were able to manipulate human beings with hidden forces that significantly surpassed the abilities of any machinery. All these phenomena were very seriously examined! They sent even scientific expeditions searching for this knowledge: from the studies of the mysteries of ancient civilizations to the search for the legendary Shambala."

"Shambala... it sounds familiar... What is it?" Andrew asked impatiently.

"Shambala? Well, it is kind of an abode located high in the mountains. But it is famous because the group of scientists living there have long surpassed mankind in their spiritual, scientific, and technical levels."

"Now I recall," said Nikolai Andreevich. "Legend says that Shambala is an abode of Wise Men. But what has science to do with that? Do these Wise Men study something in particular: astronomy or mathematics, or just philosophy?"

"¬In Shambala, they study only the most ancient primordial science, the Art of White Lotus, which includes everything, and exact sciences as well. Moreover, it is a source of all sciences studied by mankind."

Nikolai Andreevich distrustfully looked at Sensei.

"What do you mean, 'only the most ancient'? The majority of exact sciences appeared quite recently; well, maybe two or three hundred years ago."

"You are wrong. All this knowledge was given to people time and again for the development of their civilizations, in ancient times as well. Long before written history there were other human civilizations that achieved a level of development much higher than ours now. Some of them were destroyed, some reached the Absolute. However, remnants of their existence are still being found today. Read about strange archaeological findings and you'll become certain of that. In the future, people will find even more interesting proof of what has happened a long time ago on the globe. A lot is written in ancient literature about the existence of this knowledge. For example, ancient nuclear explosions, the results of which scientists now find in the most ancient strata, precise maps of the stellar sky, identified planets that weren't discovered by us, the 'vimanas', aircrafts, and so forth. It means that this knowledge was given to people before and it originated from one source: the science of Shambala."

"And how far ahead is this science compared to modern knowledge?" Nikolai Andreevich asked arrogantly, crossing hands over his chest.

"Considerably far ahead," replied Sensei simply. "Much farther than you can imagine. But to put that into perspective, I will give this example. At the time when people still piously believed that the Earth stood on three whales and the Sun turned around it, the scientists of Shambala had already conducted scientific experiments and different tests on the Sun. Modern civilization is still very far from that, and it's not clear whether it will ever reach such a level. Why do you think people at the peak of their power so actively searched for Shambala? For instance, in the span of time known to you, such celebrities as Alexander the Great, Napoleon, Hitler, Mussolini, Stalin and so on, searched for it. Because according to all ancient legends and myths of different cultures, all the knowledge of the Universe and cultural heritage of extinct civilizations is concealed in Shambala.

"I wonder why was it searched for only by tyrants?"

"Not tyrants, but people striving for absolute power over the world. All people in power possess true information, they knew and know about the existence of this abode, about the existence of this powerful knowledge concealed in it. They perfectly understand that the real power over the world is concentrated in Shambala. That's why many people searched and still are searching for it. However, Shambala itself never gave anyone the possibility to conquer the whole world. It balanced, in a way, certain forces. And if a man standing at the peak of his power zealously tried to realize his dream of domination over the world, he simply ended his existence. Many people in power contacted with representatives of Shambala and fulfilled their requests. Everybody tried to help, because it's simply impossible to give up the temptation to know more than mankind knows... Aside from public leaders, many ordinary people were also in search of knowledge of Shambala."

"Does it mean that nobody has ever found it?" Kostya asked.

"Not exactly. The paradox is that Shambala has never hidden its existence. It doesn't interfere actively in people's lives unless it concerns something globally important for all of mankind and in particular for Shambala. But if it's necessary, its scientific society decides itself whom it is reasonable to contact."

"Well, let's assume that. But if this abode of Wise Men doesn't hide its existence, why couldn't it be found by people who were at the peak of power? After all, they had everything at their disposal: equipment, finance, and human resources!" Nikolai Andreevich was puzzled.

"Yes, you've listed everything but their hard hearts and greedy thoughts. The unalterable rule for contacting Shambala is the high morality and purity of a person's intentions. Only possessing the first of all these qualities can get someone access to the required knowledge.

"You see, we come back again to our starting point. Why can't a human develop these phenomenal abilities consciously when it is quite possible? Because there is too much egocentrism, vanity, greed, anger, envy in him. In other words, too many qualities inherent to a beast, to animal nature. And if he comes into contact with this inexplicable psychic phenomenon, his animal nature turns against logic because it fears losing its power over the human mind. That is, animal nature tries to preserve its power over the human by rationalizing the phenomenon or criticizing it, when all that is necessary is simple childish faith.

"In some cases, of course, people spontaneously discover their phenomenal abilities, as a result, for example, of some kind of trauma, intense stress, and so forth. But, if negative qualities prevail in the human mind, it's the same as if a Neanderthal finds a monkey wrench and, not knowing how to use it, applies it, from his negative point of view, to his friends."

The guys smiled, and Eugene asked, "Will he hit them on their heads?"

"Even worse, on the big toes. Then his friends will completely forget about their heads."

"And if at that moment a good, spiritual nature prevails in the human?" I asked with curiosity.

"And if there prevails a spiritual nature in a person, then he will correctly perceive new information on a subconscious level, using his phenomenal abilities for good intentions. Because in this case, faith gives birth to knowledge, and knowledge strengthens faith. And without faith no miracles are possible in this world."

"It's an interesting thought," said Nikolai Andreevich, and remaining silent for a while, added, "I wonder, when Stalin came to power in our country, did he stop research into these phenomena?"

"On the contrary, this research became even more intensive and continued even after his death. This interest hasn't waned, even to the present day. This subject is examined by many scientific institutes."

"Hmm, but I've studied works of many well-known authors of different institutes specialized in my sphere, but I haven't run into subject."

"It's not strange because this subject belongs to the sphere of hidden control over the masses. I think that you understand well enough how secret these works are. I can give you an example of the Leningrad institute named after Vladimir Mikhailovich Bekhterev. By the way, the work of Bekhterev was continued by his granddaughter, Natalya Petrovna Bekhtereva. There they study closely the human brain. And one of the priority directions of that institute is research into people's psychic phenomena."

"But the Leningrad institute is one of the leading in...," Nikolai Andreevich froze, saying half a word, evidently shocked by his guess. Having coped with the excitement, he continued, "Well, but if it has been studied for so long, if the military has shown such an interest in it, and if huge amounts of money were spent, then probably there should have been huge scientific progress in psychic studies."

"Progress?" grinned Sensei. "What kind of a progress can there be with such motivation? Their institute still can't explain the phenomenal effects of this biomass that weights a little more than a kilo - the cerebrum, just like other world scientists. It has remained, despite all of their efforts, the mystery of mysteries. Space is investigated much more than the human brain."

"I agree... But you say that the sacred knowledge can be given only to people of high moral standards. Not all the scientists are complete egotists with excessive megalomania. For example, that very Bekhtereva..."

"Absolutely correct. And if you carefully follow the work of academician Bekhtereva as a human and a scientist, you'll see that after having studied the human brain all her life, she came to the conclusion that she knows very little about it, about its potential. Nevertheless, the deeper she delves into the study of the brain, the more she believes in the idea of its extraterrestrial origin, that is, of its true source of origin, based on the exceptional complexity and superfluity of the brain. I'm pretty sure that soon she will publicly announce it, just as it was announced by the great scientists of the world not just in the sphere of psychic research, but in other natural sciences, for example, by Einstein, Tesla, Vernadsky, Tsiolkovsky, and other great scientists. This list is huge and would take a long time to go through. But all those people came to the conclusion that humans are very unique and mysterious creatures and in no way could have originated on the Earth from some kind of infusorium!"

We stood silent, slightly shocked by what we had heard.

"So, it means that the power of extraordinary, phenomenal people is concealed simply in their thought?" Kostya asked again.

"Absolutely right. Thought is a real power. A lot greater than humans can imagine. Thought is able to move planets, to create and destroy entire galaxies, which initially was proved by God Himself."

Nikolai Andreevich smiled and said ironically, "It's a very convincing answer, I can't even argue with it."

"Really?!" Andrew expressed our general amazement. "Then why don't we feel the presence of this gigantic power in ourselves?"

"Because you don't believe in it."

"Is that so? The beginning was so complicated, but the end is so simple," stated Kostya.

"What can I do? So is the nature of knowledge," answered Sensei with a smile.

"Well, how can it be," Slava was struggling to understand, "if I felt such a power, why wouldn't I believe in it?"

"The whole trick is that first you should believe, and then you will feel it."

"And what if I believe but don't feel it?" Slava couldn't calm down. "What then?"

"If you really believe in it, then certainly you will feel it," answered Sensei and added, "All right, we can discuss it for a long time, but it's time to begin the meditation."

"And what is a meditation?" asked Tatyana. "I've read that it is psychic training during a trance. But what it actually is, I still don't understand."

"In a few words, a simple meditation is the training of thought and a deeper spiritual practice is the training of spirit."

"Does it mean that thought and spirit are the same?" Kostya broke into the conversation again.

"No."

The cat sitting close by stirred at its place, as if making itself more comfortable.

"Now we will practice the simplest meditation on the concentration of attention, so that you can learn how to control the Qi energy. But before that, I would like to repeat again for those who came late. In addition to the material body, the human also has an energy body. The energy body consists of an aura, chakras, energy channels, meridians, and special reservoirs for energy accumulation. Each of them has its own name. I will tell you later in detail about all of them, depending on the meditation."

"And what is a chakra?" I asked.

"Chakra is a tiny spot on the human body through which different energies enter and exit. It works...so for you it would be easier to understand... like an iris or diaphragm in a camera. Do you know what that is?"

We nodded assent.

"It is the same way with chakras; they instantly open and instantly close."

"And does all that energy really come out in that instant?" Slava was surprised.

"Well, it's not like emptying a bucket of water. After all, a human being is an energy and material creature, where energy and matter exist by their own laws and time, however they are fully interconnected and interdependent. Any other questions?" Everyone was silent. "Then let's begin. Right now, your objective is to learn to feel inside of yourselves the movement of air, the movement of Qi. You all think that you perfectly understand

and feel yourselves. But I'm pretty sure that you can't see right now, for example, the toes of your feet. Why? Because you don't have internal vision. Internal vision, just like internal feeling, can be trained with time, in everyday training. That's why we will start with the simplest and easiest meditation. We'll try to learn to control thoughts and feelings, to evoke them and to guide them.

"All right, now make yourselves comfortable and relax. Calm your emotions. You may close your eyes, so nothing will distract you. Dissolve all your thoughts and everyday problems in the emptiness."

As soon as that phrase was spoken, I recalled a pile of tiny household chores. "Gosh! Those impudent thoughts again," I thought. "You were told to get dissolved." I tried again not to think about anything.

"Concentrate on the tip of your nose..."

With closed eyes I tried to "see" the tip of the nose, guided more by my internal feelings. I felt my eyes slightly strain.

"Now breathe in deeply, slowly and gradually. First, with the bottom of the stomach, then with the stomach, chest, raising shoulders... Slightly hold your breath... Slowly breathe out... We concentrate our internal vision only on the tip of the nose... You should feel and imagine that the tip of your nose is like a small light bulb or small flame, and it flames up with your every breath out... Breathe in... Breathe out... Breathe in... Breathe out... The flame flares up more and more..."

At first, I felt a slight burning and pricking in my nose. There was such a feeling as if I were filled with something material, like a jug with water. Later it seemed to me that in the area of the nose tip appeared a dark distant contour of a purple tiny spot. At first, I couldn't clearly focus on it. Finally, when I was able to get it fixed, it started to lighten up from inside. Moreover, when breathing in, the light narrowed, and when breathing out, it widened. When I got used to breathing this way, I heard the words of Sensei.

"Now switch your attention to another part of meditation. Slightly raise your hands a little forward, palms facing the earth. Breathe in as usual: through the bottom of the stomach, then through the stomach and chest. Your breath out should be directed through the shoulders, hands, to the center of your palms, where the chakras of the hands are located, and through them into the earth. Imagine that something is flowing through your hands, Qi energy, or light, or water, and then overflows into the earth. This flow rises from the bottom of the stomach up to your chest, and there it is split up in two streamlets and overflows into the earth through your shoulders, arms, hands. Concentrate all your attention on the feeling of that movement... Breathe in... Breathe out... Breathe in... Breathe out..."

A thought flashed across my mind, "What does it mean to breathe through the hands? How can it be?" I even panicked a little. Sensei, obviously feeling my confusion, came up and placed his palms over mine, without touching the skin. After some time, my palms began to burn, like two stoves, spreading warmth from their center to the periphery. And what astonished me most of all was that I really felt how tiny warm streamlets were pouring through my shoulders. In the region of my elbows they weakened, but I felt them very well overflowing through my palms. Deep in these new, unusual feelings, I asked myself, "How am I doing this?" While I was thinking it over, I lost the feeling of the steamlets. I had to concentrate again. In general, it worked with variable success. After one of my next attempts, I again heard Sensei's voice.

"Close the palms of your hands in front of you, firmly grip them so that the chakras of the hands are closed and the movement of energy stopped. Take two deep, fast breaths in and out... Lower your hands and open your eyes."

After the meditation, when we started to share impressions, I understood that everyone experienced it differently. Tatyana, for example, didn't see the flame; instead of it she felt some kind of light movement through her hands. Andrew had a shiver in his legs and light dizziness. Kostya shrugged his shoulders and answered, "I didn't feel anything special, except a pins and needles sensation. But that is quite a normal reaction resulting from the oversaturation of the body with oxygen."

"After the third, fourth breath in, maybe," answered the Teacher. "But at the beginning the brain becomes fixed by the thought, in particular before the movement of the Qi. And if you listen to yourselves, relax and breathe in deeply, you will immediately feel a widening or paresthesia feeling in the head, or in other words, a certain process that develops there. That is exactly what you need to understand, what is moving there, and learn to control it."

"Why didn't I feel anything?" asked a disappointed Slava.

"What did you think about?" Sensei asked half in jest.

It turned out that Slava didn't really know what he had been expecting, maybe some kind of a miracle. Sensei replied, "Right, that's the reason you didn't feel anything "because you concentrated your thoughts not on the work but on waiting for some extraordinary miracle. But there won't be a miracle until you create it yourself. You shouldn't wait for anything extraordinary when you breathe correctly or concentrate on something. No. The biggest miracle is you, yourself, as a human! After all, where does all great spiritual art lead? It helps you become human so that you gradually wake up and recall the knowledge that was given to you primordially. These meditations are only a means of awakening from spiritual lethargy and recalling long-hidden and forgotten information that you knew and used once upon a time."

"What do you mean knew?" Slava didn't understand.

"Well. For example, everybody knows how to read, write, count, if, of course, he is normal, without mental disorders. Right?"

"Right."

"But first he had to be taught. While later he already easily reads, counts and so forth. That is, he already exactly knows that, for example, one plus one equals two, two plus two equals four. It seems so simple and real! But at the beginning he was taught all this, although in reality he simply recalled. These are hidden, subconscious abilities. Or, here is another easier example that has to do with the physiological level. If a man who doesn't know how to swim is thrown into the water, he will drown. But it has been proven and confirmed by deliveries in water that a newborn baby, when lowered into pool, swims like any other animal. Does it mean that he already possesses these reflexes? Indeed. But later it's simply forgotten. It is the same with a human. He has a lot of knowledge that he doesn't even suspect he has.

"But... all of this works only with a positive factor. If some mercenary interests prevail in him, for example, to learn to cheat somebody or to be able to hit someone with energy from a distance, or maybe he wants to be able to bend everyone's spoons so they throw him money for that, he will never achieve anything. Only when a person learns to control his thoughts will he really become human, and only then will he be able to achieve something."

"So, does it mean that spiritual practice is a method of awakening a human?" asked Andrew.

"Absolutely right. Spiritual practice is only an instrument for repairing your mind. And the result depends on how you use this instrument. In other words, it all depends on the desire and skill of the master. And in order to learn how to hold this instrument in your hands it is necessary to control your thought, to concentrate it, and to see it with your internal vision. In our case it means to learn to control our breath, to feel that you breathe out through the chakras of hands. You need to learn to evoke certain feelings so that later you will be able to control the internal, hidden energy."

"In my opinion, this is a hallucination," remarked Kostya.

"Yes, a hallucination, if you regard it as a hallucination. But if you regard this energy as real power, then in reality it will be real power."

"It's strange, but why?"

"Because, I repeat, a thought controls an action. While energy itself is an action. That is all. Everything is very simple."

We remained silent for a moment, while Nikolai Andreevich asked, "From the point of view of psychology, is it nevertheless an objective factor or a subjective feeling? For example, I clearly felt the concentration on the tip of the nose. But movements through the arms I felt only partially, where I was focusing my attention."

Sensei started to explain something to the psychotherapist, using terms unknown to me, probably from his professional language. And as I understood from their speech, they touched on the problems of sensitiveness, including healing and diagnostics of different diseases. The latter interested me very much.

During this discussion, while the other guys were listening, Slava was carefully examining the palms of his hands. And as soon as a lengthy pause appeared in the discussion, he hurried to ask, "I do not completely understand about chakras. You said that there should be opening points. But there is nothing in here!"

The senior guys laughed.

"Of course," said Sensei. "Visually there is nothing like that."

Eugene, standing next to Slava, couldn't help it, turned his hands around and seriously asked like a doctor, "Well, patient. Do you see bones and tendons there?"

"No," replied Slava, still puzzled.

Eugene smacked his lips and mournfully said, "He is hopeless!"

The guys laughed.

"You see, chakras are certain zones on the human body that are more sensitive to warmth," patiently explained the Teacher. "They, of course, can't be seen, but this is real and can be registered by modern equipment. For scientists, just like for you, these zones are still a mystery: the cells are the same, the connections are the same, but their sensitivity is higher. Why? Because chakras are located here while chakra belongs to the astral body, that is, to another, more profound physics. A thought is a binding link between the astral and material bodies. That's why it is very important to learn to control your thoughts... Then you will be able really to guide Qi moving inside of your body."

The senior guys joined the conversation, discussing some kind of their own meditation issues. At the end of our meeting, Sensei asked Eugene and Stas personally to accompany us to the tram stop and help us to get to the tram.

"And no tricks of yours!" Sensei ordered jokingly to Eugene.

"Yes, sir," Eugene saluted, "no freaks!"

Sensei hopelessly waved his hand. When the whole crowd moved laughing towards the path, the Teacher called the cat. But it grandly walked out in a different direction. Sensei tried to run it down to catch it, but to no avail. That prankster slipped into the nearest bushes.

Squatting down, Sensei tried to pull it out. Using this opportunity, I came up to the Teacher, as if helping to catch the cat.

"Can you diagnose..."

Without letting me finish, Sensei replied, "You mean that wound in your head, my dear... Samurai! Now you want to scratch. You naughty cat. Come out!"

"How does he know?" I thought to myself, simply shocked. Inspired by hope, I thought, "If he knows about it, then maybe he'll help heal it!" Meanwhile Igor Mikhailovich asked, "What is the diagnosis of Aesculapius?"

"My parents say nothing serious, something with vessels. But as far as I understood by eavesdropping in the conversation between my mother and the doctor, I have a malignant growth in the cerebral cortex. And it's not clear how it will progress."

"An impressive argument," said Sensei, shaking off his hands and looking towards the bushes as he addressed the cat. "Well then, sit there as long as you wish. When you freeze, you'll come out yourself!"

The crowd, noticing Sensei's "trouble" with the cat, started to come back, offering to help catch it.

"Never mind!" Sensei waved his hand. "He will come home on his own."

To my complete disappointment, for that small amount of time that could have been used for conversation, we walked with Sensei keeping silent untill we joined the others. I expected him to show some kind of a reaction, some sympathy, some hope for a possible cure. But in vain did I think that he was about to say something. His answer was only silence. Inside of me there was a small hope that I would hear some kind of hint or advice or moral support during general conversation. But he was simply walking and joking with everyone, followed by loud laughter of the crowd. That made me completely furious.

10

All the way home, I was terribly angry. And at home I simply couldn't sit still. "Everything is over, everything is over!" I lamented in my mind. "Just when some kind of hope appeared, it all collapsed. I'm fed up with it, I'm tired of everything. Everything in this world is so senseless! I can't stand it anymore, it's too much for me. Damn it all, this struggle for life with this stupid school, meaningless training, and indifferent Sensei. The end is always the same!"

My imagination was already drawing a horrible, terrifying picture of my own funeral, the bitter tears of my mother, relatives, and friends. I clearly visualised the nails hammered into my coffin and its lowering into a damp pit, thrown over with dirt. There was an absolute scary darkness around, emptiness and hopelessness. And that's all!

What happens afterwards, above me, where life runs like a full-flowing river? Another picture appeared in my mind. Everything was just like before, nothing has changed. My parents as usual continued going to work. My friends went to training, looking cheerful as usual, laughing happily at their endless jokes. While

Sensei, just as before, continued his interesting training, demonstrating and telling the amazed crowd about their own abilities.

Nothing has changed in this world! Except, I was not here anymore. That was the point, the reason for my resentment and sorrow. This was only my personal tragedy. And in general nobody else but myself needed my thoughts, my worries, my knowledge, and my life. I was born alone, and I will die alone. Then what is the purpose of this senseless existence? Why are people even born? What is life for?

This mixture of the philosophy of life and the fear of death was going on in my head. A horrible melancholy seized me, and it was quickly changing into depression. I was fading under the pressure of my depressive thoughts. My health rapidly became worse, and horrible headaches appeared again. I missed school and all my hobby classes, including my favorite dances. I really didn't need anything in this world. But...

The time of the next training was drawing near. Despite the external squall of negative emotions, I had somewhere deep inside me a permanent, unchanging feeling of confidence in my own strength and full tranquility. That's why I argued with myself, to go or not to go. This exact internal feeling for some reason irritated me most of all.

My friends appeared at my home and settled my doubts. Before that I didn't even think of getting ready. Their inspiring laughter, discussion of simple problems, and exchange of impressions about how they had worked on the meditation at home distracted me from my heavy thoughts, raising my mood a bit. My friends were finally able to drag me out from my "graveyard" to the training, declaring that I was being an incorrigible pretender. Andrew also lectured me for a while using his eloquent examples, and made a conclusion at the end:

"I understand when we miss school classes. That's clear, it's boring. But the training?! It's a real adventure that you won't read in any book or see in any kind of a movie! It is so interesting and cognitive! While you, sleepyhead, say 'Don't want to; I'm not going to go.' Then you'll sleep over the best years of your life and you would have nothing to remember later."

"Aha," I thought gloomily. "If that 'later' will ever come."

11

As usual we came early. Having greeted Sensei, the guys ran to the changing rooms, while I unwillingly dragged myself behind everyone with my head hung low. And suddenly very close to me I heard the voice of Sensei:

"You've mastered yourself, well done!"

It was so unexpected that I even got embarrassed, surprisingly looking into his eyes. He was carefully looking at me, and his eyes shone with endless kindness and sympathy. And as usual, without giving me time to collect myself, he added, "Well, it's time for you to go change."

Meanwhile another group of people came up and greeted him. They started to tell him about their problems.

"There you are!" A thought flashed across my mind. "Is it possible that he knew about all my thoughts, doubts, and torments?! Then if he knew, maybe that's normal, maybe that's the way it should be? And if he said well done, it means that not all is lost yet." Nevertheless, the words of Sensei affected me like an elixir of youth given to an old woman. I rushed to the changing room, having forgotten that very recently I hobbled all broken and tired through this life.

"Where are you rushing to?" Tatyana asked puzzled, looking at my wild speed of putting on my kimono. "I can't believe my eyes, just recently you were dying, and now you are rushing headlong into the sports hall."

"Ah, Tatyana," I smiled. "Andrew was right when he said that we shouldn't worry too much."

Looking at the surprised expression on her face, I added, "I'm in a hurry to live, so that 'I won't later regret the senseless years of my life...'"

Tatyana laughed, and I ran into the sports hall full of overflowing energy and joined the other guys who were warming up. To tell the truth, I myself didn't expect such activity from my almost dying body. Where did it come from?

Five minutes before the beginning, Eugene, who was warming up next to Stas, looked in through the door and shone in the rays of his blinding Hollywood smile.

"What good luck! I see a familiar face." Eugene moved his hands apart.

A sturdy built guy, not too tall, with a strong-willed face and military bearing, entered the sports hall. The amazed exclamation of Eugene made others look around. Sensei and the senior guys came up to the newcomer:

"Hi, Volodya!"

"Welcome back!"

"We're glad to see you!"

When the delighted participants calmed down a little, Sensei asked, "So, how was your trip to the south? Did you warm your bones thoroughly at the resort?"

"Aha, I have even burnt myself. I wouldn't wish such a trip on anyone. As they say, if you have nothing to worry about, your command will help you with it."

"What's going on down there?" Eugene asked.

"What, don't you watch television, country boy?" Stas said with a smile.

"What? What? What is a "tilivision"? You should know that news is spread in our village only through rumors. And if somebody doesn't understand it, one fist punch in the ear, and the heads of brothers get clear. That's it!"

The guys laughed. Eugene transformed into the role of priest and addressed Volodya, "Confess, my son, confess in detail, about your overseas sufferings and about the sorrowful deeds of hell. Relieve your soul!"

"Well, Eugene! Even the grave probably won't change you," remarked Volodya, laughing with everybody. He added more seriously, "What can I say, people are getting mad there, they can't share even a piece of earth... They ruined such a resort!"

"They know well how to make a tempest in a teacup," Victor agreed. "They learn it from birth."

"Yes," Eugene drawled, "they couldn't avoid the bloody front, unfortunately. I suppose you also chattered your teeth with fear?"

"We are used to it, holy father. It's not my first time," Volodya comically mimicked him.

"All right, guys, we'll have enough time to talk." Sensei stopped this funny exchange of impressions. "Go change. It's already time to start the training."

The warm-up went by at an active tempo with moderate exercise stress. I noticed that Volodya, despite being a stocky guy, moved softly and easily, like a snow leopard. When the main crowd finished repeating the basics, Volodya and the "speedy" guys started emotionally discussing something with Sensei. Having finished our exercises, we also hurried to join them, trying to grasp the subject of the conversation.

"Was it possible to undertake something over there?" Volodya argued hotly. "We had to work mostly at night, in complete darkness, and often in cellars. There you can't light a flashlight or even a cigarette or you would instantly get a lead bullet. So many of our guys died because of that! The only thing you try to do under such circumstances is to fire back at every sound in the darkness."

"But you are supposed to have special equipment for night vision," said Stas.

"Aha, they only show that in movies. But in reality, maybe they have it in anti-terrorist units... but where can we get it from?"

"Why do you need special equipment?" Sensei asked, shrugging his shoulders. "The human is a lot more perfect than any piece of iron."

Volodya reflected and remained silent for a little while before adding, "Well, I think I tried it all. I tried to narrow my eyes, so my vision would adapt faster. We tried to train in the darkness in order to improve the perception of sounds. But all in vain. Still, in most cases we were caught by surprise despite the fact that we seemed to be ready."

"Vision and hearing here are absolutely irrelevant," ascertained Sensei. "Humans have a completely different level of perception, thanks to which you can control your surrounding space at a desirable distance around you."

Volodya briskly glanced at Sensei and said, "Sensei, show me." He placed his palm against his heart and added with a smile, "My soul missed your examples so much."

Sensei smiled ironically, waving his hand as a sign of agreement, "All right, kamikaze, come on..."

Volodya and the guys developed a whole plan for how to disorient Sensei. Meanwhile the crowd got excited about the unusual demonstration. Someone brought a thick scarf to blindfold Sensei's eyes, checking its light impermeability. Others discussed how to create more noise and vibration in the air. Our company observed that process with interest, standing next to Stas.

"Who is this Volodya?" Andrew asked.

"Volodya? He is a friend of Sensei's. One of his old disciples," Stas replied.

"And how long has he been training with Sensei?"

"Well, I've already been training for five years. When I met Sensei, Volodya had just come back from the army. Actually, he had trained with him even before the army."

"He is a serious man, athletic," remarked Andrew.

"Well, I would think so. Volodya is a master of sambo, served in the marines and in the intelligence service. And after that, in the Ministry for Internal Affairs."

"Where does he work now?" I asked.

"Right now, he trains a newly created special force," Stas explained. He added, "A fine fellow indeed!"

Our entire group, under the supervision of Volodya, sat on the sides of the sports hall, forming a circle. Sensei walked into the center. Volodya blindfolded his eyes with a scarf, thoroughly closing every possible chink. After this preparation, he disappeared into the crowd. Meanwhile Sensei took an odd stance. He looked like a tired pilgrim who took a rest for a while leaning over an imaginary staff.

"Wow!" Eugene exclaimed with admiration, rubbing his hands in anticipation of something special. "Shortly we'll see something very interesting."

"That's for sure," confirmed Stas, carefully looking at Sensei.

"What kind of a stance is that?" Andrew inquired.

"If I understood correctly, this is from the style of the 'Old Lama'," Stas answered quietly.

"I have never heard of such a style before."

"Hmm, and probably you'll never hear of it. It is an ancient, dead style. As Sensei says, it was forgotten even before the birth of Christ. Today there is left only a poor remnant of this school. In China it is known as the style of the 'Dragon'."

"Not bad for a poor remnant," Andrew was astonished. "As far as I know, the style of the 'Dragon' is the most powerful style, as it absorbed the wisdom and power of all of the martial arts schools..."

Looking once again at Sensei he added, "How do you know about this ancient style?"

"I had an opportunity to learn about it two years ago. Some tourists came to us. So Sensei, as a polite host, regaled them with the style of the 'Old Lama'. That was quite a show, I tell you, we couldn't tear ourselves away from it!"

After such an advertisement, we stared at Sensei in order not to miss something thrilling. Meanwhile, Volodya gave the signal, and our entire crowd started to make an unimaginable noise, chaotically clapping our hands and stamping our feet.

Making use of this cover, Volodya started to come near Sensei, going around him clockwise. His movements were soft and light. He stepped like a panther before the jump, getting closer and closer to the enemy. When Volodya neared Sensei's right side, with a quick, light under-step, he started to execute a strike of mavashi-geri in the head. Practically simultaneously, Sensei moved his right leg behind and, rotating his right hand into an arch, slightly touched Volodya's face with the edge of his palm. Sensei just touched him, like a light feather, and didn't hit like I expected him to. Judging by what we had seen, it wasn't an accident or a miss. All movements were executed by Sensei with ease, smoothly and with special accuracy. Volodya reacted to this light touch as if he had been hit by a cannon-ball. His legs sharply flung up, and he was catapulted backward, crashing down with force against the floor. Everybody in the sports hall was completely silent. Volodya moved, sitting up on the floor. People exhaled and buzzed, like a beehive, discussing what had just happened.

"How did he manage to fall down?" Kostya asked Andrew with curiosity, but he shrugged his shoulders.

"Maybe he just lost his balance. He was standing on one foot. Probably so, because it seemed like the strike was very light. And you can't even call it a strike."

Sensei, shedding the scarf, asked Volodya, "Are you alive, masochist?"

"Alive," Volodya drawled, holding his right eye. "I don't understand, where did I make a mistake?"

"Your mistake is that you tried to get me from what you thought was my most unprotected side, in other words, from the most vulnerable point."

"Of course!"

"That's why you got into trouble! If you had attacked me from the front, you would've had more of a chance than attacking from behind or the right side. Had you attacked from behind left, you would've been hurt even more."

"But why?"

"Because you think like a human, possessing vision and hearing. How many times did I tell you, you must take into consideration your opponent's way of thinking. Since I see and hear nothing, you could logically assume that my mind is controlling the worst protected places a lot better and stronger."

"And how about the front?"

"In front of me, there is weaker control because the body is already prepared for attack. A human, without natural perception, is more physically ready for the fight in front of him and spiritually from behind, and that's a lot more dangerous. It means that the more vulnerable the side of the opponent seems to be, the more it is protected and, correspondingly, the counter-attack can be more unpredictable."

"And what if I had had a gun?"

"If you had had a gun, we would have greater use for you tomorrow."

"What do you mean?"

"Exactly what I've just said. We would have eaten pies from your fresh meat."

Volodya smiled in reply to Sensei's black humor.

"Well, no need to, I will better bring pies to you myself..."

When Volodya took his hand away from his face, we were taken aback a little. A big bruise has swollen under his eye. The skin around his eye became dark blue and was covered with blisters, as if after a burn. Girls from our group began to bustle about and brought Volodya a towel, which they had wet in cold water. But even this compress didn't help him. Nevertheless, it seemed that Volodya worried least of all about his eye. He stood up, shook his clothes off, and merrily joked with Sensei, while we were commanded to exercise our techniques.

After the training, almost at the very end of the additional training, we again heard something interesting.

"Sensei, is there such a technique to control the surrounding space that can be taught in a simpler form, so that it could be understood and practiced by the guys of my sub-unit?" asked Volodya.

The Teacher thought for a little while and replied, "Yes, there is such a technique, although you will need a partner for it. Best of all is to practice it sitting in the lotus pose. You should do the following: on the level of your head suspend a soft tennis ball on a rope, so that during its swinging or pushing by a partner the trajectory of its flight would coincide with the location of your head. Your objective is simply to learn to dodge it without using your common organs of control in the surrounding space, and to rely more on intuition. You should perceive the ball in its spiritual interpretation. Try to feel the object approaching the back of your head and, guided by your internal intuition, move your head before it hits you. The most important thing is to train your mind, and again we got back to our subject," smiled Sensei. "Speaking frankly, you should bring your mind to a complete calmness so that it reminds you of the mirror-like surface of a lake. And in that full silence of your consciousness, the approaching object, in our case the ball, will be like a pebble thrown into that glassy surface, causing ripples, or like a boat, call it as you wish. But it will be cleaving your space. All the rest that is located farther, such as people standing in the circle, will be like trees or people on the shore, whatever you prefer. And you are the center of that lake. You should learn to feel any vibration on your surface, any penetration in your space. Finally you will learn to feel the approaching alien object and all that's happening around."

Andrew, who stood with us next to Sensei, asked, "Can we also train in this way?"

"If you have such a desire, certainly, train yourselves," answered Sensei.

"And in this case, what kind of a perception will it be?" Volodya asked.

"Almost the same as the one during this demonstration. The most important thing is to come out with your consciousness over the boundaries of your body."

"And how is that?" Andrew didn't grasp the idea.

"Well, I'll give you this simple example. Any human, when he sits down, relaxes, and tries to calm his thoughts, will start to feel that his consciousness is widening and comes far out over the boundaries of his body. Consciousness becomes three-dimensional. It covers enormous spaces. In this case, you simply limit it with a certain place. In the example that I showed you, it was the sports hall. Although, if you train hard enough, you will be able to feel what is going on at the other end of your district. Actually, it's not that difficult."

"In other words, the most important thing in the exercise with the ball is to achieve a complete calmness of the mind, like in the example with the lake?" Andrew asked again.

"Absolutely correct, and make an effort so that not a single thought could enter that space."

"That's hard."

"Hard, but possible."

"Stas said that the style of the 'Old Lama' is very ancient. Is that true?"

"Yes."

"Does history record the names of those who mastered it?" asked Kostya.

Sensei smiled, thinking about something and answered, "You might know only Buddha. And, of course, his first followers."

"Buddha?" said Kostya, surprised. "But I thought that he had a different kind of philosophy, the philosophy of good. Why did he need to fight?"

"Even good people may need to fight," Sensei answered calmly. "But to master that art doesn't always mean to attack someone. For them it was sort of a stage in spiritual development."

Thus our additional training ended, and again we became witnesses to the valuable knowledge and abilities of Sensei. Our delight was endless. Having changed, we awaited the others near the sports hall. When the crowd came out to the street, Eugene glanced at Volodya and exclaimed with horror, "My god! Oho... What a shiner you have, beautiful."

At these words, everybody turned their attention to Volodya. His eye was completely swollen, turning into a big, black spot.

"Don't worry," Eugene tried to cheer him up, puffing up his chest, and declaring, "Bruises make men more attractive!"

Volodya replied with a smile, "And how about you, don't you want to become more attractive?"

Everybody burst out in laughter.

"Of course he wants to. And I'll be like a witness in that joke," Stas was developing the situation. "When he was asked, 'Did you see how one man hit another on the head?' he replied, 'I don't know if I saw, but I heard a sound, as if somebody hit something empty'."

Victor added, "And I will be a second witness. If I am asked why I didn't come to help the victim during the fight, I will answer with a clean conscience, 'How could I know who the victim was when they were fighting with each other so hard?!'"

Another wave of laughter rolled through our crowd.

"Come on, guys," Eugene mimicked everyone. "Your jokes are good only for soldiers in barracks. Did you see, Sensei, I hardly said a word, and they have already fabricated a case!"

12

Joking and poking fun at each other, the guys moved on. The weather was calm, and the sky was covered with scattered stars. Enjoying the evening cool after the intensive training, we didn't noticed that our group was a little stretched out. Kostya and Tatyana had gone far ahead. Volodya, Eugene, and Stas dragged somewhere behind. And Victor, Andrew, Slava, Yura, and I were walking in the middle with Sensei chattering about trifles.

Just around the corner, we came face-to-face with a group of miners, about eight of them, all considerably drunk. They seemed to have seriously angered Kostya in passing, as when we approached them, his face was red with rage. Kostya kept snapping at them, obviously annoyed with the drunks. Andrew added fuel to the fire in an attempt to defend his friend. The most impatient of the miners rushed towards the two to fight. Andrew and Kostya dashed at him. But Sensei arrived just in time and stopped them, addressing the miners, "Calm down, men! Why should you curse here, in the presense of women? Noblemen do not swear."

"What are you talking about?" A furious miner croaked, having seized Sensei. "Move along or else I'll break all your bones!"

At this point we could not stand it any more and moved in a crowd to the instigator. Even I flew into a rage towards these drunkards and was ready at that moment to tear them to pieces. The senior guys ran up to us, but unexpectedly Sensei stopped all our attempts and gave a sign to Victor for everyone to leave. We grumbled with indignation. But Victor, Stas, Eugene, and Volodya took us away like diligent shepherds leading a flock of sheep without letting us stop.

I kept turning around, waiting for the Teacher to show off one of his supertricks against eight enemies. But Sensei only stood there smiling and explained something with gestures as if he were making excuses. When I glanced back the next time, I saw that the smiling miners were fraternizing with him, saying goodbye to him as good friends. "Well, really!" I thought. "What is the point of practicing Kung-fu for so many years?" Judging by the puzzled responses of my friends, I was not the only one who thought that.

When Sensei came up to us, Andrew said with indignation, "Why did you make excuses to them? They were the ones who bothered us and stirred up trouble. We should have beaten them to teach them not to do it again. If you hadn't stopped me, I would..."

"Surely," Sensei interrupted him, "if I hadn't stopped you, they would have been seriously injured, not only in their soft tissues but also in their organs, and they might have even gotten a concussion of the brain. Do you realize that these are men who have families at home, who are probably the only bread-winners of these families? Do you realize that they are miners? Have you ever been in a mine?"

"No," Andrew replied.

"I have been there... These guys, whom you wanted to break to pieces, they go down to a mine like to hell, to a depth of up to one kilometer and more. Just imagine the pressure on their bodies. Not to mention," Sensei started to list on his fingers, "heat, lack of oxygen, very harmful methane... And despite all of this, they realize that they risk their lives every second. Because any moment they can be crushed, injured, or even killed. Injuries happen regularly in the mine. And people take it hard. Their mind is always on the brink, so to say, at the breaking point. This state of mind is comparable with the state of mind of soldiers on the front line during the war. That's why Stalin used to say, 'The mine is the second front.' Do you know why they drink? In order to relieve somehow this stress, this internal feeling of permanent fear. That is why highly qualified specialists in psychology and medicine should work with miners for them to overcome this psychological block. But of course they don't get this help. That's why many of them drink."

"Yes," Kostya sighed, "Thus it apereth what great unhappynes / And blyndnes cometh to many a creature / By wyne or ale taken without measure."

"Exactly... Besides, every miner who has been working for a long time in the mine has a clear understanding that he has no future. You have some chances; for example, you may finish high school, have a career. And they have no chance; only to croak in the mine or to die of diseases they contracted there. They understand it quite clearly. But they have their own pride and megalomania, the same as yours."

"No," Andrew negated. "I do not posess any megalomania at all."

"Really?! But you just wanted to beat them up only because they bothered you. This is evidence of your megalomania, that you, such a king, have been offended. They have the same pride. But unlike you, they don't have any future. And you wanted them to lose everything? Just imagine what would have happened with them, with all their stress, unrealized ideas, dreams, and lost chances, if they had come to in the emergency room after your beating. It would have brought them additional suffering, much stronger even than physical pain. What for?"

We hung our heads, feeling ashamed. Although Sensei directed this explanation mainly to the men, all of this was quite applicable to me as well. His words had completely shaken me. I felt some internal discomfort caused by my recent aggressive thoughts, and I felt very ashamed of myself. Suddenly I perceived the whole depth of Sensei's thoughts and realized how well he understands and feels each person.

"What for?!" the Teacher repeated. "Because you felt uncomfortable? You could have calmed them down and walked away, right? Nothing happened to you. It's quite clear that you are able to smash all of them just with your legs."

"Of course, I would..." Andrew started to flare up again.

"You see, it's your megalomania again. But I teach you to train your body, not to beat up people on the streets. The main sense of the martial arts is completely different, and all these tricks may never be used by you in your life. I hope that they will be never used. Your task is to learn to understand the reason and the effects, the depth and the sense of the situation, and to solve it peacefully."

"What did you say to them?" Kostya asked.

"It's very simple. I explained to them that they had children like you and that another group of drunken men like them might bother their children and beat them. I described this case from the human point of view. Notice that their megalomania has not suffered. And what is more important, they left satisfied, with the intention to defend others like you. Every situation like this may be solved much more easily, with peace."

After a small pause he added, "Every fool can snap and punch... But do not give in to your animal instincts. It's much more important to be human in any situation, to understand why and by which reason this aggression is caused. And how to solve the dispute in the right way in order to find a friend and not an enemy."

As we came to the tram stop, Sensei concluded, "Remember that any blow caused by your rage will come back to you at the end."

We stood in silence and looked ashamedly at Sensei. After making a new appointment, we went home.

13

Almost the whole way home, we were silent. When coming to the center, Andrew, who had sat all this time with a thoughtful air, burst out, "I feel so guilty after Sensei's speech!"

"Sure," Kostya agreed. "I'm thinking why did I get involved with those guys? As they say, no wisdom like silence!"

"Don't worry," Andrew reassured him. "You see how it turned out. Every cloud has a silver lining... Yeah, Sensei has done a tough brain reboot."

"It will take a long time to digest it", I thought. All the way back I was tormenting myself, not with thoughts about the incident but about myself. Something in my ordinary internal state was unusual. But what exactly? I rehashed the conversation with the Teacher over and over again and felt this discomfort and... Stop! It dawned suddenly on me. Of course, it was a new feeling! When this powerful blow shook the huge underwater rock of ignorance and egoism, suddenly a long-forgotten, deep feeling emerged in me. But I could not completely realize it. When it arose to the surface of my mind, I understood what Sensei wanted to say. It happened to me for the first time. I understood clearly his simple truth. It was the real discovery for my internal world. I was so happy to feel it as if I had managed to reconcile with myself.

I came home in an elated mood. It turned out that there was a surprise for me as well.

"We have got good news," my mother said with her shining, charming smile. "Uncle Victor has called us today from Moscow. He managed to arrange treatment with the best professor from that clinic. So we just have to set up an appointment."

If I had heard this news before, I would have been extremely happy. But now it struck me that I didn't really care what was happening to my head on the physical level. The main thing was the feeling I realized in myself. It was some new level of perception that concerned the soul more than the body. But in order not to ruin my parents' good mood, I spoke out, "That's great! I had no doubt. It comes easy to uncle Victor with his high standing and connections! He is a nice guy and a real go-getter."

The whole next day, I pondered this new feeling. I returned to a normal life, so to say, with my body and especially with my soul. And when it was time to go to meditation practice, I couldn't wait to get there as soon as possible. This time it was I who hurried sluggish Tatyana to pack up her things more quickly.

We came to the tram stop and met the boys there.

"Girls, just imagine," Kostya said laughing. "Sensei has almost spoiled our Andrew."

"What happened?" we asked.

Andrew stood, silent but smiling, and Kostya continued with excitement, "After we saw you to the door, we went home. And when we were almost over there, some guys started to bother us. They seemed to feel an urge to light up a cigarette at night. They insisted so as if it were a kickback for twelve years. Andrew was a real gentleman and did his best to explain to them that we don't smoke and would not recommend it for their own health. Besides, he added that the public health ministry warns that smoking is bad for their health. He concluded that instead of poisoning their lungs with this disgusting thing and hanging around and idling, they should instead go in for sports, for example, Kung-fu. It would be more useful for both their souls and their bodies."

"And?" Tatyana asked impatiently.

"They started to ask for trouble."

"And Andrew?"

"Just picture it, our Andrew began to deliver a speech about their miserable life, and he said that their words would boomerang against them. I thought that he was lost. But then I saw it was all right."

"What happened next?"

"What happened next? Tensions were growing. Andrew kept his patience for a while, enduring their insults, but then in order to be more convincing, he whacked them in the face and made a moralizing conclusion, saying, 'You see, all your bad words boomerang against you with the same force'."

"How could he blurt it out," I wondered.

"And what was at the end?" Tatyana asked with a smile. "Any victims?"

"Everything was all right," Kostya waved his hand. "Ah! I forgot to tell the funniest thing. Later they asked him if they could be his disciples."

Everybody laughed, but for some reason I was uncomfortable. First, I didn't expect such a stupid thing from Andrew. And second, I felt sorry for Sensei.

"Yeah, Andrew, you are a pervert," Tatyana said laughing.

"Right, exactly," Kostya kidded. "He is a dangerous man, we can even say an old offender. He usually perverts even my great sayings and puts them into the most inconvenient position."

"Don't exaggerate telling us about your great sayings," Andrew teased him. "Our new Socrates, so to say."

"Why Socrates? There were more famous people in this world..."

This funny dialogue would have continued endlessly but just then our tram came.

14

We left early for the training, and as it turned out, it was not in vain. Andrew tried to bring us to the secret glade, reassuring us that he knew the road. For about half an hour, we strolled about the streets of the village, teasing all the dogs around. Finally, desperately arguing with each other where the turn was, our company came to a small lake.

"You are a dunderhead!" Kostya said. "Where is your glade?"

"Theoretically it should be here," Andrew shrugged his shoulders.

"Aha, so it was driven by a flood to the other side? Let's go back."

On the way back we bumped into Eugene.

"Finally we have found at least one other living soul," Kostya sighed with relief.

"Have you been lost in our Shanghai?" Eugene poked fun at us.

"Yeah, we relied on the memory of this dunderhead."

"Where is the glade?" Andrew asked.

"Over there," Eugene waved his hand in a completely different direction.

"I told you we turned to the wrong way! There was no hillside," Andrew reproached Kostya.

"And how did you happen to come here?" Tatyana asked Eugene.

"Don't you know? I can spiritually locate any man, I need only think about it."

"Don't joke with us," Kostya said with a smile. "But really what are you doing here?"

"Do not ask me twice. I live here, l-i-v-e!" Eugene said in a funny way. "I had just left and saw your flock rushing to the lake. I didn't even have time to open my mouth. Well, I thought, they will figure it out soon and go back. Just so! I saw you coming back five minutes later. I went to the road so that you didn't take me for a sign-post."

We beamed with smiles after such a successful meeting and arrived together at the glade. In that secluded nook, created with love by nature, almost everyone was there, including Sensei and Volodya. We loudly joined the others, greeting them.

Having noticed that it was again Eugene who brought our company to the place, Sensei asked jokingly, "Has this muddle-head organized an excursion for you again?"

"No, we have a new one now," Kostya nodded to Andrew. "This one surpassed even Eugene."

And then Kostya started to tell eloquently about our adventures. He was so carried away by the overall laughter of the crowd, he became so expressive that he blurted out at the end something unnecessary what we had decided to hide from Sensei: "Well, really! Now imagine entrusting him with disciples after that. He will lead them into such a dead end that he will not know how to get out of it."

"Which disciples?" Sensei caught on the word, although it seemed to me he had not been listening too carefully before.

"Yeah," Kostya became confused after he realized he had said too much. "There was a story..."

"Which story?" Sensei showed interest.

Kostya could do nothing but reluctantly tell all the facts. Andrew also joined the conversation, making an attempt to justify his behaviour with good intentions. Sensei shook his head after hearing all this baby-talk.

"You see... There is an old very ancient legend: Once upon a time a king had an only son. One day he heard that there was a great martial arts Master who was famous even among kings for his Wisdom. He was said to work wonders because he made an excellent Master from an ordinary village boy in just one year. The king made up his mind to send his son to him.

"One year passed and the king asked, 'Well, has he grasped the way of the warrior?'

"'Not yet,' the Master replied. 'He is too self-confident and he wastes his time on pride. Come back in five years.'

"In five years, the king asked the Master the same thing.

"'Not yet. His eyes are still full of hatred, and his energy boils over excessively.'

"Another five years passed. The Master said to the king, 'Now he is ready. Look at him! He is so strong, as if he were carved from a stone. His spirit is stainless. His internal virtues are full and perfect. His challenge will not be accepted by any warrior, as they would run away in fear just from his glance.'

And the king asked the Master, 'Why did it take so long with my son? He is much smarter than that village boy.'

"And the Master replied, 'It is not the mind but the heart is important. If your heart is open and your thoughts are pure, your spirit is stainless. And this is the main thing in the way of the warrior... The village boy came to me with a stainless spirit, and I just had to teach him the technique. Your son has spent years learning this Wisdom. Without this source of power, he would not be able to make a single step on the way of the warrior.'

"Rejoicing at his son's success the king said, 'Now I see that he deserves to take a throne.'

"'No, father,' the young warrior replied. 'I have found something greater. Before my mind was limited only to material wishes, but now it is endless in spiritual cognition. The greatest power, all the gold of the world, fades compared to it like a gray dust under the foot of the wanderer. And the wanderer is not interested in the dust, he is fully devoted with each step to the new discoveries over the horizon.'"

Andrew hung his head ashamed. There was a long pause. But then Nikolai Andreevich joined our company and the discussion switched to other problems, including the meditations practiced by us at home.

"I felt again this paresthesia," Kostya said. "Is this all right?"

"Of course. What is the main point in it? You have to feel these ants that appear with the first breaths in your head. You have to feel how they 'run' inside of your arms and, most importantly, how they jump out of the centre of your palms to the earth. That is, you have to feel your inward and outward breath. And you should not have any outside thoughts at all."

"This is the most difficult thing to do. When I concentrate on the tip of my nose, the ants start coming to my head, catching on each other. And the most amazing thing is that I even do not notice when they appear."

"Right you are. It means that we are not used to controlling our thoughts in our daily life. That is why they guide us to any direction they want, confusing us in their 'logical' chains. And the uncontrolled thought may lead mainly to negative things as it is managed by the animal nature of people. That's why there are different spiritual practices and meditations, to learn to control the thought first of all."

We talked a little more about the striking points of our home practice. And then it came to the next meditation.

"Today we will unite two parts of the meditation into one," Sensei said, "so that you understand how it should work and try to reach it in your individual training. Now find a comfortable position..."

Following his words, we relaxed as usual and concentrated on the meditation practice. First, we concentrated on the tip of the nose as the last time. Then the Teacher said, "Do not distract your attention and vision from the tip of the nose. Take an inward breath through the bottom of your stomach, through your stomach, breast... Outward breath through shoulders, hands, chakras of the palms to the earth. With the outward breath, a small light flares up more and more. Breathe in... Breathe out... Breathe in... Breathe out... Concentrate on the nose tip... Breathe in..."

I was completely confused. As soon as I had concentrated on the 'streamlet', which I could feel clearly as partial movement through the arms, I immediately lost control over my nose tip. And as soon as I had concentrated on the 'flashing' nose tip, my 'streamlet' disappeared. It all happened when my 'outside' thoughts came to me. I was unable somehow to unite it all. During one of my next attempts, I heard Sensei's voice, which informed us of the end of the meditation. As it turned out, this incident happened not only with me but with my friends as well.

"It is natural," Sensei said. "You should not think it over, just observe. Then you will succeed."

It seemed completely unreal to me. But I was encouraged by the fact that Nikolai Andreevich and the senior guys didn't have any problems with this meditation. "It means that not everything is so hopeless," I reassured myself. "If they can do it, why can't I do the same? I just also have to practice hard. That is the point." There I caught myself on the fact that even in my thoughts I had started to speak with the words of Sensei. While I was reflecting on this, one of the guys asked a question.

"So you want to say that the way to self-recognition starts with observing yourself and your thoughts?"

"Of course. Self-observance and control over your thoughts can be practiced little by little during everyday training. And for this you need an elementary knowledge base. It's a natural way of any training, either physical or spiritual. Just a simple example. A man lifts a weight of 20 kg. If he trains for a month, he will easily lift 25 kg, and so on. The same happens at the spiritual level. If you are prepared, it will be much easier for you to master more difficult techniques."

"But there are a lot of different meditations and modifications. It's difficult to understand which one leads to the peak," Kostya as usual made a show of his erudition.

"It's too far to reach the peak. All these meditations that exist in the world practice are just an alphabet that has been never a secret. And the real knowledge leading to the peak starts from the ability to put together words from this alphabet and to understand their meaning. Reading the books is a privilege of the chosen ones."

"Not so bad! Everything is so complicated," Andrew said.

"There is nothing complicated in it. You just need the desire."

"And if you have the desire but hesitate?" Slava asked.

"If you have doubts, someone should beat your head with a heavy hammer so that you understand that you're a dunderhead. A person who hesitates is very much stuck in the material world, in the logic and egoism of his thoughts, his mind... if he possesses one at all."

The guys smiled at these words, and Sensei went on, "If you sincerely strive towards self-recognition, with pure belief in your soul, you will surely succeed. It's a law of nature... And the spiritually developed individual will succeed even more."

Andrew said with a thoughtful view, "Well, the alphabet is clear, but I don't quite understand about the composition of words. Is that also a meditation?"

"Let's say it's something higher - a spiritual practice, an ancient primordial technique that allows us to work not only with the consciousness but, what is more important, with unconsciousness. There is a set of certain meditations that lead to a respective spiritual level... It's simple. The main point is that an individual should overcome his guard, his material thinking, with the desire to conquer the whole world... The same eternal truth as usual, and the same eternal stumbling-block. If an individual is able to overcome it, he will become human."

"I wonder, if someone reaches perfection through training his body, does it mean something?" Yura asked.

"It's one of the ways of alphabet learning."

"Recently we watched video about martial arts with Yura," Ruslan inserted into conversation. "And before it they showed a documentary on people's achievements in self-perfection of their body. Just imagine such a trick, one guy put a spear edge to his throat, fixed its handle to a minivan and pushed it without hands, not injuring himself. Another one lay on his back under heavy things. And nothing happened! The third one smashed bricks with a blow of his hand. But the most interesting was in the end. They took an ordinary bull bone and poured highly concentrated acid over it. Of course, it was destroyed. Then they poured this acid over a man. It immediately destroyed his clothes but brought no harm to his body."

"Incredible!" Andrew exclaimed. "I can't believe it!"

"It's not unusual," Sensei said, evenly as always. "The potential of a human is limited by his fantasy."

"And what was that, Qigong?"

"Well, let's say, aside from Qigong, there are a lot of similar techniques. But the source of the knowledge, including Qigong, is the same. That is, this is a work with energy 'Qi' – the constructive energy of the air."

"I have read somewhere that 'Qi' is life energy, and you call it constructive. Why?" Kostya asked.

"Because energies, chakras, channels, and even energy centers in different teachings are known by different names. For example, under the energy 'Chi' in yoga, they mean noble recoverable energy. But in the science of Lotus under the 'Chi,' initially it meant a powerful destructive energy. The same is true with 'Qi'."

After keeping silent for a while, the Teacher added, "People just assume but they don't possess precise information about the real nature of this knowledge.

Therefore they mix up the meanings. As they say, it's better to stand on the head than to hang in the air."

"Hmm, that's true," Volodya agreed. "If to paraphrase my favorite poster that is an eyesore to all in front of our house, 'There is no such obstacle that we can't create for ourselves!'"

The guys smiled.

"What is Qigong in relation to the art of Lotus?" Andrew came back again to the serious issues.

"For you to understand it, Qigong like kindergarten and the Art of Lotus is like an academy. One of the first stages in learning the highest art is full control over the thoughts. If you can control your thoughts, everything will be under your control.

"Oh, it will be possible to..." Slava started to talk with excitement.

"No, impossible, because you will control your thought. That is, you will not be able to do something negative and wrong. That is the whole sense. We learn and practice Qigong, but in the Art of Lotus we don't train, we recall all things hidden in our soul.

"And those body phenomena we have seen in the film, is it possible for us to learn them?" Ruslan asked, thinking about something.

"Of course. It's easy if you can use this energy in the right way."

"And what is needed for it?"

"Elementary skills, concentration of breathing, a certain understanding of the essence of this phenomenon..."

"I just can't grasp it," Jura said in a thoughtful way. "How did that guy manage to break bricks with his hand?"

"Did you want him to break them with another part of the body?" Eugene poked fun at him.

"It's possible to break them with another part as well," Sensei smiled, "if you want strongly enough to do so. The point is that with a certain concentration and breathing exercises you can accumulate the Qi energy in any part of the body, in this case in the hand. And at the moment of the blow, the chakra opens up in the palm, and all this power is released to break something. It's very important, I say it again, the very process of mind concentration, that is, the process of focused concentration.

"Does it have any effect on the change in the level of brain activity?" Nikolai Andreevich asked.

"Sure. It launches a very interesting process in the brain. To put it in medical terms, a beta rhythm may be registered at the moment of the blow preparation and full mental concentration. A few minutes before the blow itself, an individual stops thinking about what he is doing. At this moment, his mind activity changes from beta rhythm to alpha rhythm, and it's similar with the shock state. In this state, a blow is being struck. It is like a stoppage of time, perhaps. It's not difficult. Just physics. That's all."

"We have one soldier in our platoon who breaks bricks," Volodya joined the discussion. "The others tried to imitate him but didn't succeed except with board punching."

"It's natural," the Teacher uttered. "The mistake of many people is that they try to think too much, to analyze the situation. That's why they are not successful."

"Can you break bricks?" Andrew asked, unable to resist a temptation to see everything with his own eyes.

"It's easy, just take a hammer and go forth," Sensei joked.

"No, I meant with a palm," Andrew specified.

"Why should I dirty up my hands? It's better to break them with a piece of paper."

"With a piece of paper?"

"Yes. I'm not sure about the bricks, but if it's something wooden, easily. Does anybody have a sheet of paper?"

We started hastily looking for it in our pockets. Volodya tore a piece of paper out of his notebook, about five centimeters wide. Yura found a dry branch not far from us, around 3-4 centimeters in diameter.

"Does anybody want to try?" the Teacher suggested.

The guys in turn waved a piece of paper over the stick like true card-players, but nothing changed. Volodya had to tear off another piece of paper. Sensei wanted to give a piece of paper to me and Tatyana.

"No, no, no," we waved our hands. "If these guys were unable to do it, what we can say of our muscles?"

"Muscles don't play any role. It can be done by anybody who doesn't doubt his abilities."

With these words, the Teacher gripped a piece of paper between his forefinger and thumb in his outstretched hand. He concentrated and started to do a range of breathing exercises. After that, the paper started to vibrate a bit, its movement was gradually slowed down, and soon it stopped moving at all, becoming straight. In less than a minute, Sensei raised his hand slowly and cut the stick with one smooth movement. The cut looked as if it were made by something iron and sharp."

"Gosh!" our amazed group exclaimed.

We looked first at the branch, then at the paper, and after that at Sensei with one silent question, "How did he do it?"

Nikolai Andreevich assumed with doubts in his voice, "Was it a trick? You might have broken the branch with your finger in the very last moment."

"Really?" It was Sensei's turn to get surprised. "Have you ever seen a trick like this?"

He threw a piece of paper that went into the nearest tree just like a knife blade, complete with a metal sound. We had hardly put our lower jaws back in place as we rushed to the tree, as if there were an answer to the eternal question from Shakespeare, 'To be or not to be?' Nikolai Andreevich himself took out a paper-blade, even tasting it. It was circulated. This piece of paper seemed to be an ordinary iron plate, with all typical features. We stood completely at a loss, unable to believe our own eyes. Suddenly the plate in Slava's hands started to lose its shape, gradually turning into an ordinary piece of paper. Slava noticed it, threw it into the air, and jumped quickly away with a piglet scream, causing the same reaction not only in us but in the senior guys as well. Volodya was the first who collected himself. He carefully picked up the former page of his notebook and said in a bass voice, "Why are you making noise? It's just a piece of paper."

We looked at the Teacher.

"It's all right. It has just lost its power."

When we calmed our stormy emotions, Sensei explained, "You have seen one more feature of the energy Qi - its ability to accumulate ions of metal. Since Qi is constructive energy, I concentrated and mentally inserted ions of iron into this piece of paper. My thought was implemented by Qi which, through my breath, brought these ions from the air into the paper. That's why the paper turned into a metal plate for a time. Qi is a free energy - that's why it dissolved in a few minutes, thus returning this plate to its original form."

"Great!" Ruslan said with admiration. "And is it possible to Qi something like 2 kg of gold?"

The guys burst out laughing.

"Theoretically it's possible." Sensei smiled. "But in reality it's like the saying in the Winnie the Pooh cartoon, 'If there is honey, there is no honey.' Remember physics: in order to retain ions of metal, you need strong molecular links. And these ions are connected by the energy Qi mixed up with psychic energy. Qi is the connecting link between ions of metal, and psychic energy creates any shape for a short period of time. But there will be no density at all."

"Wow!" A hum buzzed through the crowd.

"That is the practical use!" Kostya discovered for himself. "And here I was thinking what's the use of all of this? That's great!"

"We can do so many things with it," Ruslan said with a smile.

Everyone's eyes shone with joy, and the guys started to discuss how to make use of this knowledge. Sensei observed all our excitement, keeping silent. And the more we boosted the situation in jokes, the gloomier and more serious his face became. Finally he said, "I see, guys, that you have too much animal nature in yourselves."

"We're just joking," Ruslan uttered, trying to make an excuse for all of us.

"Many a true word is spoken in jest."

"Right," Volodya agreed while he was silently observing our jokes. "Otherwise it will be the same story as with the ninjas."

We didn't understand whether he was joking or telling the truth.

"What do you mean?" Andrew asked.

"What I've said," Volodya said in a bass voice.

We looked at Sensei with a question in our eyes.

"Yes, there was such a story," Sensei said. "Once a whole clan of ninjas was liquidated because they used spiritual knowledge with selfish motives."

"We have not heard about it," Ruslan said. "Tell us."

"Yes, tell us," we backed him up.

"There is nothing to tell... So long as ninjas trained their body and mastered their skills, they flourished. Nobody paid attention to them, actually. They were just hired assassins. But when ninjas started to master spiritual practices and learnt something, they started to use this knowledge for their material enrichment. It was a real hour of triumph for ninjas, so to say, their heyday and decline at the same time. They won fame immediately as invincible superkillers. Due to spiritual practices, ninjas developed their extraordinary abilities. They were able to turn everything into a weapon: any piece of paper, anything available. They learnt perfectly how to camouflage, to jump into a space and from a very big height, without any harm to their health and so on."

"That's great!" Slava burst out.

"Do not admire them," the Teacher said after Slava's exclamation. "And moreover do not create idols from them. They were just a gang of hired assassins who killed from behind, from an ambush. They were foul dregs and nothing else. They were directed by their material nature... They didn't have any honor. And honor is one of the features of the general spirituality of a human, not just of a warrior, that is, when he is guided by high moral values. A man without honor is nobody and nothing.

"And what happened to the ninjas?" Jura asked.

"As is usual in such cases, when they started to use spiritual practices for gaining their own material enrichment, they were liquidated."

The guys bombarded Sensei with questions. But Ruslan was the most insistent of all, "How did they get this spiritual knowledge if they used it for their own devious purposes?"

"They didn't get it. Ninjas stole it. More precisely, they wormed out the technique of meditations through deceit. And then they grew this seed of knowledge themselves. But they used it for bad things. That's why they were punished."

"Who punished them? You said yourself that they reached such a height that they became invulnerable to people," Andrew put his question to Sensei.

Sensei grinned and cited his favorite saying, "You see, for every Vijai there is a Rajah... If there is military science, there is somebody who guides it. The same thing happens with spiritual practices. If there are spiritual practices, there is someone who controls the use of these practices. This knowledge is thus called spiritual as it is meant for spiritual enrichment of the individual, not material enrichment, especially not through killing living beings."

"I have read that ninja schools still exist," Kostya remarked.

"Yes, but the truth is, modern ninja schools are just a miserable parody of those that existed in ancient times. They still have their techniques and instruments. But all this training is focused on the material physical level. And the door to further perfection is closed. As the law says: spiritual for spiritual... And if you guys strive to learn the Art for material profits or satisfaction of your megalomania," Sensei shook his head, gazing upon us, "no good will come of it."

"Why?" Slava asked.

"First, you will never learn anything. Second, if, of course, you are lucky enough, you will gain at least schizophrenia."

"Yes, it's a nice future," Ruslan said smiling.

"Well, there is no such threat for you," Eugene said chuckling.

"But we are not going to kill anybody," Andrew was looking for excuses.

"Physically, maybe not. But your thoughts contain too much of a beast. And this is the first step towards aggression and violence."

"What should we do now?"

"Control your thoughts every second."

Keeping silent for a while, Sensei added, looking at Andrew, "Have you ever thought about who you are in fact? Who you are in essence? Have you thought how you perceive the surrounding world? Not from the point of view of physiology, but from the point of view of life... Who are you? How do you see, how do you hear, why do you feel, who in you understands and, who exactly perceives? Look inside of yourself."

Sensei continued addressing the guys, "Have you ever thought at all about the infinity of your consciousness? About what is the thought? How is it born, and where does it go? Have you thought about your thoughts?"

"Well," Andrew became confused, "I think all the time, reflect on things."

"It seems to you that it's you who thinks and it's you who reflects. But are you sure that these are your own thoughts?"

"Whose else? This body is mine, therefore the thoughts are mine as well."

"Try to analyze them, if they are yours, at least for one day. Where do they come from, to where do they disappear? Dig through your thoughts thoroughly, and what will you see there except shit? Nothing. Just violence, just ugly things, just the desire to gorge yourself, to put on fashionable clothes, to steal, to earn, to buy, to raise your megalomania. And that's all! You will see for yourself that all thoughts generated by your body end with one thing: the material supply around you. But is it really you inside yourself? Look into your soul and you will face the beautiful and eternal, your true "I". All this external vanity around is just nonsense... Are you aware of it?"

We stood silent. Suddenly the scene seemed very familiar to me. It already happened to me once, in exactly the same way down to the smallest details: this word-for-word discussion, and this glade, and these bright stars, and most importantly, this voice familiar to the innermost of my heart, this kind face... I knew that it had already happened. But when, where? I tried to exert my memory, but I was unable to recollect it. I shook my head a little to get my mind out of this deadlock and back on track.

Sensei went on, "You have lived 16, 22, 30 years, and you, about 40 years. But each of you, do you remember how you lived? No, there are just some miserable scraps connected by emotional splashes."

"Yes," Nikolai Andreevich said in a thoughtful way, "life passed so quickly that I didn't manage to notice it. All the time I spent studying, working, dealing with insignificant, endless family problems... There was no time to think about myself, about my soul, since there were always urgent matters."

"Exactly," Sensei agreed. "You think about the future and about the past. But you live in this very moment called 'now'. And what is now? It's a precious second of life, it's a gift of God that should be rationally used. Tomorrow is a step into uncertainty. It's not improbable that it may be your last step in this life, a step to the abyss, to infinity. And what will happen there?

"Each of you believes that he has plenty of time on the Earth, that's why you don't think about death. But is it true? Each of you may die any second, for any reason, as on the one hand you are a biological being. But on the other hand, you are not just a biological being, you are a human who possesses a particle of eternity. Having realized it, you will understand that your fate is in your hands and a lot of it depends on you, not only here, but also there. Just think it over: who are you, a perfect biorobot or a human, an animal or a spiritual creature? Who?"

"Well, a human... maybe," Ruslan said.

"Exactly, maybe. And what is a human, in fact, have you thought? Go deep inside of this question. Who feels in you, how do you move in the space, who moves your extremities? How do your emotions arise in you, why do they arise? And do not shift the blame onto someone who bothered you, offended you, or vice versa, if you envied, gloated, gossiped. Is it your spiritual nature in you?

"Find a crystal source of your soul in you, and you will understand that all this material glare – cars, flats, villas, social status – all this material wealth you spend your conscious life reaching for will turn into dust. Dust which immediately will be transformed in this source into nothing. And life passes by. Life which might be used by you to be transformed into the endless ocean of wisdom.

"What is the sense of life, have you ever thought about it? The highest sense of life of each individual is the cognition of his soul. Other things are all temporary, passing through, just dust and illusion. The only way to understand your soul is through your internal love, through moral purification of your thoughts, and through the absolutely firm self-confidence to reach this goal, that is through internal faith... Until you have a glimmer of life in you, it's still not too late to recognize yourself, to find your basis, the holy life-giving spring of your soul. Get know yourself, and you will understand who you are in reality."

15

After all we had seen and heard during that meditation, there was something to seriously think about, especially for me on the verge of death. "God, these are the answers to my questions, which I have been looking for for so long. Is it possible that this formula of achieving immortality is so simple? Control your thoughts, believe and love. Is it possible that I will reach a saving shore, an edge of eternity from which the immortals already observe life, all those who have recognized themselves and their divine nature?! Is it possible that my "I" will be able to break loose from death's grip? Even if I don't have time to "re-conquer" my body, I will still be able to become free, and at least I will be prepared to meet with the unknown." Such thoughts raised in me an unusual inspiration and a burst of internal power. I decided not to lay aside things for tomorrow but to start working immediately, right now. Because who knows what tomorrow will bring for me.

First I tried to examine my thoughts. But I felt so enthusiastic and inspired that I was unable to stop at something specific, as all my material thoughts suddenly disappeared under such a force. Then I started to investigate my feelings. Only now did I notice that I was so absorbed with my internal feelings that I started to look completely differently at even the outside world. This was some kind of a new vision, an unknown point of view for me on the old and, as they say, shabby problems.

A new vision surrounded me from all sides, like a cocoon, seizing my consciousness away from grey, everyday commonness with its trivial worries. I had the impression as if I existed by myself and the rest of the world by itself. Moreover, I observed for the first time the workings of my body from the outside. It was making its usual movements, as if it were on autopilot: it came home mechanically, took a shower mechanically, ate mechanically, and went mechanically into its separate corner, that is into the room. The real "I" at that time was observing it and thinking about its salvation. This small discovery shocked me. I found out that there is a true "I" in me and a kind of physical autopilot.

But the further the better. Once again having restored the conversation with Sensei to my thoughts, I recalled his words: "Have you ever thought how you move in space and who moves your extremities?" Examining myself from a new point of view, I reflected, "And really, who moves my extremities: the "I" or the autopilot?"

I looked at my open palm and decided to conduct a simple experiment. I thought, "I need to clench and undo my fist," and my hand obediently executed it. "And now I am not going to move my fingers." But this time, a wild thought flashed across my mind, "I'm still going to clench my fist." My fingers, under the influence of this "order," gripped and released again. "Oh!" I was surprised. "And who was that thinking in me? Who is there playing boss in my thoughts?!" Gathering myself up again this time, I was more persistent and concentrated my thoughts: "I won't move my fingers. That's what I want, and let it be so." Strangely enough, my hand didn't even move, and this wild, mad thought pretended to have never existed in my mind.

"Oho!" I was surprised even more. "It means that when I was relaxed in my thoughts, this someone started to invisibly manage my consciousness and my body by his will. And when I strictly control a thought, he disappears somewhere without a trace. Gosh!" Nevertheless, I was so happy to find out this fact, it was as if I had traced a spy thoroughly camouflaged for many years in my most secret department. "Yes, this clever boy is much more dangerous than that stupid autopilot. I should be more vigilant!"

It's easy to say but hard to do. When I started to practice meditations, I understood that this dodger visited my thoughts all the time in the moment of relaxation, and especially during concentration on meditation, constantly diverting my attention on outside matters. He carried it all out in such a clever and logical way that I didn't notice when I went off track in concentration. But when I concentrated my thoughts on meditation deeply and clearly, the dodger disappeared. But I needed only to weaken control and he would appear again. "What a skunk! Impudent and bothersome," I thought, trying once again to concentrate on meditation. When I finished a meditation, I understood that it was not easy to fight with my number one enemy. "I will need to ask Sensei how to find justice for this dodger," I thought, falling asleep. "Otherwise he is going to spoil everything for me."

The next morning, when my splash of emotions had faded away a little after yesterday, I began again to observe myself from outside. Once again, my body somehow came off the warm bed and started to mechanically perform its morning ritual, getting ready for school. My mind, as it seemed to me, was sweetly sleeping, and that's why I didn't feel like thinking about anything. Walking the usual road to school through the city square, I was enjoying the surrounding stillness, the morning freshness, the rustling of fallen leaves. I really liked this state of peace. My mind slept, my body walked in a given direction, while I just felt well and cozy inside of myself. I felt that this was my true "I".

But in school, the situation changed immediately. I flew into a tornado of events, information, emotions. As a result, I was completely confused about the nature of my thoughts because they came in a continuous torrent, and it was hard to sort out them, what was mine and what was foreign. And the whole day passed in this wild rhythm.

16

In the evening when I met the guys at the tram stop I started to share my achievements with them and asked with interest, "How about your results? Did you think after yesterday's training?"

"There is nothing to think about," Kostya said arrogantly. "My "I" is me, the whole, one and indivisible... I am not a maniac to divide myself in two parts."

"Oh, yeah, you're not a maniac, you're a genius....from ward six. Does Napoleon bother you too much?" Andrew teased him with a smile.

"Stop it. I don't have excessive megalomania." He added, "Great people don't suffer from it."

"Of course," Andrew laughed, "I didn't expect another answer."

"Calm down or you'll start with the same old song and dance. Tell me more about your experiences," I said impatiently.

"There's not much to tell," Andrew answered. "Sensei said a lot of useful things yesterday. There's enough to think over for many years. That's what I was doing yesterday, I was reflecting on whether I had correctly formulated my goals for the future or whether I had to adjust them, taking into account the new information."

"Oho! You really mind your language," Slava said sarcastically. "Are you going to join the Academy of Science?"

"Oh no, Sensei is quite enough for me."

"That's true," I said. "Did you succeed with meditation?"

"A lot better than yesterday. Thoughts didn't crawl too much into my head. My concentration improved right away, and all the feelings became clearer."

"Tatyana, did you manage with it somehow?"

"Well, to tell the truth, I didn't do meditation and even didn't think to try with it. I was so tired yesterday that I barely reached my bed. In the morning I had to take my younger brother to kindergarten, then I went to buy milk, after that to school. There's no time for reflection when you have so much to do!"

"Right," Kostya backed up her excuses. "You should not think but act. Youth is given for action and old age for reflection."

"Aha," Andrew teased him, "and when old you will be squeaking with your decrepit voice, thinking with the last remnants of your brain, 'Ah, if only youth knew, if only old age was able to.'"

The guys laughed again, teasing Kostya.

"And what about you?" I asked Slava.

"All right."

"In which sense all right?"

"Just the same as all of you."

"All is clear," Andrew smiled, hopelessly waving a hand towards him.

17

At the next training, we warmed up before the beginning of the exercises as usual. A crowd of men with imposing appearances headed by Volodya entered the hall.

"Oho, what a crowd!" Andrew was surprised.

Victor smiled and said to Stas, "This is what's known as 'a couple of guys.'"

"What do you mean?"

"Volodya called me yesterday and said that he would come to the training with a couple of his guys."

"Not so bad, there's half a regiment here, I'd guess," Stas said with a smile.

"Exactly, that's what I'm telling you."

Volodya came up to greet Sensei, who was standing not too far from us. The senior guys hurried to join them.

"Sensei, do you mind?" Volodya pointed towards his guys.

"No problem," as always, Sensei answered easily.

"Did you watch TV last night?"

"When? I barely have time for it."

"Would you believe they showed our San Sanych yesterday?!"

"Our San Sanych?!" Eugene was surprised. "It's been ages since we last heard from him!"

"Oh! But now he is really famous! He says that he lived in a cave somewhere and learnt a Russian martial art. And now he calls himself a Russian ninja. What's most interesting is that he demonstrated your techniques, Sensei. With the only difference being that he tells everybody that it is a long-forgotten Slavic style revived by him."

"Not bad!" Stas grinned. "You see, Volodya, if you hadn't kicked Sanych so hard last time, you would've been his partner."

"No, he wouldn't," Eugene said archly.

"Why not?"

"What do you mean why not? If Volodya hadn't beaten him down so well, he would never have seen the light."

The guys roared with laughter.

"You shouldn't have treated him like that last time," Sensei said. "He is an old man, and we should respect our elders."

"It was his own fault; why was he asking for trouble?" Volodya began to make excuses but added softly, "I barely touched him, just struck him by accident."

"Exactly, exactly, Sensei, that's the way it was," Eugene joined in. "I remember it as if it happened yesterday. Volodya put forward his fist, and San Sanych was knocking it with his head for almost five minutes. And now look how useful it was! The man saw the light and became a Russian ninja."

The guys burst out laughing again.

"Ah, let him amuse himself," Sensei waved his hand with a good-natured smile. "The man found his gold mine, let him live."

"Yesterday we were on duty in the barracks," Volodya continued the story, "and saw on TV how Sanych flapped his legs and kicked his opponents. We had a good laugh, recalling our youth. Even my newcomers are far and away better... That's why we decided to come today, in order to gain some knowledge of the real Art, to enrich our reserve knowledge."

"It's a noble deed," Sensei agreed.

The guys continued to tell stories of bygone trainings and a whole range of funny incidents during them. At the very end, Volodya's guys joined the conversation, and it turned from martial arts issues into a philosophical dispute about relations between people.

"Well, I dealt with them this way on principle," one of Volodya's guys impulsively defended his point of view.

"Principle is a stupid resistance to reality, akin to idiocy. Principle..."

Sensei had hardly finished this sentence when the senior guys almost as one continued his thought, "...is applicable only in exact sciences as synonym to axiom."

"Exactly," the Teacher confirmed.

Volodya got a bit embarrassed, "Well, I've done my best to explain it to them."

"Well, then you haven't tried very hard. And what can't be understood through the mind..."

"...will be hammered in through the body!"

"Good, since you all know this so well, you shouldn't laugh."

I realized the meaning of Sensei's last words when the training began. Sensei warned that that day we were going to train in full power, and those who couldn't endure that tempo should step aside to the left corner of the sports hall and polish strikes there, without disturbing the others. We ruffled up, like sparrows, and whispered with pride among ourselves.

"We couldn't endure?!" Andrew said quietly.

"Don't even say it," Kostya added. "We will show right now what we are able to do!"

"It wouldn't be the first time," I uttered carelessly, remembering the warm-up of the senior sempai.

But our arrogance flew away immediately after the first few minutes of the warm-up. I have never before seen such a tough training. It was a real school of survival. The crowd was running through the sports hall in a mad tempo, overcoming constantly changing barriers. In less than forty minutes, many of us already were crawling over these barriers almost grappling, including me.

Groaning nearby, Tatyana murmured, "It's so awful! Almost like a joke, 'Dear ladies and gentlemen! Colleagues and colleagues! Koryak crooked girls and boys...' The last one is for sure related to us. I feel like I'm a native of that region."

The first 'victims' appeared in the left corner of the sports hall. But our group carried on stubbornly. However, later it became even worse. After that marathon race with a series of different exercises, we did so many push-ups. I don't know how many times, I just remember that it was over one hundred. My hands were shaking as if I had been using a jackhammer, and my body curved like a caterpillar when trying to get up, not so much due to the vibrations, but due to the jerking of my gluteal muscles. Because it seemed to me that only this part of my body had any power left. I started to look more and more often towards the left corner, where a growing number of people crawled to this saving oasis. Tatyana traitorously joined them and was alluringly waving at me.

At that time, the senior sempai counted push-ups. In order to raise people's mood, he jokingly kept saying, like a toastmaster, "Sensei has a sheep dog that lets everybody into the house, but doesn't let anyone out. So let's do ten push-ups for the quick wit of this smart dog that doesn't eat its bread in vain."

While everybody was getting more exhausted with each counting, Sensei walked around the big human circle of sweating people, searching for someone to whom he should add weight with his palms. When he presses you with his palms, it feels like a truck has driven over you. During the second round, when he came up to me jerking through the push-ups as if in convulsions, I thought, "This is the end! If he puts his hand on me, I will surely be flattened like a fly against the glass." Despite my expectations, the Teacher seized me by my kimono from above like a kitten by the scruff on the neck and started to help me come up from the ground, evoking laughter from the surrounding guys.

While Victor went on, "Sensei also has a cat Samurai, which became so self-confident that it started to fight with dogs. Let us then push-up ten times for his desires to always correspond with his abilities."

My bones were aching because of the strain. While Victor continued telling his funny puns, I was cursing Samurai's flea Mashka that jumps so far, and the mice that live in the shed and run so fast, and those Siamese battle fishes that have lightning reactions and a piranha's manners, in other words, all those living creatures that dwell in Sensei's house. Finally, the last round of push-ups was for the parrot Keshka, which made an effort to breed five nestlings, and we felt down to the floor completely exhausted. However, in less than one minute, we were laid out again in stacks, and the crowd started to jump over its long-suffering brethren, accidentally crushing our extremities on the way. In the hall every now and then under staring eyes, one could hear a restrained howl. I couldn't stand it and joined the left flank of weak-nerves.

"It's high time," Tatyana said.

But our rest didn't last for long. When the warm-up was finished, we started intensive work on base techniques and exercises of strikes and movements. I noticed that Sensei devoted more time to Volodya's guys, explaining and showing them a series of new techniques. They were throwing each other so easily while practicing strikes that I was simply shocked by their endurance and inexhaustible force. It was as if there had been no wearisome warm-up.

After two and a half hours of intensive training, we had power enough only to think about how to survive additional training. Of course, nobody forced us; if we wanted to leave, we could have. But our curiosity was bigger than physical tortures. Since Volodya had brought his guys, the most interesting should be ahead. And we weren't mistaken.

18

When the main crowd left, Sensei started to show some special techniques on how to use counterforce. Divided in pairs, the guys started to practice them. Tatyana and I also tried, but our feeble bodies ended up hanging on each other, like tired out boxers in the last round. Having seen our parody of sparring, Sensei separated us, placing us into pairs with the guys. I immediately mobilized all that was left over of my power. Who could have expected it?

Exercising one of the kicks, Ruslan, who looked like a skinny ant against his partner Eugene, complained to Sensei, "Is it even possible to knock out such a giant? He is so impenetrable, like solid armor. If he initiated an attack on me, I could at least use his own force against him, as you said. But what if I need to attack him? Then what can I do against this stubborn rhino? He's a heap of muscles!"

"A heap of muscles is nothing. In martial arts, power is not essential. In the East there is a saying, 'Hands and legs are nothing more than a continuation of the body, and the body, in its turn, is a continuation of the mind.' In other words, the most important things are knowledge and skills. Then even the weakest woman, with just a touch of one finger, can knock out the strongest athlete in the world or even kill him."

"Well, theoretically it's possible," Eugene smiled. "Especially if she is beautiful, then one glance is enough... But seriously, in my opinion, it is practically impossible."

"It is possible," replied Sensei.

"An athlete?"

"An athlete.".

"With one finger?"

"With one finger."

"Without force?"

"Without force."

"I don't beli...."

Eugene had hardly finished his sentence when Sensei touched one of his throat muscles, a little below the right ear, with a light movement of the middle finger of his left hand. Unexpectedly for all, Eugene's face distorted as if he had chewed a dozen lemons with the right side of his mouth. His right leg quickly gave way, and he fell on the ground, with no time to understand why. His right hand was not obeying and looked like a rag. Eugene glanced at Sensei with frightened eyes, twitching with the left side of his body.

"Ohsh, notsh shou bash," Eugene could only mutter, trying to say something coherent. We stood shocked by this scene, as a young, healthy man was turned into a helpless, half-paralyzed old man.

"Whash shush i shu?"

Sensei bent over the living corpse of Eugene and touched some points on his back and stomach. He did it so quickly and skillfully that I didn't even see where exactly he pressed. Eugene started slowly recovering, massaging his suffering extremities.

"Notsh sho bash!"

"So, how are you doing, doubting Thomas?" Sensei asked.

"Shenshei! You should have letsh know beforehand. I gotsh almosht crazy," Eugene hardly enunciated in his broken, hissing language.

"What a pity you didn't," the Teacher said jokingly with disappointment. "At least once in your life you would feel good. Sometimes it really helps."

"Sensei, tell us the recipe for this poison," Stas jokingly joined the conversation, evidently being the first to recover after that shock.

"Well, the recipe is simple. You need to know where, when and how."

"It sounds logical, but could you give us more detail?" Volodya made an attempt to clarify.

"In detail? There is a great number of BAPs in the human body."

"Whatsh?" Eugene didn't understand.

"BAPs – biologically active points."

"Thshey are not pointshs, damn itsh! Thshey are balishtic misshiles!" Eugene said it with ironic indignation. "Moreover, witsh auotshopilotsh."

The guys smiled at his zealous speech.

"Absolutely correct. It proves once again that any knowledge can be turned into a weapon. So, this effect of ballistic auto-piloted missiles is caused by no other reason than an accurate point impact on biologically active points of a human body."

"And what are these points?" one of the guys asked with interest. "How do they work?"

"Well, it's a certain area of the skin with common innervation. Located in this zone, receptors send signals through nerves which in turn transfer these signals not only into the spinal cord but also through centripetal and extraspinal tracts up to the cerebrum. There happens to be a certain fusion of seemingly unconditioned reflexes. Moreover, this process is reflected in cortical analyzers as well, with the formation of conditioned-reflex connections. In other words, to put it simply, a certain order for the body is being formed there."

"If so, will it lead to such an effect?"

"Not just one effect. A man can be frozen for some time or knocked out, or finally programmed to cease existence on the physical level in a definite amount of time."

"And do you only need to hit this point hard?"

"Not at all. All processes inside of the body take place at very small energy levels. If you affect these points with a threshold stimulus, that is to say, with a weak stimulus, it brings a much bigger influence on the body's function than a strong stimulus."

At that time, Eugene stood up and tried to walk around, all the while limping on the right with his right hand shaking. "My dshear mothsher, thshish gripsh, ash if I were laying on thshe right sidshe."

"This lazy lie-abed," Sensei joked. "He just wants to sleep and to eat well... You should train more!"

"Well, I kindsh of sweatedsh ash muchsh ash everybodshy."

"I mean, you should train your mind more so as not to make an ass of yourself."

"At which point did you 'kick' him so easily?" Volodya was interested.

"This is a so-called Botkin-Erb point. If I had pressed in a bit another way, the effect would've been completely different. If I had affected the plexus of nearby splanchnic nerves with the same impact power, then I could've caused a spasm of the thyroid artery, which in turn would cause a disorder in the thyroid gland. This would've led to overall weakening of the immune system or its complete cessation. In that case, he would've died on his own from any infection."

Eugene stopped moving after hearing such a speech, "Shanks, you shealy calm me witsh shuch a chsheerful pershpective."

"You also said, 'Where, when and how,'" one of Volodya's guys uttered. "What do you mean, where?"

"Well, apart from the fact that you need to know the exact location of the point and the power of applying impact to it, you need also to know the time of the day when this point is most active."

"Hmm! And that's all," Volodya smiled.

Even now Eugene didn't miss an opportunity to joke, still in his hissing language, "Tshell me, and doesn't it come witsh the latesht map of the universh?"

Sensei smiled, "It depends for whom. For a dummy, even this won't be enough."

"And how can one understand all these points and use them?" Stas asked.

"The simplest way to understand something is, of course, to examine and to feel it in yourselves, especially the impulse of pressing, this is very important."

"Aha, and if we screw up something in ourselves," Victor made an assumption half in jest.

"You won't screw up. There exist points-antagonists on the human body for this purpose, which neutralize the given stimulus or spasm. Everything in nature is maintained in equilibrium."

"It's better to try it on others," Kostya proposed smiling.

"It won't work," Sensei said. "No matter how many times you try on the others, you'll never achieve the right effect until you feel for yourself the power of this impact."

"May we try it right now, during the fight?" some of Volodya's guys asked.

"You may."

"And may we?" someone else in the same company added.

"Yes, please."

Three volunteers from Volodya's team and Ruslan came up to Sensei. Stas, who also joined them, offered the same to Volodya who refused, saying, "I'm not your everlasting makiwara, you guys!"

"Well, well."

Eugene hobbled, sitting next to Volodya on the sport bench, and addressed Stas, "Come on, guys. One shecondh and zhthere is no thongue nor head anymore. Andth itsh will be your own faultsh."

"So, anybody else?" Sensei asked, looking at Volodya's guys.

This time I screwed up my courage and put myself forward, evoking a smile on the faces of the surrounding guys.

"And what are you going to do?" Sensei was surprised.

A cowardly thought flashed in my head, "And really, why did I come up?" But it was too late to retreat:

"May I try?"

"Aren't you afraid?"

"Only of tickling," I got confused and blurted out my dad's favorite joke.

"Alright, if you want to join the ranks of kamikaze, you are welcome."

Already addressing the other volunteers he added, "Let's work in full contact. Your task is to win this fight by any means."

"May we work in a group?" one of Volodya's guys asked.

"You may. Fight as you like, you have absolute freedom of actions."

While Sensei turned around, Volodya's guys came together into a circle, negotiating something in their own military language of gestures. Ruslan and Stas also whispered to one another. I stood among these giant athletic bodies like a mouse, without any idea what I could do, with my power of a small fly against a hurricane wind. Unfortunately nothing special came to my mind. "Alright, whatever will be, will be," I thought.

The guys took up their fighting positions around Sensei. Only I stood in the same place. When the senior sempai gave the order to attack, Volodya's guys surrounded Sensei from all sides and started to attack him at the same time on different levels. Surprisingly, Sensei easily avoided their strikes. He launched a counterattack so quickly, that all I saw were chaotically falling bodies. Terrified, I was shaking in my shoes. Then Ruslan and Stas tried to attack the Teacher. In fighting with them, Sensei turned with his back to me, only the distance of an outstretched arm. I made up my mind to do something immediately. Nothing else came into my mind but to catch hold of Sensei's back, like a flea, so that he wouldn't touch me. But when I tried to do my best to realize this idea, it turned out that my hands went through the emptiness, and instead of Sensei I caught air. I didn't believe my eyes, right now he stood in front of me! "It's easier to catch a ghost than Sensei," I thought.

But then all my thoughts about the soul left suddenly when I realized Sensei had already completely bewildered the next unfortunate fighters. I turned around and ran away with all my might in the opposite direction. But having hardly made two steps, I got a light painful push somewhere in the vicinity of my first and second vertebrae. A bright, blinding light momentarily flashed before my eyes, as if I were illuminated by a bright powerful projector of some yellowy-pink color. All my body stood motionless in a rather unusual position with arms frozen wide, torso bent forward, and right leg half lifted. How I was balancing, I didn't understand. But that time it worried me least of all.

I observed terrified what was happening to my muscles. They all as a single mechanism started to spasm despite my will and desire. And this overall spasm crept over all of my body. It seemed that the strain intensified with every second, and nothing was able to stop it. My body was being squeezed with such a strength that it seemed I heard my spine crackle. The most extraordinary thing was to feel the tension of my internal organs. It had never happened to me before. Even my strongest former headaches were trifles in comparison with this unbearable pain. The muscles of my face got so strained that it was distorted into a dreadful grimace.

Amazing, but despite all these transformations in my strained body, I kept a clear mind. I continued to clearly see and hear everything. I saw how guys from our group, observing all of that, changed their expressions, looking with fright at our frozen figures. I could clearly hear the words of Kostya addressed to me, "Oho! What a beauty you became, I can't take my eyes off you."

I wanted to reply to him sarcastically, but I couldn't say a word, couldn't even move my tongue. It seemed to me that an eternity passed while Sensei was bringing us back to life. But in reality, I hadn't even stood one minute in this position. My whole body felt like pins and needles in all directions, as if I had simultaneously crushed all my extremities. My accomplices were actively rubbing their bodies. I hastily followed their example, though not so emotionally. My body was aching and hurting.

"Don't worry," Sensei reassured us. "In a couple of days, a maximum of three days, this pain will be over."

Until the end of the additional training, all six of us were doing nothing but rubbing our extremities while suffering the tireless jokes of the other guys. When our company of cripples came outside, Volodya, who stood close to Sensei, said with admiration, "Splendid! It was a great training today. I warmed up my muscles well."

"Oho, he warmed up his muscles!" I thought, hardly moving my legs. "If it continues like that, next time I will arrive in a wheelchair." Our group of unfortunate fighters slowly toddled down the road, accompanied by funny jokes of our company.

"You don't look bad, guys, just like in that joke," Victor commented ironically.

"Which joke?"

"Well... two guys meet each other in the ER, bandaged from head to toe. One asks the other, 'Where did you manage to get hurt like that?' 'I crashed into the garage.' 'Your car is probably smashed,' the first one felt for him. 'No, I was walking!'"

"But it's not a joke, my body hurts," I complained to the Teacher.

"Just don't think about the pain. Because any pain is an illusion."

"How can it be an illusion if I really feel it?"

"It just seems to you that you feel it. It's possible to stop feeling any pain at all, if you wish strongly enough."

"Really," Slava asked with distrust, "even if they cut you up?"

"Even if they fry you," Sensei answered with smile and added more seriously, "Because pain is a reaction of certain nerve endings to irritation, delivering a signal into the brain. If a man controls his body and mind perfectly, he can regulate his pain barrier. By the way, there is a 'katedo' school in martial arts in which masters specially teach their followers not to feel pain."

"Lucky guys who learn in this school," Ruslan mentioned dreamily.

"They are not so lucky," Sensei uttered jokingly. "Before they learn something, they get hit in the neck with a stick at least one hundred times."

At that moment, Yura wanted to say something approving to his friend. But as soon as he opened his mouth and clapped Ruslan on the shoulder, his friend yelled out at the top of his voice, "A-a-a! Don't exuch my totremities!"

The whole crowd burst out laughing at such a precisely perceived absurdity.

"Well said," Stas said laughing.

Eugene continued, "Such trainings will inspire people to invent a new language."

"Aha," Victor added. "And they will speak with words of unknown letters."

We walked on, more cheerfully now with a host of new jokes, partially having forgotten about our unfortunate extremities. Just my stomach was jerking from laughter in evident pain convulsions. Andrew spent this time thinking about something and didn't participate in our mutual conversation. Not paying any attention to our laughter, he asked Sensei, "And this style, the points style that you showed us, is that a style of the Old Lama?"

"Ah, don't mix up a stone on the road with the Himalayas. In the style of the Old Lama, the Art is brought to perfection. There is enough one hand shake or simply a mediator, to do anything you wish to a person.

"Not bad!" Andrew got surprised.

"This is just rubbish. There are more serious things, and maybe someday I will tell you about them."

When saying goodbyes at the tram stop and shaking everybody's hands, Sensei suddenly took Kostya aside and started to whisper something to him. We tried our best but were unable to hear anything. When Sensei and his company started to move away down the street, we began to torture Kostya with questions. But he tried his best to laugh off all the attacks and ascribed everything to his personal secrets.

We were silent on the way home. Only Kostya tried to joke and cheer us up. I was deep in thought about my pain. What's strange, as soon as I started to think about that purposefully, my body began to ache and to hurt with new power. I thought about only one thing - how to get back home faster. Fortunately my house was in the center, five minutes away from the stop.

But having accompanied me home, the guys didn't hurry to leave. Or to put it more precisely, it was Kostya who was not in a hurry and who burst out with jokes and other funny stories from daily life. I already was shifting from one foot to the other, mechanically smiling and showing with all my appearance that it was time to say goodbye. But Kostya in no way reacted to that and went on with his jokes, only nervously looking at his watch from time to time.

Less than in ten minutes after our conversation about nothing, Andrew unexpectedly huddled himself up with wild cry of pain and almost fell on the ground, but he was caught in time by Kostya, who stood close to him. But Kostya himself couldn't keep balance and fell down on the ground, holding his friend on his body. Frightened, we bent over them trying to help Andrew somehow. Out of fear, I forgot about all my aching muscles. Only Kostya seemed to keep quiet.

"It's alright, it's alright, just let him sit down and rub his temples, now it will be over," he said, raising Andrew.

While we messed around and seated the almost helpless guy, Kostya glanced at the watch and pronounced thoughtfully, "Exactly as Sensei said... What power!"

We looked at him puzzled.

"What did you say?"

"I will explain it later," Kostya pronounced quickly and started to help intensively rub Andrew's temples.

Gradually, Andrew's color began to return to normal. The yellow-blue spots disappeared, and his cheeks became slightly red. His breath became natural. In about a minute, which for us lasted for eternity, Andrew recovered more or less. Grabbing his head, he mumbled in confusion, "I don't understand what the matter is... That has never happened to me before... Maybe I overtrained or something is wrong with my body... Well, but I'm still young."

Kostya grinned shaking his head, "Wow! Sensei foretold even these words... So, have you come back to life, fellow?"

"Which words?" We didn't understand.

But Kostya was entirely absorbed in the conversation with Andrew. "Sensei told me to ask whether you liked what happened to you?"

"What?!" Andrew looked surprisingly at Kostya.

"I say, did you like this fall?"

When Andrew grasped these words, he became furious and was covered with red spots out of rage, "Did I like it! Go to hell! If you were dashed against the asphalt like me, would you like it?!"

"Oh!" Kostya uttered with smile. "If he's cursing like mad, then for sure he came back to life." And then he added, "Why are you boiling and puffing like a teakettle? Cool down. This wasn't a simple fall, but a punishment from Sensei for your thoughts."

"What?!" Andrew got even more astonished.

This time I got boiled up, "What do you mean, a punishment?! How could he treat the guy in this way? He just decided to make a helpless creature out of him. What does Sensei do? How can he be good, if he is doing such things? He drones on about love thy neighbor, while he acts like that!" I recalled a couple of cases with demonstrations of strikes during trainings – they were harsh, ruthless, and rude towards a sparring-partner. Immediately a wave of despair and anger covered me.

Andrew continued, "What?! Punishment by Sensei for my thoughts?! For which thoughts? Are you crazy? And it means you knew all this time and said nothing to me? What a friend, damn it. And I was puzzled why he was cracking jokes here looking at his watch. Just so he could relate Sensei's words on time. So, have you told? Enjoyed the spectacle enough, you idiot?!"

Now it was Kostya's turn to blush, "You are stupid! Sensei asked me to stay close to you so that you wouldn't break your empty blockhead against the asphalt. And then, if you were able to listen, I had to tell you these words."

Andrew was taken aback as if doused with a bucket of cold water. We stared at each other. The conversation came to a strained pause. We also stood bewildered by such a turn of events.

"And what did Sensei ask you to tell me?" Andrew asked, still irritated, but already more self-retained.

"Sensei asked me to tell you that even a thought is material and that one should not use the Art against people."

"What does this have to do with the Art? Which thought? What do you mean?!" Andrew was dumbfounded.

"You must know which thought. You were thinking over something the whole way, not me."

"When?!" He was surprised even more. "Well I, I, I,... in the tram I was scrolling in my mind the whole training from beginning to end," Andrew said, full of indignation.

"I am not speaking about the tram. When we walked with Sensei, what were you thinking the whole way over?"

Andrew frowned, intensively trying to recall that stretch of time.

"Well, we were laughing and telling jokes..."

"That was us, and you?"

"And I...And I... What was I thinking about? Hmm..."

After a time of concentrated thinking Andrew spoke out, amazed, "Shoot! Is it possible that it was for..."

He stopped in the middle of the sentence and his indignation quickly changed to reflection on some shocking discovery. This event intrigued us even more and our curiosity brimmed over.

"What for? What for?" We threw questions at Andrew.

At first, he tried to get rid of our intrusive questions, but he confessed, "Well, it's an old story... I found some freaks who beat me up hard five years ago. Do you remember, Kostya, those lanky fellows?"

"Ah, those whom you swore to revenge all your life."

"Well, that's an exaggeration."

"Your words," Kostya said, shrugging his shoulders.

"Well, yes, mine. But let's say it this way, those guys were the reason to start my intensive karate trainings... So... When I was walking that time... I was thinking over..."

Andrew got somewhat embarrassed, hanging his head. Evidently, it was not easy for him to confess it. But plucking up his courage, he continued, "In general, I thought... that with the help of this Art... they can't hide anywhere... from my... revenge."

After his words, silence fell. Kostya said with a sigh, "Yes, well... You see, it's your own fault, you dream about God knows what, and I turn out to be guilty."

"Are these also the words of Sensei?" Slava hemmed, trying to joke.

Kostya looked at him in such a way, that Slava at once was confused.

"And now imagine," Kostya continued addressing Andrew, "how shocked those lanky fellows would be. Because they are ordinary people, with their own merits and demerits, just like us. But you are at least somehow prepared mentally, or rather you know about this power. And they?... Even if one of them survived after such a fright, just imagine what would happen to them later. Each of them would have thought that he was sick with epilepsy... You felt unpleasant, and how would they have felt? Sensei asked me to remind you that any blow caused by your rage will come back to you in the end... And something else, 'You should not wish bad to other people, even in your thoughts. Because with the power of your thought, you are setting a trap for yourself, for your body and mind. And the more you think about it, the stronger it keeps you, the tighter its loop becomes. The only way out is to become a friend to your enemy and to forgive his deeds because you are also imperfect."

Pondering a little more, Kostya added, "Well, I don't think I forgot anything to say... That's all, now you can be free."

"In what sense free?" Andrew didn't understand. "Does Sensei drive me out?"

"Well, he told me nothing about that... It's me who lets you go."

"Ah," Andrew drawled with a smile and started to get up from the ground with Kostya. "And why have you fallen?"

"Why? You shouldn't be so fat and heavy. I'm not Rambo to catch such a bull!"

We laughed and said good-bye to each other, in a cheerful mood. I was very happy that everything ended so happily. In my soul there was another revolution of feelings. And really, whose fault is it that there is so much evil around us? We are guilty ourselves. Because we don't control our desires. And then we just get what we deserve. And then we yell and rebel, but what for? We should think more often about good things and be good to people, and maybe the world around us will change. At least in our mind. And our mind is our real world... If I had realized that earlier, I wouldn't be paying now for my egocentrism and megalomania with my own health and life... Oh! If only I had known it before, I would have been more confident in tomorrow. But since I'm doomed to such a destiny, at least I will try to live this time with dignity, as a human... Sensei was right when he said once, 'The quality of instants lived by you in this life are much more important than senseless years of existence. How you lived, and not how many years you lived, is important.'

Yes, we are responsible for all that we think and do. Why was I angry with Sensei? We are guilty ourselves, and he is just an observer of our reality, our irresponsibility and disorder. He judges from the point of view of his internal world, his knowledge, and his high moral values. In order to understand him, we first need to become humans.

19

At home I pondered over the events that had occurred recently. And then I remembered my body. All the time that my thoughts were distracted, the pain was hidden and existed on some distant level of thought. But as soon as I thought about my overtrained muscles, they immediately replied with a sharp pain, just as a loyal dog responds to the call of its owner by barking. My entire body started to cry out and break apart, and my mind began to feel intensively sorry for my poor body, blaming my real "I" for the trial I sentenced it to, to sympathize with and be compassionate to my extremities.

I forced myself to sit in the lotus pose to meditate. It was very hard to relax and even harder to concentrate. But still, my persistence brought me small results. In one of my attempts at purposeful concentration, the pain was forgotten. Meditation went smoothly. Only when a foul thought flashed across my mind did the pain commence again. At that time I clearly was feeling a streamlet down my hand. I thought, "This hand muscle hurts the most. Stop! Aha, I got you, leader of distemper. It's you who spoils all my attempts. Alright, alright. This time I didn't manage to start a conversation with Sensei, but next time at the meditation training I will certainly find out how to cope with you."

When I came out of the meditation, I started to reflect logically, "I wonder if I have schizophrenia. I start to speak with myself and try to catch someone inside of me. Maybe I am already going crazy?" And at the same time another thought appeared in my mind, "It's a good indicator. If I were to think like that more often, I would reach my goal faster." At some internal, inaccessible level, I understood what it meant. But my mind yelled, "What goal? Who's speaking again?" Completely confused by my thoughts, about who is who and what I really wanted, I fell asleep, following the example of my flesh, which was ruthlessly exhausted during the training.

The next day, my body became completely alien. Not only that, it was hurting and moving like a rusty robot. I got even more interested, as I had never seen myself in such a state. The autopilot evidently got turned off. I had to invent new ways to operate my body, even just to put clothes on. It was good that my parents went to work and didn't see all of my comic horrors. Since I was busy with this disobedient machine, I was almost late to school.

I felt pretty much fine during the lessons, although it was strange to feel like a robot. The very last lesson was gym class. This was the end of everything. I tried to obtain leave from the teacher, but he was a rather conservative man and an awful bureaucrat. Our pains didn't worry him. My only chance of leaving was by bringing him an official permission slip. I had an official note at home, hidden far away from my parents, because I liked gym class and didn't want to sit aside during them, despite the opinions of the doctors. Even more so, the exercises we did were never very difficult, in my opinion. During the trainings with Sensei, we tortured our bodies much more. But today for the first time I regretted that I didn't bring this paper with me.

Though during the day I had managed to move somehow, I had a hard time with the warm-up. And today, as if on purpose, there was a test on push-ups. "I certainly won't survive. I won't be able to do even one, especially after yesterday," I thought. "He is such a bureaucrat and will not even listen to me without a note..." And I began upbraiding this man in my evil thoughts.

During the next break, while thinking of a word worse than the previous one, suddenly the words of Sensei softly arose in my mind, 'You should not wish bad to other people, even in your thoughts.' "Oh! What am I doing," I woke up, "I am creating a trap for myself." Cooling my temper down a little, I started to think soberly, "What's the point of swearing at him in my thoughts and looking at him gloomily? I will just be more upset and will be rude to him during the test. He will return the favor, will give me a bad mark, and will call my parents. My parents will find out that I haven't brought my paper to school and also will become upset. Why do I need all of this? And what if, as Sensei says, I try to put myself in his shoes? After all it's not his fault that I came to the lesson down and out. Does he know that all yesterday evening, I was in fact preparing for the test? He doesn't know. Then why should I be angry with him? He simply does his best to fulfil his job. And as far as my doctor's note is concerned, he also needs to report for his lessons. What if the director or some revising commission comes to check on him? I can understand his position in this case." Thus having put my thoughts in order, I noticed that my anger vanished and now I was able to think about how to solve this problem in peace.

After the warm-up, I again went to the teacher and calmly explained the situation to him. I said that the day before I had trained intensively and had suffered terribly, but for the next lesson I would certainly do push-ups, even twice as many. I also added that I completely understood that he's fed up with our constant complaining.

"Well, you understand, you were also young once."

That last sentence burst from me by accident, but obviously stirred up some good memories from the teacher's past, because the next fifteen minutes we listened to stories about his active youth. And when the test finally began, I asked him, "So, should I do push-ups?"

"Alright," he genially waved his hand, "you will do it next time. We'll consider that you didn't have time today."

To the great joy of the others, half of the class also "didn't have enough time." When the bell rang, my classmates said with smiles, "Great! Listen, maybe for the other lessons you'll evoke the teachers' memories of their far-away youth, and maybe they won't have time to ask us about homework. That would be great!"

"I'm not a wizard," I answered jokingly. "I'm just learning."

After class, I had a rather pleasant feeling inside. Nobody suffered moral damage and, more than that, all remained satisfied. This pleased my vanity, and my megalomania started to grow by leaps and bounds. I didn't notice, though, until my friends listened to me in the evening and joked around.

"You inflated this story like a soap bubble," Andrew remarked with a smile. "What's so special in that? I do such tricks almost every lesson. You simply need to act with ingenuity and humor."

"Yes, but do you tame your anger every lesson?"

Andrew thought about it and said, "That's true... but humor so far has always helped me to understand teachers."

"Listen!" Kostya tapped him on the shoulder. "This is a brilliant method to fight with anger... Do you remember Sensei's guys: Eugene, Stas, and others? They never stop joking."

"Exactly!" confirmed Andrew.

"You see, everything is simple, as Sensei said. You were wondering the whole night how to fight with your anger. Here is an answer for you... Well, now you'll have to joke with your mind all your life."

And then Kostya added calmingly, "Don't worry. We will bring you tasty cakes at the mental hospital..."

"Stop it! You always confuse everything."

The guys laughed and we went to attack the overcrowded tram. On board of the tram, Kostya said to Andrew, "By the way, I have also spent this night not in vain."

"With whom?" Andrew inquired with a smile.

"Dirty mind! Not with whom, but on what, think deeper. I made a brilliant discovery!"

"In the sphere of self-love?"

"I'm serious. Listen, I've discovered a chain of events. If you weren't beaten up by those lanky fellows five years ago, you wouldn't have started to practice karate. And if you wouldn't have started to practice martial arts, you wouldn't have pulled me into this business. And if you hadn't dragged me, we would have never met Sensei and wouldn't have found what we have found and what we are now learning. At least, if we had read about this information somewhere, then certainly we would've considered it complete nonsense. While this way we were convinced and have seen it, as they say, with our own eyes. In short, if you hadn't been beaten up, we wouldn't have found this gold-bearing spiritual vein! That's it!"

"I agree. But what makes you think that it's because of you we met Sensei? The address of his school was given to us by a complete stranger from that previous school of Wushu. Neither you nor I knew anything for sure. We simply started a conversation about psychic phenomena by chance, and later found out about Sensei."

"Yes. But I dragged you to this training," Kostya defended his theory. "You were so resistant, remember, and didn't want to go. And that guy appeared exactly that day by chance. He was waiting for his friend in the changing room."

"Yes, he was waiting, but he would've kept silent if he hadn't seen our magazine with an article about psychics."

"Which magazine?"

"Well, remember, Tatyana brought it from home that day. You and I were indignant that we would have to drag this burden with us all day instead of just giving it back in the evening."

"Ah! Exactly!" Kostya recalled.

"Well, I put it on the windowsill. And that guy was probably just bored sitting around, so he asked if he could read it. As you know, one word led to another, and he gave us Sensei's address.

"Right, that's exactly how it was." Having sighed, Kostya added, "It is always like that: such small facts kill the most beautiful hypothesis... Alright, then my theory will look this way. If you hadn't pulled me into martial arts, I wouldn't have brought you to this training. And further, had Tatyana not brought a magazine, our group wouldn't have met Sensei, and so forth."

"Still, everything started with the magazine," persisted Andrew, further developing his thought, "and with the article. We became interested in these articles because... why?"

"What do you mean why? Because... Ah! It was she who launched all of that, she infected all of us with stories of phenomenal people," said Kostya nodding towards me.

"Exactly!"

The guys looked at me. "And why did you become interested in them?"

"Me?" I was a little confused and right away wiggled out. "Me... I was inspired by movies."

"Oh! And movies were shot by..."

The guys were carried away, untwisting the whole chain of imaginary events.

Tatyana smiled and said, "You guys, I'm ashamed to say, will come soon to primitive man," and she mimicked them in a funny way. "If that man had been caught by a saber-toothed tiger, then you wouldn't have existed and therefore wouldn't have met Sensei."

"Hey, that's a thought," smiled Kostya.

"Men," complained Tatyana. "They always find logic in everything. We have met Sensei, that's great. That's the way it should be, it's destiny. And that's all. There is nothing to argue about."

20

Our company reached the glade, this time accurately determining its location..

"Listen, there is nobody here," Slava said doubtfully. "Maybe this is not the right glade?"

"It's the right one. I remember it well from the last time," Andrew nodded affirmatively.

"Of course!" grinned Kostya.

We laughed recalling our last adventures. In about ten minutes, the senior guys started to arrive, joining our good mood.

"Oh, the Teacher is going to come now," Victor livened up.

"Why do you think so?" I asked looking at the stars.

"Because of Samurai," the senior sempai replied smiling.

I shifted my gaze to the ground and only then noticed how the cat paced grandly on a lonely fence in the light of a distant lamp, all the time almost falling down and trying to maintain his balance with his claws.

"He always comes to the meditation," continued the sempai. "He sits calmly aside in full trance, and then without wasting his time with our conversations and impressions, leaves right away."

"The first time we came, he stayed until the end. Sensei was trying to grab him out of the bushes," I remarked.

"Well, that was probably a small exception from his rules."

"Strange how it came out that time," I thought, "Even the cat took direct part in that."

The guys joined our conversation.

"Why did Sensei get a black cat?" asked Tatyana.

"He didn't get him on purpose. When Samurai was still a kitten, the village kids would throw stones at him. So, Sensei picked him up from the street and cured him. Since then, the cat has lived with him and doesn't leave him."

"Who tore his ears up so much?" Andrew asked with a smile.

"Ah, he was sparring with dogs."

"With dogs?"

"Yes. Samurai not only trains spiritually, but also practices martial arts," said Victor, making everybody look at the cat. "Sensei has been teaching him, one could say, from childhood, the Wing Chun style, which is opposite to the Cat style. So now he picks fights with both cats and dogs."

"You must be joking?" Andrew was sincerely surprised. "How is it possible to teach a cat Kung-fu? Not every human will understand it, and this is just a stupid animal."

"It depends how you look at it," the Teacher interrupted the conversation, coming out from the dark. "Sometimes a stupid animal proves itself to be cleverer than some Homo sapiens."

"Still, though," Nikolai Andreevich was interested in the unusual fact, "How did you teach him?"

"Oh, it's easy," Sensei simply said as if we were talking about something ordinary. "In the form of game.

First I would clench his claws with my fingers and then in the same way would show him how to unclench. That's how he learned... Now, he not only fights with cats but also picks fights with dogs. You see, he is not interested in mice anymore, they are not the right level. But why did I teach him? Now I have to run around with the mouse traps myself!"

Everyone laughed. I still didn't understand whether that was a joke or not. If that was a joke, then why was it so serious? And if true, then one really needs to have remarkable talent to teach a cat.

During his story, Sensei was simultaneously shaking everybody's hand, and when it was Andrew's turn, he didn't give his hand, but instead bowed politely.

"What happened?" Sensei was surprised.

"Well, I'm afraid to touch you after the other day's events," Andrew replied half-jokingly.

"What do I have to do with that?" said Sensei, smiling and shrugging his shoulders. "It's not me that you should be afraid of but him. He was next to you and not me."

While Sensei was speaking with the other guys, Andrew pushed Kostya slightly to the side, "So it was through you!"

"What!? I'm smart of course, but not to that extent."

"I'm serious."

"And I'm serious."

"Honestly?"

"Honestly."

Andrew waited until Sensei answered another question and asked, "Is it true that you've done it through a handshake?"

"Of course. Some day I will tell you about this."

Then the conversation moved on to our home meditations. At first I wanted to call Sensei off to the side and speak to him alone about my thoughts because I was afraid of the reaction of the senior guys. Who knows, maybe they'd ridicule me with their picky jokes, like my friends. But Sensei patiently examined and explained every situation that happened to the guys. From Yura I heard a similar story, but not exactly so acute. Seeing the serious mood of the others, I finally decided to tell Sensei everything in the presence of everybody. And when another pause appeared in the conversation, I timidly started to share my achievements. Everyone listened calmly and carefully. Then I grew bold and told them about the dodger.

After my story, there reigned a short silence. "That's it," I thought, "Now Nikolai Andreevich will diagnose me with schizophrenia. Why did I blab it out in front of everyone?" But, to my surprise, Sensei said the following:

"It's a good result. To catch a thought of your animal nature is hard and to fight with it, even more so. It is impossible to fight with this category of thought in principle because violence generates violence. And the more you try to kill it, the more intensively it'll appear in you. The best way to defend against it is to switch to positive thoughts. In other words, the principle of Aikido of smooth withdrawal should be used here."

"What if they are chasing me the entire day? Can't I just chop them off with some swear word?" asked Ruslan.

"No matter how you chop them off, negative thoughts will keep appearing according to the law of action/counteraction. That's why you needn't fight with them. You should withdraw from them, artificially developing in yourself a positive thought. In other words, concentrate on something good or recall something good. Only in this way of smooth withdrawal will you be able to win over your negative thought."

"And why can thoughts sometimes be absolutely the opposite of each other? Sometimes I too get confused by my thoughts."

"Let's say it this way: in the human body, there is a spiritual nature, or soul, and a material nature, or animal, call it as you wish. The human mind is a battlefield of these two natures. That's why different thoughts arise in you," Sensei replied.

"And who am 'I', if thoughts are alien?"

"Not alien, but yours. You are the one who's listening to them, the one who is choosing your nature. If you prefer the material, animal nature, then you'll be evil and nasty, and if you listen to the advice of your soul, you'll be a good person, and it will be pleasant for other people to be around you. The choice is always yours, you are either despot or saint."

"And why did my admiration for taming my anger lead to pride, to the growth of megalomania? Because it seemed like I did a good deed, but the thought got carried away in a different direction?" I asked.

"You turned to the soul, your desire was fulfilled. And when you weakened your control over yourself, you were pulled over by the animal nature by your own favorite egoistic thoughts. You liked that you were complimented from all sides that you were so smart, so judicious, and so forth... There is a permanent war of two natures inside of you. And your future depends on which side you choose."

I pondered a little and then specified, "In other words this dodger who reminded me about the pain and prevented me from concentrating, who inflated my megalomania..."

"Absolutely correct."

"But there is an entire pile of these thoughts there!"

"Yes," confirmed Sensei. "An entire legion. That's why it's impossible to fight with them. It's not Kung-fu,

it's much more serious. It is possible to fight with the one who shows resistance. But fighting with a vacuum is senseless. Against a vacuum of negative thoughts, it is only possible to create the same vacuum of positive thoughts. In other words, I repeat, shift your mind to positive and good thinking. But always stay vigilant, listening what your brain thinks about. Observe yourself. Pay attention to the fact that you don't do anything but the thoughts in you are constantly swarming. And not one thought. There can be two and three or more at once."

"It's like in Christianity, they say, on man's left shoulder sits the devil, and on the right, an angel. And they are always whispering something," remarked Volodya.

"Absolutely correct," confirmed Sensei. "But for some reason, the devil whispers louder, he probably has a rougher voice. What's called the devil in Christianity is the manifestation of our animal nature."

"When I discovered this division of thoughts in myself, I thought that maybe I caught schizophrenia, because it also has to do with the splitting of consciousness," I said more bravely.

Sensei smiled and jokingly answered, "There is no genius without a sign of madness."

Nikolai Andreevich laughed, "Yes, indeed. I observe something similar in myself as well."

Stas joined the conversation, reflecting aloud about his experience, "Well, if the mind is a battlefield of two natures, and as far as I understand it, their weapons are thoughts, then how can you distinguish who is who? How do the spiritual and the animal nature manifest in thoughts? In which way?"

"The spiritual nature means thoughts generated by the power of love, in the broad sense of the word. While the animal nature means thoughts about the body, our instincts, our reflexes, megalomania, desires, entirely devoured by material interests, and so forth."

"Well, then we should live in a cave," Ruslan expressed his opinion, "So that we have nothing and want nothing."

"With a head like yours, even a cave won't help," Eugene teased him.

"Nobody forbids you to have all of this," continued Sensei. "If you want, please, follow the modern world, use all the goods of civilization. But to live just for that, to place the accumulation of material goods as the main purpose of your existence on Earth, it's stupid, it's unnatural to the spiritual nature. This goal is an indicator of the predominance of the animal nature in people. At the same time, it doesn't mean that you should live as a bum in a cave. No, I already told you that all these high technologies are given to mankind so that humans could free up more time for their spiritual perfection. But certainly not for a man to collect a pile of these iron things at home and blow up his megalomania because he possesses all that dust."

After keeping silent for a while, Sensei thoughtfully pronounced, "A human is a complex synthesis of the spiritual and the animal nature. It's a pity that in your mind more of the animal nature than the one from God predominates. The other day, I decided to give you one ancient practice to help you balance these two natures, so that the animal won't burden you so much. It has existed just as long as humans have. This spiritual practice is not just for working on yourself, on your thoughts, but what is very important, it is for the awakening of your soul. In relation to life, it can be compared to a dynamic meditation because it is constantly functioning, regardless of where the human is located or what he does. A part of this human should always be in this state, controlling all that happens around or inside.

"This spiritual practice is called a Lotus Flower. It consists of the following. You imagine that you plant the seed of a lotus inside yourself, in the regions of the solar plexus. And this small seed grows due to the power of love generated by your positive thoughts. Thus, controlling the growth of this flower lets you get rid of negative thoughts that constantly turn over in your head."

"Do we really think about negative things all the time?" Ruslan asked.

"Of course," Sensei answered "Just follow your thoughts carefully. People spend a lot of time visualizing different conflict situations, negative memories of the past, they imagine as they quarrel, prove something, deceive someone or hit back, they think of their illnesses, material deprivations, and so on. It means they always keep a lot of negative thoughts in their mind.

"By doing this practice, you intentionally get rid of all these negative thoughts by internal control. And the more positive image that you keep in your mind, the quicker the growth of the seed of Love. In the beginning, you imagine that a seed starts growing, and a small stalk appears. It grows further, leaves cover the stalk, then comes a small flower bud. And finally, getting more and more of the power of love, the bud blossoms out into a Lotus. The Lotus Flower is at first golden, but on growing it becomes dazzling white."

"How much time does it take it to grow?" I asked.

"Actually, it depends on you. Some people need years, and others just months, or days, or even seconds. It all depends on your desire, whether you will make an effort. It is necessary not only to grow this flower, but also to support it by the power of your love so that it will not fade or die. This constant feeling of growth should be held at the level of subconscious or, to say it more precisely, at the level of a controllable, remote consciousness. The more love you give to this little flower, the more you cherish it in your mind, take care of it, protect it from surrounding negative ¬influences, the more it grows. This flower is generated by the energy of love, I emphasize, by the internal energy of love. And the more you feel love towards the whole world, to all the people and to your surroundings, the bigger the flower becomes. And if you start to get angry, the flower becomes weak. If you yield to anger, the flower fades and becomes ill. Then it is necessary to put forth the maximum effort to restore it. It is a kind of control.

"Thus, when this flower blossoms and starts to increase in size, it starts to emit vibrations instead of a scent, the so-called leptons or gravitons, call them as you like, that is, the energy of love. You feel the moving petals of this flower that bring vibrations to your whole body, to all the space around you, radiating love and harmony to the world."

"And is it somehow felt at the physical level?" Eugene asked.

"Yes. The Lotus can be felt as though the regions of a solar plexus are burning, spreading heat. That is, these feelings arise in the regions of a solar plexus where, as legends say, our soul is hidden. These regions start getting warmer and warmer. The main sense of all of this is that wherever you are, whomever you are with or whatever you do or think, you should always feel this heat, heat that warms not only your body but also your soul. This internal concentration of love is located in the flower. Finally, the more you take care of it and glorify this love, the more you feel that this flower expands and tightly surrounds your body with its petals, and you stand inside of the huge Lotus.

"And then it comes to a very important point. When you reach the stage when Lotus petals surround you from all sides, you feel two flowers. One is inside under your heart that is warmed all the time by the feeling of internal love. Another one, the bigger one, is like the astral shell of this flower that surrounds you. On the one hand, it radiates the vibration of love to the world and on the other hand, it protects you from the negative influence of other people. Thus the cause-and-effect law works. To put it in the language of physics, there is a wave effect. Briefly, you radiate waves of good feelings, intensifying them manifold and thus creating a graceful wave field. You can feel this wave field all the time supported by your heart and soul of love, and it positively impacts not only you but also the surrounding world.

"This happens with everyday practice. First, you always control your thoughts, learning to concentrate on positive things. Therefore you are not automatically able to wish bad things to anybody or to be bad. This practice should be done every day and every second for your whole life. It is some kind of distraction method, as nobody can fight with negative thoughts by force. Love cannot be compelled. Therefore you should distract your attention. If a negative or undesirable thought comes, you concentrate on your flower, you start to give your love to it, that is, you forget all the negative things. Or you switch your attention to something else, to something positive. But you feel the flower all the time: going to bed, getting up, at night, during the day, whatever you do, when studying, working, doing sports, etc. You feel how love flares up, how currents of love are moving in your chest and are filling your body. You feel how this flower starts heating up inside with a special warmth, the divine warmth of love. And the more you give, the bigger the love is inside. Constantly radiating this love, you perceive people from the position of love. That is, second, what is very important, that you tune yourself into the frequency of the good.

"And the good means success, luck, health. It means everything! You start feeling happier, and that has a positive impact on your mind. The central nervous system is the main regulator of all vital activity. Therefore, first of all, this practice improves your health. Besides, your life becomes smoother as you start finding reconciliation with everybody. Nobody wants to quarrel with you, you are welcome everywhere. You won't have any major problems. Why? Because even if you have some troubles in life, as life is life, you start perceiving them in a completely different way than just ordinary people. You already have a new vision of the life that helps you to find the most optimal decision for the situation. Because the wisdom of life awakens in you, you start feeling yourself becoming human, you come to understand who is God, that God is an all-encompassing substance, and not just a fantasy of a few idiots. You start feeling the divine presence in yourself and strengthen this power by your positive thoughts and feelings. You will never feel alone in this world anymore as God is in you and with you, you feel His real presence. There is an expression, 'If you are in love, you are in God, and God is in you as God is love.' It is very important that you start feeling the aura of the flower that is inside and outside of you.

"How is the aura felt around the body?" Stas asked.

"With the lapse of time, you see this vibration around yourself as a glowing light. The air seems to become lighter and more transparent, and the surrounding world turns more intensive in its colours. The most fascinating thing is that people start noticing these transformations in you. There is a common expression, 'a man glows, shines.' That actually means the glow of this wave field resulting from the workings of love in the individual. People surrounding him also start feeling this field. They are glad when this individual is somewhere near, as they also start feeling joy, internal excitement. Many people are getting better. They will feel good even in his presence, however sick they have been. Everybody is attracted by this person, wishing to open their hearts and souls to him. That means that people perceive love. This is the heart's open gate towards God. This is what all the great souls said and what Jesus meant when he said, 'Open your heart to God.'

"This spiritual practice of Lotus has been used since time immemorial. Since olden times, the Lotus was said to beget God, as God awakens in the Lotus. A divine substance – a soul – awakens in the Lotus flower, in harmony and love inside of you. You should always take care of your flower, controlling at all times your thoughts and feelings so that the Lotus flower does not fade."

"Is there a real flower?" Slava asked with surprise.

"No. The material flower does not exist there, of course. It is imaginary. This process can be discussed in a different way: the awakening of divine love, the reaching of enlightenment, full unity with God – moksha, dao, shinto. Call it what you like. But all of this is just words and religion. And in fact it means that you create by your positive thoughts and feeling of love a certain force field that, on the one hand, affects the real world around you and, on the other hand, changes the internal frequency of your mind."

"And the soul?" I asked.

"The soul is you, it is a kind of eternal generator of divine power, if you wish, but it needs to be activated by your constant thoughts of love... Later I will tell you about the soul and its meaning in detail."

But then Kostya joined the discussion, "You have said that this practice is very ancient. How old is it?"

"I have already told you that it has existed as long as people have existed as Homo sapiens."

"Well, how long, seven, ten thousand years?"

"That's too short a period of time. Mankind in its civilized form has existed a lot of times before, with much better technologies than now. Another thing is why these civilizations disappeared. At some point, I will tell you about that too."

"But if this practice is so ancient, there should be some memory of it in our civilization."

"Certainly. The fact that the spiritual practice of the Lotus Flower has existed for so long may be proven by various ancient sources. The Lotus was given, for example, to some Pharaohs of Ancient Egypt. And if you look for the literature on this issue, you will find evidence that Egyptian myths and legends say that even their Sun God was born out of the lotus flower. This flower served as a throne for Isis, Horus, and Osiris.

"In ancient Veda, the oldest Hindu books written in Sanskrit, the Lotus is one of the central issues. In particular, regarding the three main male incarnations of God – Brahma-Creator, Vishnu-Protector, and Shiva-Destroyer – they say the following, 'The body of the God Vishnu bore a giant golden lotus with lotus-born Brahma-Creator on it. The golden thousand-petalled lotus was growing and the universe followed it growing.'

"In China and India, this flower depicts purity and chastity. The best human qualities and intentions were

associated by people with the lotus. In China, they think that there is a special Western heaven with a lotus lake and that every flower growing there is bound to the soul of a dead person. If an individual was virtuous, his flower blossomed out, otherwise the flower faded.

"In Greece, the lotus was considered to be a plant devoted to the goddess Hera. Hercules made his voyage in a lotus-shaped boat.

"However, all these legends and myths are not made up by people. They appeared because of people's self-development with this ancient spiritual practice. As earlier the animal nature prevailed in most people, the Lotus Flower was given only to the chosen ones, spiritually mature individuals. It is natural that other people later regarded these individuals as gods. An individual with a grown-up Lotus and awakened soul becomes God-like as he can create love just by his thought.

"And when it was time to spiritually educate people, the Bodhisattvas of Shambala gave this spiritual practice to Buddha. Due to practicing this technique of the Lotus, Siddhartha Gautama reached enlightenment sitting under the Bodhi tree. On approval of Rigden, Buddha gave it to his disciples for further dissemination within people. Unfortunately, over time, people distorted the teachings of Buddha and created a whole religion based on this practice. The Buddhists imagine their paradise as an unusual place where people are born like gods on the lotus flower. They are looking for this place, although it is always inside of them. They made Buddha into a god, even though he was just a human who had known the truth due to this spiritual practice. In such a way, the Lotus became a symbol of Buddhism. There is even an expression, 'Buddha sits in a lotus' or 'Buddha stands in a lotus.' He has shown people by example what an individual can reach by defeating his animal nature. He has really done a lot of useful things for the spiritual development of mankind by disseminating this spiritual practice among people in its original form.

"The same prayer was given by Jesus Christ to revoke the divine love."

"Does it mean that prayer and meditation are the same thing?" Tatyana asked.

"Actually, yes. The prayer 'Our Father' is the same. It is just so simple, people ask for bread and so on, but the main sense is the same: an individual develops himself, grows out his soul by controlling his thoughts, by his desire, by his firm belief and love.

"In general, Buddha, Jesus, Mohammed, and all the great souls knew this spiritual practice, as they used the same source. It helped them not only to become themselves but also to help other people know their divine nature. Why was it so pleasant for all to be near Buddha, Jesus, Mohammed? Why are saints said to shine? Why don't we like to leave strangers on meeting them? Because they radiate this love. Because they always strengthen this power, the power of good, the power of love, the power of this divine emanation in people. They say that God is in this human. And it is true."

"So, does it mean that you should just think with love about this flower?" Andrew asked.

"No. You should not only concentrate yourself and think over it but, most importantly, awaken this feeling of warmth in the regions of the solar plexus and support it at all times with your positive thoughts. Not everybody can reach it at once. Therefore you should go into the root of the matter, get the more realistic view of it, and, I repeat, awaken all these feelings. Why do I draw your attention to it? Because when an individual awakens these feelings, he starts supporting them not just with his mind but also at the level of his subconscious. And it leads to an awakening of the soul. It just can't help but awaken. And the more love you share, the more it will be awakened, and the faster you will become yourself, as you have always been inside, and not in your external mortal body shell."

After keeping silent for a while, Sensei added, "Life is too short, and you'd better progress in glorifying your spiritual nature."

Our entire group of different ages stood silent, thinking about Sensei's words. I felt some kind of tingling sensation in my body from the sudden delight and inspiration. I was so amazed by all I had heard, so shocked by this unexpected information, that it was hard for me to believe that these words were spoken by an ordinary man. His deep knowledge, from my point of view, was evidently not of this world. I wanted to ask about that, but something was holding me back. I suspected that this something already knew about everything because it was pulling me towards this creature with all my heart and soul. But as soon as I thought about that, my mind again started to argue with me, assuring me that this is an ordinary, simple man, just competently understanding philosophy, religion, psychology, history, physiology, medicine, and physics. "Stop! Where am I heading?" I thought. "Is it possible that a man can accumulate so much fundamental knowledge at one time? But on the other hand, why not? There happen to be talented people, like Lomonosov or Leonardo da Vinci, who was far ahead of this time in his knowledge. But I don't remember them speaking clearly about the soul. And in general, why do I rack my brains wondering who he really is? The main thing is that I got answers to the questions that I had been asking for so long. It's true, as they say, the one who searches will always find."

I was sincerely happy, like a child. Can it really be? This is the way to reach that edge of eternity where the great contemplate the world! This is my only chance, my only straw. It's not just a straw, it's an entire saving ark, in which even physical death is not to be feared, in which it's not scary to swim into eternity.

"So, any more questions?" Sensei asked.

We kept silent, looking at him with admiring eyes. Only Nikolai Andreevich, who was more or less the sober-minded man in our group, replied, "Well, let's assume that I don't believe in God. From the point of view of psychology, though, this is quite an interesting variant. Everything needs to be pondered... There is a lot of information, and I need to examine everything. Questions will arise later."

"All right," the Teacher answered genially. "Then, I suppose, it is enough for today, let's go home."

21

I was in an excellent mood. All the way home, I analyzed what I had heard, reviewing it in my thoughts from different points of view. And then I started examining my good mood. Something was strange with it, and I felt as if I were completely healthy. Analyzing my impressions a little, I suddenly realized what the matter was. Before I thought that my soul, that is my "I" which would go to eternity, was located in my material brain. And it seemed to me that I think with it, and all my thoughts arise from it. But I was having serious problems with my brain lately, as the doctors said. It didn't really depress me physically, but more spiritually. I assumed that if my brain was damaged, then my soul might also malfunction.

I couldn't wait to get home and plant my small seed. Sensei, of course, said that one can do this spiritual practice in any place. But I decided to start this noble doing at home in peace and quiet.

At home I quickly finished with all my petty tasks. When my parents settled down to watch TV, I sat comfortably in the lotus pose. Finally came the long-awaited time. Concentrating, I thought: "Let's begin with planting..." but I panicked a bit. First, I didn't know what the lotus seed looked like. I had seen the flower in a book, but not its seeds. And I didn't know either what this planting would look like and what I would plant it in. I saw how seeds sprouted in the soil. But for some reason it didn't satisfy me, as the soil in the soul, even an imaginary one, somehow didn't coincide with my notion of eternity. Reflecting on it a little, I found an acceptable way out. One day I saw how my mother was germinating kidney beans by placing them in wet cotton wool. I liked this method a lot. "Then let it be a bean," I thought. "After all, it's my imagination. And the most important thing is what I do, the essence, as Sensei said."

Having concentrated once again, I started to imagine that I placed inside of myself, in the area of the solar plexus, a small white bean, immersing it into something soft and warm. Then I repeated endearing words internally, nursing my small seed. But no feelings followed. I started to recall all the good words that I knew. And here I was astonished to discover that I knew many fewer good, beautiful words than bad, swearing ones. This was because I heard them everywhere on the street and in school and they enriched my vocabulary more often than the good ones. My thoughts again unnoticeably switched onto the calculation of some conclusions, logically clinging to each other. Discovering this, I again tried to concentrate on the flower, but nothing happened. After about twenty minutes of fruitless efforts, I thought that I wasn't doing something right. Finally, I went to sleep, having decided to ask Sensei later in detail about my mistakes.

But I couldn't fall asleep. Darkness covered everything around me. Objects and furniture in the room lost their natural color. A thought came to my mind, "Our world is really so illusory. It just seems to us that we really live while in fact we are like children, imagining a game and playing it. But unlike children, adults don't grow up, because they get so used to the created image that they begin to think that everything else is the same kind of reality. And in this way, our entire life passes in imagination and vanity. But, as Sensei said, "The real you is the soul, that eternal reality which exists in actuality. You need only to wake up, to awaken from illusion, and then the whole world will change..."

As soon as I went deeper into the contemplation of the eternal, I began to feel somehow light and good. And I felt how something started to warm up in my chest and even to tickle pleasantly. Small ants started running through my whole body from my coccyx to the back of my head. Such a pleasant, peaceful state came over me that I wanted to embrace the entire world with my soul. In such a sweet slumber, I fell asleep. I slept like in a fairytale because when I woke up in the morning, I felt such inspiration, such lightness that I had never experienced in life.

At school, I tried again to evoke the previous day's state of mind, but I couldn't really concentrate because of the constant circulation of school information and contradictory emotions. I was successful only in literature class when the teacher droningly explained a new topic. Half of the class carefully listened to her with drowsy eyes, and the other half tried to fight off sleep. Meanwhile, I again concentrated on the area of the solar plexus, focusing all of my attention on evoking warmth and a state of happiness. My good thoughts wandered somewhere in the background of my mind. The important thing for me was what was going on inside. I felt very comfortable, my body somehow relaxed, and in my chest I started feeling light pressure turning into warmth. After that I simply sat enjoying this state and continued listening to the new topic. A few days later, I found out that, starting at that moment, I clearly and easily remembered everything the teacher was telling us. This was a very pleasant discovery for me.

After the lessons, I ran into the library to fill the gap in my knowledge about the lotus flower. But what I read about it from different sources really staggered me. I found out the following: the lotus is a water-resistant perennial herbaceous plant with a long stalk and large flowers reaching 30 centimeters in diameter and resting upon big leaves. The leaves of the lotus have interesting, peculiar properties: they are covered with a special waxy covering and don't get wet in the water. I interpreted this fact in such a way that the soul can't be spoiled by bad thoughts, or in other words, by the impact of animal nature. It will just keep sleeping.

The lotus flower has twenty-two to thirty petals, faintly pink at the foundation and bright at the top, located spirally around the seminal box. I glanced at the photo of the flower. This seminal box, located in the center of the flower, looked similar to a golden cork, with multiple fibers around of the same color. It is interesting that the lotus flowers are always facing the sun: a little lower than the point of the pedicle attachment, the lotus has a so-called reaction zone that catches the light.

I read even more stunning information about its seeds: lotus seeds possess the extraordinary ability to retain their germinating power a few hundred (and sometimes even a few thousand) years. This peculiarity of the lotus is supposed to be the reason for using it from the time immemorial as a symbol of immortality and resurrection.

Also, I managed to clarify one interesting detail. The lotus possesses homothermy. It means that the flower is able to maintain its internal temperature just like birds, mammals, and people do. The lotus flower has a significant place in the beliefs of different nations.

And that's all that I succeeded in finding out. But this was enough to partially grasp the meaning of why the Art of Lotus constantly mentioned by Sensei is named in honor of this flower. However, the complete understanding of its meaning I felt somewhere inside of myself, in the very depth of my true "I".

.

22

In a few days, when we were all going to the training, the guys started to share their impressions and results. It turned out that everybody understood Sensei and grew this internal love in a different way. Kostya imagined that he planted a lotus seed, as he said, "into some kind of a live substance of the universe." He did it yesterday, while previously he was diligently searching through the literature looking for proof of Sensei's words. He didn't have any kind of feelings; he simply imagined the process and now is waiting for the result.

Tatyana imagined this love as the birth of Jesus in her heart, since she was brought up by her grandma as a faithful Christian. She had feelings of happiness, internal delight, and light pressure in the area of her heart. But her heart began to ache a little.

Andrew tried every day to concentrate purposefully on the area of the solar plexus in order to achieve at least some kind of feeling by thinking about the lotus. Only on the third day did he feel a slightly noticeable, light warmth, not warmth really, but as if "something was tickling in that place, as if touched by a feather." And Slava wasn't even able to imagine how all of this happens "inside of the organs."

Before the beginning of the training, our company waited for a moment when Sensei wasn't busy and came up to him with questions. We started to tell him about our feelings. Tatyana broke into the conversation out of turn and complained to Sensei about her heart. The Teacher took her hand and felt her pulse like a professional doctor.

"Right, tachycardia. What happened?"

"Don't know. It started to ache after I concentrated on the birth of God in my heart..."

And then she spoke with more details about the awakening of her divine love.

"I see. You concentrated on the organ, on the heart. But you shouldn't concentrate on an organ. The heart is the heart, it's only a muscle, it's the pump of the body. By concentrating on it, you bring it off its rhythm and interfere in its work. When you learn to control yourself, only then you will be able to concentrate on the work of the body and organs. By doing that now, you'll only harm yourself. You need to concentrate exactly on the solar plexus. Everything is born from it. That is the primary chakra in Lotus, called Kuandalini."

"Well, I read that when Kuandalini begins to awaken there, some kind of snake crawls along the spine," Kostya bragged a little with his erudition.

"This definition is from yoga," answered the Teacher. "It's typical for people to mix up everything with time. Originally, in the Lotus, Kuandalini was a chakra located in the area of the solar plexus. What I told you about the lotus flower, I repeat, are just images, nothing more, so that for you it would be easier to understand, perceive and feel."

"And in general, what does it look like in reality? Tell us, please, one more time, specially for dummies," Andrew asked jesting.

"You simply feel the fibers, growing the internal power of love. Let's say, you feel as if you were waiting for something very, very good. For example, you are waiting for some huge, long-awaited present you've dreamt about. And now you receive it, you're happy, you're overfilled with gratitude. You feel tingling all over your body, in other words, you perceive this feeling in the area of the solar plexus, as if something beautiful, good emanates from you, or you are waiting for that. You should have a feeling like this that you evoke artificially and permanently maintain in the area of the solar plexus. Finally, it becomes natural for you. And people begin to feel it. In other words, you radiate this happiness... And that's all. It's not necessary to have a flower there. These are just images for easier perception."

"And the flower that should be around the body. How does that work?"

"Well, are you familiar with such notions as the astral, mental, and other energy bodies, simply saying, the multi-layer aura around a human?"

"Yes."

"So, when this power field of good expands in you, then you start to feel a kind of multi-layer of petals. You feel that you are covered, protected, that you flourish in lotus. And at the same time, you feel that you are like the sun over the world, you warm everything with the warmth of your vast love.

"This is a permanent meditation, wherever you are and whatever you do, you evoke these fibers, these feelings, these flows of energies. The main sense is that the more you practice, the stronger they become. Finally, this process becomes material and you'll really be able to have a positive effect on people. In other words, you'll be able to do it only when you completely change yourself internally in thought, and externally in action.

Andrew wanted to ask another question, but a lanky old man appeared in the doorway of the sports hall.

"Alright, guys," Sensei said before Andrew could say anything, "We will discuss it later."

We moved aside. The old man, greeting Sensei, started to speak with excitement, taking him aside, "You know, the academician from Leningrad called today," he said, out of breath, "George Ivanovich. He asked me to tell you that he will come here for sure in three days..."

I did not quite catch the following words because "Lanky" coped with his excitement and switched to a whisper. I was extremely surprised by this message. What does an academician need here? One from Leningrad even? What does he need Sensei for? I was full of curiosity. But the training had started and Sensei entrusted the senior sempai to head it. There was no time to satisfy my curiosity.

During the training, having thought about Sensei's words about waiting for a big present, I felt that these feelings worked a lot better in me because I remembered them well from childhood. Just when I had revived these long-forgotten feelings in my memory, I felt a pleasant tickling in the center of the solar plexus, spreading in different directions with light winding streams. It was really a nice and very pleasant feeling at that moment. But I couldn't keep such a state even for a minute, and it disappeared by itself. My attempts to revive and to evoke these feelings took up a lot more time than I wanted them to. Thus, absorbed in my internal state, I didn't notice that the training was over. My body wasn't still aching after that memorable training, and the pain had gone away, like Sensei said, in exactly three days.

23

For the next few days, I tried to evoke these feelings while doing different things. But it worked well only when I specifically concentrated on the lotus flower, doing some kind of physical work. Furthermore, I began to keep track of my thoughts a bit. One day, while sitting at home and doing homework, I tried to recall all I had thought about that day but could not do it; not only thoughts, but also all of my actions. I was able to recall some general things while details surfaced with difficulty. Most importantly, my good deeds went under the category "that's the way it should be," and I hardly remembered them. However, negative moments, negative emotional upsets were engraved in my memory in detail. That was the case when I deliberately felt the power of the animal nature. Sensei's words came to my memory by themselves, "A thought is material because it's born in the material brain. That's why a bad thought oppresses. This is the first guard, which always tries to defeat the human. One day I will tell you about it in greater detail, about how your thoughts are born and why their power is so strong over you." I thought, "Why doesn't Sensei say everything at once? Why does he keep postponing it until an indefinite later? This later may never happen for some of us...

But on the other hand, the way I perceived his words at the first training and now is completely different. Before, I simply listened, and only now have I begun to understand things because I started to practice and to work on myself. I already have some results, some experience and, therefore, I now have concrete questions. Sensei always gives detailed answers to concrete questions. Suddenly I had an insight: "He just simply waits for us to understand his words, so to say, when we let them work through ourselves, when our minds conceive everything on their own and take the side of the soul. Otherwise, all this knowledge, as Sensei says, will remain for us as an empty ringing in an empty head. Sensei said that we have to work constantly on ourselves, that every minute of life is valuable, and we should use it as a gift of God for the perfection of our souls." These words strengthened my confidence and optimism. Later on, I recalled them often, when my body was seized with apathy.

24

Despite the bad weather and traffic problems caused by the year's first snow, which heaped up like never before, everybody came to the meditation training on time. Without wasting time, Sensei started discussing our attempts to bring up the flower of lotus. Nikolai Andreevich admired his results, in particular from the psychotherapeutic point of view, as one of the best ways to control thoughts. At the end of his story he said thoughtfully, "I was trying to analyze everything you said in more detail, and a question arose in me. You said that these vibrations of love protect a human from the negative influence of other people. From which one exactly, and how does it manifest?"

"Negative influence can be various. It can be an evil eye and, as people say, bedeviling..."

"An evil eye? Bedeviling?" Nikolai Andreevich was sincerely surprised. "I thought that the evil eye and bedeviling were just folklore, which is profitable enough for some enterprising people."

"Folklore exists only for the reason that this phenomenon of thought really exists but doesn't yet have sufficient, steadfast, scientific acknowledgement. But in fact, the manifestation of a negative thought exists. I've already said many times that a thought is material. They try to prove it today. Later on they will find more and more scientific proof. A thought is an information wave. Its information is coded on a certain frequency, which is perceived by our material brain, or rather, by its deeper structures. And when someone thinks something bad towards you, it's natural that it is received by your brain at the subconscious level. During the deciphering of this code, the brain starts to model this negative situation, which is implemented later into life as an unconscious order of the subconscious. That is the bedeviling, which manifests itself in a form of illness or something else. That's on the one hand. But on the other hand, when an individual creates around himself a wave field with certain frequency characteristics - well, simply saying, an aura of love - then, by all the laws of physics, negative information won't be able to penetrate into this power field, not even to reach his brain and to manifest there in the form of a command. Why? Because this power field is much stronger. The human as a social creature is a pretty complex structure. He exchanges information with others not just by means of mimicry, gestures, voice. Do you know what the voice itself is? It's the same vibration heard by us in the range of the same waves, just at different frequencies than thoughts."

"So it means that our ability to perceive sounds is limited only by the peculiar illusion of the mind?" Nikolai Andreevich enunciated, thinking about something else.

"Of course. For example, science officially proved that a human is limited in frequency range and only hears in the range from 20 hertz to 18 kilohertz. But for some reason, when people discovered the world of ultrasounds, then they learned to communicate with dolphins. It simply proves one more time that a human consciously perceives only a small part of that diverse world that surrounds him. But his subconscious... it records much more from the surrounding world."

"And does a human somehow feel it?" Stas asked.

"Yes. It's just that an ordinary human feels it at the intuitive level. In other words, as people say, with a sixth sense, while a more spiritually developed individual perceives more consciously. By forming in himself the power field made of the vibrations of love, he becomes invulnerable to negative informational flows. In other words, to put it more simply, he is impervious to bad thoughts. Consequently, he is not distracted by the struggle inside of himself and doesn't waste his precious time and power on it."

"How does it manifest in life? It doesn't always work so smoothly, sometimes you have good or bad luck," Victor showed his interest.

"Good or bad luck exists only in your mind; it is you who created it yourself in your imagination. When everything is wonderful in your life, you subconsciously expect something bad and negative. And since you pre-tune yourself to it, finally you get it. It's we who invented such a game for ourselves, to our own misfortune. It doesn't exist in nature. Good means good. Bad means you are dumb. No exceptions."

The guys smiled, having heard this indisputable answer to all objections.

"Can this spiritual practice help us cleanse ourselves from...well..." Eugene faltered a bit looking for the right words, "from a sin, or something? In general, from all the bad that you already managed to commit in life?"

"Of course. A human, as you say, cleanses his sins, because not only does he repent what he has committed in his life, but what's more important, because he no longer commits and doesn't want to commit, for him these actions have become alien. He simply casts aside everything negative, forgetting this at the conscious and subconscious levels. If he is oppressed by some past actions that constantly pursue him, he automatically cleanses himself with the help of the growing power of Love, working over the awakening of his soul."

"Why do they say 'sin will destroy you'?" Andrew asked.

"Yes, it will destroy. If a human commits a sin, this action doesn't let him rest at the conscious and subconscious levels, and like a worm it nibbles at his brain. Finally it bursts through in the form of an ulcer or insult, and so forth. In other words, whatever one may say, if nothing is done to stop it, this bad thing destroys the human from inside."

"And if the human doesn't understand whether he committed a good or a bad thing?"

"Everybody understands pretty well what he did wrong and what good. No matter how he swaggers, no matter how he shows off in front of others, how tough he is, how good, what a superman he is, in reality, when he is left alone, he is afraid for himself. He is afraid when he goes to bed at night, especially if he is alone or walks along a dark path. He clearly feels that someone is looking at him. He feels this gaze at himself and it oppresses him. He is afraid of death because there will be... Well, to put it mildly, he will have bad time."

"What happens after death?" asked Stas.

"For the one who's good, let's say, who's cleansed, who's with God inside, for that one there is nothing to be afraid of, it will be good for him there. Even though he didn't achieve much success in spiritual development, even though he didn't manage to reach his final freedom of the soul, to unite with eternal love, with God, Nirvana, call it as you wish, or to get to heaven or to the kingdom of God in the interpretation of religions, but he was developing his soul, he was striving for this... Heaven is not a place where you physically hang out with your friends, the ones who, like you, prayed in church, because it's fashionable and consider themselves enlightened. All that is rubbish, even if you pray like that all your life. The most important thing is not what you show off to the outside world, but what you think and do. The most important thing is who you really are and how you carry yourself, how you devote yourself to your spiritual growth. And if you reach a certain level of freedom, when you come to God as a mature child, then, indeed, it is clear. This is the primary goal that draws you. You left, you are free, the stars are in front of you, and endless perfection await you. But it's difficult for you to understand this state.

"If you are a bad, negative fellow, if a material nature predominates in you, if you try to obtain material goods for yourself at the expense of oppressing others, that is, by harming them, and at the same time you don't try to change yourself, then you will be in trouble there."

"Ah, just bribe priests in the name of God, they will forgive all sins at once," Eugene tried to joke.

"Priests, maybe, will forgive, but God unlikely. In general, if you try to give a miserable ransom, even by building a church, but don't repent for what you have perpetrated and won't make peace with your conscience, then all your recompenses will be senseless and foolish, because God is more interested in the cultivation of your soul, that is, of his own particle, than in recompenses in the form of material goods that were created by His own will for the cultivation and trial of human souls."

"What does it mean 'to be in trouble there'?" Andrew asked.

"Well, it is hard to explain for you to understand. But approximately something like this. Imagine the most heinous thing that can happen to you, the most horrible... Imagined?"

"Imagined."

"So, this is the best that will be there, and for pretty long... I'm not scaring you; I'm telling you how things are. Every human bears responsibility for his doings. He may not even think of it, although at the subconscious level he is perfectly aware of what he is doing. He is greedy in secret. A material essence predominates in him. He steals, lies, and satisfies his megalomania. He begrudges to donate a penny or he thinks: 'I have a lot of money, I am a king!' Tomorrow, though, he'll croak, and they will look at him, deciding who and what he was... And the most interesting thing is that everybody feels and understands this. That's why many people rush about all their life, like a pendulum, from one extreme to another, from one religion to another. In reality, nobody except you will ever pray off your sins. What's needed are your real actions in respect of your internal world. What's needed is a real maturity of the soul and not some elusive self-delusions and foolish hope that no one will find out about this and you will get away with it. The guard inside of you records all of your thoughts, not even counting your actions. And the destiny of your soul will be determined according to these memory testimonies."

"Then, it means that it's bad to be rich," Slava made his own conclusion.

"No, a rich man, it's good, it's wonderful. The fact that we still have poor people, it's bad, it's sad. When people are rich it's wonderful; they have time for themselves, for their development, if they, of course, use it in the right way."

"Tell me please," Nikolai Andreevich again joined the conversation, "regarding the Lotus flower, I would like to ask if all people perceive these fibers of love positively?"

"A majority of them, yes. But there are certain individuals who perceive these vibrations extremely negatively. It makes them suspicious and causes antagonism. It means that they possess a defective state of mind. In other words, they are afraid that their soul might awaken by contact with the emanations of the positive person, and therefore their mind is activated and brings to the foreground all the negative. It means that this individual is very bad, rotten, although he might think that he is wonderful, good. He might be extolled by the whole crowd, while in reality he is a scumbag. Why? Because he reacts to all this extremely negatively. In his mind, the animal nature predominates over the soul."

We kept silent for a while.

"You know, I recently read by chance that Helena Blavatsky mentioned in her manuscripts about some kind of special spiritual practice that she called the Rose of the World, which very distantly reminds me of the Flower of Lotus," Kostya bragged about his discovery.

"Yes. It's an echo of the spiritual practice of the Flower of Lotus. However, Blavatsky brought a lot of confusion to it. And that's not strange because she wrote after hearing from different lamas and not from the genuine source."

"I also read that the awakening of the lotus is the highest achievement in Buddhism. But before it, one needs to go through numerous initiations, levels and trials."

"Ah, all that is rubbish. People made up all that stuff in order to create a gratuitous sinecure - religion. In the beginning, Buddha gave this simple practice in a pure form to the majority of people so that everyone would have access to the spiritual practice of the Flower of Lotus for awakening the soul. Everything was very simple."

"What about for his disciples?"

"At first, he also gave this spiritual practice to his disciples. Then, according to their level of awakening, he gave them more profound knowledge."

"You said last time that Buddha's knowledge was partially lost," Kostya just couldn't calm down, "and partially distorted. And I read that the Dalai Lama, who in Lamaism, one of the major branches of Buddhism, is the highest being among the reincarnated personalities, an earthly incarnation of highly respected Bodhisattva... Avalokashevara... No, not like that, Avalokiteśvara," Kostya hardly enunciated. "In other words, he is a living god, as they say. There is also written that the death of this living god becomes the beginning of his new earthly incarnation. And a special commission of the highest lamas finds him among infants who were born over a year after the death of the Dalai Lama. So, I think that if this Bodhisattva constantly reincarnates, how can this knowledge be lost?"

"Who?! The Dalai Lama is Bodhisattva?! It's not even a parody of Bodhisattva. Who is the Dalai Lama by himself? Well, for you to really understand it, I'll tell you his history. The teaching of Buddha was initially oral. It had great resonance among people because its spiritual practices were simple and easy to understand, especially the Flower of Lotus. His philosophical teaching was written down for the first time from the words of his followers, just think about it, almost 600 years after his death, on palm leaves (Tripitaka) in 29 A.D. This was the most ancient early-Buddhist collection of manuscripts that had been written in a distorted version in relation to the real teachings of Buddha. It was written by people pursuing their personal goals of getting rich due to this knowledge, and in particular, of creating the basis for a religion. Moreover, after the death of Buddha, dissidence happened between his disciples. A part of them adhered to traditional views, the so-called doctrine of Hinayana, which in Sanskrit means 'the low vehicle,' or 'the narrow way' of salvation. In its initial form, this way was more or less closer to the truth because it emphasized the significance of the personal efforts of the practitioner to liberate himself from the bonds of Samsara (the transition of the soul from one body to another) on the way to final salvation (Nirvana). And still, it was heavily distorted with time by people who turned it into a complicated, fluffy cult.

"Another doctrine, Mahayana, which in Sanskrit means 'big vehicle' and 'wide way of salvation', is the beginning of our story about the Dalai Lama. The doctrine of Mahayana reformed all sides of Buddhist teaching, turning Buddha from the wise man and the Teacher into a typical deity, and the Bodhisattvas into his emanations. By their understanding, anyone could become a Bodhisattva by reaching the ruling clique of that religion, even though the very word 'Bodhisattva' has a completely different meaning. This word originates from Shambala.

"The word Bodhisattva translated from Sanskrit means: 'The one whose essence is knowledge.' Buddha introduced this concept among people, taking into account the level of spiritual development at that time. But even in his decoding of that word, its meaning sounded like this: 'Bodhisattva is the being of Shambala who reached the highest level of perfection and came out of Nirvana having the will again to submerge into it but refused it because of his love and compassion to living creatures and a desire to help them attain perfection.' So what did these fake Bodhisattvas do? They took out only a few words from Buddha's definitions: 'of Shambala,' 'came out of Nirvana,' 'having will' and also 'help them attain perfection' and changed that to their own interpretation. They changed the entire meaning of the words in such a way that they could benefit from them. They hoped that the world would never find out about this. But this fact points out to their immeasurable stupidity in regard to true knowledge. True spiritual knowledge, no matter how much it is distorted, no matter how much it is hidden, no matter how much it is destroyed, will still be brought by Shambala to people in its pure form because this is the only crystal source of spiritual knowledge on the Earth from which all the teachings of the world originated.

"It is impossible for a person to become a Bodhisattva. Although, in the history of mankind, there were a few unique individuals who were able to grow with their soul to the level of Bodhisattva. But these unique people can be counted on the fingers of one hand for the entire history of the existence of mankind, not just for that tiny period of so-called history known to you. So, the highest level that people can achieve in spiritual practice by working on themselves, I emphasize again, by working on themselves, is to develop their soul through love to such a degree that death won't be able to rule over them. In other words, they can liberate themselves from the chain of reincarnation and unite with divine love, with Nirvana, call it as you wish. For you it's hard now even to understand the meaning of this word 'Nirvana'. But no earthly pleasures can be compared even with a thousandth of this highest state."

"So, Bodhisattvas are really beings from Shambala?" asked Andrew.

"Yes. They created their small world, known to people as the Abode. From there the world is given knowledge, both scientific and spiritual, so that people can grow spiritually and develop their souls."

"Are messiahs also Bodhisattvas?" inquired Stas.

"Sometimes, Bodhisattvas, when giving their basic teaching, had to become messiahs. But this is very rare. More often, as a rule, messiahs are their disciples brought up from the ordinary people."

"In what sense?"

"Well, one day I will tell you about it. Because we deviated from the subject too much... So, Bodhisattva will not prove to anyone who He is, and moreover He won't create a religion. Bodhisattva may give a teaching about the spiritual essence of the human, how to develop it. But in no way a religion... In fact, any religion is just a show business begotten by the megalomania of the ruling class to fleece money from a crowd of stupid asses."

"Well, why stupid?" Ruslan said resentfully.

"Because these people become very limited in their knowledge. They are constantly being told that they should listen only to the speeches of their religious leaders, they should read only their literature and stick only to their herd, because all other religions are wrong. For example, let's not look for something else but return to the subject of our conversation, what did these showmen do with the teaching of Buddha? First, for their convenience and in order to have fewer questions from the crowd, they turned Buddha into a god. Second, they introduced complicated religious ceremonies, worship services, prayers, pointing out to the masses the wide and easy way to salvation, due to their show cult of bodhisattvas-mentors. The ordinary man not only has to perform the rituals, spells, vows and all their multilayered nonsense invented by them but also has to pay them for their lie and obey them implicitly. In fact, these false bodhisattvas, who are actually just sly and clever people, simply created another religion.

"And now we'll return to the question about the Dalai Lama. So, it was Nagarjuna, who lived in the second century and started all this mess about reforming Buddhism. He was a pretty smart but cunning man with mercenary-minded interests. He was a Hindu philosopher, theologist, poet, and he founded the school of Shunyavada (Madhyamaka). And now the most important part. As Nagarjuna made a complicated thing from a simple one, he greatly distorted and partially pocketed for himself the knowledge given by Buddha for the masses, he turned upside down the essence of the very teaching, and he was severely punished by Rigden Jappo and sentenced to eternal conscious reincarnation."

"Who is Rigden Jappo?" asked Kostya.

"Rigden Jappo leads a commune of Bodhisattvas in Shambala... So, later Nagarjuna was known under different names. In 1391, his soul was reborn in a man named Gendundub, who became the first Dalai Lama. He wanted to be worshipped, admired for being a great teacher... He was drawn by wealth, luxury, and worship. Now the Dalai Lama has plenty of wealth; he is worshipped by a quarter of the world. But on the other hand, he is not happy and will never be. He is doomed to eternal conscious reincarnation and eternal internal suffering. He cannot leave for Nirvana, cannot liberate himself from the continuous vicious circle of conscious rebirths. Nobody will let him free from this earthly life. Every lifetime, when he is 13 years old, during puberty when the life force begins to awaken and connect the human with the universe, when he begins to awaken as a personality and realizes who he is, for him it's a big pain for the rest of his life."

"What kind of pain?!" Kostya blurted out. "He is the Dalai Lama, he has everything! It's a big joy to have everything and to be reborn constantly. How can he be bored of such a life?!"

The Teacher wearily looked at Kostya and said, "Well, how to explain it to you... Have you seen, for example, the movie 'White Sun of the Desert'?"

"Yes."

"Do you remember how the customs official, Vereschagin, sat down to dinner and when his wife put before him a whole plate of black caviar, he glanced at it and said, 'Again this caviar! I just can't eat it any more, damn it. Can you go and swap it for bread?' In other words, everything becomes boring very quickly with time. And life becomes boring even much more. If you remembered at least a part of what you experienced in other bodies, you would be fed up with the monotony of bodily forms. To be reborn consciously and to know that this is your eternal destiny is scary, and you can't even imagine how scary it is. That's why Jesus punished the Wandering Jew with immortality. Do you remember this story?"

Kostya shook his head in embarrassment, "No."

"When Jesus was whipped on the way to Golgotha, He felt very bad; He was very thirsty. And when He stopped on the threshold of the house of one of the Jews, whose name was Ahasuerus, and asked for water, he rudely banished Him, being afraid for his life that he would be punished. Jesus said to him: 'You are afraid for your life; so you will live forever!' Ahasuerus cannot die and wanders all over the world, no matter how much he's bored by it."

"So, will he never be forgiven?" Tatyana asked, feeling pity for him.

"Not until there is overall forgiveness, until the entire world repents. But that's already another story."

Sensei glanced at his watch.

"Alright guys, it's time to begin a meditation, otherwise our conversation might go on for a long time. Today, we will repeat for some of you and some of you will try to work through the chakras of legs and the chakra Hara."

"Where are they located?" asked Stas.

"The chakras of the legs are located in the center of the feet, and the Hara chakra is three fingers lower than the navel in the point of Dan-tian. Translated from Japanese, Hara means belly. This is a center of the human and it practically coincides with the center of gravity, both in the physical and the geometrical sense. This meditation, just as the previous one, is focused on concentration of attention... And now stand up, relax, put your legs as wide as your shoulders..."

We stood up in a comfortable way, relaxed, and concentrated on performing the meditation.

"Now we'll breathe in as usual, in other words, voluntary, and breathe out into the bowl-like Hara, as if filling it with Qi energy until you have a feeling of light heaviness. When the Hara fills up, you should let this Qi energy pass through from Hara into the legs through the center of the feet into the earth..."

For some time I drove this energy only with my thought. But then my imagination switched to an evidently real feeling of my belly bursting as if water had been poured into me. Meanwhile Sensei reminded us, "When Hara is filled up, you should pour this energy out through the legs, through the center of your feet into the ground."

I tried again to do it in my imagination, mentally working on my body. Gradually, I started to feel some kind of warmth, starting with a small streamlet. It wasn't wholly but only partially felt in the area of my shin and my foot. Even though it was pretty cold outside, my feet in my boots started gradually to warm up. When I noticed that I switched to thinking about how I was able to do it, the feelings somehow disappeared as soon as I gradually deepened my mind into logic. But just as I tried again to concentrate, Sensei notified us that the meditation was over.

"Take two deep breathes in and out. Sharply clench your fists, open up your eyes."

I looked at my watch; only about ten minutes had passed. To me it had seemed like a lot more. Someone noticed that the snow had melted under us. We looked around with amazement. Under some of the senior guys, the thawed patches were about 40 centimeters in diameter, and under us just ordinary ones.

Eugene glanced at Stas and declared, "You see, and you complained, 'It's so cold, it would be good now to be in Africa.' There's no need for you to go to Africa. There are already palm trees starting to grow under your legs."

Addressing Sensei, he added, "I suspected a long time ago that something was not right with his origin; he is always drawn to Papuans."

After another series of jokes, when everybody calmed down a bit, Sensei said that we could work on this meditation on our own at home.

"And on the Flower of Lotus as well?" asked Kostya.

"Of course. Pay special attention to it and do it every free minute."

"When will we see results?"

"Don't worry, if you aren't lazy, the results won't make you wait."

"I'm sorry. I wanted to return a bit to our conversation before the meditation. You said that all scientific knowledge is given to the world by Shambala. I didn't quite understand how is it given?" Nikolai Andreevich pronounced it with a faint note of arrogance in his voice. "I always thought that a human is a pretty intelligent creature to invent everything on his own, including scientific discoveries."

"Well, what should I say, in general, a human, undoubtedly, will one day become a perfect creature... But as long as the animal nature prevails in his mind, he won't even be able to invent an ordinary chair if he were not told how it should be done."

"How can it be?"

"Well, simply. It's only now that people are so smart because they use the knowledge of the ancestors. But how did their ancestors find out about that, have you ever thought? Even in the most ancient legends of the Sumerian civilization, written on clay tablets, it is mentioned that people from the sky told them how to organize the household, how to build houses, how to fish, how to cultivate vegetative food for themselves, and so forth. Before that, people lived like a herd of animals... Let's take for example, the modern world. How do scientists make discoveries?"

"By intensive work on the given subject of research."

"Certainly, externally this looks exactly this way. But the very instant of discovery, the instant of insight?"

Nikolai Andreevich shrugged his shoulders.

"Recall the history of great discoveries," continued Sensei. "Take for instance, the well-known periodic system of Dmitriy Ivanovich Mendeleev that came to him in a dream in its final form. He was given only a partial form that can be perceived by mankind at this stage. It's the same story with the structure of the atom discovered by Niels Bohr, with the formula of Frederick Augustus Kukle, with discoveries of Nikolai Tesla, and many, many others. Practically all the scientific ideas and theories of mankind appeared as a result of insights, intuition, and more often as inspiration from on high. In other words, these discoveries were extracted by scientists from the depths of their subconscious.

"The depths of the subconscious is the chakra called the doors or the gates, call it as you wish, which can open from one side as well as from the other side. It is just a transition to a completely different sphere, a different dimension, a different information field. So, when necessary, a ready answer can be inserted into the brain of a scientist from that side."

"Who inserts it?" Kostya inquired.

"The One who's located on that side. Every human perceives Him differently: some take Him for the Absolute, some believe it's the Collective Intellect, or Shambala, or God..."

"I wonder whether Shambala and God are one and the same?" Ruslan asked, pondering something.

"No. God is God, while Shambala is just one of His creations."

"And what is Shambala in relation to mankind?" asked Nikolai Andreevich.

"It's simply a source of knowledge. Speaking with modern language, it is a certain bank of information, the entrance to which exists in the depths of the subconscious of every human."

"So, it means that one can get into Shambala without leaving the room?" Stas was surprised by his guess.

"Absolutely correct..."

We spoke a little more about the questions worrying us until Sensei once again glanced at his watch.

"Alright, guys, it's already late; it's time to leave."

Honestly speaking, I, as well as the others, didn't want to leave. Eugene precisely expressed our mutual opinion, "The soul demands the continuation of the banquet." But, alas, we needed to go home so that our relatives would not worry about the long absence of our bodies.

25

The following days flew by uneventfully. At the next training, everything was as usual: the warm-up, the basics, the new techniques. This time we were given new techniques from the Monkey style. In order to execute a deceitful blow or to make a simple attack, we tried to copy the habits of this animal, which looked pretty funny. Eugene, as always, didn't fail to express that, for the majority of our group, there was no need to copy the monkey because our habits in life evidently surpassed the original. In short, the training went by quite emotionally and merrily.

After the additional training, when almost the entire crowd had left, we continued polishing the complex exercises Sensei showed us for individual work. Already at the very end of the training, a solid, imposing man, about sixty years old, entered the sports hall. Sensei, on seeing him, smiled and said, "Whom do I see?! How did you get to us, George Ivanovich?"

"Don't even ask me," the man said, slightly indignant. "I have been looking for you for two hours, circling half the city."

Sensei grinned, "I beg your pardon, Sir Academician. I was busy and couldn't meet you near the ladder."

Having greeted each other in a familiar way, they went deeper into the sports hall and, sat down on the sport benches, and began to talk about something.

Upon hearing the word 'academician', it was too much for my curiosity. The others around didn't react in any way to the appearance of the guest. The senior guys continued polishing their strikes as if nothing had happened and concentrated on the work. Our guys kept up with them. Tatyana and I also tried to put on a good show. But with the arrival of this man, all my attention switched to him and Sensei. I saw that Sensei, turning to the guest, started to gesticulate, saying something in quite animated form, and I couldn't bear it. Dodging Tatyana's blows, I began gradually approaching them with this improvised sparring. I heard the following words of Sensei, addressed to his guest.

"About twenty years ago you dreamt only of worldwide fame and recognition as a remarkable scientist, and you offered us your services in exchange for concrete knowledge that would make you a leader in science..."

"Oho!" I thought, dumbfounded. "Sensei speaks to him in such a familiar way! But who is this 'us'? What services?"

Meanwhile Sensei continued, "...From our side, we fulfilled the conditions of our agreement. You received detailed information from us, starting from the semiconducting heterostructure laser and ending with the converters of solar energy. Isn't that enough for you?! All your life, you did nothing and just used our knowledge, and next year you'll get the Nobel prize. Not so bad, right?! I don't understand what the problem is?"

The man sat, hanging his head. When Sensei finished, he raised his eyes towards him. His face his was all red, probably because of strong agitation.

"What's the problem, you say? You take me for a fool!" With a softer tone, he added, "I remember everything perfectly and never renounced my words... But explain to me, please, where I can find an energy source with the necessary power? In order to launch the plant, according to the blueprints which you handed me, I would have to switch off the power to at least the entire region of Leningrad. You want this plant to work from the beginning of August until December. This means that for these months Leningrad and others will be without light!"

"Dear George Ivanovich, don't worry about the source of energy, we'll supply you with it," Sensei replied.

"Are you going to bring a nuclear generator to my institute or what?! How can you imagine that? Why does it have to be exactly in the territory of our institute? Can't you do it in some other place, in Moscow, for example?" George Ivanovich was indignant.

"We can, of course. But we decided that your institute is located in a more convenient place... And we'll supply you with the source of power. You need not worry, it is very small in size, no bigger than a briefcase, so it won't take up a lot of room. Its energy is sufficient for the plant to work for the time needed."

"I apologize, but you mentioned millions of kilowatts. It'll all be in just a briefcase?" the academician was surprised.

Sensei smiled. "Don't stuff your head with trifles. I can partially satisfy your curiosity and say right now that this is a vacuum source of energy. Moreover, we will give you, as promised, a frequency converter for this equipment. But I warn you in advance, I wouldn't advise you to get in there and disassemble these devices; otherwise, it will be a million times worse than Hiroshima even though in outward appearance, they look completely harmless. But remember, the plant should begin to work continuously no later than the 15th of August."

"Alright. And when will you deliver them to me?"

"I think right after Christmas they will be delivered to you."

"Well... Just..." The academician halted a bit.

"What?"

"I'm curious to know one thing. You spoke once about noninterference in our life, while this plant is evidence of the opposite."

"We do not interfere. If we interfered, we would stop the events that are going to burst out. But we don't have the right; it's your will, do what you wish. It's just not in our interest that a third world war break out with the use of nuclear weapons. That's why we only want to smooth away the consequences of these events."

"And is there a guarantee that these waves won't harm anyone?"

"We assure you that it is absolutely harmless. People will become calmer and more reasonable. That's why their reaction will be softer and won't develop into some global conflict. But I repeat, we don't have the right to prevent these events. If you want, prevent it yourselves. It's your business."

The academician got up heavily from the bench and began to bid farewell. Sensei accompanied him to the door, one more time reminding him about the date. Shaking each other's hands, they said goodbye. I heard how Sensei, coming back from the door, mumbled to himself with a smile, "Hmm, every fool considers himself to be smart, but only a smart one can call himself a fool."

I was very impressed by this peculiar conversation. "Who is Sensei? Is he a physicist?" I thought. "He probably works in some scientific research institute. Sensei also once told us about some profound physics. In that case, it explains a lot about the extensive range of his knowledge." This was the only explanation that came to my mind and was more or less acceptable because the thousand other questions completely confused me, and I couldn't find a clear explanation for them. Nevertheless, Sensei rose in my estimation as a scientific authority because even the academician valued his opinion, even though Sensei did not want to distinguish himself from the crowd. On the way home, as usual, he joked with everybody, keeping up our happy mood after the monkey training. However, at home, I didn't forget to write down this unusual conversation in my diary with a big remark at the end, "It turns out that he is a physicist!"

26

A few days later, when I was shopping with my mother as usual, I was making plans for the evening, thinking over questions that I intended to ask Sensei at the training.

After yesterday's rain and night frost, there was a heavy fall of fluffy snow on the streets. Winter here was quite warm in comparison to those regions of the Soviet Union where we had lived before. Miners' snow looked like snow only the first day because on the second day it became grey from coal dust, and on the third day, it completely melted, turning into wet, slushy mud. Every New Year we celebrated with the same weather forecast: "Rain turning to wet snow." So I was glad to see at least this fluffy snow and feel the long-awaited freeze. It was giving me hope that next New Year, which was only three weeks ahead, we may celebrate properly, with real winter and a lot of fun.

As I was dreaming of a good future, we were walking to the next store. Suddenly my mother unexpectedly slipped and fell back so hard that even her legs flew up. It happened in a few split seconds. I didn't even have time to understand, not even to catch her. Men passing by rushed to lift her up. I also tried to help somehow, being really scared. Having thanked the men, my mother stood up, leaning on me.

"Mum, how are you, can you walk?"

"Hold on, my back hurts so much, as if something cracked."

"Maybe we should go to the hospital?"

"Just wait; it will pass."

We stood a bit and then slowly walked home. My mother limped slightly. At home, she felt even worse. We didn't want to bother father at work and hoped that it would pass. The pain kept getting stronger, and no pills helped. We tried all we could: we rubbed it with different ointments, made compress, and simply warmed it up. But she felt even worse after the last procedure. Of course, I didn't go to the meditation training. And when my dad came home late in the evening, we tried everything possible in order to relieve the pain. There was only one way out: to go to the hospital. My father made a few calls and arranged for mother to be observed by a doctor at the regional department of neurosurgery.

In the morning, her state quickly worsened. An aching, sharp pain passed into her leg. Even the slightest movement caused the strongest attack of pain. She was even taken into the hospital reclining. In the neurology department, after a series of X-rays and computerized tomography, the doctor diagnosed that she had had osteochondrosis of the spinal column for a long time, and the fall had caused the fibrous ring to burst and a 7 mm herniation of the intervebral disk. As a result, the sciatic nerve was squeezed, and the strong pain extended to her leg. After careful examination, the doctor sent her to consult with the neurosurgeon. My father again found a good neurosurgeon, who, having studied the results of the examination, concluded that an operation is inevitable.

It was a catastrophe for our family. We saw more than enough bedridden patients on the way to the consulting room of neurosurgeon. My mother also heard plenty of horror stories from her future neighbor in the neurology ward, who needed to undergo a second operation. My mother was so scared by the forthcoming operation that, after consultation we abducted her from the neurosurgery department, if our strenuous hobbling could be called an escape. Thus, unexpectedly for all of us, the future looked dark. We decided to try drug treatment, injections, and, as they say, to fight to the end.

From that day when my mother went into the hospital's neurology department, my life changed sharply. In the morning, I went to school and later went by bus to the regional neurology department. All the time I was near my mother and tried to support her spiritually. As it seemed to me, it was very important for her. The doctors were indignant that outsiders visited her, but my father quickly settled that question. The hospital became the main place where I spent my free time.

My mother was all the more sad that misfortunes, one after another, chased our family. Moreover, a message came from Moscow that the date was fixed and I was awaiting an operation after the New Year's holidays. My mum greatly worried that I had given up my favorite hobby classes and trainings and even tried to insist that I should return to my usual life. But I didn't listen to her. It seemed to me that nobody would take care of her like me and that without me she would simply fade away from her bad thoughts and the oppressing atmosphere of the ward where all her neighbors just spoke about their diseases.

At first, I, as well as my family, was a little bit shocked. "How could such a thing happen?" I thought. "So unexpectedly, and to my mother. Our life is so unpredictable! It only seems to us that we can forsee and plan everything in it, and that everything will be exactly like we imagine. In reality, every day is a trial, as if somebody wants to test us, how reliable we are, how steady we are internally in various situations, whether it's joy or grief. Maybe these stresses that make us their unwillingly witnesses and participants appear to us as reminders from above that life is too fragile and that we might not even have time to do the most important thing in it. We are so accustomed to put aside the important things in our soul for an indefinite 'later' that we don't realize how quickly life passes and that we do not have time to do anything serious in it.

Why do we start to really value something only when it is irretrievably lost: youth, in old age; health, on the hospital's bed; life, on our deathbed? Why?! Maybe these sudden situations make us think over our perishable existence, make us wake up from our unrealizable fantasies borne by our laziness and bring us back to reality. Reality shows that nobody clearly knows what can happen to him at any minute. So, maybe it's not worth tempting fate and we should start to value each moment right now, value it as if we were people doomed to death. Maybe then we'll be able to understand more deeply the sense of life itself and do a thousand more useful things for our soul and for surrounding people. "It's foolish to think that tomorrow is waiting for us, it may simply never come." Only now did I understand the real meaning of Sensei's phrase, which once I believed to be a joke: "If you want to make God laugh, tell Him about your plans."

In the first few days with mum on the ward, we listened to the life stories of her neighbors, and I found proof that nobody is insured against Mr. Accident. The woman whose bed was next to the window was called Valentina Fedorovna. Just one instant had turned her entire life upside down, and it happened unexpectedly as well. She and her husband were living from hand to mouth, with hardly any money. They decided to join a wave of the cooperative movement, so her husband quit the factory and registered his own furniture cooperative. Her husband was enterprising and hard-working, and the business was successful. In just one year, they made so much money that they bought new cooperative apartments, a car, and even a country lot. Everything couldn't be better and they had no troubles.

But two months ago, when Valentina Fedorovna was coming back with her husband from a relative's birthday party, they got into a big car accident. It happened in a split second. Three cars crashed into each other at full speed because of a drunken driver in the oncoming lane. Her husband died immediately. Thanks to being fastened by a seatbelt, she miraculously stayed alive. However, she was told that the doctors later diagnosed a subluxation in the cervical area of her spinal cord with a hematoma. After that, her hand hardly moved, while she couldn't feel her legs at all. The subluxation was cured in the neurosurgery department. However, the hematoma remained as a consequence of the spinal cord injury. Valentina Fedorovna was transferred from the neurosurgical to neurological department about one month ago.

It seemed to me that she suffered more in her moral state than in her physical state. At that moment, her life was destroyed. She had to mortgage a part of her property because all the money she had was quickly spent on treatment and on paying off her husband's odd debts. But most of all, she was shocked by the strange attitude of her friends.

She told us that she had many friends and relatives, but as soon as they found out that her husband had died and that she remained disabled alone, everybody for some reason immediately forgot about her existence. She had been in the hospital for two months and had been visited only by her old grandmother and her sister, who, despite the fact that she lived in poverty, always tried to bring her something delicious. Valentina Fedorovna now understood who is who, but it was already too late. That evening, I wrote down in my diary her old grandmother's interesting expression regarding careless friends, "When the pot is boiling, the house is full of friends. And when the pot is gone, nobody comes."

Valentina Fedorovna was in despair and didn't find any other way out for her grief except slandering her former friends and relatives. I felt uncomfortable when hearing such speeches. These bad words spoilt her own mood and made her very nervous, and she inflamed hatred in herself and people around her suffered. We didn't even want to mention the word 'friend' because this woman would explode and resume her non-stop complaints.

Another woman, Anna Ivanovna, was kind. She didn't curse her destiny, though her health wasn't any better. She had almost the same kind of disease as my mum. One day, her back simply began to ache. The doctors found a herniated disk. They performed an operation and eliminated the vertebral herniation. After that, she felt a lot better. But some time later, she again fell ill and felt even worse. The doctors recommended her for a second operation, but she was afraid that she wouldn't be able to walk after it. Anna Ivanovna was quite reserved in telling her story, but the details, especially the consequences of her operation, scared not just my mother but also me because I, most likely, would be operated on by neurosurgeons as well.

Anna Ivanovna hardly moved. Her husband, a happy plump man, often visited her. Their children had grown up a long time ago and lived with their families in different cities. But Anna Ivanovna had her own distress, as she was most of all afraid to be bedridden; after all, she was only fifty. She was afraid to become a burden to her husband and even more to oppress her children with her illness. That's why this woman tried very hard to recover, swallowing all the assigned pills and performing all the prescribed procedures. But sometimes, when the pain became unbearable, optimism left her and she would weep bitter tears, repeating the same question, "Why?!"

The third neighbor, a young woman about five years older than me, had afterbirth trauma. Lena had already felt pain in her back during the pregnancy. Her right leg completely stopped moving; she couldn't even move her toes. As it turned out, she had a protrusion of two disks. At home, she left the baby in the care of her retired mother-in-law. She also was visited by her husband. He was a good guy: calm, and probably a meek person. Her mother-in-law, on the other hand, was rushing like a hurricane, always grumbling and dissatisfied with trifles.

This complication after the delivery, which nobody could foresee, put the young family on the verge of collapse. Apart from the fact that Lena had serious health problems and couldn't physically take care of the child, her mother-in-law regularly provoked conflicts, telling her son that he didn't need a cripple wife, that it would be a burden for all his life, and that he should ask his wife for a divorce. Lena couldn't rely on anyone else to be with her child but her mother, but the mother lived far away in a different city and seldom visited her because she worked all the time in the factory, barely making ends meet. In general, Lena's life had turned to a continuous tragedy.

Having heard plenty of all these stories, I realized that not one of these patients had expected such an outcome; everyone lived and planned something, but the events came like thunder amidst a clear sky. Everybody complained about why it happened specifically to them. In the evening, after having heard all of that, I randomly opened my diary and came across Sensei's words, "There is no such thing as chance. Chance is only a natural consequence of our uncontrolled thoughts." "That's it!" I thought. "Strange that I simply didn't pay attention to these words before." In order to improve my vigilance, I marked them out in the diary with bold italics.

I really wanted to visit Sensei's trainings, but I just couldn't get out from this whirlpool of events without feeling guilty. I regularly called my friends, who effusively bragged about their successes. At home, I continued doing meditations, and I tried to do the Lotus Flower every free minute. It worked well to evoke feelings when I thought about a desirable present. At that thought, a wave of tiny ants would arise in my solar plexus and spread through my whole body in different directions. This feeling was quite pleasant. Even though I wasn't near Sensei, his words in my diary constantly circled in my mind.

In the hospital, I decided that, at any cost, I would change the unhealthy atmosphere in the ward because listening to talk about diseases and oppressive existence could quickly weaken even a healthy man. Visiting my mother, I tried to tell all the funniest stories I knew, starting from school life and finishing with different amusing incidents from literature. But this method was ineffective, since the women remained deep in thought about their own problems. One time, talking to Lena, I told her what I heard from Sensei about good and bad thoughts, about the essence of our soul and our life. Amazingly, the women started listening to these words with such attention, as if they weren't Sensei's words I was telling but rather a confession that concerned each of them. My mother said that after my departure they continued to discuss these words and reflected on their meaning in relation to their life experiences. Strikingly, in just a week after my conversation, there were some unexpected results.

Valentina Fedorovna, who more than everybody groaned and grieved, transformed herself into a completely different person, an intelligent organizer of her destiny. My mother said that after these conversations she intensively pondered something. The result of her decision surpassed all expectations. She offered Lena's husband the official position of director of the furniture cooperative with a correspondingly good salary. This was a complete shock not just for the young family, but especially for the mother-in-law. They simply didn't know how to thank Valentina Fedorovna for this present of destiny.

Although Lena's husband was a meek person, when he was entrusted such an important business, he showed the talents of a good manager. As the mother-in-law told us, he worked with great enthusiasm and efficiency twenty-four hours a day, and due to his efforts, the production of furniture was restarted in less than two weeks, and they even got their first big profit. The mother-in-law blossomed from happiness, and her attitude towards Lena immediately changed for the better.

Moreover, Valentina Fedorovna hired her sister in this cooperative, turning her from a simple bookkeeper with a tiny salary in a state enterprise into the chief bookkeeper of a privately owned enterprise, with a good salary. And since the woman was honest, punctual, and accurate, order was guaranteed. In general, such smart and simple decisions made by Valentina Fedorovna pleased everybody, and especially herself. Her health and her life in general began to improve. Even her old friends began to visit her, offering various services. But Valentina Fedorovna, completely without anger, let them know that she no longer needed their services or help.

The atmosphere in the ward after that got significantly better. Now, the women smiled more often, joked, supported each other. The atmosphere in this ward became pleasant for everyone. Even the hospital staff lingered for longer than usual just to chat with our jolly women. What's most striking, not only did the women's mood improve, but also their health; they quickly started recovering. I understood that this terrible pain was begotten, first of all, by their imagination, by bad thoughts and fear of the unknown. It was like a worm eating them up from inside, intensifying over and over again their physical pain. As soon as these women drew their attention away from these thoughts, they became pleasant not only to those around them, but also to themselves. They received an opportunity not only to reason soberly, but also to try to adapt to the new conditions of their lives and their relationships with people.

I was simply shocked by this discovery, since I didn't suspect that Sensei's words would cause such a revolution in the thoughts and feelings of these women doomed to suffering. The positive thoughts of one of them begot an entire chain of events in the destinies of several people, bringing happiness and wealth into their lives. This proved to be evidence that Sensei was absolutely right in telling us about the power of our thoughts and how much they affect us and our destiny.

Also, I noticed that it became significantly easier to practice the Lotus Flower in the ward. I did my best to support this spirit of optimism, which grew every day. I brought library books of the great classics, with good endings of course, as well as humorous stories. The women read them with pleasure, retelling each other the exciting moments. It turned out that many of Sensei's words also found their proof in works of the classics of different epochs. Finally, I realized that Sensei actually spoke about the eternal truth that was always known to humankind. He just explained all this simply and clearly.

I also noticed one more curious moment. Anna Ivanovna, who had been working for twenty years in a university as a teacher of literature, knew many of these books almost by heart. But now she said that she reread these books with pleasure, as now she perceived them completely differently. In particular for her, for her soul, as she later confessed, she made interesting discoveries, noticing in the books those things that she hadn't paid attention to before.

Sometimes our readings would turn into real literary soirees. Amazingly, when I spoke to the women about Sensei's theory of control over thoughts, they listened to these words with unusual attention. At first, it embarassed me because I simply couldn't answer many of their questions about life. But at home, looking through my diary anew, I found the words of Sensei, which, in my opinion, more or less matched the answers. Strangely enough, the women perceived these words in their own way, depending on their life experiences, and these answers quite satisfied them. So, although Sensei wasn't with us, his presence was felt clearly in his deep thoughts which we constantly came back to.

New Year drew near. The women decided to organize a holiday party right in the ward. My father settled all the formalities with the chief doctor. We even installed a small, real Christmas tree, decorating it with various toys and, just for fun, with syringes and droppers. Our family celebrated New Year in mother's ward with the other women and their close friends and relatives. It was so merry, and everyone was so kind to each other that I had the impression we were all a big, friendly family. I remembered one interesting toast, proposed by Lena's mother-in-law.

"They say that how you celebrate New Year, so will be the entire year. And despite the fact that we are celebrating it in the hospital, the most important thing is that we are celebrating it in the company of such wonderful people. I am thankful to God that all the misfortunes of my son are finally over. Thank you so much, dear Valentina Fedorovna, for your kind and keen heart. If it weren't for you, we would never have gotten out of that nightmare. So let's drink to you, to unpredictable destiny, which gathered all of us in such an unusual place. To your health!"

A lot of kind and beautiful words were said that night. Close to two o'clock in the morning, we were even joined by the chief doctor and his wife, who were coming back after visiting their friends. But as I later understood, he was more interested in talking to my dad rather than staying with us. Having drunk a few glasses of wine, the women began pouring out their souls to each other. I was really shocked when Valentina Fedorovna was telling us how she had taken her vitally important decision.

"You know, girls, I long thought about what had happened to me and how to get out from that trouble. And one time, after one more heavy pondering, I had a strange dream. A beautiful young man with blond hair to his shoulders came up to my bed and started speaking with a melodic voice, 'Why are you suffering? Look at the people surrounding you. When you see their best features, your problems will disappear.' After that, I woke up in a completely different mood. I began thinking. And really, as it turned out later, I couldn't have found better candidates for my business. Although, honestly speaking, in the beginning I had doubts, there was still a great risk. But recalling this dream, something pushed me to a final decision. Honestly, girls," she made the sign of the cross, "it's the genuine truth!"

"Would you believe that this blond man was also in my dream?" confessed Anna Ivanovna. "I was just too shy to tell you. He was telling me something with such a pleasant voice. But in the morning, I could remember nothing of his words. I just remember that afterwards I had such a nice feeling. I still keep feeling appeased. What could it mean?"

"They were angels from heaven who came to help you," exclaimed the pious mother-in-law. "They show you, my dear, the right way..."

She then started the whole homily of church teaching. But this case clearly intrigued me. Coming back home, I hurried to write it down in my diary.

27

Soon after the New Year holidays, my mother felt a lot better, and she was discharged from the hospital. Parting from the women, who were also getting ready to be discharged, was very warm. These days I had more free time, and I decided to go to the training. But my friends said that Sensei had left on a business trip for a couple of weeks. So, our meeting was postponed for an indefinite period of time because in three days we had to fly with my mother to Moscow.

I took my diary with me on the plane. As my mother slept during the flight, I turned its pages over and over again. Of course, I worried a lot before the forthcoming operation, but Sensei's words warmed my heart and were honey to my soul.

Uncle Victor met us at the airport and informed us that grandfather had come from Siberia to support our moral spirit. My grandpa was the most respected, most esteemed, wisest man among all our kinfolk. Everybody listened to his opinion. It was considered a great honor if he visited one of the relatives. It pleased me to see such a touching demonstration of care from grandpa; it was not so easy at his age to travel more than five thousand kilometers, even by plane.

When we had happily greeted grandpa, we began the traditional feast, where mother told him about all the misfortunes that had befallen our family. They continued to discuss the problems for long time but I, fairly tired after the trip, went to take a rest because the next day was going to be quite hard.

In the evening, when I was reading my diary, somebody knocked on the door. It was grandpa. He sat next to me and began inquiring about some trifles. Gradually, our conversation moved on to more serious subjects. Grandfather was trying to console me before the forthcoming operation. He said that regardless of the results of the second examination, there was no need to be upset. Many people who got into worse situations came out of them as winners precisely because they didn't lose their self-control and willpower and fought to the end. Grandfather started to cite eloquent examples from his front-line life during the war. To be more convincing, he supported his speech with his favorite proverb, "As long as life in you glimmers, hope still shines." All that time I carefully and calmly listened to grandpa. When he finished his speech, I sincerely told him what I actually thought and felt in my soul. I expressed all my opinions about life, which, thanks to Sensei's teaching, had formed me from the inside and had become an essential part of myself. Grandfather was so startled, so amazed by this simple truth that he again asked me if I really wasn't afraid of death.

"Of course," I calmly replied. "For me, death is just a change of conditions, a transition from one state to another. I know that I will always be with you, with my relatives, because my love for you lives in me, in my soul. And wherever I am, whichever form I take, this love always will be with me because I and my love are eternal... I began to appreciate this feeling most of all in life because in life, the quality of the instants lived is more important than the senseless years of existence.

These words affected grandpa's feelings because he was touched to the depths of the soul. I realized that everybody is afraid of death, even those who are as courageous as my grandfather. Apparently, he was also afraid of the unknown, of what will happen after death, but had never told anyone. Grandpa pondered for some time and then said, "Yes, probably, wisdom is a virtue of the soul and not of the age."

The next day, I noticed that grandpa changed. He became happier, more cheerful, and looked as if he had found answers to questions that had been tormenting him for years. We headed to the clinic together. I was examined for almost the entire week, passed various analyses and X-rays. And finally, one day, my mother and I came to the professor, an old, pleasant man. I thought he greeted us strangely, slightly confused. Looking at him, I thought that my body had very little time left to live. A tense pause reigned.

"You know," he began, still looking through my films. "I don't understand anything. There is a clear pathology in these September films that you brought, and the tumor had already begun to progress slowly. But if you look at the ones we just took, everything is clear. I even had repeated films taken... Either there was a mistake in the first films, which is unlikely based on the fact that the girl has been regularly examined, or... I even don't know what to think."

Addressing me, the professor asked, "When was the last time you had headaches?"

"Me? Well..," I did my best to recall, "Probably, some time in October, I clearly remember it. While later..." I shrugged my shoulders.

And really, I had completely forgotten the last time that my head ached. The previous months had been full of events, especially in the case of my mother, and I had completely forgotten about myself and my disease. The only thing that was significant for me was the spiritual and physical care of my mother.

"Strange...Very strange," said the doctor. "According to our films, the girl is completely healthy, though the old films show that, at a minimum, right now she should be bedridden. Did you get any other treatment beside the doctor's recommendations?" the professor asked with evident interest.

"Well, no," my mother replied in confusion. "We did what we were prescribed."

"What my colleagues prescribed would only slow down the growth of the cancer cells but not completely destroy them. Paradoxical! This is the first such unique case in my entire long-term practice. Evidently, it didn't happen without providence," the doctor kept saying, once again going through the films and the results of the analysis.

"So, does it mean," my mother asked shyly, clearly not believing all she heard, "you can't confirm the diagnosis?"

The professor drew his attention away from the films and glanced at my mother with amazement.

"Of course. Your daughter is absolutely healthy!"

My mother, for one more minute, sat clinging to the chair. When the professor's answer finally sank in, she rushed to thank him and to shake his hand as if he were an angel with wings. I was also happy. But unlike my mother, I knew who my angel and savior was. Even my mind didn't resist that definition. The only question that worried me in that moment was: how did Sensei do this?

After such news we didn't just walk out of the clinic, we flew out of it. Our relatives waited downstairs, including grandpa. There was no limit to their joy. My mother made the sign of the cross and silently thanked God, which unspeakably surprised me because I could hardly believe that my mother, an officer, a major, who had been brought up in the ideology of communism and atheism, would do something like that. But I realized that everybody, whoever or whatever he or she is, first of all, remains an ordinary person with his or her fears, grief, and faith in a higher power.

For the whole next week, we celebrated my "second birth." All those days, my diary was full of pages of joy, excitement, and one and the same question: "How did Sensei do this? Why did my life change so sharply? Is it thanks to his presence in it? Who is he actually? And where do I know him from?" One question begat another series of other questions. But I left Moscow with a firm intention to find out everything, even if it took years.

28

At home, I first asked my friends about the next training. It turned out to be that evening. We agreed to meet at the same time on the tram stop. I barely had the patience to wait until the appointed hour and took all my medical discharges and films.

The gang greeted me with elation and a flow of news. When the long-awaited tram came up, they held me back.

"We have to take a different tram now," Tatyana said smiling.

"How come?"

"Surprise!" they yelled almost in unison.

"We have now moved to a different sports hall," Andrew explained with pride. "It's a lot better, a lot more comfortable, with mirrors. Besides, it is located almost twice as close."

"What news!" I was surprised.

All the way my friends told me about the many interesting things I missed when I was, as they thought, healing my stomach in a health center. Andrew, vying with Kostya, shared news about the trainings, about original cases in Sensei's regular demonstrations, and about his unusual philosophy, which he was telling them during spiritual trainings.

While Tatyana and Slava echoed the especially thrilling moments and supplemented them with their impressions. I was listening to them with attention and great regret that I hadn't become a witness to such interesting events. But, on the other hand, an entire life was now ahead of me.

Having reached the final stop, I saw a huge, modern building, the palace of culture, though the locals simply called it a club. There was a movie theater and many rooms for various hobby classes, and a good sports hall with mirrors on the wall.

"Great! Now we can practice the Monkey style in front of them as much as we want," I joked, examining my multiple reflections.

Sensei entered the hall together with the senior guys. He warmly greeted us, including me. Shaking his hand, I was looking into his eyes with admiration and one silent question, "How?" Not that I didn't believe, I simply knew that my cure happened due to Sensei, due to interference of higher powers, as the professor said, "divine providence." But how could he do it so quickly? Why did the disease disappear so quickly?

My soul was overflowing with feelings of gratitude. But I could express them only with my eyes because there were too many curious people around. When the guys went to the changing rooms, I gathered all my courage and asked Sensei to speak with me alone. He agreed willingly.

We walked into the vestibule, and I started showing him my medical records, telling him about the events in Moscow. I tried to express to him the feelings flowing over me, but my strong emotions caused me to speak only some incoherent mixture of grateful phrases.

Igor Mikhailovich quickly flipped through all the films with the professional movement of a doctor, and

having read the documents, genially asked, "Are you satisfied?"

"Very much! Even more than satisfied."

"That is the most important."

"I nevertheless don't understand, it seems as if this disease never even existed. But all these films, the confirmation of the doctors, the medical records," I uttered in confusion.

Sensei smiled and said, "You know, there is a Latin proverb, 'What doesn't exist in documents, doesn't exist in the world.'"

"No, I'm serious. I know for sure that you did this, but how? Why so quickly?"

"What do you mean?" grinned Sensei. "Did you think that one needs to open a skull, cut out a piece of brain, or get stuffed with pills just for you to really believe that you were cured by some kind of action?! Any action is begotten, first of all, by our formed thought... Have you ever heard about stigmata?"

"Somehow it sounds familiar..."

"Stigmata appear in people of deep faith. In minutes, bleeding wounds appear on the hands and feet. These wounds appear in exactly the same places that appeared on Jesus Christ when he was crucified on the cross. And literally in three days, these wounds disappear without leaving a trace. In some of the faithful, stigmata appear not only as wounds, but also as nails. These nails have been taken for analysis and proven to be not simply some wart of bone and meat, but real nails, made of the material typical for those times, in other words, made around two thousand years ago... Faith really creates miracles. And there is nothing impossible for believers, regardless in whom or in what they believe... And you say, why so quickly?"

"But I wouldn't say that I am a believer, an especially deeply faithful person, because I really believed

in..." Here I almost said, "in you," but I continued, "a higher power only when I heard the words of the professor in Moscow who confirmed that I'm absolutely healthy. In other words, when everything had already happened."

"Everything is a lot simpler. When a human can't deeply believe in his recovery, then there should be someone else to believe in him, someone who is more spiritually developed than he is. And then the result will surpass all expectations."

"Is it possible to overcome any disease?"

"Absolutely."

"What needs to be done for this?"

"Just simply and sincerely believe and think in the right way. But believe deeply, with love, with positive thought. Not something like, 'I want to be healed,' but from the position of an already healthy person who can create by asserting this positive thought, well, let's call it, 'the matrix of one hundred percent health.' This matrix is saved in our subconscious thanks to the power of our faith... And exactly due to this matrix, as a result of its healthy scheme, a body regenerates its functions on a physical level because it simply fulfils the order of the subconscious. Everything is simple."

"How can one cure another person by faith?"

"In the same way. It's just that this matrix, or rather it would be more rightly to call it a hologram, is transmitted by thought as a healthy image from one person to another..."

"Can everybody do this or only those who strongly believe?"

"Of course... I can tell you about a case that happened to our Volodya, but I will tell you just because you have already gone through this yourself. But don't tell it to anyone. If you want, you can quietly ask Volodya but so that no one will hear. His father was a fireman at the Chernobyl atomic power plant. Before that, his stomach ached, and they thought that it was gastritis. When he came back, he felt bad. The doctors unanimously diagnosed stomach cancer. Of course, he needed urgent surgery. Volodya came to me that evening and asked if it were possible to help somehow. I told him about this technique. He relaxed, removed all unnecessary thoughts, thanked God that a mistake had happened and that his father was completely healthy, and everything was fine with him. Volodya asked God to forgive his sins, the sins of his father, everything that he had done wrong. He repented and at the same time thanked God."

"Is a human really sinful before God?"

"Well, let's say it this way, in fact, a human is sinful only before himself, before his soul... The problem is that the factor of sin is placed in our subconscious from childhood. We are told that, regardless of the religion we belong to, all of us are guilty before God. But none of us is guilty before God! We are guilty just before ourselves. God, He does only good. We push ourselves into the dirt. That's why when we admit that we are animals stuck in the dirt and when we pray for forgiveness from God, we admit the fact of His existence, we admit His power, and, what's most important, we get tuned into love, to the positive. So, Volodya practiced this technique for a couple of days, going to bed, waking up, whenever he happened to have a free minute. He pronounced this prayer in the deepest faith, in great love for his father. As he confessed, he had never before experienced such an internal state, although Volodya had been practicing meditation for a long time. What's most amazing is that, in seven days following our conversation, I emphasize, on the seventh day, when his father was opened up during the surgery, there was no tumor, and they sewed him up and sent him home. The diagnosis wasn't confirmed, and it was considered to be a medical mistake. To this day, his father is alive and feels wonderful; he works just as hard as he did when he was young. This old man, for his entire life, believed in no one and relied only on himself, on his powers. This is an example from real life that deep faith can work wonders."

And being silent for a bit, Sensei added, "Faith: It's not just a word, it's a huge internal power generated by the human himself. In its union with the divine power of love, about which we spoke in the Lotus Flower, it gives birth to such a power that can really create impossible things. Although all these words - miracle, impossible - are just the words of people. Because the science of Shambala explains everything by the laws of nature, which at the present are not fully known to mankind. The power of faith and love, begotten by thought, is a power initially inherent to a human being. This is what distinguishes him from an ordinary biped.

"That's why, throughout history, all great teachers of mankind summoned people to faith and love, giving them this knowledge on their level of perception. Recall at least the words of Jesus, who said, 'If you have faith the size of a mustard seed, you will say to this mountain, "Move from here to there," and it will move; and nothing will be impossible for you.' These are not empty words; this is true knowledge for those who can listen: 'Those who hear will hear.'"

"Interesting. But if this huge power can be explained by natural laws, then it means, as far as I understand, there should be some kind of formula," I countered.

Sensei smiled and replied, "Undoubtedly, formulas do exist, but people are still not ready for this knowledge to be given to them in formulas because thoughts of the animal nature predominate in the majority of people. In reality, to prove that this power really exists means to discover the laws of the universe, to discover the reality of the existence of God. Even simple, blind human faith with limited impact is capable of doing a lot, while true faith opens up unlimited possibilities. It not only moves planets, but also creates, destroys, and rules many worlds with only a thought."

"Oho... With such power, one can probably restore health just by thinking about that!" I said in admiration, discovering for myself a completely new world of thought.

"Absolutely correct."

I recalled the miraculous healings performed by Jesus, and suddenly it dawned on me, "So it means that Jesus alone with His positive thoughts healed people! And before I thought that these were just fairy tales."

Sensei laughed, "Yes, yes, yes. That's why He said, 'You will receive from God according to your faith.' Jesus created with His power a hologram of health, while a man was holding it with the power of his blind faith. And the stronger man's faith was, the firmer it held this hologram in the man's subconscious."

I reflected a little and then asked, "And why shouldn't I tell anyone about this?"

"You see, telling other people, a human sows in himself a grain of doubt in his subconscious after hearing their answers and opinions, but doesn't even notice this. This negative power, gradually cultivated, begets in consciousness the logic of parasitic thoughts, which occur when a human, based on his little knowledge about the surrounding world, tries to formulate at least some kind of common sense, searching for an explanation in his scanty bag of knowledge. So-called common sense is the first enemy to a human, his faith, and his spiritual development, because it is an abundant field for the cultivation of doubts, negative thoughts, and negative emotions. God and common sense are two completely antagonistic notions. So, finally, these doubts, with their negative power of logic, win on the battlefield of the mind and destroy the blind faith together with its matrix of health. And then the disease comes back. If you are not strong in your spiritual knowledge, you need simply to believe, to thank God for this gift of health and not to speak to anyone about this cure. Only then will you have a chance to save this hologram of health, created by the power of love, for a very long time."

At that moment, Victor came out from the sports hall and, seeing Sensei, asked whether he could begin the training.

"Yes, of course," answered Sensei.

We hurried to join the group. Throughout all the exercises, I thought only about our conversation. I was amazed by this simple truth. It seemed like I had read about it before, but just read and had not deeply understood it. Sensei showed me a new kind of vision of these ideas that had existed for thousands of years.

At home, carried away by this subject, I dug through our entire family library and finally found a magazine with abstracts from the Bible about people Jesus had healed. I reread it now with completely different eyes, with completely different thoughts, from the point of view of those extraordinary events that had happened to me in such a short period of time. Gradually, a new world was opening to me, a world begotten by the mighty power of thought.

29

On the way to the spiritual training, I noticed that the vocabulary of my friends began to change. It now consisted more of good words, positive moments, and wise thoughts. They even decided to get rid of the bad words that they had often used in their expressions. They decided that if someone uttered something bad, he or she would buy a cheesecake or patties for everybody. I, having slipped a couple of times myself, decided to carefully watch over my speech and over all my thoughts.

A small but quite packed-down snowy pathway had been treaded to our secret glade. Volodya, Stas, Eugene, Sensei, and Nikolai Andreevich already stood in the glade. Having joined them, we heard the continuation of the conversation, which had been interrupted by our arrival.

"... but using hypnosis in our practice, we found out that it turns off consciousness and works simply with the subconscious," the psychotherapist said with enthusiasm. "And we made the conclusion that there is no concrete knowledge in the subconscious. It perceives everything as is: if we suggest to someone that he is a singer, and he has never sung in his life, he will sing. If we give him an onion and say that it is a sweet apple, he eats it with pleasure, not even making a wry face, and so forth. We even repeated a series of experiments performed by our colleagues from the capital regarding the inhibition of irritant reactions in cells of the cerebral brain cortex in the state of hypnosis. We placed an ampule with hot water (+65° C) into the hand of a man under hypnosis and rang a loud bell. There was no reaction in the vessels of the hand. The level of the plethysmogram didn't change. The man hypnotized not to respond to these irritants answered that he felt nothing, and this was obviously seen in his physical reaction. We also suggested somatic effects that are impossible for a person to cause by himself. For example, we said that a piece of ordinary paper was a mustard plaster. A corresponding redness appeared on the surface of his skin where we had applied the paper. In other words, a man in a state of hypnosis literally executed all our commands, beginning with a psychological image and ending with the reactions of the body."

"Absolutely correct," answered Sensei, "because hypnosis is a clear manifestation of the animal nature in the human, it is a liberation from intellect and a disconnection of the soul. Hypnosis is only a function of the subconscious. In hypnosis, a human becomes who he really is if he is completely overwhelmed by the animal nature, a zombie, an obedient piece of meat, or, as Omar Khayyam correctly remarked, 'a bag with bones, tendons, and bloody mucus.'"

"Who are zombies?" asked Tatyana.

"Zombies were what Afro-Caribbean tribes called people whose mind was oppressed by certain narcotic substances and who were programmed by special psychic influences. These people implicitly executed any order of the chief and could kill not only themselves, but their own mothers, their children. In short, a zombie is a body of a human whose soul has been taken out or disconnected and who has been deprived of intellect," answered Sensei. Addressing Nikolai Andreevich, he continued, "Hypnosis is the breaking in of the individual, it is aggression, it is slavery. And you will find no knowledge there except that of a dumb, obedient animal."

"I don't completely agree with you in regard to a dumb animal obedience," protested Nikolai Andreevich. "Because as far as I know, the "I" of the hypnotized person keeps control of reality all the time and can be restored at any moment. The hypnotizer can affect only something with which the patient subconsciously agrees. As it's written in medical research, the mechanism of resistance and protection is not completely turned off."

"If all this were so, as you say, in reality, then hypnosis wouldn't have been used so actively in the secret services of all of the developed countries of the world. Do you know that all the newest discoveries, technologies, and the best ways of fishing out the information and methods of control over the human mind are used, first of all, in the military interests of states and only a small, not a significant part, in peaceful goals?"

"Alright, well. But hypnosis can be used in medicine to cure some diseases. Will you deny this fact?"

"I will. What is disease? It is, first of all, a signal from the body about a possible serious disorder in its functions and tissues. Posthypnotic suggestion, left by the hypnotizer and later executed by the human mind as its own idea, simply eliminates this signal of pain but doesn't remove the cause of the disease. And a human, indeed, for some time won't feel the pain, deceiving himself with elusive hopes. While practically, he will make himself even worse because the disease will keep progressing and in the end will appear again in an even worse, neglected state. To be cured by hypnosis doesn't mean to be healthy. By such healing, even a light form of one disease can beget another disease, a more serious one."

"What about the patients who get into a habit when the medical effect shows itself? It has been proved many times that bad habits disappear and, on the contrary, good ones are formed, implemented, and the mind itself begins to work differently. Why? How can you explain it?" Nikolai Andreevich asked.

"Everything is very simple. The mind under hypnosis is, as a rule, in a state of the trusting listener. In other words, it looks at everything as an outsider, absolutely without any analysis. And if it's ordered in this state not to listen or to forget, or to change habits, it will execute all this precisely. And afterwards, it will perceive this order as its own idea. Our mind isn't perfect, very imperfect. The soul is perfect and its possibilities are unlimited. But the soul gets disconnected when a human is mesmerized because it evidently awakens the animal nature in the human. The soul, of course, loses and cannot then have an impact on the mind. That's why hypnosis is, in general, awful for people."

"What if a human is suggested to do good?"

"It doesn't matter," Sensei said simply.

"But the hypnosis response is unique in all people, simply of a different degree and in different forms."

"Of course, just like the presence of the spiritual and the animal nature is unique in all people, to different degrees," Sensei replied.

"But hypnosis has common features with other altered states of consciousness, such as dream or meditation. Hypnosis is also achieved by a reduction of the influx of signals into the brain; the subject concentrates on one sensor stimulus before it..." Nikolai Andreevich was cut off by Sensei.

"Yes, but you listed features that are peculiar to the beginning of any method of altering the state of consciousness. The main distinction of hypnosis is in this state itself, which is reflected on a physical level as well. I would call hypnosis a state of 'doubling of command'. Take a look at how it manifests itself on a physiological level. If it is compared with a dream or meditation, then the content of oxygen and carbon dioxide doesn't change as in those other states. Unlike the other altered states of consciousness, hypnosis isn't accompanied by a physical deviation from the state of wakefulness. Waves of the electroencephalogram - brain waves - most often remain the same, as in an alert person, and so forth. But these are only facts that our science can actually detect at this stage.

"Meditation, on the other hand, is a completely different altered state of consciousness. Even the term meditation, which comes from Latin, means reflection. Meditation is a state in which the highest degree of concentration of attention on a certain subject is achieved, or, conversely, the complete deconcentration of attention. In this state, the processes of perception and thinking are halted. It is a peculiar form of isolation of the human from the external world and a full concentration on the internal, spiritual world, the spiritual essence. It's natural that psychic immobilization on a physical level is associated with the temporary disconnection of the major integrative mechanisms of the brain. It facilitates the recovery of the nervous and psychic functions of a human, bringing a feeling of freshness, internal renovation, and joy of life. Hypnosis, on the other hand, brings about depression on the subconscious level, forming in this way the slavish psychology in the consciousness of a human.

"One more curious consideration in regard to meditation: the normal functioning of the sense organs during wakefulness creates in the central nervous system a high level of internal noise that impedes the flow of processes of integration and association. During meditation, this level of noise of the brain becomes extremely low. Consequently, a human gets an opportunity to use the associative and integrative processes for completion of certain tasks that he has formulated for himself. So, hypnosis and meditation are two completely different states of consciousness. Meditation is one of the ways of awakening the spiritual nature, while hypnosis, I emphasize, is just a function of the animal nature."

"But are we allowed to suggest a human self-confidence and self-reliance at least for psychotherapeutic goals?" Nikolai Andreevich just couldn't calm down.

"Hypnosis is a bad instrument for that, as it increases suggestibility, compliance to the will of other people. This is something unnatural to the essence of the human, to his true predestination in life. Because internally, on the subconscious level, he strives for true freedom, freedom of his soul. That is why people always strive for independence, for self-assertion in any form of external freedom.

"If you really want to help someone change, to believe in his own powers and potential, convince him with your word, your thoughts, and your argumentation. Because the power of words begets the power of thought, and the power of thought begets action. But hypnosis is not the answer, not with its open order into the consciousness of a human. Because you don't know what you do, because you are not aware of the true nature of hypnosis and those negative forces it awakens in a human."

Nikolai Andreevich stood still in thought. Meanwhile, the last guys arrived at the glade. Greeting them, Sensei said, "Alright, everyone is here. Perhaps we'll begin... Today, we will do the same meditation as last time, to purify thoughts. For those who were absent, I will repeat. So, stand more comfortably, legs as wide apart as shoulders. Hands should touch each other with the tips of the fingers at the level of the belly. Tip to tip, in other words, thumb to thumb, forefinger to forefinger, and so forth. Like that."

Sensei showed me this connection.

"It is necessary to relax by taking away all thoughts and to concentrate only on normal breathing. Then, when you have reached a state of full relaxation of all extremities and a feeling of internal peace, you begin to imagine that you are a jug. In other words, the top part of your head is as if cut off like in a jug. The source of water is the soul. This water fills the whole body and, in the end, overfills it, spilling over the edge of the jug, streaming down the body and into the earth. During the process, when it fills the body and flows out into the earth, all bad thoughts, all problems leave you with it; in other words, all that dirt and unease present in your mind. It is as if you are cleansing yourselves inside. And when you do it, then you begin to feel a clear division of soul and thought: the soul located inside of you and the soul located above the jug that observes the process. And finally, practicing this meditation every day, you cleanse your thoughts of the negative ones and further learn to control them, all the while keeping your mind in a clean state. Any questions?"

"Why should the hands touch exactly this way?" I asked.

"Because during this meditation certain energies circulate inside of the body. I will tell you more about them later. The tips of the fingers need to enclose this circle. Moreover, there is an irritation of the nervous skin receptors located on tips of fingers, which positively and calmingly affects the brain. Are there any more questions?"

Everybody remained silent.

"Then let's begin."

Under Sensei's guidance, we began to perform this meditation. I tried to imagine myself as a jug, but my imagination formed this image somehow half-way, because my mind just couldn't agree with this definition. I stopped trying to prove anything to myself and simply thought, "I am a jug," and concentrated on the internal source of water. An interesting feeling appeared, as if my consciousness went inside of me, went into my soul, and concentrated in the form of a point in the area of the solar plexus. That point began to widen gradually while crystal clear water spiralled in it. Finally, there was so much water that it boiled over, filling my entire body with its pleasant moisture. Filling the vessel this way, this pleasant feeling flew over the edge. A wave of small ants started to run over my body from top to bottom, as though going into the earth. I imagined that my body was cleansed of all bad thoughts. And in one moment, I felt so nice inside, so cozy, and so joyful that I couldn't resist and slightly deviated from the meditation, thanking God for all that He gave me in life, for all His love for His children. In the next moment, I suddenly found out that my consciousness, in other words, my real "I", was seemingly above my body. But my body didn't look like a body at all. From its jug-like head emanated thousands of thin, multicolored threads, which constantly moved and went into the earth. In the depth of the jug, something bright was shining, transforming these threads into more vivid colors. The beauty was of course simply charming. But then I heard the melodious voice of Sensei, reaching me from somewhere far, "And now take two deep, quick breaths in and out. Quickly close and open your fists. Open your eyes."

I quickly came to my senses, though the state of this internal euphoria stayed somewhere in the depth of my "I". As it later turned out, each one of the guys experienced this state differently. The senior guys did it better than I did, while my friends practiced it only in their bare imagination. Sensei told them that at first, it often happens this way with many people. But if they train intensively every day at home and if they have a desire to improve their moral qualities, then in a certain time they would experience new feelings and learn to permanently control their thoughts. The most important thing is to believe in themselves, in their powers, and not to be lazy.

When we were leaving the glade, I snatched a moment and quietly asked the Teacher, "The guys told me that when I was absent, you gave them new meditations. I probably missed out on a lot. What should I do now?"

Sensei, glancing at me very kindly, replied, "Believe me, the one who acts with good intention has no need to be upset about what he has missed because he acquires a lot greater power for cognition of his soul than when doing nothing."

At that time, of course, I did not understand what Sensei meant by that because everything that I did, I simply considered common everyday care. Nevertheless, these words sunk into my soul, and the very same evening a corresponding record appeared in my diary.

The days flew by in the twinkling of an eye. I liked this new meditation so much that I performed it with pleasure before going to bed though, just like all the previous ones, in turn, one by one. One day, I asked Sensei whether it's harmful to do them one after another in one evening. He replied that, quite on the contrary, it was very useful because then a human works more on himself spiritually, while the Lotus Flower also awakens the soul. "It's better to perform them in the evening before going to bed and in the morning when you wake up. These are the simplest meditations to work on the concentration of attention, the awakening of internal sight, and the control over thoughts. They are absolutely harmless; that's why everybody can learn them, even those who have never come across any spiritual practices. And at the same time, these meditations, being simple and clear, bring the most results."

30

At the training, I tried to catch up with the guys, doing all my best to study both the new and the old techniques. These days, everything interesting and cognitive was happening at the spiritual trainings. At one such training, Nikolai Andreevich began to argue with Sensei about reincarnation. It seemed to me that he wasn't really arguing but rather provoking the Teacher in order to start a conversation about it. I noticed that despite the fact that Nikolai Andreevich was a psychotherapist, zealous atheist, and the common sense of our company (as we jokingly nicknamed him), he didn't miss a single training and treated Sensei with delicate respect.

"Reincarnation is a fable invented by people, because most of them, I would say, have pathological thanatophobia. That's why they imagine different tales about reincarnation, about life after death."

"Not at all," objected Sensei. "Concerning a fear of death, it's begotten solely by the animal nature in a human being, by the instinct of self-preservation and the power of imagination, cultivated by egoistic negativism. Fear is just an emotion, switched on only where information is absent or where there is too little of it. The phenomenon of reincarnation really exists in nature. And you can't even imagine how long it has existed."

Sensei had begun to speak with Nikolai Andreevich in a familiar way recently, like a friend.

"No, if it were really so, we would remember something, some excerpts or something else."

"And do you remember what happened this very day a year ago?" Sensei asked.

Nikolai Andreevich reflected and uncertainly said, "I was probably at work, if it wasn't Sunday."

"So then you can't exactly remember this day?"

"No."

"Right. So why do you speak about another time, whether you had a previous life? We already examined, in regard to your hypnosis, that there is mind, and there is an animal nature and a soul. You are located in the soul, exactly you, the genuine you. The mind is that part of you which perceives. And it also has a particle of your "I". It means that you are divided: in your soul you feel yourself as one person, while you think completely differently. You should reflect on yourself, who you really are, how you think, how you speak, how you see. Not in the meaning of brain activity, verbal, nonverbal, excitation of acoustic fields: all that is rubbish. But exactly you! Look inside of your consciousness. It is endless. Think about that, how the universe is endless. And try to explain the fact that the universe is reflected in every atom of your body."

"Is the universe really reflected in every atom?" Nikolai Andreevich was surprised.

"Of course. If you doubt, read the corresponding literature on atomic structure and compare it with the organization of the universe. Even today, there is enough evidence to support the realization of this fact. Or take, for example, a vacuum. It's empty, it looks like there is nothing in it, at first glance. But life is born in it. What from? From emptiness? Think about these global questions seriously. But what's most important is to find out: Who are you? Then you'll understand that the body is only a carriage, which carries you from birth to death, first in one reincarnation, then in another. Where you arrive will depend on how you use this carriage. Either it will run by itself, or you will drive it.

"A human - that is, his soul - is just the coachman of this carriage. If your soul is asleep, the carriage will rumble in the same direction as others. The coachman will be riding in circles. But if the soul wakes up, he will ride in the right direction, the direction of spiritual development, in the one he himself chooses. But what's most important is for a human to understand that he is the driver of this carriage. Having realized that, he will be able to simply stop riding in circles and go to Nirvana. In other words, he will be like God."

All the guys carefully listened to Sensei, while I, having gathered enough courage, asked the Teacher my acute question, "Tell me, what is the sense of the existence of the soul, in other words, of myself?"

"The sense is simple: in the end, to arrive before God as a mature creature. A human is the synthesis of the spiritual and the animal nature. This synthesis is necessary so that the soul can obtain a certain form; it has to go through matter, in other words, to ripen. A human, like a butterfly, goes through the stages of development of his soul. Metaphorically speaking, at first, hatching from the egg, a human goes through the material stage of larva or 'animal human' when he crawls on Earth with mostly material interests, like a caterpillar. He doesn't see a soul in himself and considers himself to be one and the same with his matter, in other words, with his body.

"Then a certain time of realization passes, either in the course of several reincarnations, from one to another, or during one life - it is different for everyone - when his soul matures from good thoughts of spiritual love. Gradually, a human changes into a cocoon, into the stage of 'human human,' when he clearly realizes his true "I" (soul) and "cocoon" (body). Now the body is regarded just as a material for the ripening of his soul. Externally it may not be shown in any way, but internally, rapid, global changes take place in him.

"Finally, when the soul ripens, the cocoon bursts open and a glaringly beautiful, divine creature flies out of it, the butterfly or soul, which is free in its flight. Joining other beautiful creatures, it takes part in the creation of new souls, the creation of new larvae that will follow the same path. This is the stage of 'God human.'

"That's why the whole sense lies in the development from animal to divine, in order to become a full-fledged particle of God. This is implied in us primordially and deep inside. That's why we search for God; that's why we know about God."

Smiling, Nikolai Andreevich said, "And if I am an atheist and deny God?"

"Nobody denies God really, whoever that one is. Because everyone feels it in his soul. Everyone is scared in darkness, however courageous he is. Everyone thinks about eternity, about death, about the sense of his life and his existence. Many people just don't have enough information and turn on the protective functions of their mind and try to muffle these thoughts."

"Well I'm like that, I need real proof. If only I really could come across a case, at least in a memory, of past reincarnation, I would believe in it, making sure of myself."

Sensei thought for a little and answered, "Alright, I will grant you such an opportunity. After training, I will tell you about one interesting technique of altering the state of consciousness, which will let you awaken a human soul and evoke a conversation with it. But I'm warning you, nobody else should know about this technique, because society is still in the stage of 'animal human.' People will receive this knowledge in the future, when the majority of them will change to the stage 'human human.' You can do it with any of your patients, do everything exactly as I tell you. But, jumping ahead, I'm warning you right now that in reincarnations, the notion of time is absent. In other words, one man, for example, lived two hundred years ago, and was reborn only now. Another died a year ago and was born in a minute, and a third one maybe lived in the distant, distant future, and was born in our time, and so forth. In other words, there are certain laws there, so don't be surprised too much. Alright?"

"Of course!" Nikolai Andreevich uttered with admiration.

Suddenly Stas, who had kept silent before, thoughtfully asked, "Concerning reincarnation, do people in Shambala also undergo it, or do they exist eternally?"

"If you mean the life of the Bodhisattvas in Shambala, they exist under completely different laws. And they don't have such bodily, rough matter as people. Shambala is a completely different side of reality. Well, for you to understand it better, their bodies are subtle matter, which exists under its own laws in time and space. And if in the human world the mind serves the body, at home - I mean in Shambala" the Teacher quickly corrected himself, "the body serves the mind. Why can't Shambala be found? Because it exists at a completely different frequency level of perception."

"So, a human cannot get there in his body?" Andrew asked with surprise.

"Why? He can if he knows and is able to transform his body to that frequency of the perception of reality."

"It sounds like a fantasy," Kostya sniffed quietly.

"For today's human perception, maybe. But it's a fact. If people believe that this is science fiction, let them... But a human cannot make up anything on his own because all this knowledge was, is, and will be in spite of his desires. His capabilities of perception are limited only by his egocentrism. In general, science fiction is only an unrealized reality."

"How do higher creatures come into this world? You said that they, if needed, can get into contact with people."

"Simply, through reincarnation. Their soul enters the body of an infant on the eighth day, in other words, just like all people are born."

"I wonder," remarked Nikolai Andreevich, "What made you think that the soul enters a human on the eighth day of life? In the Christian religion, for example, it is believed that the soul enters him while still in his mother's womb."

"It's a wrong opinion. Evidently, someone understood something incorrectly and another one incorrectly translated it. A third one added his own thoughts coming from his logic; in this way, the real knowledge was lost. In reality, the soul enters the human body on the eighth day. It can even be materially traced. A soul, though being an energy substance, enters the body, acquires a quality of subtle matter. That's why the weight of a newborn baby sharply increases on the eighth day from three to twenty grams, and sometimes, in exceptional cases, up to fifty grams. This can be traced if one exactly measures the weight of an infant starting from the seventh day, taking into account the nutrients he ingests and expels. In other words, on the eighth day, there occurs a sharp increase in the weight of a newborn baby. Moreover, exactly on the eighth day, the gaze of a child becomes alive, luminous. It is impossible not to notice that."

"How do Bodhisattvas differ then from ordinary people?" Kostya asked with interest.

"They don't. They are consciously reborn into the matter of the human in order to experience all the severities, hardships, and also the temptations of the world. During their human lives they make their contribution, which they should do. Sometimes they come to Earth with a certain goal, to realize a decision made in Shambala, but most often as observers. Bodhisattvas live as common people, quietly and modestly performing their work, though inside, this human is quite aware that he is a Bodhisattva. But he will never yell this and drum on his chest. As a rule, no one around knows this. This could be anybody: your close friend, your acquaintance, relative, and so forth."

"Why do they come as observers?" asked Victor.

"Yes, why?" I thought. "Our world probably seems like a dirty and egoistic place to these higher creatures."

"Well, they have such a rule or, to be more precise, a responsibility. Each one of the Bodhisattvas of Shambala should, at least once in a thousand years, reincarnate into this world. What for? In order to live a human life, to see how and what mankind thinks about, at what level people should be given knowledge. In other words, to know the human nature because in Shambala the animal nature is absent in individuals. In Shambala, there is a completely different reality. So, for a Bodhisattva who lives there, to understand what is going on here, he is thrown out into this world so that he won't forget, so to say, won't relax too much. Even Rigden Jappo cannot avoid this rule, this fate. However, he comes, as a rule, to this world before the beginning of global changes in the course of human civilization, approximately once every ten or twelve thousand years, not as a Messiah, but as a judge. He checks the work of his forerunners, assessing the level of human perception, the degree of their spirituality or absorption by matter. Depending on that, Shambala then returns a verdict, to be or not to be, for mankind."

"What do you mean?"

"Well, if mankind in its majority is evaluated as a spiritually progressing society, then it is preserved. While if more of the beast, in other words, the material nature, predominates in it, then the same story of global cataclysms that affected previous civilizations is repeated. Less than one-tenth of the total people are left for the breeding of matter for the souls of the next civilizations. Mankind chooses the path for itself, while the actions of Shambala are just the consequences of that choice."

"As I understood it," Victor joined the conversation, "their main predestination is the spiritual development of humankind."

"Almost right," answered Sensei. "Their main predestination given from Heaven, in other words, from the Cosmic Hierarchy or God, call it as you wish, is the cultivation of the human soul during all cycles of its reincarnation. They actively help develop it when the spiritual nature awakens in a human."

"I bet this egoistic world seems horrible, from the point of view of their spirituality," I spoke my thoughts aloud.

Sensei grinned and continued, "Right, it's not quite a gift. This reincarnation is similar to if a butterfly were stuffed into a caterpillar - that is inconvenient for both the butterfly and the caterpillar. But these are the rules. Each Bodhisattva should serve his time here, live an entire life. Any Bodhisattva is free to go to Nirvana any minute, though; it is a big temptation for them."

"You once said that a Bodhisattva is a human who left Nirvana for the sake of humankind."

"Certainly. That's why this is a double temptation for him, because he felt this state of peak of unearthly happiness. You simply can't imagine yourselves, what kind of a... feat it is to leave Nirvana and to come here. Metaphorically speaking, Bodhisattvas can be compared with those who are the best of the best volunteers that were sent to do the most crucial work. Bodhisattvas stay here for the sake of people, for the sake of the cultivation of human souls so that these souls can develop and become free, really free. Because our internal nature, our soul, strives for this every moment of life."

Sensei glanced at his watch and said, "Alright guys, it's time to start a meditation. Otherwise, we could continue debating until morning."

I also looked at my watch. Time flew by in this conversation as if it were just one second. There was a strange feeling too, as if time were completely absent, as if it were the moment of eternity, slightly opening the curtain of its mysteries.

We performed the same meditation as last time, cleansing our intentions. I already started to feel more clearly the water streaming over edge of the jug, with some kind of wavy movement. After the training, the Teacher reminded us that we should permanently learn to control our thoughts and fish out negative parasites of consciousness. He also emphasized that we shouldn't give in to our aggression, if it appears. And the most important thing, we should constantly cultivate in ourselves divine love by performing the Lotus Flower. Nikolai Andreevich remained in the glade while we said good-bye and went home.

31

I was so amazed by this knowledge that Sensei was so simply and lucidly telling us that I wrote down this whole conversation into my diary, marking out for myself the most important moments: "The sense of human existence is the perfection of the soul!!!" I felt this but wasn't sure. Now, once again I thought that this was changing everything that I had known up to now and that I considered so valuable and important in life. I looked around and thought: "We really live life entirely for the body. Even at home, whatever you look at, everything exists for the service and satisfaction of the needs of the body. Books are probably the only exception. Of course, Sensei said once that all these attributes of civilization are necessary for us to have more time for the perfection of our souls. But how much among all this unnecessary stuff is completely redundant! And still for us it isn't enough. We still want more. What for? Why? After all, tomorrow we could die and in that other world they will value what we have cultivated inside us and not how much dust we've gathered by the tireless work of our shell, half rotten in the earth."

I went on to revalue everything, even at school. The girls, as usual, showed off what fashionable rags were bought for them and with evident envy told about what they saw on others. Listening to them, I was surprised with myself, because before I was just the same. I was chasing some kind of illusive fashion that didn't completely suit me. But my megalomania was increasing, as at that time I had an opportunity to stand out from the crowd. In reality, though, fashions are only those things that nicely suit a person. Once fashionable clothes, after a momentary presentation, are now hanging as dead weight in my closet. Why does one human need so much stuff? What do I need it for? Maybe somewhere people don't have anything to wear. In my own class, for example, there are three girls from poor families. Two of them didn't have fathers because they had died in the mines. And the third one's father was a drunkard, which is even worse. Why can't I share all this stuff with them? They need it more than me.

I asked the advice of my mother, although I lied to her a bit, telling her that our school had organized a charity action. But my mother wasn't against it. We even found shoes for the girls. I gathered all this and then had to solve another problem: how can it be given to them? Putting myself in their place, I considered that the best variant would be to ask my class teacher to pass the clothes to them as if from some charitable organization. I suppose that she liked this idea, because in a week the whole school, under the initiative of our teacher, announced a charitable action to benefit children from the city orphanage. Having heard this news, I recalled once again Sensei's words that one kind thought and one kind deed give birth to a chain reaction of kind thoughts and kind deeds. I thought that if everyone could understand this and did whatever good deeds he could, then perhaps poverty and hunger would disappear in the world. Otherwise, it's somehow shameful to be called civilized when nearby somebody is starving or extremely needy.

With such thoughts of universal love, brotherhood, and mutual aid, my body was embraced by some kind of stirring quiver. A feeling of light, pleasant pressure began spreading in the area of my solar plexus. Reaching a certain size, it started to radiate waves, which brought consciousness to an even bigger excitement, to an increasing feeling of endless love to the whole world.

32

At the next additional training, we learned the new kata with interest and diligence. The "speedy guys" never ceased to impress us with their mastery. With captivating beauty and thunder-like speed, they sparred with each other. Andrew, observing their movements, complained to the Teacher, "How do they move so quickly? It seems like we do same kata, but no matter how hard I try, I still fall behind. They move practically twice as fast as I. Why?"

"It has to do with balance. This is the trick," answered Sensei.

"But I keep balance as I was taught earlier with my first steps in karate. In my opinion, I follow all the rules; the center of gravity is distributed as it should be. But it doesn't work like with them."

"Because you move the center of gravity while they follow the center of gravity."

"How is that?" Andrew was surprised.

"Well. In 'hara,' or as it's also known, the point of Dan-Tian, which is located three fingers lower than the navel, is the center of gravity. Remember, one time I told you about this. Everybody is taught to rightly hold it, to step, to move, and so forth. You were told that, for example, a standing man doesn't fall down until his plumbing line from the center of gravity is located inside a platform limited by the edges of his feet. Walking is a series of falls forward, prevented by timely moving of the supporting leg. Running is a series of jumps from one leg to another with a corresponding shift of weight of the body and the center of gravity. Right? Right... In other words, everyone is teaching the general rules of moving the center of gravity. But that is why they lose in speed. Because in order to increase speed and to teach the body to move, one needs to learn, first of all, to move the center of gravity."

"Can I learn it, or am I hopeless?" Andrew asked with a smile.

"Only the fools and the lazy fellows are hopeless," Sensei replied with irony. "Otherwise, everybody can learn it. There is an elementary technique to shift your center of gravity. In other words, it's almost the same as dynamic meditation. At first, you learn the breathing technique. In any arbitrary movements, when your hands move away from you, inhale. When your hands come towards you, exhale; step forward, inhale; step back, exhale. You exhale into the bottom of the belly, into the 'hara,' which is similar to how we exhaled through our hands in meditation. In other words, during the exhale, concentrate your attention and completely concentrate on this point of the belly, as if slightly straining it exactly in the area of 'hara.' In the end, you begin to control your derived breathing in this way. And the most important thing is to feel this place, to feel in particular your center of gravity."

"What kind of movements does one need to perform? Is there any sequence?"

"Any, whatever you want, it doesn't matter. If you want, warm up or polish kata, or simply walk in circles, or make bows, it doesn't matter. The important work is done by your thought and concentration. This is the first phase: to find your exact center of gravity and to feel it during movement.

"The second phase is aimed at increasing the point of gravity concentrated in the 'hara.' In other words, you mentally send Qi to it. At this point, due to the concentration of energy of air, it spreads and becomes round and dense. And now it turns into a small ball, in the shape of whatever you like or imagine. The important thing is that you almost feel it physically, as if something is there, for example, a big, round ball.

"And the third phase is the most important. With the power of your will, you move this center of gravity, and everything follows it. Wherever you are and whatever you do, you constantly perform this dynamic meditation."

"Just like the Lotus Flower?" Andrew asked.

"Absolutely right. Just like that. Besides, to practice one meditation doesn't mean to neglect another. No matter how you move, wherever you go, first, you should move not the body, but your center of gravity with your mind. Later, the body should learn to keep up with it. That is all. Everything is simple."

Andrew reflected and started to move with his breathing.

"Look here," Sensei drew his attention, "that's how you move usually. You first bring forward the shoulder, the leg, the head, and so forth. In other words, at first you bring forward a part of the body before the center of gravity. And now look at the guys. See, they start all movements exactly from the point of 'hara,' the bottom of the belly first goes forward, while later the body follows it, no matter how they move around, quickly or slowly."

"Aha, now it's clear," Kostya caught up, carefully listening to the Teacher with us. "We couldn't understand why your unusual walk differs so much from other people's."

Sensei shrugged his shoulders and said with a smile, "It's a habit."

Our first attempts ended with loud laughter because everyone tried to learn everything at once. But all that we were able to do was to walk like penguins. That's why Sensei remarked, "Guys, I told you, you at first need to learn to breathe, to feel you center of gravity and later to move it."

"But how do they accelerate their movements?" asked Andrew, nodding towards the speedy guys. "Do we need to do something special?"

"Actually, no. You can accelerate just with the exhale, in other words, with the power of your thought pushing forward the center of gravity. You move your hand just by thinking about it. It is the same: you should freely move your center of gravity by mentally sending it an order. And when you learn to move your center of gravity at the speed of thought, you will be able to move as quickly as your physical condition will permit. You'll only need to have time for your body to catch up with your center of gravity."

"Great!" pronounced Andrew. "Any sprinter competition can be won in this way."

"That's for sure. If this technique were known to sportsmen, they would win the gold at world championships," Sensei answered half in jest.

"Don't any of them know about this?"

"Unfortunately, not."

"I have never heard about this and never even read about this," Kostya confessed honestly, to our surprise. "Why not?"

"Well, this is a very ancient technique for the development of human abilities and is the secret knowledge of superiors of ancient monasteries. They don't tell even their disciples about it and save it for their own use as a peculiar, secret technique. Though, in reality, there is nothing special about it. It's not even the art. It's an ordinary technique easily learned by anybody, although it is more effective among others."

The entire way home, our company was very proud. We were so happy to find out the secrets known only to masters of ancient monasteries. It was much more than we could have hoped to have learned. I was amazed once again by Sensei's knowledge of ancient techniques. When guessing who he is, I wrote down in my diary that Sensei was probably a talented orientalist, or he knew those regions very well, or he grew up there. Otherwise, how did he receive this knowledge? Mystery gave rise to yet another mystery. Sensei undoubtedly knew a lot, starting with philosophy and finishing with exact sciences. And all that was on a foundation of some kind of unknown science of the fundamental knowledge about human beings, starting with the micro-universe of the endlessly dividing atom and finishing with the invisible soul, or rather with the mystery of its creation. "Who is he?!" I asked myself once again.

33

The next day, I received quite unpleasant news. My mother again fell ill with a sharp, horrible pain in her back. Lately she was greatly nervous because she, as a good specialist, was simply overloaded with work. Moreover, she had to finish the work that had piled up during her absence and they had regular inspections at her workplace. In general, due to sitting for a long time, her back and nerves couldn't endure such an overload. That day she got up from bed with great difficulty, with horrible, unbearable pain in her waist.

This was, of course, a shock for us. We worried horribly. Each of us tried to help her in his own way. My father started to call all our relatives and consulted about other methods of treatment because my mother didn't want to undergo surgery. Most likely, she was scared not by the surgery itself, but by the consequences that she had seen and heard from many people while in the neurology ward. My mother didn't at all like the prospect of becoming disabled for her entire life. But the pain became so strong that she agreed to do anything.

Meanwhile, my father called his direct commander, the general, to obtain leave for the following day. My father was saying that this general was a good man.

He, with fatherly concern, took care of and worried about all his subordinates and always helped them and their families as much as he could. This time, he didn't betray his principals and didn't ditch his deputy officer. The general, having listened to father, advised him to visit a good chiropractor, giving him the corresponding address. Then he asked my father to calm mother down because he had had a similar story when he pulled a muscle in his leg. He received treatment from this chiropractor and was able to move, and after two years, everything was still all right.

After that call, my mum and dad unanimously decided to drive there the next day. I, honestly speaking, was doubtful. In my mind, I simply couldn't grasp how my mother could be treated just with bare hands if even injections and pills didn't help her. I decided to treat my mother in my own way, as Sensei had said. He told us that any man can make a matrix of health with the power of his deep, internal love, if he believes in it very much.

Before going to bed, after all my meditations, I concentrated on an image of health for my mother. I imagined her completely healthy, happy, cheerful, with her beautiful, sweet smile and kind eyes. I silently asked forgiveness from God for all my sins, if I had such in His opinion. I sincerely asked Him to help her, because I greatly love my mother. I was asking so strongly that I shed tears. I wanted so much for mother to recover quickly that after this peculiar meditation, I ran to my parents' room to see if maybe something had already changed.

My father was working on some papers at his writing table while my mother was already sleeping. Her face was slightly frowning. Her back was probably hurting her, even in her dreams. I came back to my room and thought, "Maybe my power alone is not enough. Of course, I will continue doing this technique to create a matrix of health, but it would be great if Sensei would join this. Then success is guaranteed. He has such spiritual power, such solid internal faith, and such knowledge that can do anything, if he was able to save me from death just with his power of thought. I will need to speak with him at the next training. He is kind; he will help." With these good thoughts, I fell asleep.

The next day I went to the chiropractor with my mother. The general cared for us and provided us with his black Volga car and personal driver, who knew that place and the roads well. On the way, I imagined how this decrepit (in my imagination) old man, the chiropractor, having looked at mother, would tell her that everything is well with her, that this is a mistake, and she is healthy. Meanwhile I noticed that the driver turned towards the district where we went for spiritual meditations. "Familiar places," I grinned to myself. "It's strange that such a remote district is so famous for its people." And again I concentrated on a desirable result.

We arrived at a private sector. I noticed from afar the house where evidently the chiropractor lived. Or rather, I did not notice the house itself, but rather a huge crowd of people who stood near a small but tidy house. There were a lot of people there. The driver could barely park his car among the multitude of other cars, drawing his professional attention to the many license plates that were not just from different regions, but even from different republics. It so surprised me that this god-forsaken place was so famous.

People stood in line as if a thick wall. It didn't even help us that we came in a black Volga. No matter how we tried to break through the crowd, we weren't able to. We had to stand in line like everybody else. My mother, meanwhile, was half-lying in the car. Our number was four hundred seventy-three. But when people found out that my mother had a sharp pain, we were told that the chiropractor takes those with such pain without waiting in line, and that we need to stand in a different line, which was ahead. We hurried to join the out-of-turn people, and there were only fifty of them. My mother was even given a place on the bench by those who at least could stand on their legs. And we began waiting.

I was very surprised by such a large number of people and even got a little flustered. People in line were of different ages, from seniors to young people with children. Ahead there stood a woman with a tiny baby. They said he was only five days old and already had plexitis. His hand didn't rise due to some kind of pathology of delivery. In general, the public gathered here had various illnesses of the spinal cord that I'd never even heard of before.

A senior lady sitting next to my mother said that the chiropractor takes twenty women, twenty men, and later ten out-of-turn people. The line, she said, wasn't very long; according to her estimations, we would be taken in only two hours. I thought that in this case I had time to concentrate on my healing meditation for mother. For around ten minutes, I tried to do it. But concentrating wasn't easy because the crowd was silently buzzing in unceasing conversation, creating an obstructive noise. Unwillingly, I began listening to the conversations.

"We had such misfortune, such grief," lamented an old woman standing next to a girl around fifteen years old. "It is horrible even to recall. There is nothing more bitter in the world than to have a sick child. My grandchild had a horrible kyphoscoliosis, a real hump. The doctors prophesized that she would be disabled for her entire life. The girl came back from school in tears every day. Though she had a beautiful face, her classmates teased her, calling her a freak. And we went everywhere, showed her to all doctors, and even took her to psychics, but it was all in vain. We were all in despair. One time we just barely managed, God help us, to pull the girl out of a noose. She was crying about her life, that nobody would ever fall in love with her. She was crying, we were crying, such grief, in a word, can't even tell it..."

The woman's voice trembled and she furtively wiped a rolling tear.

"Don't cry, grandma," pleaded her granddaughter. "Everything is already over."

"Yes... So, I went that... day to the church, prayed to God. And the next morning, I received a fresh newspaper and there was an article about our chiropractor. We, of course, at first doubted whether we should go and entrust our child to just another doctor, because she had already been examined by many specialists. But... all these last events... At the end we decided that if God gives us one more chance, we shouldn't refuse, because it can't get any worse...

"We worried when came to the reception. But the people in line spoke well of him. And when we entered and I saw his eyes, all doubts dissolved for some reason. He has such luminous, blue eyes, such a peace-giving gaze that even a light shone in my heart..."

"Yes," said another woman. "His eyes are really somehow unusual, so bottomless. As if they know everything, as if he feels your pain."

"I have also never seen in my life such calm and smart eyes," pronounced a young woman standing next to her.

The women nodded their heads, agreeing with the opinions.

"And what a pleasant, melodic voice he has, a calm manner of speaking. He speaks so politely with everybody..."

"After speaking with him, my mood always gets better. After all these endured pains, even I want to live."

"I too have such a feeling."

"That's what it means to be a good man."

Listening to these words, I halted all my fruitless attempts to concentrate and began carefully listening to the conversation.

"That's what I'm saying," pronounced the old woman. "Something in him was quite unusual, hope-giving. He looked at the girl and said that he will fix her back, but we will have to come here and perform all his recommendations at home. You can't imagine how his vivifying words affected the girl. We came for treatment a lot, for almost a year, even though we live in another region. Sometimes there was foul weather and it was hard to come, but Anna always insisted on the trip. She became so purposeful that we just rejoiced and crossed ourselves. Every day at home she diligently performed the entire complex of curative gymnastics recommended by the chiropractor. And in a year, there wasn't a trace left of her hump! You can't imagine how happy we were. Anna blossomed; so many fiancés appeared right away; now they are running after her in crowds... Now we have come for a check-up. Oh! We pray God to give him great health. His golden hands simply created a miracle!"

"Yes, his hands are really golden," confirmed another woman around forty years old. "He is a professional in the full sense of the word. Rarely can you find such a specialist who possesses a talent from God and such fine knowledge of medicine... I, for example, suffered from headaches for ten years. I passed through a lot of hospitals with no result: sleepless nights and even loss of consciousness because of the headaches. And two years ago, I'm even afraid to recall those days, I couldn't walk. You wouldn't wish this experience on your enemy, this state of confusion and helplessness, and such a strong pain in the waist, in the legs. Again sleepless nights, injections with no result. There were even horrible minutes of despair from pain and suffering. Even though by nature I am a courageous woman and always was a leader, suddenly my entire life stopped, everything froze, I felt only pain and suffering.

"The doctors of course, insisted on surgery and were convinced that nothing but surgical intervention would help. But they couldn't guarantee a full recovery. To put it briefly: disability for life. And then my mother came to me and began telling me about our chiropractor, persuading me to go to visit him. I consulted with my doctors, but they just laughed in my face and said that nobody in the world, even among prominent doctors, could cure a herniated disk or neck in a nonsurgical way. They said, go if you want, but you are going to come back to us. But my mother insisted.

"When I was brought here, I didn't have hope after the doctors' verdict. However, surprisingly, after the first seven visits, I started to move one toe and the pain was relieved a little. That's when I really began to believe in recovery, though the chiropractor even on the very first day said, 'It's hard and long, but we will fix it.' With each day I started to notice small but stable changes for the better. Slowly I began moving without assistance and dressing myself. So, in half a year I returned to a normal human life, and now I'm finishing up treatment. I can't believe that my horror is over and everything turned out so fortunately. To cure such a serious and terrible disease without surgery is really a miracle!

"When I returned to a normal life, I came to my city and went to show the result to my doctors, who hadn't believed in the chiropractor. They only shrugged their shoulders. Can you imagine, none of them even asked about how I achieved such results even though all of them once yelled that it would be impossible. Here is this knowledge, just introduce it into medicine. It may help so many people! But no, their pride doesn't let it... I will be grateful to Igor Mikhailovich to the end of my days for everything that he did with his golden hands! How many people did he put on their feet? When I came here, I saw a lot. People came here with their last hope for recovery. Even those doctors and professors bring their kids and grandchildren here."

I flinched at the mention of the name of the chiropractor. "Is it really... No way, it can't be!" I thought, getting lost in guesses. Everything inside of me strained and turned into a listening ear. Then the line buzzed in a new wave.

"Yes, he is a man with a big soul!" said another woman. "People say that his great-grandfather also was a famous chiropractor in the Orlovsk region. They say that he was a man with a gift from God and diagnosed disease unmistakably."

"Our doctor is also very strong, he looks as if with X-ray. I had a dislocation of the disk and he said right away, 'six millimeters.' And later I had films taken, and really, everything coincided."

"It is because his hands are especially sensitive. I read in the newspaper that he can find a child's hair, akin to a human nerve, hidden under forty pages of paper. Journalists conducted this experiment. 'This is the same' he said, 'as finding the exact place of the strangulated nerve and releasing it by manipulations of the hands.'"

"Thank God there is such a man. Thanks that He led us to him," the old woman, who was talking about her granddaughter Anna, crossed herself.

"You know, last year, I had osteochondrosis that he treated," an old woman with white-grey hair said. "This year, I lifted a heavy weight and again disrupted my back. It was so painful that I could not sleep for two nights. I had a gnawing pain and fainted because of it, as I completely ran out of power. And our chiropractor came up to me in a dream, touched me on the head, and said, 'Don't be afraid; now you'll feel better and tomorrow come to me. Everything will be all right.' So, what do you think, I stood up in the morning completely different, even the pain slightly let go. Now, I have visited for a third time, and I feel completely revived. Otherwise, I just couldn't find a place for myself... But what's strange is that in the dream he had hair down to his shoulders, as an angel, and his eyes were so kind..."

"Yes, he has an unusual hair color, such a blond color is so rare."

"What would we do without him? Really, probably, God sent us an angel."

After these words, the very decrepit old woman who, up to this moment, had been dozing on the edge of a bench, unexpectedly squeaked, "Not an angel but an archangel."

She again submerged into her drowsiness. This unspeakably surprised the whole crowd.

Finally some miner, judging by the black edging around his eyes, said, "I don't know what kind of angel or archangel he is, but he is a great man! He put me back on my legs, though I don't believe in God."

"I also didn't believe," remarked a tough old man. "Thirty years I had the Communist Party membership card, and now look..." He pulled out a cross on a string and showed it to the crowd. "I have this cross. All this happened after one case. I will never forget it... That memorable day, I had to go to the shift. While the night before this I had seen our Igor Mikhailovich in my dream who said, 'Tomorrow come to visit me, don't go to work. If you go, you won't come back.' Well, before that, I was receiving treatment from him, but then I had a break in treatment. I woke up in the morning and my back was hurting. Well, I thought, it probably ached at night; that's why I dreamt of him. I got ready to go to work, and then I thought, why should I go? I will need to lift heavy weights. How can I do it? My back will collapse. Well, I decided to go to the chiropractor and obtained a leave permit. Can you imagine, that day there was an explosion in the blast furnace and almost my entire brigade perished. If I had been there, because I stand next to the blast furnace hearth, I wouldn't be here now. So, how can all this be understood by a common mortal? I wanted to talk about this with Igor Mikhailovich, but he put his finger to his lips, hinting at me to keep silent. And that's all... How can I not start believing in God after this?"

"Oh, you know, a similar incident happened to our neighbor," said a woman around thirty years old who had joined the conversation. "He, by the way, gave me the address of the chiropractor. He was receiving treatment one day. And last year, our neighbor got into a trouble. Remember, if you are local, that explosion at the mine? He was buried under the support. As he told me, 'I was lying alone in the darkness, buried by rock. I was terribly afraid of being buried alive. I had already bid farewell to life, to all my relatives. Suddenly I saw before my eyes, as if from the fog, the figure of our chiropractor, who said so calmly with his melodious voice, "Don't be afraid, don't be afraid. It's too early for you to die. I will stay with you, until you are saved..."'

And when he came back to consciousness, he said he was already being pulled up by rescuers. He alone survived out of the entire crew. After that case, the man completely changed. He stopped drinking, started to believe in God. His wife and kids can't stop rejoicing. He became a really nice guy!"

Meanwhile, the line moved ahead. In front of the crowd someone came out in a white smock. I was so surprised that my bag almost slipped out of my hands.

"Sensei," I silently whispered, but in the next instant yelled at top of my voice, "Sens...oops, Igor Mikhailovich!!!"

Sensei turned around and, on seeing me, gave a sign to come up. I barely squeezed through the crowd. My heart was beating fast in my chest. Having greeted me, he asked, "Why are you here? What happened?"

"Well, my mother has problems with her back..."

We moved off to a corner, where Igor Mikhailovich lit a cigarette.

"My father's general gave us this address," I let out all the 'state secrets' in a single breath. "He even gave us his Volga."

Sensei glanced at the cars.

"Ah, Alexander Vasilievich. How's he doing?"

"Well, as he said to my dad, he has had no problems with motion for two years."

"Alright. And what happened to your mother?"

I began telling everything in detail, actively gesticulating with my hands from excitement. Having listened to me, Sensei pronounced, "Alright, take your mum and follow me."

I ran up to my mum with joy and said that Igor Mikhailovich will take us out of order. My mother was happy, of course, but she was very surprised. She got up with difficulty, and we returned with her to the chiropractor.

"This is my Sensei, Igor Mikhailovich," I introduced him to my mother with indescribable pride.

We walked deep into the house, filled with people waiting. In the waiting room stood a trestle-bed, and in the corner there was a small icon with a lit lamp. I helped mother undress to the waist and lie down on the trestle-bed. Walking out of the room, I saw how Igor Mikhailovich inclined above mother's back, palpating her vertebrae with his hands. Already behind the curtain in the neighboring room, I heard Sensei's voice, "Yes, you know, here is a serious problem, a dorsolateral prolapse up to seven millimeters in segment L4-L5 that's causing stenosis of the intervertebral foramen. As a consequence, it leads to a compression of the spinal root."

"Can you explain it more simply?"

"Simply saying, it's a disk herniation. As a result of the destruction of the disk, its sequestrum, in other words, small pieces of this disk, dropped into the spinal canal towards the spinal foramen and are pushing on the spinal root. That's what caused these pains... This, of course, is a serious problem, but curable."

Behind the thick curtain, I heard a light crackling of vertebrae and a few unusual claps. In a few minutes, Sensei called me so that I could help my mother get dressed. Having agreed on the next visit, we bid farewell and slowly walked towards the car.

"How are you?" I asked my mother.

"It's all right," she replied.

When we were driving home, the entire way I couldn't calm down, thinking about Sensei. I considered him everything: physicist, chemist, philosopher, historian, orientalist, physiologist. But an ordinary chiropractor, that was too much! Well, not ordinary, but pretty famous... And still, with his inconceivable potential of knowledge, with his phenomenal abilities and, in the end, with such unusually pure human morals, he could become a prominent scientist, politician, or whoever, moving up the ranks of society with his level of knowledge. But what is he spending his potential on?! If it weren't for how he helped my mother, my mind would have kept rebelling longer.

Driving out of this god-forsaken place by back roads, we drove past a shabby, half tumbledown church, evidently built before the revolution. My thoughts switched to thinking about the eternal, about God, about faith, about the Great. And suddenly a thought flashed across my mind, "Sensei really helps people! With his hands he cures thousands of bodies tormented by pain, thousands of souls seized by sorrow, restoring people's health, faith, and joy of life... God, that's how all the Great acted! Each of them went to people with an open soul and performed good deeds. Sensei one time mentioned about... Can it be that he...? Oho!"

I feverishly began remembering all the moments, supporting my guesses. After coming back home, I reread in my diary everything concerning Sensei's personality. Yes, the fact that he is a chiropractor supplemented the main missing link in my logical chain in proving it to my own mind. "It is most important that he cures the bodies and souls of different people. Consequently, speaking with such a huge number of people, each of them with his concrete destiny, problem, and pain, he knows much better than all politicians the intentions of the common people, their attitude towards life, as well as their spiritual level of development. It's not possible to imagine any better profession for the earthly life of a Bodhisattva." These discoveries caused a wave of small ants on my skin while my solar plexus began tickling with its spiral waves.

As soon as my agitated thoughts began to calm down, my common sense hurried to take up the vacant place. On the other hand, I thought, "Why did I exalt him so much? Maybe all this is just my imagination. I got tired, worried too much, had heard in line the different conversations, and have made hasty, fantastic conclusions. Alright, he helps people, he has a talent for this and abilities, so what? Simply, he is a good professional, as that woman from the line said. That is all. By appearance he is a common man, with a common face that looks like all other human faces. His appearance does not differ from others. He is the same like everybody..."

And here I noticed that the deeper I developed my common sense theory, the more something bad appeared in me, some kind of anger or something, some kind of dark envy that Sensei possessed such talent and abilities and I didn't. And here, my thoughts became so dark that I even got scared of myself, "Stop, stop, stop! Who is creating a tempest in a teapot? Comrades, it isn't me! Can the soul really think so badly? No. It is kind by itself. Where did all this filth come from? It is not my opinion. Some kind of fixed ideas, thoughts which impudently keep coming back again and again, and they awaken in me anger and hate... These are the instincts of the animal nature!" And here I completely got angry with myself and thought, "I am fed up with them! For how long can I keep being a dumb, stubborn beast?! I've had enough, simply had enough. If I continue like that my whole life will pass in evil intentions and vanity..."

Then I was visited by another thought, "Maybe because of our blown-up egocentrism, we don't notice what wonderful chances destiny grants us. And for the soul, wandering through the centuries in darkness, maybe, such a chance occurs only once in a thousand years. Who knows what we don't see because of our envy and anger. God, why are we so blind? Why do we start really valuing something only when we lose it? Why do we praise the Great only after their death?"

Christ was crucified because of somebody's blown-up megalomania and our gregarious egocentrism. And what a great man He was, how many good deeds for human souls He could've done. If He were alive and people opened up their hearts at least a little, maybe human civilization would've made such a jump in its evolution that we, their descendants, would already live in a real, united, free society, without borders and government, without violence and terror, in a world of harmony. But no, even during the life of Jesus few people really valued Him. But the majority, probably, were envious of Him, gloated and upbraided Him with their animal vanity, with rottenness, with hate and indifference. But after His death everybody started to believe in him right away!

Just take our contemporaries, the prominent individuals. When are they all being acknowledged? In general, after death. It is only after their deaths that people speak well about them, even those who, during their life, did many mean things. However, these people are probably glad in their private thoughts that their rival has died. That's authentic animal nature.

When will we finally wake up, when will we be thinking with our souls and not our bodies? Because then the whole world will change and will become completely different! I just want to yell this to the entire world. But what for?! I shouldn't yell but instead do something and change myself and not permit these parasites to enter into my consciousness or mind. Yes, if only this could be understood by the majority of people then, maybe, we could all learn together to value and respect those geniuses who are so rarely sent by nature to the world! As one great classic stated, "Mother Nature, if you didn't send such people to the world, the field of life would've died."

34

The next day, during our trip to the spiritual training, I was telling the guys the entire way my great news that our Sensei is the famous chiropractor and what I had heard and seen while visiting him. For them it was also a big surprise. In our secret glade, almost everybody had already gathered. Sensei, having greeted us, politely asked me how my mother was doing.

"Thank you, a little better. She has strong pains still, of course. But at least she slept calmly last night."

"This is good. That's all right, she will slowly recover her health."

I didn't have a slight doubt about this. For the most part, I was very happy that everything turned out exactly this way. I could not wish a better doctor for my beloved mother. Now my soul was calm.

"And you know," I continued, "I was so surprised to have seen you. I thought that chiropractic was only practiced by dilapidated old men and women."

"Many people think this way."

"Why is that so?"

"Because in chiropractic, real knowledge and experience comes with years, and that's why most of us are older."

I noticed that none of the senior guys, including Nikolai Andreevich, was at all surprised by the word "chiropractor." They had probably known about this for a long time.

"Tell me," I continued, looking with admiration into his eyes, "Can spinal diseases be cured with the help of faith?"

"Faith is capable of moving mountains, not just curing spinal problems. But few people have true faith."

"Why?"

"Doubts gnaw, our animal nature suppresses. That's why it is very hard for a human to acquire true faith. But for a soul dominating in the mind, it is very simple."

"If a human simply blindly believes in his recovery or in the recovery of those close to him, will treatment be faster?"

"Of course. And not just faster, but a lot lighter and more efficient."

"I apologize," Nikolai Andreevich joined the conversation. "I have long wanted to ask you, why exactly did you choose this profession?"

"Well, what can I say?" answered Sensei. "Just like any man, when I needed to choose a profession, I began to think. You will agree with me, what can be better in the world than to restore people's health, and what can be more complex in a body than the spinal cord, perhaps only the brain... What is the spinal cord? Take a look at a picture of its nerve plexuses - it is a real tree of life that goes with its top to the brain and is connected with roots to every organ of the human body. Figuratively speaking, this tree of life nourishes the entire body with health. And if, God forbid, it has some kind of disorder, this immediately affects the work of organs and the entire body as a whole. Because practically more than ninety percent of all diseases appear as a result of the malfunctioning of the spinal cord, from the most insignificant to those that are fatal. Almost everybody has problems with his spine during his life... The spinal cord, for today, remains the mystery of mysteries in science. And it is, just like the brain, insufficiently explored."

"In general, yes," pronounced Nikolai Andreevich. "Honestly saying, I never thought about this... But since it's such an important and complex organ in the body, one needs to possess considerable knowledge to treat it."

"That is indeed so. The spine is a very interesting, perfect biomechanical structure. Its treatment is a great responsibility because a doctor has to precisely diagnose the patient, considering information, age, weight, and a whole range of various factors, and then make the right decision and calculate the corresponding power and dose of impact because this is a sort of microsurgery, only without opening. The revitalization in the process of exploitation should be also taken into account. Chiropractic is a very serious profession. One needs to thoroughly know everything: biomechanics, anatomy, pathology, genesis, morphogenesis, physics, and chemistry of the cell. To put it briefly, one should perfectly know vertebrology."

"What?" Ruslan asked. "What is this for... 'brology'?"

"Not 'brology,' but 'vertebrology,'" Sensei answered with a smile. "It is the science of the spinal column, which includes all those sciences plus specific knowledge about the spinal cord."

"What kind of specific knowledge?" Nikolai Andreevich got interested.

"You also need to know the details and techniques of different manual ways of treating vertebral pathologies, osteopathy, chiropractic, and so forth. In other words, it's necessary to know the experiences of previous generations in the area of chiropractic because it is a pretty ancient and interesting profession." Sensei added, "And, of course, it means communication with a large number of different people."

I don't know about the others, but I clearly understood that Sensei's last words were the main reason for choosing his profession. I was absolutely sure about it.

Meanwhile, Sensei changed the subject of our conversation to meditations. We started discussing our home results and then tried to work intensively on ourselves, approaching with tiny steps our far-away cherished goal: to become human.

35

I noticed that the days started flying by, as if in one instant. I felt that I did not have enough time for everything. I even stopped visiting a few hobby groups so that at least, somehow, I could manage to do everything. Our exercises and trainings continued to gladden me with their novelty and uniqueness. At one of the trainings, Sensei began explaining a new subject.

"Today we'll study and, as usual, partially will learn the style of Tai Qi Quan, considered to be from the soft style of Wushu. This style originated in one of the most famous monasteries of China, located in the Wudangshan mountains. It is noteworthy that the local mountains used to be called the Mountains of Great Stillness. But then a man, whose name was Zhen Wu, flew to heaven having reached Dao (which in Daoism is considered to be the internal divine power and primordial substance that created everything in the Universe). The mountains were renamed in his honor.

"According to one of the legends, a monk named Zhan Sanfeng lived in that monastery in the twelfth century. One day, hearing an odd sound in the yard, he looked out of the window. The monk saw a crow sitting on the tree and a snake on the ground, both looking at each other. Each time, as soon as crow flew out of the tree to attack the snake, the snake would quickly turn its head and would curve in such a way that the crow wouldn't be able to peck it. While observing them, Zhan had an insight: an opponent can be defeated by dodging attacks.

"According to another legend, he received this wise hint from Zhan Wu in a dream. As the proverb says, 'A saint said, a wise man understood.' Having perceived the main principle of martial art, Zhan Sanfeng, after many years of training, developed the soft style, which received the name Supreme Ultimate (Tai Qi Quan). To translate it literally, 'tai' means supreme, 'qi' means ultimate, and 'quan' means fist.

"According to another version, the development of this style is ascribed to another Zhan Sanfeng from Wudang who lived in the fourteenth century, a disciple of the famous master Ho Lung (Fiery Dragon). Of course, there are other legendary versions of the origin of this style. Bur the main principle of Tai Qi Quan didn't change and is stated in the following principles: Statics begets dynamics; the pliable overcomes the rigid; the slow defeats the fast; the short defeats the long. In other words, for example, you should respond to the sharp attacking movement of your opponent with soft pliancy, in this way amortizing the strike by letting it pass into emptiness. As a result, the opponent loses balance. And then a few grams are enough to overcome the power of a ton. The ancient writings of the masters of Tai Qi Quan say about this style, 'Little movements lead to big changes. The pliable overcomes the rigid: make use of power of your opponent; attack suddenly, affecting points.'

"Tai Qi Quan is similar to a smooth dance. At the highest level of mastery of this style, there are no fixed movements or complexes, only the major principles remain. The body moves as if on its own, performing in dynamic meditation an undefined peculiar dance.

"But to reach something big, one needs to start with something small. That's why we'll start with the simplest exercise, pushing hands. It is done in pairs. Here, it is necessary to slightly touch with the hands, softly, taking turns to push each other, for the beginners under the known trajectory of movement, and for the more experienced, arbitrarily. This exercise develops reaction to the actions of the opponent by foreseeing his intentions. In other words, by 'listening' to where he wants to move, you should attempt to trick him by breaking free from his 'stuck' hands. With the inaccurate movement of your opponent, for example, if he moves roughly or loses balance, you, with a light push, can cast him to the ground. Movements should be relaxed, but the consciousness stays vigilant. Also I'll show you the corresponding complex of breathing.

"These and the following exercises can be used as health-improving gymnastics. Especially for medical goals, Tai Qi Quan is helpful to people who are in a constant nervous stress because these smooth movements with even speed align potentials in the cerebral cortex, protecting it from overload. Moreover, the concentration of thought on movements distracts man from everyday problems, restoring his nervous system. And, of course, gymnastics trains all joints and ligaments. It is helpful for everybody. So, coming back home, you can show it to your mums and dads, grandmas and grandpas, so that they will never be sick.

"I want to draw your particular attention to the fact that the ancient masters of the Tai Qi Quan gymnastics insistently demanded from their disciples 'purification, stillness, absence of wrong actions, preservation of purity of heart, restraint in their desires.' In this way, a human not only will defeat his diseases but also will destroy his ego, thus clearing a path to the perfection of the spirit. They were strongly convinced that Heaven sees the 'de' (spirituality, love) of man and that, based on his 'de,' he gets a reward. The wisdom of the masters that reached us from the depths of centuries is relevant today. Each one of us can use this knowledge to the maximum, and not just for self-defense, but also for the opening of his own internal world, for the perception of the mysteries of nature and the universe. You always need to remember that a human can achieve anything if the goal is clearly defined. Now let's proceed to the practical part."

We lined up, and the Teacher showed us the breathing exercises for 'stuck hands.' After individual demonstrations of the techniques by Sensei, almost everybody in a few seconds landed on his back hearing the laughter of his friends, who found themselves in the same position a few minutes later. More serious fighters, using the wrong techniques, were flying away as many as three to four meters. Most interesting is that during the first ten minutes we laughed, but after twenty minutes we were rising up slowly, groaning. After half an hour of more engaged, serious work, we completely concentrated on the movement and accuracy of our performance. Nobody wanted to be seen as a clown by excessively falling.

The speedy guys, including Stas and Eugene, worked especially beautifully. Evidently they had practiced this art for a long time. Their completely nonrecurring, improvised movements were similar to a grandiose dance, full of unpredictable and at the same time rational movements. And if one of them made a mistake, then immediately he flew far away, knocking down a lot of people on the way. In order not to harm other people, these guys were moved to the end of the hall, almost to the exit. But even here, Eugene and

Stas surpassed themselves. Working at sparring, Eugene for one second got distracted by the opening door and right away received a powerful blow from Stas, which not only threw him into that unfortunate door, but also placed him before the exit on his knees. At that time, an imposing man of indefinable age, with a stately face similar to that of Ramses, entered the hall. Some kind of fine eastern aroma wafted from him. He was dressed in a stylish coat under which an expensive suit could be seen. "Ramses" looked at Eugene with surprise. But Eugene quickly composed himself and, touching the floor with his forehead, ritually uttered, "Oh, we welcome you, great Zhan Wu, the most desirable guest of our tribe!"

Eugene quickly jumped back on his feet and, bowing to the gentleman one more time like a fighter, turned around and went toward Stas, who could hardly control his laughter.

Sensei, with a smile, came up and greeted the man.

"For how long did he practice this form of greeting?" asked "Ramses" with a strong accent, in broken Russian.

"Don't get mad at him. He is young and always confused."

"Ramses" was surprised even more and asked with a slight resentment in his voice, "Do I really look Chinese?"

"No, of course, but...," Sensei continued in some unusual language.

"Ramses" laughed and added something in reply. Speaking in this melodious and very pleasant language, they went into the private room for coaches. I noticed that the guest walked the same way as Sensei.

As soon as the doors shut behind them, Stas couldn't keep it in and laughed aloud, immediately receiving in return a punch from Eugene. Having fallen with a rumble on the benches, he couldn't stand up for five whole minutes, rolling from his laughter attack. They might have kept laughing like that until the end of training, but the senior sempai, who was responsible for discipline in Sensei's absence, showed them a fist, and the guys quickly hushed up and got back to work.

I was bursting with curiosity to find out who that mysterious guest was. But my attempts to ask the senior guys weren't successful. They let me know that they don't interfere in Sensei's business.

In thirty minutes, closer to the end of training, "Ramses" and Sensei came out of the room, confirming something on the way with a smile. They bid farewell as old, good friends, warmly shaking each other's hands. After the departure of the mysterious guest, Sensei, with the same ease, switched back to Russian and, as if nothing had happened, started explaining the guys' mistakes he'd seen. His mood was clearly raised.

At home I wrote down, as always, the most interesting things in my diary. The visit of this unusual foreigner raised in me many unanswered questions. I decided to leave this mystery to an undetermined later. As Sensei would say, "There is nothing mysterious on Earth that one day won't be revealed." With such an optimistic forecast of the future, I continued to be an observer.

36

At spiritual lessons, we polished old meditations. Everything was as usual, except that Nikolai Andreevich was absent for almost a week, which was unusual for him. At last our psychologist appeared in full health and high spirits. He came before the beginning of the training when our merry party was standing in the glade with Sensei, Eugene, and Stas. Nikolai Andreevich's eyes shone with extreme pleasure and delight..

Having greeted everybody quickly, he addressed Sensei and began telling him excitedly, "We finally finished the experiment, everything proved to be true. The results are simply tremendous... This technique of altered state of consciousness that you gave, in fact, it radically changes the picture of our world, the whole conception of our existence... But I will now tell you everything in detail..."

Our guys looked in wide-eyed astonishment at the unusually excited behavior of Nikolai Andreevich. Sensei listened to him attentively while smoking a cigarette.

"...In my opinion, I picked a more or less suitable candidate. One guy, a full-fledged alcoholic, was treated at our clinic. Two years of boarding school was his entire education. He grew up in an orphanage, one of those post-war orphans. Army, then a coal mine, and hopeless alcoholism, that was his life. But when I brought him into the altered state of consciousness, he told me such unusual things. He was also speaking some old Russian language, and all my colleagues who were present during the experiment were just shocked by his answers. We recorded all that he was saying and brought it to a professor, a historian, a great expert in this area. The result surpassed all our expectations. Even the professor was surprised. It appeared that this alcoholic spoke the language of the Drevlian people, who the professor told us were an ancient east Slavic tribe. Our subject regaled us with amazing details and household trifles of the seventh century. Many of them coincided with data from archaeological excavations, but some are still unknown to science. He also mentioned some geographic district and the river Sluch where he said he used to live. And finally he told us about some big conflict with someone from the Dregovich tribe. All this coincides with amazing accuracy with the available data... You can't even imagine what a great achievement in science it is! But it is necessary to confirm these data some more times for the validity of the experiment. We need to prove it scientifically. Look, I have picked up one more candidate..."

"Wait, wait, we agreed that I would give you an opportunity, and you would try. That's all," Sensei said firmly.

"Just try to understand me. This is so valuable for the world science..."

"I understand everything," Sensei said calmly. "However, we did not talk about the world science but about you. You wanted to be sure, and now you are sure. It's not the right time for the world science yet."

Nikolai Andreevich became silent, got calm and uttered, "Sorry... But the experiment was really tremendous. I was such a zealous atheist, but now... It really proves... Why do I say all this, it completely changes most everything."

"That's good. The main thing is that you understood it."

"Understood?! You are putting it too mildly... It is a complete revolution in my consciousness, it is a significant revolution of mind. Indeed, I'm not only convinced of the veracity of your words, but I also believe in you with all my heart and soul!"

Sensei smiled and said thoughtfully, "I have heard this before... Ah, yes... exactly. Peter spoke to Jesus the same way before he renounced Him three times."

Nikolai Andreevich insistently tried to make Sensei change his mind, convincing him with the help of forcible arguments. Sensei only smiled silently, and then changed the topic of conversation to meditation.

37

Spiritual lessons gradually became more and more important to me. Being so simple and accessible at the same time, they gradually changed my vision of the world. Some new feelings grew inside of me. I started to perceive everything in another way as if I had opened the other side of reality for myself..

Even nature, the air that I never noticed before, turned into a special material substance that I felt as light pressure from all directions whatever I did. This feeling was somewhat similar to the sensation of water elasticity when you dive into it. But in the case of the air, everything was much easier. Nature around me became brighter, colors became richer as if an invisible dust veil had been removed from my eyes.

Spring was storming outside. It animated the grey space of cities with its fresh, salad greenery. The world of nature existed according to its own cycle as if wishing to show greatness and independence from the tiny creatures occupying it. This living creature had its own secret of life and death, which was carefully protected during its long existence.

The time spent in trainings and conversations with Sensei flew by so quickly that imperceptibly I came up to the point of final examinations. To tell the truth, I didn't want to spend any precious time on them even though I had realized that examinations and further studies were not trifles, they were necessary. As Sensei used to say, a human should constantly develop his intellect and enlarge his mind, meaning he should expand his knowledge everywhere and in everything wherever it is possible, to strive for the knowledge of science. Because the mature human comes to God through knowledge, namely the knowledge of himself and the world around him.

At spiritual and common trainings, Sensei continued to surprise us with his personal examples, with the breadth and depth of his knowledge. During common trainings, he mostly taught those skills that our brain perceived easily, as they say, without any shock. There were strikes, techniques from different styles, health-improving gymnastics, which were demonstrated by his narrations from the various points of view: medical, strategic, and philosophical. At the additional trainings, we were lucky to contemplate his mysterious demonstrations to a greater extent when most people were leaving. But once there was an incident.

During one of the trainings when most people were practicing strikes in pairs, Sensei was standing right next to us, showing Andrew a difficult strike with a hook. It is necessary to note that that day the Teacher was a bit thoughtful, absorbed in his ideas. Unexpectedly he stopped his movement and turned back, abruptly peering worriedly into the opposite side of the hall. Volodya and Victor were sparring there, but their sparring was a little bit strange. Volodya conducted an aggressive and rigid attack. He attacked his sparring-partner dexterously and quickly with his hands and legs. Meanwhile Victor was somehow perplexed and hardly had time to fend off missing strikes. Sensei sharply clapped his hands, shouting "Yame!" that means "Stop!" But Volodya was obviously captured by the passion of sparring and did not hear him, though the rest of the crowd turned to Sensei at this call. And then something happened.

Sharply waving his hand, Sensei made a movement in the air simulating a blow. At the same instant, Volodya flew aside with such a force and along such a trajectory as if Sensei stood near him and not near us. We were all astonished by what we had seen. Silence was established in the hall. The Teacher had interfered right in time. If Volodya had hit him one more time, Victor would have been in trouble. Writhing in pain, poor Victor tried to restore his breath by a special technique used after dangerous strikes, which Sensei gave us once at additional lessons. Meanwhile Volodya, having flown about five meters head over heels, also tried to reestablish himself after his unexpected flight. He was strenuously rubbing the place that Sensei's blow would have struck if he had been standing next to Volodya.

Everything happened in a split second in the presence of everyone in the group. Though I saw it with my own eyes, I could not believe it even though my mind was used to such surprises from Sensei. In a minute, the crowd burst out with emotions. Andrew pulled Eugene by a sleeve, without taking his eyes from Volodya, "Hey, what was that?"

Eugene was probably in shock too, "Wait, my spirit trembles in me from a queer vision."

Meantime the Teacher's face changed, as though he was annoyed with himself for this negligence. Coming up to Volodya, he made a number of gestures above his body. He was scolding him quickly, obviously indignant at the attack. Volodya answered something, shrugging his shoulders and bashfully hiding his eyes. The crowd was riled up based on what they had seen. Sensei was bombarded with questions that he was reluctant to answer.

"What kind of a blow was that?" The guys asked eagerly.

"Well, how can I say it," the Teacher said with a sigh. "It is connected with the mental energy of a person. It isn't anything worth your attention. It is only one of the steps of spiritual development in the martial arts."

"So we can learn it, can't we?"

"Certainly, maybe you can if you are patient."

Sensei quickly continued the interrupted lesson, hushing up this incident as it seemed to me. At the end of the training, the majority of people present had increased adrenaline in their blood and corresponding optimistic forecasts concerning the future.

Unlike the others, our company silently observed the agitation because we were sure that at additional trainings Sensei would not avoid our direct questions.

Before the additional training, the Teacher's mood improved a little bit, and his good mood was a good sign. The senior guys hastened to take advantage of it. During the additional training, they tortured Sensei with inquiries to "contemplate personally" something like that. At the beginning, Sensei laughed the matter off but then he agreed under their pressure to show us the so-called 'saving screen.' He told us first to find some objects for ourselves.

We ran to the room used for sports stock and armed ourselves with what we could find there. The guys grabbed poles and basketball balls. Andrew even took his nunchaku. I thought for a long time about what to choose. Finally I decided to take a tennis ball, as I thought that if Sensei failed and the object hit him it would not hurt him. But Sensei had never made any mistake in his actions before, which inspired special respect for his abilities.

When we had armed ourselves, Sensei stood 7 or 8 meters away from us. Concentrating, he lifted his hands forward and placed them slightly to his sides. In turn, we started to throw various objects at him as hard as we could. It was fantastic but no matter how hard we tried, all objects simply missed Sensei, changing the trajectory of their flight in the distance of half a meter from his palms. Victor, Stas, and Volodya decided to challenge Sensei by throwing the objects at him from behind. But Sensei didn't even change his position, he only opened his hands wider to the sides. To put it briefly, we experimented a lot, but all the objects missed Sensei.

I didn't understand whether all of us became cross-eyed or there really was some invisible powerful wall around him. My mind resisted the last reason and was indignant in trying to prove that it could not be. This conclusion forced me to try throwing the tennis ball again and again. Now I was throwing it without any pity into this invisible wall to be convinced for a second that an obstacle really existed there. I think all other guys also had similar feelings because their passion gradually changed into confusion.

In my opinion, again Sensei began to turn from a normal person into a supernatural creature. My head really started to go crazy from all this improbable plausibility. Meanwhile Sensei had removed the screen and began to explain the principle of its action, in this way bringing the logical work of our consciousness to a normal, natural rhythm. Then I noticed that while listening to Sensei, some signs of envy (the animal nature) began to slip into my head again. First it happened accidentally, and then they got stronger and stronger. Then some doubts rose in my head, although Sensei explained everything in a simple and understandable way based on what we had just seen with our own eyes.

I caught myself on the idea that while listening to Sensei talk about spiritual opportunities, I was thinking dirty thoughts with the inflated mania of my own egocentrism. "Wow!" I thought. "With such an underlying basis of egoism, all valuable knowledge will pass by my ears. My mind will choose out of Sensei's words only those ones that are necessary for the animal nature instead of the spiritual one. That means I will never succeed... So I need to concentrate on good... This knowledge is necessary for me only for good purposes, for learning my essence. I do not want to cause any harm. Let all people live in peace and love. I do not wish anyone evil and do not envy them. All of them are good and worthy in their lives. The main thing for me is perfection of my soul." Adjusting myself in this way, I began to listen to Sensei more attentively. The conversation had already moved on to creating blows in the distance.

"...this blow is very powerful," Sensei said. "Mental forces of the person are involved in it."

"How is the blow itself committed at such a distance?" Stas asked.

"Basically, distance is an illusion. Therefore in your understanding it acts like the projection of a blow. In fact, there is another type of physics in which space and time are compressed. Therefore a person who delivers such a blow, like a person who really receives it, feels direct physical contact."

"Does this knowledge come from the Art of White Lotus?" asked Victor.

"Yes. This is a special technique of Lotus from the Art of the 'Punishing Sword of Shambala.' People of Shambala knew and still know this Art... Once a very long time ago, Masters of Lotus came out to our world rather frequently. They perfectly knew not only the Old Lama style, but also knew the Art of the Punishing Sword. Such a Master could gain a victory over an entire army. Until now in the East there are legends about warriors who appeared from nowhere and returned to nowhere. But in the area where they stopped, they enjoyed great honor and respect among the local population because better protection for the peaceful inhabitants could not be found. These Masters possessed an energy power much more serious than any modern weapon. For people who don't have knowledge of this Art to receive such a destroying blow from nowhere is more than awful.

"Time passed, and the necessity of such Masters' arriving disappeared. But certainly it does not mean that the Art of the Punishing Sword vanished. In the gate of Shambala there is a specially trained person who carries out decisions made by the council of Bodhisattvas. If you remember once I told you that Shambala will never allow somebody to capture the whole world or to use spiritual knowledge to harm mankind. So this Master realizes such decisions without leaving his cell. For this purpose, it is enough for him to be in a special state of consciousness and to wave the 'Petal of Lotus,' a special ritual sword somewhat similar to a short Turkish saber. The name of the Art of the Punishing Sword of Shambala appeared because of this sword.

"Evidence of this Master's activity can occasionally be found in the modern world. Mysterious deaths still remain a secret not only to pathologists. For example, in the process of an autopsy, it was discovered that the heart was cut precisely into halves as if a sharp object had been used, but the skin and nearby organs were not injured. Or there were 'inexplicable' cases where in the presence of numerous guards a body was cut into pieces as though from a sword and the clothes were undamaged. It doesn't matter how thoroughly a guilty person had been protected by the newest technology or the whole army, he isn't able to evade this penalty. It is an original cause of fear before Shambala for all tyrants. Therefore people searched and continue searching for contact with it because they know, no matter how powerful and authoritative they are, they are powerless before Shambala."

Sensei broke off, and it seemed to me that his words still echoed in my ears. All the guys stood in thoughtfulness perhaps because, like me, they were also shocked by everything they heard. Nobody dared to break the silence, hoping that the Teacher would add something else to this extraordinary information. At last, Volodya lost his patience and spoke in a bass, "This Master of the Punishing Sword probably has a force similar to atomic energy if distance does not matter for his blows."

"Atomic energy in comparison with this force is only a children's toy. Mankind is far from knowing its real abilities and real forces because of the prevalence of the animal nature."

38

After such a training, our emotions concerning the things we had heard and seen stormed for more than a day. Thoughts about our abilities did not give us a moment's peace. We wished to reach everything at once. So for the next few days, this optimistic mood came out in assiduous trainings of body and mind. When it came time for the next spiritual lessons, we simply showered Sensei with different questions. Looking at all our excitement, the Teacher said:

"Guys, this distant blow, all the effects of Qi energy, and all those 'miracles' that I show you, all of them are trifles not worthy of real attention. True force lies in the soul. This is what is necessary to develop; learn and admire it. Divine love of the soul combined with the mind of the person is a true miracle. All that you saw is only a side-effect of different levels of spiritual development. It is nonsense, you should not pay attention to it."

"But why is it nonsense?" Nikolai Andreevich said. "In fact, miracles generate belief."

"Yes, they do. Miracles generate belief. But let's understand what kind of belief. What happens to a person when he sees miracles, that is, those phenomena that are inexplicable for his brain? First of all, it powerfully shakes his mind. The mind simply begins to go beyond the limits as it does not have the proper information to explain the given phenomenon. Our brain has amazing mechanisms of self-preservation and self-defense, the protective factor of our brain, so its compensatory functions are immediately activated. Using the language of physiology, zones of the brain and groups of nervous cells can't join in mental activity to their fullest extent. And there is an important point. If the animal nature prevails in person, this person internally starts to ignore the existence of such a phenomenon. He shifts the blame for everything to the unreality of an event, to trickery, or he obtains a desire to learn all these unknown things for the sake of his own mercenary interests of megalomania satisfaction.

"The person who has balanced these two natures begins to go from one extreme to another. It means that today he blindly trusts all this, but tomorrow he starts to doubt, and the day after tomorrow he starts to doubt his doubts again, and so on. To put it briefly, there is an active struggle between the two natures in the field of his mind.

"Inside a person whose spiritual nature prevails on the basis of belief grows the spirit of research into the given phenomenon, grows the knowledge of his own abilities and the secrets of nature for the sake of this process of knowledge, for the sake of perfection of the soul. His initial fear of the mystery of the phenomenon is muffled and, during the process of learning, it completely disappears and transforms blind belief into knowledge, that is, into true belief.

"In fact, guys, why do you think I show you all this? I do it to observe your thoughts, the level of your animal nature in relation to the spiritual one. The most important question is, why do I spend so much time explaining each phenomenon? I try to give your mind a hint to put away your complex of material life. I try to make you think about the eternal secrets of nature, about your obscure soul, about God. In fact, the more you learn yourselves, the closer you are to God, to those eternal, unshakeable, and everlasting things.

"What is your physical life compared to the Universe? It's nothing. In comparison with the Universe and planets, a human practically does not exist. His life is an unreal reality, just an instant in one of God's thoughts."

"How can it be?" Eugene did not understand.

"Well, someday I shall explain it to you in detail. Your bodies exist in a closed time cycle where you, that means your soul, have all the conditions for absolute maturation. You need to realize it with the help of your mind and join your soul in common aspirations to cognize it. Then your life will acquire true sense. Because it is your ripened soul, not those ashes of material bodies changed during development, that is valuable for God, for the Universe as a whole...

"So, true belief arises from knowledge. And knowledge comes through a word, through belief of your mind in the reality of the occurring phenomenon. Miracles, in fact, are only one kind of testing of the internal level of individual development. This method of testing was used in their terrestrial practice by those who possessed factual knowledge of the science of White Lotus. However we have a unique person in Satya Sai Baba, who decided to turn people to God with the help of the permanent demonstration of real miracles."

Nikolai Andreevich thought a little, "It's a familiar name... Was it he who was shown on TV rubbing Gorbachev's head with his foot?"

"Right!" Sensei grinned.

"He was called an incarnation of God on Earth... an Avatar."

"Avatara" Sensei corrected. "But generally 'avatara' is translated from Sanskrit as 'fall' or 'descent'."

"Yes, Avatara. They said Avatara takes a human body to lift the development of the person a step higher, to bring him into a new century."

"Absolutely right. He likes to say, 'If you want to rescue a drowning man, you need to jump into water, that is to be incarnated.'".

"What kind of man is he?" our company asked with curiosity.

"Well, Sai Baba is a great soul. And as human civilization is now at the point of global changes in reassessing its spiritual level of development and the events following these changes, Satya Sai Baba decided to make his contribution. He was going to surprise the world with miracles. Satya Sai Baba was preparing for this mission for a long time, he was developing the theory of the influence of miracles on the spiritual development of people. First, he predicted in the Upanishads his threefold incarnation in the epoch of technics. And then when time came he began to check this theory in practice. So he reincarnated to Sai Baba in the village of Shirdi in 1872 in India. All his life he performed miracles, read thoughts, could overcome distances, take any material form, and so forth. He died in 1918, having informed everyone before his death that he would come back to Earth again in eight years in the south of India.

"And so it happened. Satya Sai Baba was born in 1926 in Puttaparthi, a small remote village in the south of India. In 1940, he was proclaimed Avatara. And he performs miracles up to now. When time comes for him to leave, he will reincarnate again as Prema Sai. He has already predicted not only the exact date and the place of the following incarnation, between the cities of Bangalore and Mysore, but also the names of his future parents."

"They say on TV that he can levitate, simultaneously appear in different places, and, what is most interesting, he can materialize an enormous quantity of anything you like from a diamond to cookies, is it true? They say he just pulls them out of the air. Or is this merely gossip?" Nikolai Andreevich asked.

"No. It is really so."

"But it is unreal!"

"It is absolutely real. But his main mistake lies in demonstrating miracles, things that are still mysterious for mankind. Those who saw his miracles are surprised and start to think them over, and those who did not see just laugh at him and consider all this to be a trick. The latter unfortunately belong to the majority. But he certainly carries out his mission honestly, and I wish he could help as many people as possible at least wake up. Nevertheless, the true enlightenment of the soul comes through a word."

"Is he a real God?" Ruslan asked.

"You know, people ask him this question quite often. The answer is simple enough and true. As Satya Sai Baba used to say, 'You are God too. The only difference between me and you is that I know that I am God and you do not know it.'"

39

At the next training, the sports hall was so overcrowded that there was not an inch of room. Judging from the places the beginners came from, the news about energy blow had probably spread through several cities. We had never trained in such a mess. Andrew and Kostya began to express their indignation about this crowd of people that suddenly overflowed 'their' sports hall. But the senior sempai quickly put the guys down, having reminded them that recently they were exactly the same beginners in a crowd and no one objected to their practicing here. He also reproached them with words of the Teacher, that it is necessary to respect another person's aspiration for knowledge instead of immediately attacking him with bayonets of your own egocentrism. After that the guys were ashamed, kept silent, and did not utter any evil word during the entire training. As for Andrew, he decided to rehabilitate himself somehow in the eyes of the senior sempai and even diligently began to help the beginners master movements that were new for them.

While people were practicing the techniques during the optional program, a man asked Sensei to meet him outside. At this time, Tatyana and I were next to the open door, as it was very stuffy in the sports hall even with the open windows. Three humble men, one of them under fifty and the other two under thirty, had politely knocked on the open door, drawing our attention. As we appeared to be standing nearer than the others, they also politely inquired about the name of our Teacher and the possibility of talking to him. Of course, we did what they asked. When Sensei came up, they started to talk to him about something.

At first, I did not pay attention to the conversation, fulfilling my task. But the words I could hear raised my curiosity more and more. These men appeared to be representatives of some religious sect that had recently grown in our city like mushrooms after rain. Obviously, having seen the number of young people training in the sports hall, they suggested Sensei and his pupils to visit their meeting that day in a cinema hall. A free presentation of a film about Jesus Christ was to take place there. Sensei politely thanked them for the invitation without promising anything concrete. But their leader, the elder one, who turned out to be their minister, began to ask Sensei leading questions about his knowledge of Jesus and his attitude to His teachings.

Sensei started off answering politely and laconically, letting him know that the training wasn't over. But the minister was not in a hurry to part with Sensei. Every short answer of Sensei met an extremely verbose explanation of the advantages of their church and their 'true' view of the teachings of Christ. Within ten minutes, the conversation had tired Sensei because he started to break all their seducing reasons down to ashes with precise arguments, quoting dates, figures, and events which, apparently, were unknown even to the minister. By this time, our curious company had left the sports hall to listen what was going on. Eugene and Stas followed us. Then came Ruslan and Yura, who were standing not far from the door.

"...Wouldn't you like to live eternally in paradise on Earth, in the kingdom of God?" the minister uttered in a pacifying voice.

"Eternally, on Earth, in paradise?!" grinned Sensei.

"Do not hasten to reject eternal life as an unrealizable dream," the minister interrupted him. "Pay attention to how your body is created. In fact, you practically know nothing about it. Everything in it has been conceived with the utmost detail. We have hearing, sight, taste, the sense of smell and touch. There are so many things in the world that bring pleasure due to our sense organs: tasty food, pleasant friendly relations, picturesque landscapes, and so on. We can enjoy this all due to our amazing brain. Do you know that our brain is perfect and it surpasses any computer, any supercomputer?! And do you really think that our Creator wants you to die and to lose all this? It is logical to conclude that He wishes eternal life for His righteous men, doesn't He?"

"Happy and eternal life on Earth in a body?! Do you think at all when you are speaking to people?" the Teacher said. "What kind of eternal paradise can there be in a body? Any body as any biological structure demands your constant attention. It wants to eat, it is sick, it is tired, it wants pleasure. And you call this matter a paradise and dream of living with its biological needs eternally?! For sure it is an eternal hell instead of paradise!"

"Then if you think so, why did God create the human body?"

"God created the human body as the most convenient form and protection for the maturation of a still weak soul. Even the Bible you hold in your hands says, 'And the Lord God created a man from the dust of the ground and breathed into his nostrils the breath of life; and a man became a living soul.'"

"Right, but the true sense of these words is a bit different," the minister spoke instructively. "The authors of the Bible, when using the word 'spirit' in this context, did not mean an intangible soul that continues to live after death."

"Really?!" Sensei was surprised. "How do you know the true sense of these words? Do you know it from the literature and instructions that the leaders of your sect present and put into your heads in ready-made form? Did you think it over yourself? Do you know your leaders personally, do you know their inner world? Did you reflect on why do they need all of this, in fact, this unlimited power over you? For them and their special agents..."

As Sensei spoke, the minister's nostrils dilated more and more.

"Let's not speak about it further," he sharply interrupted Sensei. Having come round, he softly added, "We say that, according to the interpretation of the Bible, the spirit is a vital force. When a person dies, this vital force ceases to support the life in cells of his body, just as a light becomes dim when you switch off the electricity. When the vital force ceases to support the human body, the person - the soul - dies. It is written in Ecclesiastes 12:1,7; in Psalm..."

"It is written in Ecclesiastes 12:1, 'Remember now thy Creator in the days of thy youth, while the evil days come not, nor the years draw nigh, when thou shalt say, I have no pleasure in them.' These words do not even relate to the topic of our conversation. And Ecclesiastes 12:7 only proves what I have already told you, 'Then shall the dust return to the earth as it was: and the spirit shall return to God who gave it,'" Sensei quoted by heart. "If you read ancient scriptures of different religions, you will see that the same eternal truth about the development of the soul in a body, about its numerous reincarnations in achievement of perfection, can be traced everywhere. Read something besides the Bible; for example, the most ancient sacred book of Hinduism, Veda, from the end of the second or beginning of the first millennium B.C.; or one of its commentaries, the Upanishads, which are the basis of all the orthodox religious and philosophical systems of India; or the Buddhist canon Tripitaka; the sacred book of Islam, the Koran, written around 650 A.D.; the sacred book of Shintoism, Nihonshoki, from 720 A.D.; or the book of wisdom Zhuangzi, the treatise of Laozi Daodejin, the works of Confucius from the 6th to 5th centuries B.C. You will see in all these works a single grain of wisdom that was given in different times by different people for different levels of human formation."

"All religions of the world are from Satan, therefore they are not even worthy of our attention," the minister said with a hint of rage in his voice. "Satan influences political forces and promotes religions in which people without knowing it worship him instead of God. Only our belief is the true belief. It is the only path to the salvation of mankind."

"Well, every religion and sect considers their belief to be true, otherwise they would not create a separate organization for themselves. But don't you think that it looks slightly egocentric on the part of religious leaders? In fact, they get their knowledge from the same books and simply transform this information according to their level of moral perception and their vision of the world.

"Your idea that all religions of the world are from Satan is absolutely wrong. Yes, religions were created on the basis of teachings of great people by others who simply used their point of view and benefited from it. From the time immemorial, religion has been a powerful political lever in the world, and consequently it has rendered a huge influence on the consciousness of a crowd. Each religion has its own exaggerations, complications, and even wrong views. But for many centuries, the relations between God and mankind were conducted basically through religion. Though world religions have greatly complicated the knowledge given to people for salvation of their souls, nevertheless all of them were based on it. In the past, it was only through religion that people could revive a belief in themselves, a blind belief but sincere, and they could slightly improve their souls. During those dark times when the consciousness of our society stood at an absolute low, religion was the only engine in the progress of mankind."

"Isn't it the same now?" one of young novices of the minister asked with interest.

"Now the time of blind belief has passed. The time of global changes has come. And the basis of future progress in knowledge of God is the science."

"But how can it be science if it officially rejects God?" the novice asked in surprise.

"Science is only partly understood by mankind. If science still cannot explain the original source of the electromagnetic field, what can be said about it? Its current level can be compared to the stage of development of a one-year-old child who crawls in the space limited by his parents so as not to injure himself and learns the world through toys that are given to him. But it does not mean at all that he does not have any prospect of growth and true comprehension of the present values of the world."

"An interesting definition. Who are these parents in your opinion?" a young interlocutor got interested.

"Everyone has got the Father, God. But beside the parent, there are also tutors who look after children and give them these toys."

"This is even more interesting... Who are these tutors?"

"These creatures are known by different names. In Christianity, they are called angels, archangels who are next to God and take care of people. In the East, they are perceived more realistically and are called Bodhisattvas from Shambala..."

"My brother, you are falling into heresy!" the minister cried angrily at his novice. Addressing to Sensei, he threateningly added, "You are a deeply stray person. You are absolutely wrong. People can not transform the world nor aspire to learn about God through science. Science is the intrigue of the Devil, who convinces people by his discoveries that God does not exist. Satan covered the world with a net of technologies to catch people, to dull minds with TV and devilish literature and to make a person worship only him as today he is the Prince of this world. Only the word of God written down in the only sacred book, the Bible, is true and right. And only through it you can learn God..."

"Yes, in your instructed interpretation," Sensei grinned. "How can science come from the Devil?! You are fooling people's heads with this nonsense. The Devil can't give anything to people at all. Who is God, and who is the Devil? The Devil is nothing more than the animal nature that is a part of each person, generating negative ideas. Even the translation of a word 'satan' comes from Hebrew, where originally this word meant 'counteracting'. The manifestation of the Devil is just what we notice in ourselves, in our bad thoughts. It simply seems to us that we are good. But in fact, look how many times a day in actions and thoughts we awake in ourselves the animal nature, that is, we appeal to the Devil, not to God. How many times a day we cherish vanity and flesh in our thoughts."

"The Devil is not in thoughts, it is an awful creature, a beast..."

"A creature? People defaced him and presented him as a beast, having made a scapegoat out of him. People are afraid of his attack from the outside. But he is inside of us, he is our integral part. He strikes a blow where it is not expected, that is from our thoughts. To defeat the Devil does not mean to renounce everything in the world. To defeat the Devil means to defeat your negative thoughts, to put things in order in your mind. As ancient people said, the biggest achievement that every person can reach working on himself is to kill a dragon inside. Have you heard such an expression, 'Know yourself and you will know the whole world'? All outstanding people came to comprehend God through cognition of themselves. God is an omnipresent substance existing everywhere. God is an almighty, united, reasonable force. Everything that is given by God is given for the good of mankind. Why, for example, are science and technologies given? They are given to people for collecting information for communication, for exchanging experiences without difficulties. They are given for the constant development of a person and saving time for every possible versatile cognition of the secrets of nature. All this will inevitably result in comprehension of God and the real fact of His existence.

"And what do you do? You limit the consciousness of people: do not read this, do not do this, do not go there, do not engage yourself with it. People, do not make trouble! Do not follow your mercenary ambitions. You impede the development of human souls, you are throwing them again into the hell of reincarnation."

"Reincarnation does not exist in nature!" the minister exclaimed in a rage.

"Brother, brother, calm down," the novice hastened to interfere in the conversation. "You said yourself that anger is evil."

The minister hissed at him but nevertheless pulled himself together and continued the conversation, "It is necessary for you to read the Bible more and to clear your mind of sinful thoughts because you are a terrible person. Come to us and repent because Satan has seized your mind. We shall teach you the true understanding of God, we shall teach you how to save your soul."

With those last words, Sensei's face changed, and he said calmly, articulating each word, "Explain to me how a man drowning in a bog can save a man standing on the bank of the river?"

But the minister grasped only the first word, 'explain,' and for the next several minutes he tried to 'teach' Sensei with his admonitions, quoting different chapters from the Bible.

"... and if you will take it as a rule to attend our meetings, it will be the most powerful protection against demon attacks. You will apply pieces of advice that are given at meetings, and it will help you to be saved from Gehenna. Be sure that God will completely compensate everything you will sacrifice for the sake of worshiping Him. It is written in Malachi 3:10. For the time of the Armageddon will come soon and will destroy the sinful of mankind. Only the righteous people will remain alive in the world. We should wait with obedience and humility for the day when the Lord Jesus Christ will take measures against Satan and his adherents. It is written in Revelation 20:1-3. And when the last fight of God with Devil begins..."

"Not only did you not listen to everything I told you, you do not even think about what you say. Just ponder a little, how can the Devil fight with God? How can you say that? God is almighty, the Devil is nothing in comparison with him. Everything, every person, including Lucifer, serves God. People have just ennobled the power of Lucifer to have someone to blame for their stupidity. Lucifer, like any other angel, just serves God executing only His will..."

These words got the minister so mad that he did not even give Sensei an opportunity to finish his speech and screamed in fury, "When Satan comes, you will be his left hand!"

Turning his back sharply, he went away. The second novice quickly followed the tutor, but the first novice who asked questions loitered a little, obviously wishing to hear the end of Sensei's story. But the second novice called him, and he followed them.

Meanwhile, Eugene could hardly help laughing. He said with obvious pleasure, addressing our crowd, "Yes, yes, have you heard what a clever person has said? Remember what I told you!"

Now we also could not help laughing together with the senior guys, recollecting cheerfully Eugene's joke during our first visit to the glade. Laughing, our crowd went to the sports hall.

Sensei thought a bit and said half in jest, half seriously, "Why exactly the left hand? Is the Devil really left-handed? I didn't notice that."

Our young company looked at Sensei in surprise. The senior guys burst out laughing again, supplementing this juicy detail with different jokes. We quickly returned to our interrupted exercises. After that we trained without incident.

40

After the additional training, as usual we left together, and we saw the novice who had taken part in the conversation between Sensei and the minister. He stood near the club. Having noticed Sensei among us, he came up to him and inquired politely, "Excuse me, have you got a minute?"

"Yes, I am listening to you," Sensei said calmly.

"The matter is that our conversation was interrupted... And I did not have time to ask you some questions that are of great importance for me. You have rather an unusual world outlook, at least I have not heard anything like that. And I feel that your words are not groundless, as they coincide to some degree with my concept of essence of things. If it will not bother you, could you answer some questions?"

"Yes, of course," Sensei responded with the same politeness.

These words encouraged the novice. He grew bolder and said, "What is the true belief, the way to God in your understanding?"

"The true belief is knowledge. Certainly, there are a lot of ways to God, but you can wind along the pass repeatedly or you can go straight. A direct way to God is a way through knowledge and love."

"How is this knowledge expressed?"

"It is expressed through versatile cognition of the world in its various aspects: beginning from microlife to the macroexistence of space systems; through cognition of yourself both as a biological and spiritual structure and accordingly the essence of things around you. Certainly, to learn everything is impossible, but you should aspire to it. A human should constantly grow in his knowledge, he should develop his intellect. The most valuable way is the cognition of God through your mind when true knowledge, overcoming the animal nature, opens the gate of the subconscious with the help of the key of love. It is an eternal unshakable truth that has always existed in the days of all highly developed human civilizations ever existing on the Earth."

"Sorry, I have not understood everything. Could you explain it in a little bit more detail?"

"In general, it means complete maturation of the human soul, a full victory over the material essence, that is, over the Devil. In Christianity and in Islam it is called enlightenment, holiness which leads to paradise after death. In Buddhism, it is called awakening and coming out of a chain of reincarnations into nirvana, and so on. Actually everything is much simpler.

"I shall try to explain it to you in general. Figuratively speaking, it looks like this. We think that we are that very mind which sees, hears, thinks, and analyzes. But actually it is only a small part of our consciousness. Let us name it Something. This small Something floats on a surface of an ocean. The ocean is our subconscious where all our genetic memory is stored in various depths, conditioned and unconditioned reflexes, that is, all our stored experience. But all this concerns our material essence. This is our animal nature. Underneath the subconscious at the bottom of the ocean, there is some kind of a gateway. Behind this gateway there is a soul, a little part of God. This is our spiritual nature. This is what we actually are and what we very occasionally feel in ourselves. The soul regenerates during reincarnation, it gradually ripens through knowledge and love from our mortal Something as far as Something is connected to the soul. But the problem is that this Something is also connected with the ocean. Moreover, from the outside it is more subject to the influence of the ocean. It is thrown constantly here and there with waves that are various thoughts, emotions, desires, and so on. Sometimes it is so overflowing that Something loses its touch with the soul and then, after a storm, tries again to grasp it. But when this Something becomes stronger in aspiring to reach the soul, without paying any attention to the storms of the ocean, and it pushes through the thickness of the waters into the bottom, having given up fear, then it finally reaches this gateway. With the help of a key of love, it opens this gate, joining the soul. Only then will a human understand who he really is. He fully realizes freedom, eternity and God. Only then is the soul free to go to nirvana, paradise, that is, into the world where only love reigns."

"So it means that this Something that is our consciousness determines the destiny of our soul, doesn't it?"

"Absolutely right. Everything depends on our choice and on our aspirations."

The novice thought a little and then said quietly to himself, "So real paradise is not in the body."

"The body will never give you paradise, as the body is an eternal worry, an eternal problem. Paradise can be reached only through the connection of the soul with God."

"You said that very rarely do we feel ourselves being real, those who we actually are, our soul. How is this divine presence felt? Is it possible to understand with the help of these sensations what paradise is?"

"Only the human who looks at the world through a prism of love can understand divine presence. And to understand what paradise is... Well, for you to have a slight notion of it... If you choose the happiest moment in your life when your true love comes, when your life storms with waves of happiness and all-embracing joy, all these sensations will be equivalent to a small divine droplet of love scattered on you. But when a human enters nirvana, paradise, that moment when the soul joins God, figuratively speaking, is the same as if a human swims like a dolphin in the ocean of this infinite divine love. It is impossible to describe with words the fullness of these sensations, just as it is impossible to imagine it in full scope. Unfortunately, the human mind is limited, but in this limitation lies its beauty. Here, in a limited mind, an endless love should be born."

"Yes, everything is so simple and clear... You said that it is possible to reach the gateway through love and knowledge. In fact, people became saints in different times. It was through love, of course. What should we do with knowledge? In those times, people did not have all the information we do now."

"People even now have too little information. But the matter is that when a human reaches this gateway, any knowledge becomes accessible to him with the help of it. There are no restrictions there."

"I thought that if I limited my consciousness the way it was told to us in my sect, I shall come to God."

"Well, first, when you are limiting your consciousness with blind belief, you need incredible efforts to resist the attacks of your animal nature. Why? Because blind belief gives the animal nature freedom of actions.

At any moment, it can overflow your mind with unexpected doubts, and your belief will fail like a house made of cards. But if your belief is based on the strong foundation of knowledge, which allows you to prove to your mind in a well-reasoned and thorough way the real fact of the existence of God and by that to bring your animal nature in the corner and to leash it there, then you will receive real freedom and will be able to come to God.

"Second, Jesus never limited His pupils as your religious sect does. Your leaders try to build a small empire of authority based on the teachings. They force you to kiss their hands, to bow down in front of them. Who are they? Even Jesus, in spite of the fact that He was a Great Soul, was always a friend to the apostles, and if you remember this story, He even washed their feet. He did not bring people the enthrallment of a crowd but mostly the freedom of personal choice. He gave people a precept of love, this very key to the gateway. Recall His words, 'Love the Lord your God with all your heart and all your soul, and with your entire mind.' In this way, he showed that high morality, soul, and reason are the three components for maturation of a soul and its union with God. This was told by prophets of all teachings, for there is a sole source of knowledge. Let's choose Mohammed as an example..."

"Mohammed? Do you think his religion brings us closer to God?"

"Religion is created by people, but Mohammed preached the teachings. His true teaching is based on the same knowledge that Christ gave us."

"It can't be true!"

"Why can't it be? Do you know anything about Mohammed?"

"I don't know about him, but I have met in person his fanatic, violent followers when I worked as a journalist in Afghanistan. Believe me, it left in my soul bad memories. I saw what Islam is."

"You did not see Islam, you saw how the teaching of Mohammed was transformed by mercenary politicians. You can find fanatic believers in every religion. Is it possible to judge the teachings looking only at those people? Blind and furious fanaticism is the worst sign of any religion, the worst distortion of any teaching inasmuch as it completely awakens a person's animal nature, covered by a shield of good intentions. It is a manifestation of politics, a longing for world domination that is inherent in the ruling clique of each religion. Study the teachings of prophets yourself, did they call for it? All of them called for the spiritual development of a human. They called for the whole world to be united in sole love for God, suppressing in ourselves our animal nature, a devil, call it as you wish. A human, being in God, can not do evil things.

"Mohammed was a very unique person. I advise you to read about his life simply from a human position, without bias and conventionalities. Beginning in childhood, he aspired to self-cognition, and first he was guided by natural human desires. He was a poor boy, an orphan, a usual shepherd. When Mohammed was young, he thought that if he became rich he will fully understand himself. At the age of twelve, he began to work as a caravan escort. Along one of his routes he met a wise man who gave him a grain of knowledge and trained him to meditate; as a result, it radically changed his destiny. Mohammed began with his spiritual practices in order to understand the essence of God.

"In a while, his early dream came true. A successful marriage to a notable woman made him rich.

Mohammed understood, though, that richness was not the thing to which his soul aspired. He started to search for this something in authority, but couldn't find it there either. This fact drove him to search inside himself, inside his human essence. Mohammed often spent long hours at night in meditations, and finally they brought him to enlightenment. He understood the sense of internal essence, the sense of existence of all mankind as a whole, he found God - "al-illah" – which means "worthy worshiping," and due to that his soul woke up, having opened a source of true knowledge. Then, as the legend says, he received revelations from above, from archangel Gabriel or, as he is still called in the East, archangel Jibril. Mohammed not only received revelations from him but also became his favorite pupil. Gabriel told him sacrament of the teaching and the secret knowledge. In order to show the truth and the depth of knowledge of this teaching, he moved Mohammed in space and time, into the city of Jerusalem, where he arranged a meeting with Bodhisattva Issa and his enlightened pupils Abraham and Moses. Through these travels in time, Gabriel showed him the elusiveness and frailty of the material world in comparison with true knowledge and showed that only God has real force and is worthy of worshiping. All this knowledge sown in his strong soul bore rich fruits. The worthy pupil justified Gabriel's hopes. At that stage, Mohammed had done for mankind more good than anybody else could have done."

"But what about Jesus??

"Make no mistake, Jesus was a Bodhisattva, which means he was already born as God. But Mohammed was a person who managed to awaken the divine essence in himself. So when archangel Gabriel felt that Mohammed was prepared enough, he said to him, 'Now you should go to the world and bring this knowledge to other people.' Mohammed answered, 'How can I explain to people in words the ideas that I learnt from you in spirit?' 'Go and tell them that there is one God and He lights everything up like the sun with His Divine Love. I am like the Moon in the night of human life, I am reflecting the light of God and light the way in the darkness of consciousness. You are a guiding star showing the way to divine light.'

"Inspired by this conversation with Gabriel, Mohammed left the cave in which he meditated, and the first thing he saw was a breathtaking view of nature. In the huge evening sky, a young crescent shone dazzlingly, and a bright star glowed next to it. In that same instant, he had an insight and understood how to express this teaching to people. He understood that God is love, that God is a permanent action. God does not speak with words, He communicates with people through mediators, archangels, who bring His will to the consciousness of people. But a human himself is free to choose whether to understand God through his soul or not."

"What did Mohammed do? Did he give people belief?"

"Mohammed gave people not only belief, but also knowledge. Unfortunately for 600 years, people have falsified the teaching of Christ, having transformed it into religion. But Mohammed tried to bring people the lost knowledge in his renewed teaching. He told people everything he knew himself without concealing anything. Moreover, if you read history books, what kind of state was Arabia in before the year 610 when Mohammed began to preach? The country was in a general chaos of various idolatry and because of its leaders there often rose enmity between Arabian tribes. Mohammed did a great deed. He united militant people, Arabs, into a general brotherhood and in belief in the One worthy of worshiping. He told the truth about God, about things that Jesus taught: that God is eternal, omniscient, and almighty; that all people are equal before Him. He spoke about the immortality of the soul, about reincarnation (the resurrection of the dead), about judgment, about punishment beyond the grave for those who create evil in this world, about the necessity to establish justice, mercy, and moral duties in relations between people. Due to his wisdom, Mohammed managed to lead Arabs out of their deepest ignorance and political chaos and to show them the way to civilized cultural growth and prosperity."

"Perhaps it was really so. But what should we do with the 'sacred war against the unfaithful'? In fact, Muslim people claim that Mohammed himself preached it."

"During those dark times, Mohammed had to deal with wild tribes that understood only force. The word 'moslem' comes from a word 'muslim' which means 'obedient,' that is, obedient to Mohammed but not 'faithful.' This meaning, the word 'moslem' got much later. So, in those days, devoted people were those who were obedient to the Prophet and who followed him, spreading the teaching to other territories of Arabia to transform the chaos there into order. Unfaithful people were people who were not following his teaching. Mohammed was not only a great prophet, but he was also an ingenious commander and a wise politician. It was not easy to calm down the passion of wild militant tribes. Besides, Mohammed had to declare 'sacred war' against those religious priests who usurped authority and who were not interested in the unification of Arabs nor in worshiping their Gods. He struggled against those who had mercenary purposes, deceived people with the help of their belief, and corrupted human souls. In these actions, he is similar to

Christ. So, the Prophet struggled for the same purity of belief, as Jesus did, for worshiping the Holy One, for direct spiritual connection of each person with God."

"Well, let's admit that time was dark and tribes were wild," the novice pressed Sensei. "But now so many years have passed and still a strange 'sacred war' is being conducted. If God is the only one, why does the war still continue? How can you understand a person who winds explosives around his body and voluntarily goes into a crowd of peaceful inhabitants for death in the name of God, carrying away lives of other people with him?"

Sensei explained, "Because instead of the teaching that was given by the Prophet, the Muslim got religion, the leaders of which are more interested in mercenary purposes, personal well-being, and political influence in the world than in the souls of individual Muslims. They convince him that after his 'pious' action, his soul will get to Mohammed, to paradise. In fact, it will not get there, as the way to God is closed to everyone who creates evil. And this Muslim will be reincarnated repeatedly and again pass through all terrestrial circles of hell to make his soul as clean as it was before the creation of evil by this person. These deceived people are victims of religion. But the real guilty people are those who distorted the true teaching. This is the victory of the Devil over any religion."

"I heard that in the Koran there are some 'suras' that reject your words."

"In the Koran?" Sensei asked incredulously. "Do you know that the Koran was written after death of the Great Prophet? The adopted son of Mohammed, Zaid Ibn Thabit, collected all records of his sermons and, pay attention, he made an edition of the Koran in 651. Mohammed himself preached only orally. Sketchy records of his sermons and lessons were made by his first followers who partly remembered and partly wrote down the words of Mohammed. But even despite further additions to the Koran during the creation of religion, the knowledge that was truly given to Mohammed from the archangel Gabriel is still there. Now scientists are simply struck by the fact that while deciphering some 'original parts' of the Koran, they find real scientific knowledge..."

At that moment, Tatyana jabbed me in the side and whispered that she ought to call her parents so they didn't worry. I looked at my watch and realized that we should have been home already. We apologized and ran into the club where the nearest phone was located. After our long and persistent knocking, at last the door was opened by an old watchman with sleepy eyes. He had probably already begun to carry out his professional duties. Having scolded us a little because strangers were hanging around and he had not gotten any rest, he nevertheless allowed us to make a call. While Tatyana was speaking to her parents, I had time to jot down in my diary some of Sensei's words. Having informed our parents that we would be late, we hastened to the exit to join our company. When we came out, Sensei was still addressing the novice.

"You refer to the Bible with too much prejudice, as if it is a primary source. I understand that you were taught this way in your sect. But you are a journalist, you should be much more curious than ordinary people. The Bible, like the Koran or the Tripitaka, was written by followers. Moreover, these books went through numerous changes, meaning they already reflected religious points of view instead of the initial teaching that was given by the Great. To focus your attention, I repeat that literally for 600 years the teaching of Christ was greatly distorted and it was necessary to give a new teaching to Mohammed; it was the same, however, as Christ taught. But later this teaching was also transformed into religion by people who left only its form but changed its contents."

"But the Bible and the New Testament in particular were written from the words of Jesus by his followers."

"If you had had an opportunity to hear the teaching from Jesus Himself and to compare it to the one that you can read now in the Bible, you would find huge blanks and the absence of much knowledge," Sensei said with bitterness in his voice. "You assert that it was written by His followers, but you don't even wonder how. They were not the first followers, they were followers of followers. The teaching of Jesus was preached orally for a long period of time. Then lists of sayings of Jesus started to appear. One of the most ancient fragments from the Gospel according to St. John is dated 125 A.D., and the earliest and the most complete manuscript is dated to 200 A.D. You can imagine how the oral sermons could be mangled in two hundred years. One person understood in one way, another person did not understand, the next one concealed something, and so on. Moreover, in 325 the first Nicene ecumenical council, under the direction of the emperor Constantine, selected and canonized the four Gospels included in the New Testament out of numerous versions, with the purpose of strengthening the Church and personal authority. Exactly at that time, the teaching of Christ was completely altered, and a powerful lever of authority for managing crowds was made from it. Exactly at that Council, the orthodox point of view on corporeal revival was authorized under pressure of the emperor Constantine. All otherwise-minded Christians and the supporters of spiritual revival were declared heretics, and subsequently they were pursued and slaughtered all over the Empire, even though early Christians professed the ideology of reincarnation.

Mention of it can be found in the Bible. As a result, a natural question arises: why were authorities so afraid of it? Why did Constantine finally alter the teaching, having transformed it into religion? What was the reason behind that? Because the teaching gave people knowledge that released them from their fear of existence in our frail world. Knowledge brought people true freedom and the awakening of their souls. They were not afraid of death, they knew about reincarnation, about things beyond the border. And the most important thing is that they realized there was only God above them instead of any emperor or bishop. But it was terribly frightening for politicians and churchmen to lose their authority, for they were more absorbed by their material interests. The teaching of Jesus, which should have made people free, was transformed into religion and knocked into people's heads on penalty of death. Expansion of Christianity succeeded through violence, crusades were arranged, and so on.

"Besides, the Bible was rewritten by hand many times by different people, up to 1455 when Gutenberg's Bible was printed. Division of the text into chapters was first made in the 13th century by cardinal Stephen Lengton. The division of chapters into verses and their numeration was made by a Parisian publisher, Robert Stefan, who published the complete text of the Bible in 1553 for the first time. I won't even mention the fact that in the modern world, for example, the Catholic church considers itself authorized not only to interpret the Bible according to their opinion, but also to supplement it.

"Despite all of these corrections and distortions, the genius of Jesus lies in the fact that some of His knowledge, due to the initial duality of its sense, could reach descendants. That is why up to now the Bible awakens interest in the teaching of Christ in people. Because of the interpretation of this knowledge 'in its own way,' Christianity has never been united and at all times existed as many churches, branches, and sects struggling among themselves."

The novice thought a little and then asked, "Which expressions of Jesus do you think were kept in their dual sense?"

"Let's take even His most widespread expression frequently used in your sect, 'For where two or three are assembled in my name, there am I in the midst of them.' It is not plurality of people as your minister asserts. It is the integrity of one individual, where the soul, reason, and consciousness are gathered for the single purpose of understanding God. Or here are other words of Christ, which religious leaders use for attraction to their sect, 'No man can serve two masters: for either he will hate the one, and love the other; or else he will hold to the one and despise the other. Ye cannot serve God and mammon.' Jesus meant an individual choice of sense of life: either a human aspires to God, to freedom, or he aspires to mammon, that is, to riches, to the material world. Everything is very simple."

"It seems to be interpreted the same way in our sect."

"Yes, but under the aspiration to God, your religious leaders drum into your head that only through visiting their sect and studying their program can a person surely come to God. Actually, a person can come to God if he changes himself inside and if he grows an internal love and strengthens his belief with knowledge.

"Or, for example, Jesus said, 'So the last shall be first, and the first last: for many are called, but few chosen.' Life is given for us to grow spiritually. During it you can make a step forward, that is, to progress, or you can make a step back, to regress. Jesus said that if today God has made you a freer person and if He has enabled you to pay more attention to Him, it means that in the previous lives you deserved it. If you used this life for the regression of your soul, then in the next life He will put you in a more difficult condition for you to realize it. Any person inside, if he concentrates on his deep sensations, can feel the experience of previous lives."

"You said that in the Bible there are still some mentions of reincarnation. Which ones?"

"For example, if you remember in the Gospel according to St. John, there is an episode about Nikodemus, one of the university teachers, who secretly came at night to ask Jesus questions. So, Nikodemus asks Jesus, 'How can a man be born when he is old? Can he enter his mother's womb a second time and be born?' Jesus answered, 'Verily, verily I say unto thee, except a man be born of water and of the Spirit, he cannot enter into the kingdom of God. That which is born of the flesh is flesh; and that which is born of the Spirit is spirit.' Besides, there are also such words as, 'In my Father's house are many mansions,' meaning there is a plurality of existence of worlds.

"Christ told his pupils about the law of reincarnation, allowing them to understand that the soul regenerates for high-grade maturation. He talked about how to save the soul and how to reach the Kingdom of God, how to understand eternal life. He also said that the more spiritually advanced a person becomes, the harder the trial of the resisting animal nature or devil."

"Yes, judging by the Gospel, even Jesus was subject to attacks from the Devil. I always thought, why? How can it be if He were the Son of God?" the novice asked.

"Of course, Jesus was the Son of God," Sensei replied. "He was a strong soul. But He also named

Himself the Son of Earth as the Great Soul of Him was embodied in the ordinary body of a human. The animal nature is inherent in a human body. The animal nature is its integral part. Therefore even Jesus, being Bodhisattva, was subject to 'temptation' of the animal nature of His flesh, of His negative thoughts. He felt the same pain, the same feelings as an ordinary person. So Issa was in the same conditions. And for Him it was a thousand times more difficult than for any of you. Because He knew freedom, He knew God." It seemed to me that Sensei said these words with an unbearable nostalgia in his voice. The expression of his face changed as he continued, "And here, carrying out this mission, He finds himself in a human body with all its problems, with all these thoughts and emotions. With all the animal nature He had to put in a corner, in the depth of His consciousness, which always has to be kept like a barking dog on a leash. And your minister still says that it is paradise?!" Sensei exclaimed, "If that isn't hell, I don't know what is!"

After these words, Sensei paused and lit a cigarette.

"But does the Gospel only mention one episode of Christ's personal struggle with the Devil when He was in the desert? In fact, if Christ was put in the same condition as people were and the Devil is negative thoughts, it means that these thoughts should have been in Him all His life."

"Absolutely right. But Christ was the Great Soul full of the force of love, therefore He kept all these negative thoughts in Himself under strict control. The moment mentioned in the Gospel was His fight in His mind to consolidate the authority of His soul above his body. It was His personal Armageddon, which everyone is obliged to pass when they are born into a body. Bodhisattva unfortunately is not an exception. Why did He fast for forty days and nights? Because it takes about this long for the body to be exhausted, to become weak, for the animal nature to finally surrender. Jesus opened Himself spiritually to let His soul completely occupy His consciousness. But animal thoughts of the body constantly tempted Him, trying to win authority over the mind. They spoke in a hungry body, 'If thou art the son of God, command that these stones be made bread.' His thoughts answered on behalf of his soul, 'Man shall not live by bread alone, but by every word that proceedeth out of the mouth of God.' In this way, He emphasized His strength of mind, the essence of a real human, that is, of His soul. Negative thoughts chased Him again, '...If thou art the Son of God, cast thyself down, for it is written, He shall give His angels charge concerning thee: and in their hands they shall uphold thee, lest at any time thou dash thy foot against a stone.' Jesus answered Himself, '...It is written again, Thou shalt not tempt the Lord thy God,' thus showing His resistance of Spirit and control over crazy thoughts of the body. When thoughts of the animal nature tempted Him to own all empires of the world trying to wake in Him the main trump card, hunger for world authority begotten by insatiable megalomania, Jesus rejected them also by saying, 'And to Him alone shalt thou render worship.' Issa won this Armageddon with honor. He defeated His negative flesh thoughts with the power of His Spirit, with the force of immense love for God. The Soul of Bodhisattva was completely awakened in Him and He found himself. After that, Jesus began to carry out His mission, using in full all His knowledge and the force of immense divine love. That is why He created miracles by His belief. He cured sick people, revived the dead. As for this divine force, there are no barriers either on the Earth or in space.

"In general, during His life, Jesus had a clear, concrete division of thoughts of the soul and 'straddled' thoughts of the body. Take the time He prayed in the garden of Gethsemane before Judas's treachery. His Soul left his body, and the body exclaimed, 'O my Father, if it is possible, let this cup pass from me: nevertheless, not as I will, but as thou wilt.' The body was addressing the Soul as if the Soul of Jesus was part of God and had His force.

"Or here is another episode when Jesus was already hanging on the cross. He suffered greatly, He felt all the pain of a body with His Soul. Issa abandoned His body. When His Soul left the body, His mind cried, 'Ili, Ili! Lama savahfani?' That means, 'My God, My God! Why did you leave me?' It clearly shows how strongly Issa as the Great Soul not only owned His body but also reigned over His mind."

The novice was silent for a bit and then asked, "Tell me please, for a long time I have being tormented by this question, whether it is true or not that we are initially guilty?"

"The human is initially free, and there is no sin in his deeds. In fact, what is a sin? A sin is something that oppresses us inside at the level of the subconscious, it is something that separates us from God and makes us feeling afraid and guilty. So it is a natural consequence of an action of your mind after breaching universal moral laws and values. This is a sin. These laws are the code of your honor, your conscience. And if you have broken it yourself, you should become better and more pure in thoughts and deeds.

"Your religious leaders constantly drum to your heads that you are a slave of God and that you are initially guilty. Why? Because they profit if a person supports them financially, paying off 'sins' that he didn't commit. This is a certain psychological trick for a crowd. If you make a person believe that he is guilty, initially guilty, fear begins to grow in him. Your religious leaders use this artificially created fear for absolving your sins immediately, of course until next time.

"But a human inherently is not a slave of God; he is a son of God. A Father cannot hate His son, He can only love him. For God is love, and love can not have any fear. God gave people freedom of choice, and this is His most valuable gift to people as to His children."

"What about the legend that the Serpent brought harm to people?"

"This information was greatly distorted. The original legend is as follows. When God created a Human, that is a soul, He admired His creation, for it had been created in the image and likeness of Him. A human at that time was not in a body or in the world as some religions assert now..."

"Why wasn't he in a body if he was created in the image and likeness of Him?"

"How can you think that God is a constant material personality, that is, someone embodied like you and me and at the same time omnipresent?"

"Well, other religions also say it."

"What religions?! Study this question more closely. All world religions say that God is the only One, He is omnipresent. God is similar, how can I explain it, to energy, to a magnetic or any other field. This is a single field in which everything exists. God is the mighty energy of thought, which creates everything and appears to be everywhere. But He is not a person with a beard sitting on a throne, nothing of that kind, although if He wishes He can be temporarily embodied in a Human. God created us in His image and likeness, those of us who are inside of these bodies. A particle of Him, the soul, lives in each of us. Human 'paradise' was in heaven, as Jesus used to say.

"So, the Essence created by God was of a divine nature, that is, the soul. It did not know bad things, it knew only good things because it inherited divine love. It is natural that this Essence had great abilities and no barriers. Besides God, these Essences were also loved by Lucifier, angel of Light, who is the right hand of God. And he said to God, 'These Essences do not understand how much You love them because they know only good.' And Lucifer began to assert the individuality of the human, his position as a free Essence for cognition. He wanted humans to truly love God instead of simply existing in front of God as a plant pleasing His eyes. God 'ordered' Lucifer, 'If you love them as much as I do, teach them this.' God settled people on the Earth, which was specially created for humankind, with seas, land, plants, and different animals. Lucifer created a human body in which God placed a soul, giving birth to two natures: the spiritual and the animal. The power of mind was given by God to humans as the Children of God. The mind became a battlefield where the thoughts of both natures fought, which proves the creation of humans by God and Lucifer together. It also shows that Lucifer was and remains the right hand of God as he actively participated in the creation of humankind and actively participates in the education of the soul. Thus, Lucifer enabled people to understand and to learn perfectly what is good and what is bad. God gave people freedom of choice between these two natures. Since then, Lucifer has taken care of people."

"Why does Lucifer call himself the Legion?"

"It is because he acts through thoughts of our animal nature. As a rule, there are legions of these thoughts. Watch yourself because it may seem that you think only your own thoughts. But try to keep this thought in your mind for even ten minutes, and you will be surprised how many different unnecessary thoughts appear in your head. This is a legion. Therefore, figuratively speaking, Lucifer is always present in us, checking our confidence, the strength of our love for God.

"The power of thought given to us by God is huge; this force is called belief. The human who believes can really work wonders. The proof of this is not only in Jesus but also in many of His followers and followers of other great ones who worked and continue working wonders up to now. But the problem is that it does not depend what someone believes in, this force can be used for both good and evil. The result depends on the side your consciousness is inclined to take. If you are inclined to evil in your thoughts, that is, your material, animal essence gnaws at you, then a great number of problems appear in your life. They appear all the time and everywhere – at work, in private life, in your family, and so on. These problems gnaw at you because evil thoughts take the force of your belief and try to lead you away from thoughts about God in every possible way. If you turn your consciousness to good thoughts, the bad thoughts lose this force, become weak, and after that we can completely control them. With the constant support of positive thoughts in our consciousness, the course of our life will become more even. The most important thing is that a human develops himself spiritually and recognizes the force of love."

"Do evil thoughts completely disappear then?" the novice questioned.

"No, they always exist in you," Sensei explained, "but they do not have enough strength to affect you. Figuratively speaking, evil thoughts are waiting for an opportunity when you weaken your control so that they can take away your force of belief again. This sharp-sighted guard of the animal nature lives in your body as an integral part. As long as the soul is in a body, these tests of your patience will never stop. But when the soul completely ripens and leaves the cycle of reincarnation, Lucifer is also sincerely glad for it just as a strict and wise teacher can be glad for his pupil because the soul has passed all tests with honor and joined God in its true Love. God is a parent. He is always glad to see the successes of His child.

"So, our life is like school for the soul. Each embodied person experiences his personal Armageddon, taking as part of his winnings either good or evil thoughts. Therefore the knowledge given to people can lead either to freedom or to slavery. But no one prevents us from our free choice, neither God nor the Devil. If we choose God, we strive towards God; if we choose the Devil, we strive towards the Devil. That means that we pave our road to paradise or nirvana or we throw ourselves to the hell of reincarnation."

"If a human does not have original sin, then why is the death of Christ an expiation for human sins?"

"Just think thoroughly about this sentence. What kind of an expiation can it be? If it were in fact true, if only Christ took our sins, then whatever sins we commit now are already forgiven. Is that really so?! All this is nonsense. Each human himself is responsible for his sins before God.

"The death of Christ has been made the greatest secret, and religious leaders still argue about it. Why did He let them crucify Him? Jesus was the Son of God, He was able to destroy the whole planet, not just a group of miserable people, as the force of God was given to Him. People wanted it to happen when they crucified him. They said, if you are the Son of God, come down from the cross. But Christ was not tempted, He allowed them to crucify His body. Why? Because the whole purpose of Christ's coming was both to give people his teaching but also to give people a choice. Jesus agreed to these tortures in order to show the will of God, the essence of which is freedom of human choice: either decide to turn to God or decide to remain in the darkness of thoughts of his animal nature. Christ brought this freedom of choice to people. This is the greatest deed that was hidden from the majority of people and it is the biggest sin of Christianity as a whole. For both before Him and after Him, people worked wonders and preached about the One above. But people remember only the crucifixion of Jesus, and the second half of His life in the East when He preached, worked wonders, and cured sick people is partly lost in time. In various sources of ancient times, for example in the Bhavishya Mahapuran written in Sanskrit, there were a few mentions of Him as of the prophet Issa."

"Did Jesus remain alive in the world?" The novice was sincerely surprised.

"Certainly. Due to the efforts of Pontius Pilate, the body of Christ remained alive and Jesus had to return to His body. For, as a Bodhisattva being born into a body, He should be in it to his last breath."

"Due to the efforts of Pontius Pilate?!" The novice was even more surprised.

"Yes. Actually, Pontius Pilate understood who Christ was. That is why he received freedom, the release from reincarnation, from Jesus. His name was engraved in the history of mankind."

"Sounds interesting. When did he understand that Jesus was God?"

"When he met Jesus, moreover when he realized who was standing in front of him, Pilate tried to save Issa in every possible way, convincing Him to run away, warning Him that the crowd would kill Him. But Jesus refused, saying that if it was His fate for His body to be lost, then it should happen so and people should make their choice. Pilate even tried to convince the crowd that Jesus was innocent, for them to release Him, as there was such a tradition in honor of a great holiday. But people demanded to see Christ crucified and killed. It was their choice.

"However, Pontius Pilate did everything his own way. As Bodhisattva, it would be much easier for Christ to finish His mission this way in a human body. Because of love, Pilate tried to serve God according to his own understanding and saved the body of Christ, thinking it was Christ himself although there was no Jesus there anymore. When He was on the cross, He abandoned His body in order not to be tempted by painful torments. But the body still remained alive."

"How could the body remain alive if it is written in the Bible that 'One of the soldiers with a spear pierced his side, and forthwith out came blood and water'?"

"The reason is that it was specially performed for the public by Pontius Pilate's men. This blow was struck by one of Pilate's best soldiers very professionally. He hit between the 5th and 6th ribs on the right side of the body, to the left and upwards, creating the illusion that he had punctured His heart. But actually, no vital organs were hurt. The body was unconscious but still alive. This is one of the important facts confirming the participation of Pilate in saving Jesus. It was done to assure the crowd that Christ had died. The shins of the other two crucified but still alive criminals were broken on purpose. In this way, they could not stand on their feet and died painfully by suffocation.

"Moreover in those days the crucified were not allowed to be buried in separate tombs or to be given to their relatives for burial. They were thrown into paupers' grave. The body of Jesus, again according to the order of Pontius Pilate, was taken off the cross and carried to a cave. For almost two days, the body of Jesus was looked after, treated, and constantly smeared with herbal potions for bringing it to consciousness. To say it in modern language, they tried to reanimate him.

"But as a matter of fact, the prophecy of Jesus ran that He will revive from the dead and will appear shining on the third day. So Jesus should have come on the third day not in flesh but in the Spirit of God to dispel all doubts that He was sent from God. But Pontius Pilate and his supporters did not let the body of Christ die. Christ was forced to come into a body.

"In his understanding, Pilate certainly saved Christ. That is why Jesus appreciated his deed and released him from a chain of reincarnations. Pilate was the first who talked to Christ after His revival."

"Well, that is not known for sure."

"It is known. Even up to now, there are some mentions of it. Someone keeps them carefully so as not to shake his authority, but everything is in vain and he will pay for it. So when Jesus regained consciousness, Pontius Pilate talked to Him and begged Jesus to leave the country because the persecutions of the priests in power could begin again. Pilate asked Him, 'Take pity upon me, do not go out to the people.' Jesus answered that He would execute the request of Pilate but that He would leave only after He saw His pupils. And He stuck to His word. As the main mission was finished, Issa left. He went to the East with His mother and one of His pupils. Jesus lived more than a hundred years and was buried in the city of Shrinagar, the capital of Kashimir, where He settled down in His last years. This picturesque place is located between two lakes at the foot of the Himalayas. His tomb is located in a crypt of the tomb Rozabal, which means 'the tomb of the prophet.'"

"Maybe that really happened. But it is impossible to prove that there are remains of Jesus' body in that tomb."

"Why is it impossible? It can be proved. There are some traces of the crucifixion left. In particular, scratches on the bones of the hands, on the feet, and even traces from a spear on the ribs. Moreover, He has a badly healed fracture in the distal half of the right tibial diaphysis."

"A fracture? Was His leg broken during the execution?"

"Oh, there is no connection to the execution. It happened much later when Christ was rather old. That is why I draw your attention to the fact that the fracture is specific, it is badly knit. It proves that Issa lived until His old age."

"What about the idea that Jesus rose into the sky in a body?"

"Obviously such an insertion was necessary for someone to make in order to strengthen his flock's belief in the material nature. And in general, you should read the Bible more attentively: out of four Gospels, only two of them mention the Ascension. It the Gospels according to St. Matthew and St. John, they write about Jesus' meeting with His pupils on a mountain. And in the Gospels according to St. John, it is even written that, after this meeting, Jesus left with His favorite pupil. There are numerous mentions of Issa staying in the East after His crucifixion. This information is kept not only in the East, but also in the Vatican library."

"Let's say you are right. But if that happened in bad times, then why not tell people the truth now, if you say that there are numerous mentions of Jesus staying in the East and these documents confirm it. The time has completely changed."

"Time has changed, but people strive for authority just as they did thousands of years ago. Can you imagine what it would mean for the top religious leaders to tell people the truth and show the world the historical documents they hide so carefully? It would be a great catastrophe for them! It would undermine all the foundations of their religion, would shake belief of the novices and their huge flock, and consequently would undermine their authority. Nobody will ever do it. But a human who is in a constant search of knowledge without doubt will come sooner or later across these texts."

"In general, you may be right," the novice said thoughtfully. "To tell the truth, I had some doubts concerning the Ascension, but about Pontius Pilate... who would have thought it!"

"Yes, Pontius Pilate deserved the favor of God for his love, but he certainly did more harm than good to Issa," Sensei said deep in thought. "He doomed Him to more than eighty years of wandering in a body. But obviously that was the payment of Christ for the salvation of Pilate."

A short silence reigned, with each participant of this conversation plunged into his thoughts. We also stood silently, not daring to interrupt such a fascinating conversation.

"I wonder," the novice started talking again, "why did Jesus come to the Jews but not to any other nation? Were the people chosen by God? It is written everywhere in the Bible that beginning with Abraham God calls them His favorite people."

"You see, God has no distinctions of nationalities, color of skin, and so on, as all people are children of God. God loves them all equally. But when one of your children falls ill, you give all your attention and love to this sick child so that he recovers more quickly. The same is true with God. Recall the words of Jesus, 'They that are in health need not a physician, but they that are sick.'"

"Is the number of His pupils somehow connected to mysticism or numerology? In fact, there were twelve of them and Jesus turns out to be the thirteenth?"

"No, there is no mysticism in it. He simply searched among people for pupils with more or less ripened souls. He was lucky to find at least twelve individuals among those people, but one of them betrayed Him."

The novice grinned, "Yes, if you follow the words of Jesus in the Bible then you are right, a sick person needs a doctor, not a healthy one. Though today, it seems to me that the whole planet needs a doctor and not just this nation."

"Absolutely right. Just look at what is going on in our country – materialism has been cultivated for more than seventy years. The slightest freedom of choice appeared and people plunged into various religions like fishes as their spiritual nature also needs to develop. Just look how many new sects, branches, and religions appeared and began to prosper at once.

"In our country, that's understandable. But take a look at what is going on around the world. Everywhere there is a splash of various religions. People are tossed from one to another. It seems like they like it. Everywhere they are treated well, everywhere they are smiled at, politely spoken to. But the soul rejects their teachings because it needs real knowledge, because it wants Freedom, while sects and religions are too limited. They give more food to the mind than to the soul. The souls feel that under this trumpery, this externally 'authentic' shell, the fruit itself is rotten. That's why the soul trembles, while man is tossing in search of wholly ripe fruit."

"I'm sorry, but you mentioned that time is beginning to shrink. What do you mean by that?"

"It was predicted by the ancients," Sensei explained, "and even Jesus said that, 'And except those days should be shortened, there would no flesh be saved: but for the elect's sake those days shall be shortened.' That is, when mankind as a whole faces the key choice or, as it is said in eschatology, when they stand on the threshold of divine justice, one of the main attributes of this time will be its compression. Basically, nothing will radically change. As the clock showed 24 hours per day, it will continue showing it. The calendar will remain as it is, and there will still be 365 days per year. But inside of the soul, something will start to tremble and the human will feel this shortage of time. He will notice that time runs faster; a day flies by as if an instant, a month flies by as if a week, years fly by as if months. Time will become more compressed and dense. It is a certain signal, a sign for the soul."

"Yes," the interlocutor said thoughtfully, "perhaps the predictions of the prophets are beginning to come true. But this is a prediction of the Second Advent. Is this time really coming? How can I find out that Christ has come? Do you remember that when Jesus came for the first time, nobody believed for a long time that He was truly the Son of God. And now just look, many people name themselves Christs or say that they were sent by Christ as the Comforter. On the one hand, all of them say it is true according to the Bible, but on the other hand there is no trust in them. How can one tell the true Christ from the false Savior?"

"It is extremely easy. In fact, the Bible says that Jesus resurrected the dead and that it was enough for a sick person just to touch His clothes to recover. Judging from this, I think the most appropriate thing would be to use the Zen practice. For this purpose, it is enough to take a big and firm stick and to hit with all your force the one who names himself Christ. If the stick blossoms after that, it will mean that it was Christ. If that does not happen, it will mean that he was only an adventurer. In that case, it would be nice to hit him one more time so that he does not take other people's glory again."

We stood silently for some seconds and thought over the words we had heard. First, the novice took it seriously. But when he got the sense of these words, he burst out laughing with all his heart, and the crowd laughed as well.

"Perhaps that is the most effective method," he said with a smile. "But seriously?"

"To put it seriously, you should not wait for Jesus to come as a human, for He will come as the Son of God into people's souls. And He will reign one thousand years as the King sitting on a throne of not only our souls but also our minds. Recall His words in the Gospel according to St. John, 'God is a Spirit'; 'I am the way, and the truth, and the life: no man cometh to the Father, but by me'; 'And I will pray the Father, and he will give you another Comforter, that he may abide with you for ever; Even the Spirit of truth; whom the world cannot receive, because it seeth him not, neither knoweth him: but ye know him; for he dwelleth with you, and will be in you'; 'At that day ye shall know that I am in my Father, and ye in me, and I in you.'"

The novice was silent for a while and then asked, "I wonder whether there will be an end to the world? Recently, the most different dates began to appear in newspapers. Our sect, as I understand, tries to match this date with predictions of various astrologers pointing to the date of the parade of the planets. So, I wonder when the Apocalypse will come, when will we appear before the justice of God at last?"

"You know, for two thousand years people have been waiting for the Armageddon and the Second Advent of Christ. Almost all religions are based on this idea that as soon as tomorrow the world will end and those who are not in their rows will all die in Gehenna. What can I tell you about this? Each human in his life experiences his personal Armageddon, but not everyone wins it and not even everyone understands that he faces this Armageddon. Therefore, you should not be afraid of the Apocalypse that will come for everybody, for it is easier to die all together. The main thing is to win your personal Armageddon and not to appear in that company."

"That's right! I myself thought that we should do something now because it is unknown what will happen tomorrow. To tell the truth, the words you have spoken have somehow relieved my soul. This absolute uncertainty, all these horror stories are already getting on my nerves. But yet, I do not understand what religion you profess?"

"I do not profess and do not belong to any religion. I belong only to God," Sensei replied simply.

After that, the conversation turned to more frank topics concerning the novice personally. I had the impression that the guy talked with Sensei as if they were alone in the universe. He told Sensei more and more about himself, about his life, as though there was no silent crowd, as though it had dissolved in the night. It seemed to me that both interlocutors were two tired wanderers who met by chance under a star's infinity. They were mutually absorbed in this conversation about the eternal, about the essence of things, as if all restrictions of space and time had disappeared.

"...It's so amazing. You know, recently, for some reason, I was unlucky in finding a good spiritual guide. Either I was not satisfied with their answers, or they were not satisfied with my questions. During our constant disputes we, as they say, beat the air, milled the wind, spending our time in vain. But the things you say... I simply catch myself on the thought that I can not argue with you because it coincides with my internal conception of the world. It would be an honor for me to have such a Teacher if, of course, the Teacher considers it worthy to have such a disciple."

"I would advise you to search for a teacher neither in me nor in anybody else. It is not because you are an unworthy disciple but because you yourself have much more of it. I see a spark in you. I would advise you to study everything yourself. Study sacred books of various religions and make for yourself a collective image of such ideas: who God is, what truth, belief, and miracles are and so on. Because if there were only one unique holy religion then all other people could not be saved and there would be no other miracles. But miracles of belief happen in other religions too. Moreover, if you have an opportunity, study psychology, biology, anatomy, morphology. It is also necessary to study astronomy, quantum physics, chemistry... In general, broaden your knowledge in the field of exact sciences as much as you can. I am sure that you will begin to understand what I want to tell you. Now you simply feel it, but then you will begin to understand. When you begin to understand it, you begin to understand God. And the best Teacher is God."

That evening we got home on the last tram. It was already late, after midnight, but I simply could not fall asleep as I was completely shocked at this conversation with Sensei. My diary, as my best friend and silent interlocutor, took all the outpouring of my soul. Our dialogue of thoughts and writing continued until the morning. Only when the sun rose in the sky and the world began to wake up slightly, only then did the bed, which had been missing me for a long time, embrace my body with its soft coverlets. Thank God it was Sunday, that is, a national day off.

41

Time flew by quickly. The stressful time of final examinations began. People were a clot of nerves and sweat. Strange enough, but during this last year of my school life, I began to take this intense process more easily. After everything I had experienced, examinations seemed to be only an ordinary check of my knowledge but not a hard trial of destiny as many of my schoolmates considered them to be. When all this was over, when at last the long-awaited graduation party came, for a long time I still could not believe that my life goes on and that all this is not a dream.

Meeting at dawn with all our classmates in a picturesque place in the country, we started talking about professions we were going to choose. Many dreamt of becoming doctors, lawyers, economists, and businessmen. And when I was asked about it, I sincerely answered, "I want to become human."

Of course, my classmates did not understand the sense of these words to the fullest extent, but many of them became more serious and thoughtful. Indeed, we stood at the beginning of our independent way of life, at the moment of our personal choice for our destiny. It was still up in the air how our destiny would change our lives. Looking closely at the destinies of different people who have already lived the greater part of their lives, it is possible to see that the net of their vital roads and footpaths sooner or later merge into one road, that is, an attempt to become human. For, as Sensei once said, it's the true sense of our lives.

42

Because of a graduation party, unfortunately I had to miss a spiritual training. The next day, I phoned Tatyana, and she told me some very pleasant news. It appeared that Sensei was planning a week-long holiday, and the guys persuaded him to travel to the seaside with them. Even Nikolai Andreevich decided to use his days off from work, which he was saving for such a rare occasion of a round-the-clock dialogue with Sensei.

"I said that you would go too," Tatyana said over the phone.

"That's great, you're a real friend! For sure, I won't miss it."

We decided to go in three cars: Sensei's Zhiguli, Nikolai Andreevich's Volga, and Andrew's old Zaporozhets that he had borrowed from his grandfather. All necessary things were found collectively. Volodya promised to get tents. Stas and Eugene turned out to be passionate scuba divers and provided a supply of all fishing accessories, including an inflatable rubber dinghy. Tatyana and I took responsibility for the dishes, and Kostya was responsible for well water supply.

43

At the appointed day at five o'clock in the morning, rattling with our bowls and spoons, Tatyana and I crept along the silent streets. We came to a place of general meeting. Ruslan and Yura were already there. Then came Stas and Eugene. They told us that Sensei would be an hour late because he had worked until morning. The guys said that usually he does not stop until he has seen the last patient. The endless queue at his door finally stopped growing at almost two o'clock in the morning. Obviously, people found out that the chiropractor was leaving for a week, so they came in droves. By five o'clock in the morning, Sensei had finally finished his reception.

A bit later, Andrew and Slava arrived in his grandfather's jalopy, which seemed to be as old as Andrew's grandfather himself. But Tatyana and I were happy to go even by such means of transportation. When you are in a good company, a Zaporozhets isn't any worse than a Mercedes. We began to put things into the steel car top carrier, having filled a trunk with our luggage almost to the top.

"Well, Kostya will have to put his bag next to him," Andrew said in a bossy way, barely able to close the trunk.

But when Kostya arrived, Andrew's jaw drooped. Kostya's luggage arrived by Volga together with a fully loaded trailer. As we helped unload these endless bags and sacks, Andrew almost lost his gift of speech. Helplessly waving his hands, he blew up at last:

"You are out of your mind! It looks like you are going to the North Pole. We are going for a week, and just the food you brought will be enough for three years! Moreover, these huge flasks filled with water! Sensei told you to take one, not four. Why not bring a tank!"

"To tell the truth, I wanted but I could not. There was no suitable transport," Kostya answered with a smile, nodding at his father's Volga.

"You're nuts! Just tell me, where can I fit all this? What do you want me to do with these barrels?! Unless we attach them to the Zaporozhets instead of wheels?!"

"But Nikolai Andreevich seemed to promise he'd take something in his trailer."

"That's it, he only 'seemed to promise.'"

"OK, don't lose your cool, we'll think of something."

For good fifteen minutes, Andrew indignantly circled the huge heap of Kostya's treasure. But Kostya only laughed the matter off, saying, "I will see how your Excellency will thank my Majesty for unforgettable comfort at the seaside."

While Andrew broke out in the next fountain of emotions, Tatyana asked Kostya, "Really, why did you pack so much?"

"Well, why not enjoy ourselves? I tried hard, not for myself but for everybody," the 'philosopher' said cunningly. "In general, all this is only ashes and vanity." Taking her gently around the waist, Kostya pensively said, "Of all, thy charming lips are most precious for me."

"Oh, you," Tatyana gently pushed him away and burst out with laughter.

Kostya made a suffering face and said with pathos, "Ah, pride of heart costs many torments!" Looking sideways at Tatyana, he added, "I have so hardly pulled my bowstring, / That I am afraid my bow will be broken!"

"He will not get away from me. I shall make it difficult for him," Andrew casually said loudly, continuing to mutter to himself.

All of us roared with laughter as Sensei, Volodya, and Victor drove up. Looking at the huge heap of things, Sensei asked in confusion, "Guys, are you going to the North Pole?"

All our company burst out laughing again, but Andrew, having found an accomplice in Sensei, started to complain.

At last Nikolai Andreevich arrived with the long-awaited trailer. But it appeared that the trailer was too small for all of Kostya's goods. Somehow we pushed things into three cars and began to ram our bodies inside. Slava sat in Sensei's car. Tatyana and I placed ourselves among the bags on the back seat of the Zaporozhets. And Kostya as the most guilty person got a vacant seat. It was in front, near Andrew, on a sitting which was not only non-standard, very low, but it also rocked here and there being fastened with only one screw. So Kostya, because of his height, felt all the charm of the three-hour trip in the Zaporozhets. But the never-ending humor of our guys smoothed all discomfort with friendly, cheerful laughter.

Our Zaporozhets rumbled ahead of the whole column. Andrew tried to squeeze all possible force out of it by pressing the gas pedal. Sensei and the senior guys followed us, keeping a distance. Nikolai Andreevich, being loaded up to the top, slowly drove somewhere behind Sensei. It was not enough for Andrew to head the line, so he made up his mind to show us that that Zaporozhets was the coolest car on the road. He began to overtake one car after another, speeding and throwing his chest out with pride. Kostya crossed himself for fun at these maneuvers, clutched at the front panel, and started to pray about the salvation of all drivers suffering from such an inveterate driver of this jalopy.

We rushed forward a little bit. On the way we saw a small roadside market. In the distance, Tatyana saw strawberries in baskets on the ground and shouted to the guys through the noise of the roaring engine to stop the car. When we stopped at last, Kostya gave a sigh of relief trying to get out, as he said, from this tin in which he doubled himself up like a mackerel. To let us get out, Kostya had to drag out his armchair again. The whole market observed this comedy. Moreover when Kostya at last slammed the door, a mirror fell off of it. Andrew yelled at him as though he had ruined the most sacred thing, "Master's fist should strike your body and his leg should strike your muzzle! Who on earth slams a door like this?! For three days, I have been collecting this car from pieces. It is a valuable antique! You should treat it gently, like a woman..."

And there was more of a lecture on this topic. The guys dispersed in the market choosing berries. I remained near the Zaporozhets waiting for others. Sensei with the guys drove up, but when they got out of the car, something strange happened.

One woman, wearing a black kerchief, about forty-five years old, stood without any interest with her goods. Her eyes were red from tears. Having noticed Sensei, she hastily stepped over her berries, practically scattering them all over the ground with this motion. Having run up to Sensei, she fell down at his feet and began to implore him, lamenting in tears, "I beg you, Gabriel, take care of my sonny. How shall I live without him now?! Please, Gabriel, take me to him. I do not want this thrice cursed life any more, I do not want it! My God, have mercy on me, let me go to my sonny..."

I was standing very close by and saw how Sensei's eyes changed. Some shine appeared in them, or more correctly, some soft, tender light that changed Sensei's features. At this moment I felt that my lotus flower began to vibrate intensively. And this pulse force came not from my thoughts but, as it seemed to me, it came from Sensei. He bent over the woman, raising her.

"Rise, woman," he told her in a very calm, quiet voice.

It seemed to me that his voice became somewhat unusual. The woman rose a little but did not stand up from her knees, continuing to beg him, but this time it was more quietly, looking directly in his eyes. Sensei tenderly put his hand on her head and said, "Do not worry, woman. Everything is fine with your Nikolai. He is a pious man. He has already been taken care of."

The woman stretched her hands to him. Her eyes were lit with some sparkle of hope, but her face became stiffened in a single impulse of begging, "Let me, Gabriel, let me go to him..."

Such words of despair made me shiver. At this moment, Sensei's face was covered with a light haze, and his face became even nicer because of it. My lotus flower pulsed even more.

"Everyone has his own time. You still need to take care of Ksyusha. You will be a guest at her wedding, you will await her firstborn, you will nurse him for a week. And on the ninth day, you will go to your Nikolai to tell him what a fine grandson he has got," Sensei said calmly.

With each word of Sensei, the eyes of the woman became lighter and kinder. Teardrops of joy began to shine on her face. The woman broke into a smile. Not knowing how to express her gratitude, she began to fall down to his feet again. Sensei tried to raise her up from the ground. Then some old women who traded next to her ran up, lifted her from the ground, took her arms, and led her to the village saying, "Hush, Mashenka, dear, let's go, let's go home..."

The woman went quietly, with her face touched, whispering something to herself and constantly crossing herself. Other old women began to collect her scattered goods. All these events happened within one minute.

At this time, Nikolai Andreevich drove up. Having come up hastily to our motionless company with Yura and Ruslan, he inquired what had happened.

"Some old bag freaked out," Eugene said, as he was standing far from the Teacher. "She fell to Sensei's feet, all in tears, asked something."

Sensei silently lit a cigarette, after everything that had happened. When Nikolai Andreevich began to ask, he changed the topic to usual things, having answered shortly, "Yes, things happen in life. A woman is in sorrow."

"I see... And why did you stop here? We did not plan it." Nikolai Andreevich asked Kostya.

"Well, we wanted to buy some strawberries."

Our company walked once again around the market with Sensei. Having chosen ripe berries, Sensei bought a big basket for all of us. Another old woman, packing strawberries into three packets, tenderly spoke to us.

"You, children, do not take offence. Not even a month has passed since the woman's son Nikolai died in a crash. He was her only son, her hope and support. Her husband died a long time ago... And such sorrow again. He, her sonny, was so young. A little daughter of his remained, Oksana, she is five. Masha's destiny is a heavy one. She brought up her son almost alone, and now she has to support her granddaughter together with her daughter-in-law. I don't understand what happened to her. She has absolutely lost her head from sorrow."

"Yes," Nikolai Andreevich agreed with sympathy. "Stress can cause even worse mental disorders. I remember there was one case..."

Having listened to eloquent examples from his practice, my consciousness calmed down a little. "Well," I thought, "it's no wonder she rushed to the very first man."

As we drove, the guys cheerfully chattered about their matters while eating ripe strawberries. During Kostya's latest joke, it suddenly dawned on me. At this moment, I precisely recalled that woman's babbling and Sensei's answers. "Stop! She didn't mention the name of her son, and moreover she did not say the name of her granddaughter. But Sensei precisely named Nikolai and Ksyusha. I nearly choked on a strawberry because of this discovery. I did not want to eat it any more. Recalling Sensei's face, my lotus started to vibrate again, distributing pleasant sensations all over my body. I physically felt the presence of Sensei nearby. More accurately, I did not feel Sensei himself, but I felt the force that came from him at that moment. And I felt so nice and cozy, as if someone had wrapped me up with soft petals. In this state of bliss I dozed off.

44

I woke up because someone was shaking me by my shoulder. "Wake up, sleepyhead, we're almost there," Tatyana said.

At the next stop, we limbered up our numb legs. The air smelt of sea and freshness. While Andrew, Victor, and Volodya tried to repair the pinging engine of the Zaporozhets, we had a snack in the nearest outdoor cafe.

In half an hour, our motorcade was at the resort area, where people with beautiful chocolate color bodies lounged around in a carefree way in their bathing suits. Sensei's car headed our column. Andrew could not concentrate on the road as he was trying to look around but not break any traffic laws.

Passing by one of boarding houses, Eugene pointed out to us a billboard he saw from the window. There was written in huge, bold type, "A well-known sensitive of international class, chiropractor, fortune teller, magician, and wizard Vitaliy Yakovlevich... carries out medical and recovery sessions. Sessions beginning at 20.00 daily."

"Who is he?" Tatyana and I asked the guys.

"I don't know," Kostya shrugged his shoulders.

"Look, isn't it that the "Neanderthal man," the one who hung spoons on himself? Do you remember?!"

"Yeh, that odd fellow?! Maybe. If I'm not mistaken he was also Vitaliy Yakovlevich. What did he call himself... the

Pantocrator of Space and the whole Earth..."

The guys began to noisy recall that case, laughing at the tricks of this 'deity-tramp.'

Meanwhile having crossed the resort area, we drove to a peninsula that measured about 12 kilometers. It was necessary here to have a car in order to get to a secluded place and camp as we wanted. It seemed the local authorities didn't want any more adventurers in the neighborhood, as a huge pipe was laid across the only road. Right there in the bushes, though, the guys found two extremely wide boards, which were left by caring drivers. After placing the boards on the pipe, our drivers rolled the cars to the closed side of the road like professional stuntmen. Only Nikolai Andreevich's trailer made them sweat.

Having reached one of the most beautiful nooks of nature, we chose a place that was not too spoilt by campers. Having collected all the garbage left by careless tourists, we burnt it and began to set up camp. Sensei again appeared to be a talented and skilled leader. He took into consideration all trifles of camp arrangement, even a possible storm. All the guys were busy and enthusiastically helped Sensei and each other. All Kostya's things turned out to be really useful, having transformed our camp into a cozy, comfortable mini-town. Kostya did not miss any opportunity to emphasize this fact, reminding us that Andrew was a sadist and tortured him the whole way in the electric chair. Tatyana and I arranged a kitchen. The guys put up a special tent for food and gave us a kerosene camp stove for cooking.

Life in our camp started at full speed. After lunch, we bathed in the sea like dolphins and warmed our bones on hot sand with great pleasure. The senior guys floated in the sea in an inflatable rubber dinghy. Nikolai Andreevich read a book and Sensei dozed in the shadow of an umbrella, having covered himself with a towel. We decided to play cards. Kostya tried to count cards, but it was practically impossible as there were too many of us and we played with two stacks of cards. At his next failure, Kostya started to count card combinations in his head according to his special arithmetic system. While doing one of these odd calculations, he raised his eyebrows as if surprised and asked, "Sensei, what is the largest prime number you can think of?"

Sensei answered without opening his eyes, "In short or in full?"

"In short, of course."

"2 to the 13,466,917th minus 1," Sensei said simply, as though the question was about a usual multiplication table. "This number can be divided only by 1 or itself. I think that is the largest prime number that I am capable of counting in my head."

Kostya turned to his side in surprise. Then he started to calculate something energetically again. Sensei, having opened his eyes, added, "If you want to calculate my IQ, you are wasting your time; it is much lower than yours."

After saying these words, Sensei turned to the other side and plunged into somnolence again. Kostya was slightly shocked, "Say! Sensei is cool! How did he know about IQ? I just thought it."

"Yeah," said Andrew, "this question remained a sweet dream in his memory until it turned into a rotten one waiting for the answer."

The guys laughed, having won again.

In the evening, Sensei failed to meet our expectations that he would tell us something unforgettable, sitting at the fire beneath the stars. Right after dinner, Sensei went to sleep, probably because his accumulated weariness had affected him. And we sat at the fire for a long time, laughing light-heartedly and telling each other different stories from our lives.

45

In the morning, I woke around seven o'clock because somewhere nearby seagulls shouted disgustingly. I heard the guys' conversation, as they had left their tent upon hearing the noise.

Stas said to Eugene in a sleepy voice, "It's so early, but Sensei is already fishing. I wonder what he is going to catch from the seacoast, moreover with a fishing rod. Let's go and check."

My curiosity became much stronger than sweet dreaming. I hastened to get out of my tent. Sensei peacefully sat on a folding chair with a fishing rod in his hands. Nearby stood a three-liter jar half filled with water. A few seagulls ran around him shouting indignantly. When we came up, the seagulls flew up and hung in the air near Sensei, examining us from above with curiosity.

"Sensei are you fattening up the seagulls?" Stas grinned, looking at the empty jar.

"Not exactly. They are teaching me how to catch fish," Sensei answered without any shadow of confusion.

We took it as a joke and laughed.

"Why didn't you wake us earlier? We could have brought a fishing net ..."

"Oh, forget about the fishing net. I just wanted some fish soup."

Just for fun, Eugene demonstratively glanced into the empty jar, turning it around in the light, and said with humor, "Yes, the soup will be rich with such fish."

At this moment, the seagull that flew above us dropped a small fish, which fell right next to Sensei's feet. Everybody laughed.

"Look, Sensei! There's a fish for you," Eugene said with humor, putting it into the jar of water.

Volodya and Victor came up and asked, "What's going on?"

"You see, Sensei with his fishing rod made even the seagulls feel pity," Eugene said. "They were already tired of watching this empty jar."

We laughed loudly again. Sensei said smiling, "Alright, those who laugh most at me will scale the fish for the fish soup and for the grill, too."

We roared with laughter, imaging cutting this tiny fish while a big crowd waited for it. Sensei laughed at us, and then said, "Well, you storytellers, pull this out..."

He pointed to a thick fishing line that was fastened with one end to the leg of a chair, while the other end was deep in the water. The guys started to pull. We were shocked when we found a pair of sturgeons about 4 kilos each and about 8 huge flatfishes. Everyone exchanged glances in bewilderment and asked almost in unison, "All this with just a fishing rod?!"

Sensei smiled. "Of course, there was no fishing rod. I just got up a bit earlier and saw that some fishermen had come in from a fish-factory to check their nets. So I thought, by the time I get there, they'll be coming back. So I went and bought some fish. Sitting with a

fishing rod was a complete waste of time," the Teacher complained with regret.

As we carried the fish to scale them, Eugene told Stas half in jest, "Yeah, sure he went. The only way to the fish factory is seven kilometers on foot."

"But maybe he went by car," I suggested my version.

"No, he didn't. First, it is next to our tent, we would have heard everything. And second, there are no traces on the sand."

While the other guys woke up, this story acquired many more mysterious details. Sensei's mood was excellent that day. After a light breakfast, he wanted to jog to the end of the peninsula. We left Kostya and Tatyana as volunteers on duty, and in order not to be without dinner, Nikolai Andreevich was also left in the camp.

On our way, we stopped a couple times to do warm-ups with intensive muscle loading. Training in nature, and with such a beautiful background, couldn't be compared with a stuffy gym. Here, as they say, the soul and the body merged in a single impulse.

Having almost reached the end, we saw a real colony of seagulls. Our company kept to the coast so as not to disturb their calm. Nevertheless, many seagulls persistently shouted and whirled above us trying to frighten unexpected visitors off their nests.

After a while, the most beautiful view, skillfully created by nature, opened up to us. At the end of the peninsula, waves met as correct rhombuses in a single chain off the distant coast. Outlines of their wavy edges were emphasized with white sea foam. All this magnificence was supplemented with an unusual play of various color scales of sea water from light turquoise to dark blue. The amazing blueness of the sky with only one whitish cloudlet created a unique masterpiece of this grandiose view.

Sensei gave us fifteen minutes to rest, but he and Volodya sat down in a lotus pose at the edge of the coastline. Some of us, including me, hastened to follow his example, placing ourselves beside them. An easy breeze blew. Coastal waves created a melodious noise, which was supplemented with the calls of seagulls reaching from a distance. Either because of contemplation of this divine beauty or because of Sensei's presence, my lotus flower began to increase its activity, distributing pleasant flows all over my body. For a short period of time, such an unusual feeling appeared in me as if I were dissolved in all this surrounding beauty and became an integral part of it. The sensation was almost instantaneous, but it was unforgettably tremendous. Sensei interrupted this state of bliss when he announced, "Let's return."

The sun was already burning. Sensei told us that, to make our way easier, we should run waist-deep in water. It appeared to be incredibly difficult. Volodya and Sensei rushed forward like two torpedoes overtaking each other. Thanks to their competition, our company could cheat a little: someone ran knee-deep and someone ran ankle-deep in water. But when we finally got to camp, only the cheaters, me among them, sprawled out in weakness on the sand. Sensei and Volodya continued to radiate their inflammatory optimism, which seemed to come from nowhere. After this marathon running, they suggested to the crowd that we play water polo. To our great surprise, the senior guys agreed with pleasure. But other ailing bodies dragged themselves along to help with cooking lunch.

Being busy with cooking, I observed Sensei. He laughed, was naughty, and rushed with a ball like all other guys. He was absolutely the same as others, a young, strong, funny, and healthy guy. On the one hand he was an ordinary person... But everybody who was present saw in him something special, some charm, found some features that attracted them by simplicity and at the same time by their refinement. His soul was like a many-sided diamond that each of us admired at his own angle of sight, at his own angle of refraction of internal light. But in fact, nobody could penetrate him up to the end, nobody could understand who he actually was.

When the guys, at last, calmed down at the hottest part of the day, our camp fell into a profound sleep. I woke up at about four o'clock, and I awakened Tatyana to help me cook something tasty for our big group. When we got out of the tent, I saw Sensei sitting on the sand with Nikolai Andreevich, talking about something. Sensei was explaining something, making three little hills from sand. After their conversation, Nikolai Andreevich and Sensei stood up and slowly walked in our direction. The first hill suddenly began to move and a pigeon, having appeared from nowhere, flew out of it. I gave a start from the unexpectedness of the action. I couldn't believe my eyes. Tatyana dropped a potato and opened her mouth with surprise. Then the second hill began to move, and a pigeon again flew out of it. Sensei and Nikolai Andreevich only turned back carelessly, continuing the conversation, not even confused. The third hill began to move, and a sparrow jumped out of it. Everything grew cold with fear inside of me. The sparrow did not fly away as the pigeons did, it jumped following Sensei. Having run forward towards him, it rumpled its feathers, spread its wings wide apart, and began to twitter loudly as if being indignant over something. Sensei stopped, observing the desperate twittering of this ruffled sparrow, and then spoke to it with a smile, "Well, let it be according to your wish."

After saying these words, he bent down and put some sand on the sparrow, making a hill a bit higher than the first one. I stood up with curiosity. But the following moment finally nailed me down to a chair. As soon as Sensei turned away, the hill began to move and a black kite of an impressive size flew out of it. It immediately flew away to the peninsula.

"Where are my thanks?" Sensei asked in surprise and made a helpless gesture, following the kite with his eyes. "Oh, as usual..."

Sensei hopelessly waved his hand and went to his tent for cigarettes. Tatyana and I sat numb with fear. When Nikolai Andreevich and Sensei were moving away to the beach, I heard the following words, "So was it an illusion of my thoughts?" Nikolai Andreevich asked calmly, as if the question was about ordinary things.

"No. This time it was materialization of my thoughts."

"Why did my attempts end only with hallucinations?"

"Because you had doubts. For materialization, purity of belief is necessary. It is very hard to achieve, for the slightest doubt will destroy everything..."

A gust of wind carried away Sensei's words so far that I couldn't hear them. I wanted so much to go after him and to listen to such an interesting conversation. But at that moment Tatyana came out of her state of shock, broke out in endless impressions, and poured them onto my poor puzzled head.

46

As the day drew on, one of the senior guys suggested that we organize an evening of entertainment and comedy. It was suggested we go and take a look at a medical and curing session of the great magician and wizard who was giving his first session that day. To get there, though, it was necessary to trek eight kilometers on foot. Only a half of our group, including Sensei and Nikolai Andreevich, decided to go. I didn't want to miss anything interesting for myself or for my diary, which was already full of unusual records, even though it was only the second day at the seaside.

By eight o'clock in the evening, we occupied seats in a summer cinema where about seventy people had already gathered. A young woman with a three-year-old boy sat near Nikolai Andreevich. Other children rushed around the rows and noisily chased each other. But this child quietly sat in his mother's lap. I gave him a piece of candy, but it turned out that the child did not see it. His mother said that her son had congenital blindness. Nikolai Andreevich started talking to her, finding out some professional information. Soon the woman had confessed the whole story of her life. It appeared that this boy also would not talk after a trauma he experienced at the age of two. Other than him, the woman had an older son and a daughter who were quite normal children. Nikolai Andreevich sympathized with her and began to write down the addresses and surnames of the best experts in this area of medicine. The woman was glad and joked that in any case she had not come to the session in vain.

At this time Vitaliy Yakovlevich went out to the stage. We could hardly keep ourselves from laughter, as it really was that magician and wizard with spoons on his belly, with whom we had the 'great honor' to get acquainted in autumn. Now he looked much more decent. His face was smoothly shaved, and his hair was accurately cut. He wore a clean summer suit. Despite this significant transformation in his appearance, his haughty look and manners remained the same.

Having come out to the stage, Vitaliy Yakovlevich gazed at the crowd with his 'magic sight' and began his lecture. For a good forty minutes, he told almost the same story as the first time in the sports hall, with the only difference that now he did not stick spoons to himself and his speech was full of different obscure esoteric and medical terms. Confirmatively waving his hands, he went about the stage and threw out his chest proudly. At last, having finished talking, he invited to the stage those people who suffered diseases on his list.

It seemed to me that he had listed almost all diseases from the medical encyclopedia we had at home, and even in the same alphabetical order.

About fifteen people came up to the stage. Someone said that he had heart disease, someone said that his stomach hurt, another one complained about high blood pressure, and some old woman said that trophic ulcers on her legs suppurated. Our woman with the child also went up. Nikolai Andreevich commented that people in sorrow are ready to believe any nonsense hoping for something.

When all interested people had gathered on the stage, Vitaliy Yakovlevich began to wave his hands strenuously from above and to talk of some 'space-fluid' character. To my great surprise, again I felt my lotus flower begin to strongly vibrate. I looked at the stage and could not believe that all this delirium of Vitaliy Yakovlevich could really cause in me this tidal wave. Having concentrated, I felt that all this vibration proceeded not from the stage but from somewhere behind and to the right. It was even more strange, as Sensei sat behind and to the left of me. I looked back, but Sensei wasn't at his seat. Then I looked back to the other side, where the source was according to my sensations. Far away in the corner, at the very end of the empty rows, I saw Sensei. He was sitting and peering with concentration at people who were near the stage. Every second I felt the stream grow in its force. Waves of pleasant sensations were already spilling about my body. But the stream still grew.

In the verbal outpouring of Vitaliy Yakovlevich came a certain pause. At this moment, the blind kid said "Mum!" – not loudly, but distinctly. The woman broke into tears, tightly embracing her son. She drew general attention. And then complete pandemonium began. A woman said that her headache eased, a man said that his stomach stopped aching. But the old woman with the squeaky voice shouted the most that her trophic ulcers began to dry up before her eyes. Not trusting herself, she tried to show them to anyone who would look. Many people in the hall also got up from their places and ran to the stage. Even Vitaliy Yakovlevich himself was taken aback from gratitude, from requests for help for people and their relatives from all directions. Meanwhile, Sensei came back to his place in the hall.

The young mother pressed the child to her breast and sobbed violently but could not get out of the crowd, as the usual crush began and nobody paid attention to her. Nikolai Andreevich hurried to help her. We got the woman out of the cinema and into the fresh air, sitting her down on a bench. Nikolai Andreevich began to calm her down. The kid sat next to her and, hearing the crying of his mother, began to pull his face with his own impressions. Sensei sat down, squatting opposite him, and tenderly stroked his head, saying something silently to himself. The child calmed down and began listening. Then he began to blink quickly with his long eyelashes. The kid then looked purposefully at the watch that gleamed on Sensei's arm as he stroked him. The boy, having caught Sensei's hand, seized the watch, trying to pull it off. He looked into Sensei's eyes and gave a short but meaningful enough command, "Give!"

The kid's mother fainted from everything she had seen. While Nikolai Andreevich and the guys tried to bring her to normal, Sensei took off his watch and gave it to the kid, saying with a smile, "Here, kid, keep it to remember."

The kid, smiling happily, began to play with it, examining and shaking it. When the woman came to, she still could not believe that her son had recovered his sight. She gave him everything that was in her handbag, and the kid examined everything with real pleasure, turning the objects into improvised toys. When she was convinced in his newfound sight, the woman grabbed her son in joy, thanked Nikolai Andreevich and all of us for the help, and ran to her building to tell her husband about this piece of news.

On our way back to camp, Nikolai Andreevich was still surprised.

"How could this Vitaliy Yakovlevich, with his chattering, wake in people so much belief that he could achieve such therapeutic effects?! In fact, I saw with my own eyes that the boy was blind. The others could be fake. But it's hard to grasp this case!"

I looked at Sensei. I was curious what he would say. But Sensei only said, half in jest, "You probably listened inattentively to his lecture. Next time, you should take a notebook with you."

On our way, we gathered dry wood for our evening fire. The senior guys picked up some half rotten wooden column that had once served as a pylon for electric lines. In general, judging by Sensei's excellent mood and the gathered stock of firewood, the night promised to be long and unforgettable.

47

On the road to our camp, the Teacher and Nikolai Andreevich started an interesting conversation. Our psychologist, being impressed by everything that happened, asked Sensei, "Well, adults with the help of suggestions under therapeutic influence can partly ease the process of disease. But children?! At such an age they practically do not understand what is said to them. In this case, though, the result is visible. Even I do not understand how it could happen. In fact, this three-year-old blind child began to see; so, as it turns out, we should logically admit the fact of treatment from a distance."

"The whole history of mankind, if we read it attentively, is full of such facts," Sensei said with a smile.

"Yes, but to read and to see are two completely different things! If it is really so, then I don't understand anything at all."

"It's not difficult to understand if you have the whole conception of the world and a human body as it actually is."

"And what is a human body?"

"The human body as well as all other matters is just emptiness. It is an illusion created by the thought of God."

"So you want to say that this tree and I are basically identical because we are emptiness?" Nikolai Andreevich asked half in jest, passing by a big tree.

"Basically, yes." Sensei grinned and added in a more serious way, "Your matter is generated by one and the same initial energy, but modified and transformed into different wave conditions. Here is the difference in material features. What does a human body consist of? A body, as you know, consists of a system of organs, organs consist of tissues, tissues consist of groups of cells. Cells consist of basic chemical elements. And the greatest part of a body, about 98% of it, is made up of oxygen, carbon, nitrogen, and hydrogen, and 2% are other chemical elements."

"I don't understand how that's possible?" These words accidentally escaped my lips.

"How it's possible? For example, for 50 kg of your weight, the scheme of division in you will be the following," Sensei looked a few seconds at my body as though estimating something, and then said, "Oxygen in different isotope conditions is 30.481 kg, isotopes of carbon are 11.537 kg, isotopes of hydrogen are 5.01 kg, and isotopes of nitrogen are 1.35 kg. That is 48.378 kg in total. Well, I shall not mention all other elements, as their weight goes in grams. In general, only 1.622 kg of the weight remains for them... To be more exact and add everything that is not digested: the remains of ice-cream, sweets, and a drink that have not yet completed a chemical reaction in your body... in total, the weight of your body will make 50 kg and 625 grams."

I was simply struck with such high-speed calculations of my body according to just one glance. I had never thought about the structure of my matter. Meanwhile, Sensei continued to address Nikolai Andreevich, "What are our chemical elements? These molecules make up our cells and exist according to their biophysical laws. Notice that there is emptiness around molecules. Let's go deeper. Molecules consist of atoms, and between them again there is emptiness. Atoms consist of a nucleus and electrons rotating around them, and between them there is emptiness. The nucleus of an atom again consists of elementary particles – protons and neutrons – with the same inherent emptiness between them. We shall notice that variations of any chemical element differ in the number of neutrons in an atomic nucleus so it has a feature of isotopy. Protons and neutrons which form the nucleus of an atom also consist of smaller particles. So look, each time when physicists make the next step, they open a new level of knowledge, removing their relative borders to the horizon of infinite knowledge. Simply, as soon as it was possible for a human to improve a microscope, he learnt the nature of a microcosm. I shall not continue mentioning what is divided into what, but finally division comes to an end, to absolute emptiness out of which everything arises. It exists everywhere, both in a microcosm and in a macrocosm. That is pure energy which is called 'energy Po,' consisting of a sole field of interaction of all kinds of energies and therefore the matter arising from it. So it is said that God is omnipresent. The pulses of energy Po generate the waves that change the curvature of material space and time. That is, in the depth of its essence, all matter is a set of certain kind of waves and exists according to laws of the wave nature."

"It is something brand new," Nikolai Andreevich said thoughtfully.

"By no means," the Teacher objected. "I'd better say these are well forgotten old things. The fact that matter is a generation of great emptiness, 'dao', was known to Indian philosophers more than four thousand years ago and to Chinese wise men about two thousand years ago. Just read their treatises. They visually represented absolute emptiness as the smooth surface of a lake in the absence of wind. The particle of matter arising from emptiness is compared with the occurrence of ripples on the smooth surface of the lake with a gust of wind."

"What then is the wind?" Nikolai Andreevich inquired.

"The wind in this case is a divine essence, it is the thought of God with the help of which He creates and destroys everything. Our soul is also a part of this mighty force that can operate the initial energy Po. Therefore, if a human recognizes his soul with his consciousness and merges them into a single unit, his abilities will become unlimited as well as his knowledge."

"Nevertheless it is new for me," the 'Common Sense' of our company said with a smile.

At this time we arrived back to a camp. The guys who had stayed in the camp were already greedily eating sturgeon barbecue, which they cooked for our arrival and which had almost entirely been eaten. We shared our impressions about the events we witnessed and had a good dinner in the open air. Then we sat near the fire and were looking forward to the forthcoming conversation.

Nikolai Andreevich hurried to come back to the topic that was consuming all his thoughts, "So it turns out that all the world is nothing more than an illusion?"

"That's right."

"But why can we feel everything so realistically, we can touch, try, that is, to be convinced, using our organs of sense that, for example, this stick is a stick, instead of emptiness and illusion."

"Because our brain, since birth, is adjusted to the frequency of perception of this reality. But it does not mean that its abilities are limited to this frequency. Different programs are put into it. If we change the frequency of perception, all the world around us will also change."

"How is it possible?" Nikolai Andreevich did not understand.

"Very simply. Let's examine what our brain is. Basically, the central nervous system is a special device for transmitting and receiving waves of various ranges with corresponding frequency characteristics. As you know, the major elements of the structurally functional organization of the brain are neurons and glia cells, out of which the central nervous system is built. The neuron has an ability that distinguishes it from other cells. It can generate a potential of action and transfer this potential across large distances. This special cell represents itself as a complex device with several conditions (rest and a number of conditions of excitation on various frequencies). This fact essentially increases its information capacity. The information on stimulus is coded by a nervous cell as the frequency of potential of the action, which is average for a short time interval. So, as a whole, the work of our brain is the work of an information managing device in which language is the frequency. Therefore, the conscious and subconscious processes of mind occur at the frequency of a neuron's discharge. When changing the condition of consciousness, for example, during meditations and spiritual practices, the frequency of pulses changes, and it also entails changes of the molecular structure of the body as a whole. That is, a person adjusts to a completely different frequency of reality and consequently perceives this world only as the lowest illusion. There is such an expression, 'When a wise man was asked what life is, he answered, "A laughing-stock for those who have tried it."' And it is a completely fair answer.

"A person who is stuck in the matter, a person with too many hang-ups in the material world of thoughts, is very limited in his perception. Think for yourself. He receives information about the world around him through his brain, which since his birth has a certain frequency of perception, which is peculiar to the animal nature. Therefore this brain, as any other animal brain, perceives information through its organs of sense. And though a person is surrounded by a whole ocean of electromagnetic vibrations, frequencies of the most various types and parameters, he perceives only a tiny part of all this variety. Basic information goes through his visual channel, but only the visible part of the spectrum, electromagnetic waves with a length from 400 to 700 nanometers. Everything that lies outside of this spectrum a person does not see, so reality is based on the limits of this range and does not find any reflection in his brain. The same concerns sound, which a person hears in a range from 20 hertz up to 18 kilohertz.

"Why have meditations and spiritual practice always been given to mankind? Why were they never secret? Because they opened a completely different real world of God to people and, as a result, a new step towards the maturation of the soul.

"So a human is a very interesting creature. He is born an animal, but in the course of his life the power of thought can transform him into a Creature close to God. The most amazing thing is that freedom of choice in his individual development is given to him... The power of thought is really a unique creation of God. There is such an ancient expression written in Sanskrit, 'The god sleeps in minerals, / Wakes up in plants, / Moves in animals / And... thinks in a human.'"

"What is the origin of a nervous impulse? Is it the birth of thought?" Nikolai Andreevich inquired.

"The same as energy Po. It is an original impulse."

"But if energy Po is a divine energy and at the same time the reason that all thoughts appear, then what should we do with bad thoughts that come from the animal nature?"

"Who told you that these thoughts don't have one root? A birth of thoughts that takes its origin from the animal nature is managed by Lucifer, the most true and devoted servant of God. Due to these thoughts, he also pushes you to various tests of your true belief. He tempts you into evil for you to learn good. But you are free in your choice, I emphasize once again, you are free! You can apprehend these thoughts as a call for action or reject them and turn to good thoughts coming from your soul. That is, what kind of thoughts you apprehend, what your observer, your consciousness, will choose, that is what you actually are."

"What is a soul? Is it energy, too?" Victor asked.

"Yes. It is divine energy, it is a part of God in ourselves. The most important thing is, the reason we have all these regenerations, the reason that bad things happen, the reason we have problems is because we are in a material body that we depend on 99.9% of the time. But if we release ourselves from it, even just a hundredth part, and plunge into the soul, we will get infinity and omnipotence. The main thing is to break through the internal guard of the gate of our soul. In the soul is hidden the true power, the power of love, which creates everything, which is capable of ruling the energy Po. All main energies are based on it because in the real world there is only love. Evil exists only in the illusory human world for the understanding of an immature soul. Therefore it is very important to generate in ourselves a constant frequency of the energy of love and good, instead of a difference of vibrations."

"It sounds interesting," Nikolai Andreevich said thoughtfully. "So, a human, on the whole, is a creature with a wave nature."

"Absolutely right, both spiritually and physically."

"How do you mean physically?" Victor asked.

"Well, in the human body, there is an informational network that, together with nervous, blood, and endocrine systems, coordinates physiological processes. A person is, so to say, pierced from the inside with wave flows by which important information is transferred with the help of bioradiation in a microwave range. All this, naturally, is connected to the magnetic field of the Earth, with space radiation and so on... But the point is that informational function for the body is fulfilled only by weak fields. Otherwise cells launch a mechanism of self-protection and do not perceive this information."

"What fields are inherent in our body?" Kostya inquired.

"There are plenty of them. For example, electromagnetic radiation of different ranges, an electric field, a magnetic one... Acoustic radiation, that is, various sounds that come from a body. Chemical discharge or chemical field, and many, many others, which there's no need to mention now."

"I ask," Kostya continued, "because I have recently read a book about the art of prophecy using the ground. It is called... geomancy. In short, it was practiced in ancient India, China, Egypt. It is mentioned that there is a certain field from which a person can gain information about the future. They say that ancient prophesiers entered a special state by getting this knowledge."

"It is really so. This field still exists. Its information was used and is still used. There are certain techniques that allow a person to reach this state of consciousness. But usual people who are engaged in hard brainwork are also capable of spontaneously entering this state of consciousness, as a rule, either while sleeping or in a state of deep concentration when their brain is switched off from extraneous thoughts. The present information is true only concerning the past or the present, and it also concerns exact sciences. Concerning the future, for example, of mankind as a whole or of any separate concrete person, it is unstable because the future depends on an individual or collective choice of people."

"How can that be?"

"Very easily. If, for example, a person changes internally then, according to his choice, his entire life changes from that point and into the future. These are laws of nature. A change in the frequency of perception adjusts a person to a completely new wave, that is to another reality. The same concerns mankind as a whole. If mankind's attitude to life, its balance between the spiritual and the animal natures, changes, then correspondingly the general frequency of energy changes, and therefore its future also changes. So both a person and mankind as a whole, by personal choices, predetermine the possible future on a daily basis."

"Then how do the prophesiers predict the future?"

"If you noticed, the great prophesiers made their predictions ciphered, with double meaning. Many of them were mistaken, many did not mention significant events because the future is changeable and exists in time and space in a multitude of variants. Prophets could be adjusted to the frequency of the wave that carried the given information. But they got data only from that reality into which they could penetrate."

"What about a personal prediction?"

"Predictions for an individual are based on the wave that his consciousness is on at the present moment. If a person does not change inside radically, the predictions will come true, as it is programmed in this wave."

We sat at the fire, listening to the Sensei's amazing story. Bright stars had shone in the sky for a long time, and the sea melodiously caressed our ears with an easy rustle of waves harmoniously filling the pauses. A set of lights from a big steamship appeared in the distance.

"Wow, what a beauty!" Ruslan exclaimed upon seeing it. "Look, it's so huge. I imagine that we could go for a voyage on it with every comfort."

Everybody turned to that side.

"Well, well. Everyone tells a story, but a sick person tells about his pills," Eugene remarked mockingly. "Go on, with every comfort. The Titanic was even huger, God rest their souls."

"I was just..." Ruslan started to justify himself, followed by everybody's laughter.

"You know, not all the details about the Titanic are clear." Nikolai Andreevich said. "I read that on board of the Titanic there was a sarcophagus with a well-kept body of an Egyptian priestess and prophetess who lived during the reign of pharaoh Amenhotep. They say that the mummy had a fatal reputation. It was excavated in 1895 and from 1896 until 1900 everyone who participated in the excavation died. Only Lord Kannervil, who was heading the project, escaped alive. So the Lord brought this mummy on board of the Titanic, planning to display the body of the prophetess at the exposition of archeological finds in Los Angeles. The most interesting thing was that the mummy was placed not in the hold but in a cabin, near the captain's bridge, as it was more convenient for passengers to look at it. In the official investigation, the reason for the collision with an iceberg was called 'bad navigation.' How do you like such coincidences?"

"That's all trifles," Sensei said lighting a cigarette, "The most surprising fact is that people were warned about the wreck of the Titanic sixteen years before the accident happened."

"What do you mean?" Stas inquired.

"I mean that Morgan Robertson's book "Futility" was published in 1896 in England. In this book, the wreck of a huge passenger steamship by the name of Titan was described in detail. It precisely specified the time, the place, and the reason for the wreck, that is, in 1912, in the Atlantic ocean, on its way from England to America, on a cold April night, the ship collides with a huge iceberg, and people die. Moreover, Robertson even gave the exact number of passengers – two thousand people – that corresponded to the number on the Titanic. He also listed all parameters and characteristics of the ship, which also coincide with the characteristics of the Titanic. There was little discrepancy. For example, he described the length of the ship as 243 m, and the Titanic was 268 m in length. The displacement was 70 thousand tons, and the real ship had 66 thousand tons. The speed at the moment of collision was 25 knots, and in reality it was 22 knots. All other details, four pipes, three screws, and so on, everything was predicted... If only people were a bit more clever, so many people would not have died."

"Yes, I recall that I also read about this phenomenal prediction," Nikolai Andreevich said. "But wait, he was a science-fiction writer, and in addition to that, nobody knew him. His book wasn't republished again. How could people have known? If only he had written that it would really happen some day, if he had named it a prophecy, I think, people would have paid attention to it. But he said his novel was science fiction."

"You know what the issue is. A person receives pure knowledge. But to save himself from the inquisition of fools, he calls these books science fiction. It was science fiction for clever people, for those who can understand it. After things happen, everybody starts to understand it, even the fools. But a clever person could have understood even then and taken a grain of truth out of this so-called science fiction."

"To put it simply, you mean to say that a clever person, having read this book, would never have booked a ticket on the Titanic."

"Absolutely right... And it doesn't just concern this book. Just read science fiction. All science fiction is divided into clever science fiction and into fairy tales for adults, but it is embarrassing to call it a fairy tale, so they write 'science fiction.' Writers of clever science fiction simply download the information from time levels of various realities. They download the future, which can come true with the right combination of certain wave conditions. They receive knowledge and describe it. This, in turn, psychologically prepares a clever person who has read this book for forthcoming events. It forms skills of multidimensional thinking, allowing them to orient themselves in the quickly changing conditions of life. All this not only expands a person's adaptable range in preparing his consciousness for a qualitatively new step in perception of the world around us, but also creates preconditions for the internal change of a person himself, simply speaking, to transition to another wave of a new reality.

"Just recall books by H.G. Wells, who correctly determined and prepared mankind for future scientific and technical progress. Or recall Jules Verne, who predicted many openings and inventions that subsequently came true. Or, in particular, take Alexei Tolstoi's book, "The Hyperboloid of Engineer Garin", written in 1925-1926 in which the laser is actually predicted. The first laser wasn't invented until 1960. And take Aleksandr Beljaev's books! For example, his novel "Star KEC" written in 1936 practically carried real prophecies about the ways of astronautics. There are many such examples... And how many grains of truth are reflected in the books of writers like Ivan Efremov, Isaac Azimov, Ray Bradbury, Arthur C. Clarke, Alexander Kazantsev, Stanislaw Lem... There are many talented people to prepare a clever reader for forthcoming events. But they have to write their books in the genre of science fiction because the clever one will understand it anyway, but the fool will not take offence."

Nikolai Andreevich grinned. "You know, to be fair, I also treated science fiction with much prejudice, reading it as you have said like a fairy tale for adults. But once I read a note in a magazine that John F. Kennedy, when he was president, invited several science fiction writers into his 'brain trust' for forecasting possible developments of the future. It was also mentioned there that a hobby of some talented, world-renowned scientists was reading science fiction. Many scientific terms have even come to us from science fiction. To tell the truth, it surprised me."

"It is a normal situation. You see, when a person reads a book he starts to live as though in its world, that is, he begins to adjust himself to the same frequency of perception as the author. Here the reader can face a surprising phenomenon, a kind of burst of brain activity. Call it what you will: generating ideas, inspiration of the subconscious, as you wish. But this burst is mostly a short-term transition to the corresponding frequency of perception of this book, which is fixed in our memory. Corresponding ideas are then born on the basis of available personal knowledge and experience. Therefore, many talented scientists, politicians, and ordinary people who aspire to understand themselves and the world around them get ideas, and the future opens right from books, including science fiction, from this unique database of non-realized realities. It can emerge in memory in any form and at any time – right at the moment of reading, or in a dream, or suddenly dawning upon you later."

We were silent for a little while. The fire quietly crackled as the branches in it burned. Its flame bewitched and fascinated us with its mysterious living beauty and bright range of light play. We could stay there for eternity listening to Sensei's unimaginably interesting stories in the open air in this finest nook of nature where, it seemed, even stars came down from heaven to hear our conversation better.

"I wonder whether there are prophetic dreams?" Nikolai Andreevich started talking again. "Or is it just the work of the mind in forecasting further events?"

"Prophetic dreams certainly exist. If a person has enough personal spiritual power or if he is tied to someone with the force of love, his brain can spontaneously adapt to that frequency that coincides with future events. He then receives these data in a dream, in a straight way, escaping analysis. But later, giving out these data, his mind participates in direct processing of the information. Therefore we can see events not in their pure state but in their interpreted version on the basis of our emotions, experiences, former impressions, images, and so on."

"You know, I had a prophetic dream once," Stas started to tell about his life experience.

For a long time we talked about different strange things in this world and its surprising cases. We recalled stories connected with it and listened to the simple and, at the same time, unusual narrations of Sensei about the mysterious human mind and its unlimited abilities. Only at daybreak did we finally go to bed.

48

Strangely enough, either because I had heard so many things at once or because of some other reason, that morning I had an unusual dream. It was bright and emotional. The most important thing was that I had never had such a dream before. I felt as though my consciousness floated above the ground, observing from a height everything that occurred in the world. At first, everything was silent and quiet. But then I felt myself somehow uneasy and frightened, as if I expected something. I noticed a bright red star that descended from the tops of high, snow-white mountains in the East. This star began to come nearer and quickly grew in size. A transparent train followed it. The closer it came to me, the more space this train covered, changing the world and making its outlines blurred and translucent. When I looked more closely, I saw that everything that was captured by the train boiled as if nature rose against human civilization, growing in its force. Volcanoes blew up and shook the Earth with their rumble. Enormous waves arose in the middle of oceans, and these waves quickly moved to megacities. Fires stormed there, where there was no water. Winds twisted huge tornados, destroying everything in their path. It was as if nature had brought down to mankind all the negative force that was produced by people during the entirety of civilization. I became frightened and closed my eyes. When I opened them, I saw myself standing in the middle of an amazingly magnificent field with different beautiful flowers. The star was still approaching and changing the space behind itself. I looked back. Behind me were cities full of people who didn't expect anything. This severe force approached to them.

When the star approached very close, I made out that it was a Horseman. His attire and amour were made of pure gold, which brightly gleamed and shone like red fire. Even his horse was covered with a horse cloth made from fine plates of pure gold. The dazzling clothes completely hid the Horseman, leaving uncovered only his eyes. In his hand he held a spear. At the end of the spear there was a flag with the image of a bud of a lotus inside, in the middle of which was a pyramid, an eye, and also some hieroglyphs and pictures. The Horseman rushed with his horse across a huge field of beautiful flowers.

Suddenly, at full tilt, the Red Horseman sharply pulled the reins to stop the horse. I saw his gaze, which seemed extremely familiar to me. The Horseman's attention was caught by a modest forget-me-not with five sky-blue petals. He dismounted from the horse and bent over the flower, as if examining and admiring it. As soon as the Horseman dismounted, all the element forces started to cease and calm down. Only an easy echo of this huge force, which moved after the warrior, came to the cities. For me it was a riddle – why was such a mighty Horseman stopped by this ordinary-looking flower? In fact, there was a whole field of the biggest, most beautiful flowers around him. Why did he stop for a long time?

Even when I woke up, the feeling of reality of this dream did not abandon me. These two questions were precisely engraved in my memory. Certainly I had had dreams before, but I had never had a dream so real, so full of sensations and emotions. The most important thing was that in the dream everything was absolutely clear, I had a real sense of all those events, I knew that it was very important. But when I woke up, I could not recall in any way what it meant and how I should understand it. There were only bright emotional impressions left and these two questions, which simply cycled in my memory.

This dream really intrigued me with its singularity. First, I thought that my brain had just shown me yesterday's information in this way. But nobody had mentioned the things in my dream in such detail. It puzzled me a little.

I chose a moment when all the guys ran to swim and came up to Sensei. He was standing in shoal water, gradually getting used to the water temperature. Taking advantage of his solitude, I began to tell him my strange dream, complaining that I could not recall its sense at all. I only remembered that it was very important for me. Contrary to my expectations that he would fully decode this dream from physiological and philosophical points of view, Sensei only smiled and, looking at me somehow mysteriously, said, "The time will come, and you will know everything."

Sensei's Aforizms

1. Life is unpredictable, and anything might happen in it, even the most unbelievable, what you yourself can't imagine.

2. A young body doesn't mean the age of the soul at all.

3. All great things are ridiculously simple, but it takes a lot of hard work to master them.

4. The human is an intelligent creature. His main force of action lies in his thoughts.

5. It is important to have a great desire, and opportunities will come.

6. For every Vijai there is a Rajah.

7. Fear begotten by imagination sees danger even where there is no danger at all.

8. With healthy thoughts, there will be a sound mind, and with a sound mind, there will be a sound body.

9. Any blow caused by your rage will come back to you in the end.

10. The potential of a human is limited only by his imagination.

11. You should not wish ill for other people, even in your thoughts. With the power of your thought, you are setting a trap for yourself, for your body and mind. The more you think about it, the stronger it keeps you, the tighter its loop becomes.

12. Become a friend to your enemy and forgive his deeds, for you are also imperfect.

13. Life is too short, and you should progress in glorifying your spiritual nature.

14. You should always improve yourself, for each minute of your life is precious. You should use it as a divine gift for perfection of your soul.

15. If you want to make God laugh, tell Him about your plans.

16. There are no accidents. An accident is only a natural consequence of our uncontrollable thoughts.

17. The quality of the instants you live are much more important than senseless years of existence.

18. Wisdom is a virtue of the soul and not of age.

19. Any action is first of all generated by our begotten thought.

20. The force of the word revives the force of thought, and the force of thought generates action.

21. The one who does good deeds with good thoughts has no need to be sad about something missed, for he gets much more force for finding his soul than if he does nothing.

22. Science fiction is only an unrealized reality.

23. True, real belief arises from knowledge, and knowledge comes through a word, through persuasion of your mind in the validity of an occurring phenomenon.

24. It is necessary to respect another person's aspiration to knowledge instead of attacking him with bayonets of your own egocentrism.

25. To learn everything is impossible, but you should aspire to it.

26. The most valuable way of understanding God with your mind is when true knowledge overcomes the animal nature and opens the gate of the subconscious with the help of the key of love.

27. A fool will be given his due for understanding-ing; for the clever one, it is silly not to understand.

Contents

Sensei of Shambala............................3

Sensei's Aforizms............................388

SENSEI PUBLISHING HOUSE

Sensei Publishing House offers a series of unique books by a popular contemporary writer Anastasia NOVYKH.

Not only do these books fascinate with inimitable content, deep meaning and impressive frank confessions, but also with exceptional combination of simplicity and wisdom in answers to the most principal personal questions of each person. The scope of topics touched amazes with encyclopaedic and analytic extent: from unique ancient knowledge to popular scientific view of the future; from effective ancient spiritual practices (including negative thoughts control) to phenomenal human abilities; from unordinary worldview and interesting parables to sparkling humor; from exciting history of the previous civilizations to profoundly intimate sacramental questions.

Sensei Publishing House was established entirely owing to the books by Anastasia Novykh.

The mission of **Sensei Publishing House** is to disseminate this unique knowledge all over the world, to translate the books into foreign languages, so that this information is maximum available to everybody.

SENSEI PUBLISHING HOUSE

Sensei Publishing House priority tasks are: enhancing intercultural dialogue, conducting educational activities, promoting spiritual way of life, broadening mental outlook on the world, developing personal spiritual potential.

Sensei Publishing House is the proprietor of SENSEI newspaper.

Please send your requests on purchasing of books by Anastasia Novykh and Sensei newspaper of Sensei Publishing House at:

e-mail: info@sensei.kiev.ua

post office box: 105, Kiev, 04205, Ukraine

In your enquiry please, include the following information:

Full name, address, phone number, name and quantity of book(s) or newspaper.

http://sensei.kiev.ua

'Sensei-II of Shambala' by Anastasia Novykh

Fascinating sequel of "Sensei of Shambala", describing sojourn of youth company of martial-arts group together with Sensei. Plain worldly vanity disappears when you happen to be beside such a unique in terms of deep knowledge and indefatigable humor Person as Sensei. An ordinary rest day turns into event, saturated with information and action: adventures of guys, thrilling world-view of Sensei, his unusual demonstrations of phenomenal abilities.

Two zests of this book – profound in wisdom Bodhisattva parable, which, owing to its underlying message, illustrates everlasting search of a human soul; and the story about a Kievan Rus Saint – AGAPIT the Unmercenary Healer, whose miracle-working relics are still kept in Kiev-Pechersky Monastery.

'Birds and stone' by Anastasia Novykh

Three captivating short stories "Night duty", "Everything is so simple", and "Birds and stone" anyway are connected with a legendary person of Sensei.

"Night duty" relates an unusual day of major Rebrov, an ordinary man, burdened with everyday concerns, but who always acts with humanity, making a matter of conscience, without stopping to think, risking his life for the sake of coming to help others. During this fateful night duty in the time of mortal danger, suddenly he encountered a phenomenon, unusual to this world, owing to which Rebrov was able not only to save other people's lives, but also struggle out of this situation alive. Starting from this moment he began to see the world with completely different eyes...

"Everything is so simple" – a story about an old man, fishing at a river-side, when an uncommon young neighbor-fisherman joined him. In their conversation, the old man imparted his uneasy destiny to him, including a striking incident that had happened to him during the war and his postwar life. And since his companion proved to be a good company, the old man shared his thoughts, tormenting him, doubts about himself and the spent life, which arise in any person, living to a great age. To this his chance acquaintance told him a wise ancient eastern parable...

pany, the old man shared his thoughts, tormenting him, doubts about himself and the spent life, which arise in any person, living to an old age. In reply his occasional acquaintance told him a wise ancient eastern parable...

"Birds and stone" is the most vivid and impressive in its information story of this triad. The narration goes about a curious meeting of Sensei with Max, who had once been a long time near Sensei. But now this man appeared before Sensei in a somewhat different look of a... girl, in whose body his soul entered after a car accident. Unusual heart-to-heart talk about the past life, values reappraisal of Max due to the past life and the present – the story leaves an indelible impression and enables to look differently at one's own life and adjust its course. Besides that, the book contains much remarkable knowledge on the human in the light of science and understanding of the ancient of where thoughts are 'born' as well as ways of controlling them. There is also information on the 'Jesus Prayer', being one of the most sacramental and effective spiritual practices of Christianity, about Saint Agapit, a resounded for ages healer monk of Kiev-Pechersky Monastery, about the present-day spiritual elder Antony. And much more information for those, who follow the spiritual path and who aspire to be Human!

'Crossroads' by Anastasia Novykh

A dynamic and fascinating detective story, relating a secret project realization via intelligence service by a clandestine Slavic organization, originating from the legendary secret service officers of the early XXth century, seeking for Shambala. The action takes place in 1994-1995. For the realization of this project, which played a crucial role in subsequent succession of events throughout the Slavic countries, the main character of the book "Sensei of Shambala" is set in motion. Owing to his professionalism and personal world-view, extraordinary powers and talent of a universal analyst – a dangerous threat, supervised by the criminal world, and menacing the project realization, was eliminated.

Along with the exciting dynamic action, the book contains a lot of fascinating information: about secret service work, about the true story of the occurred events, echoing in the present; useful informative facts on human and his phenomenal abilities; mysterious prophecies and unusual vision on problems of the mankind from a completely different universal view. And, of course, the golden thread of Anastasia Novykh works, expressed in words and acts of the central character, Sensei: regardless of the situation first and foremost – be a Human and carry this title across the life with Honor and Virtue.

Dear readers!

Being guided by the spirit of the new times, when there begin to appear such masterpieces as books by Anastasia Novykh, containing a depository of remarkable knowledge, not only supporting and helping people, but also assisting in spreading of harmony and good in the world,

Sensei Publishing House is determined to make its contribution to such a noble cause and grants to all those, who have not yet been able to look through the books by Anastasia Novykh, a free access to full-text electronic versions of these books

at **Sensei Publishing House** web-site
http://sensei.kiev.ua

Owing to this, dear readers, you will be able not only to evaluate the degree of spiritual necessity in these books at this point of your journey, but also obtain these uncommon masterpieces in the form of quality printed books with design, made by the author.

The books by Anastasia Novykh can also be downloaded for free as well as discussed at the following sites and forums:in Russian:

http://schambala.com.ua
http://schambala.kiev.ua
http://sensei.org.ua

in **English**, German, and other languages:
http://schambala.org

Good creates Good!!!

Sensei Newspaper

The main purpose of Sensei newspaper is
- thorough study of topics, touched upon in the books by Anastasia Novykh,
- dissemination of knowledge on the world and human,
- topical information on self-development, spiritual development,
- entire spectrum of various knowledge on micro- and macro-world,
- science, culture, history, and literature news,
- positive outlook,
- letters and life stories of Anastasia Novykh books readers.

The newspaper is issued 2 times a month in the Russian language in printed and electronic versions. Area of distribution – CIS and the Russian-speaking abroad.

post office box: 105, Kiev, 04205, Ukraine

e-mail: info@sensei.kiev.ua
http://sensei.kiev.ua

English version of Sensei newspaper is planned to be issued in 2010. Please check our web-site http://sensei.kiev.ua

CPSIA information can be obtained
at www.ICGtesting.com
Printed in the USA
BVHW092116020119
536779BV00029B/331/P